The Dream Life of Sukhanov

The
Dream Life
OF
Sukhanov

OLGA GRUSHIN

A MARIAN WOOD BOOK
Published by G. P. Putnam's Sons
a member of Penguin Group (USA) Inc.
New York

A MARIAN WOOD BOOK
Published by G. P. Putnam's Sons
Publishers Since 1838
a member of the Penguin Group
Penguin Group (USA) Inc., 375 Hudson Street, New York, New York 10014, USA •
Penguin Group (Canada), 90 Eglinton Avenue East, Suite 700, Toronto, Ontario M4P 2Y3,
Canada (a division of Pearson Penguin Canada Inc.) • Penguin Books Ltd, 80 Strand,
London WC2R 0RL, England • Penguin Ireland, 25 St Stephen's Green, Dublin 2, Ireland
(a division of Penguin Books Ltd) • Penguin Group (Australia), 250 Camberwell Road,
Camberwell, Victoria 3124, Australia (a division of Pearson Australia Group Pty Ltd) •
Penguin Books India Pvt Ltd, 11 Community Centre, Panchsheel Park, New Delhi–
110 017, India • Penguin Group (NZ), Cnr Airborne and Rosedale Roads, Albany,
Auckland 1310, New Zealand (a division of Pearson New Zealand Ltd) •
Penguin Books (South Africa) (Pty) Ltd, 24 Sturdee Avenue, Rosebank,
Johannesburg 2196, South Africa

Penguin Books Ltd, Registered Offices: 80 Strand, London WC2R 0RL, England

The author is indebted to John E. Bowlt's *Russian Art of the Avant-Garde: Theory and
Criticism, 1902–1934* (London: Thames & Hudson, 1988) for the quotation from
The Golden Fleece (attributed here to *The World of Art*), and to Rimma Gerlovina's
three-dimensional poems for the description of the cube-shaped artwork.

Library of Congress Cataloging-in-Publication Data

Grushin, Olga, date.
The dream life of Sukhanov / Olga Grushin.
p.   cm.
"A Marian Wood book."
ISBN 0-399-15298-9
1. Loss (Psychology)—Fiction.   2. Moscow (Russia)—Fiction.
3. Middle-aged men—Fiction.   4. Social change—Fiction.   5. Soviet Union—Fiction.
6. Censorship—Fiction.   7. Artists—Fiction.   8. Dreams—Fiction.   I. Title.
PS3607.R85D74   2005   2005043175
813'.6—dc22

Printed in the United States of America
1   3   5   7   9   10   8   6   4   2

This book is printed on acid-free paper. ∞

BOOK DESIGN BY AMANDA DEWEY

To my parents

I know your works: you are neither cold nor hot. Would that you were cold or hot! So, because you are lukewarm, and neither cold nor hot, I will spew you out of my mouth. For you say, I am rich, I have prospered, and I need nothing; not knowing that you are wretched, pitiable, poor, blind, and naked.

REVELATION 3:15–17

The Dream Life of Sukhanov

One

S top here," said Anatoly Pavlovich Sukhanov from the backseat, addressing the pair of suede gloves on the steering wheel.

The white-and-yellow columns outside his window ceased their tiresome flashing, began to slow down, and in another moment fell obediently into their assigned places. A pale orange tentacle of a nearby streetlamp pierced the plush darkness around him, and Nina, who had been silent the whole way, stirred as if waking.

"Already?" she said absently, glancing outside.

They were there. With a slight sigh, she searched for something in her purse, as she always did upon arrival. Sukhanov waited patiently while she flipped open a compact, balanced its small convex pool of glittering blackness on her palm, slid a peach-colored pillar of lipstick out of the golden coils of its case, and proceeded to bend her face this way and that, trying to chase her reflection out of the shadows. Unexpectedly he caught sight of a delicately painted eye as it flitted along the surface of the mirror, but she moved her hand, and the eye blinked and vanished. Humming tunelessly, he looked away; even after twenty-eight years of marriage, he still felt awkward in such moments, as if caught spying on some private ritual. Finally the elusive reflection became trapped in the ray of the streetlamp, and she traced the contours of her full mouth in two quick flicks of her wrist, pressed her lips together with a tiny pat, and dropped the lipstick back into her purse. He heard the lock shut with a rapacious snap, saw out of the corner of his eye a cold burst of fire as a diamond earring passed through the light—and then, with a sudden fluid rustle, she was gone, as usual without waiting for her door to be opened. Behind her lingered a smell—the elegant perfume of tonight, whatever it was, and underneath, numerous layers of other fading scents, which had accumulated over time in the backseat of their Volga like so many sweet, barely discernible ghosts of past outings.

With a slow heave Sukhanov followed her out.

At this hour of the evening, on a Saturday, Marx Avenue was starting to grow quiet. The lamps glowed like tangerine balloons let loose in the soft haze, and in their light the eighteenth-century façade of the old Moscow university shone brightly, as dramatic and familiar as the stage set of some stately, stale play. Although it was early August, the air had already acquired that special, brittle and gentle, autumnal quality that made the world seem a breath deeper and a trifle less certain, as if seen through a sheet of crystal. Infrequent cars passed. A wide sweep of their headlights brought into sudden sharp relief vague shapes of passersby, for a solitary instant imparting volume and color to a youth in a drab suit darting recklessly across the street, an old man shuffling by with a crumpled newspaper under his arm, several ageless, heavy-faced women weighed down by bloated bags, and—strikingly, incongruously—a vision: a figure in a low-cut dress of shimmering green silk, standing tall and slender and long-legged by the curb.

"It's chilly," said Nina quietly.

Sukhanov nodded, turned back to the car, and rapped on the window. The tinted glass slid down without a sound, exposing the suede gloves inside, poised at the ready.

"Wait for us over there," he said curtly. "I expect we'll be a while."

As they walked the few paces to the Manège, they tilted their heads up, to get a better view of an imposing banner unfurling above the portico of the grand exhibition hall. "THE FACE OF OUR MOTHERLAND," read the enormous red letters, and, in the line below, "Pyotr Alekseevich Malinin, 1905–1985."

"The dates make him sound dead," observed Sukhanov with displeasure. "They should make it clear it's his birthday celebration, don't you think?"

She shrugged and said nothing, only quickened her steps, and the deserted square greedily received each precise click of her silvery high heels. A broad-shouldered man who stood smoking by the entrance saw her approach and instantly, diving forward with his whole body, swung the door wide open; a waft of well-lit stuffiness and a cascading burst of a woman's artificial laughter escaped into the quiet darkness. As Nina passed inside, Sukhanov noticed the man follow her sheer silken legs with a speculative look. No one could ever guess her age, he thought, feeling pleasantly flattered. He was about to enter himself, when the man released the door and turned toward him, revealing a tentative wisp of a mustache in the middle of an insolent face.

"Just a minute," the man said in a bored tone. "This is by invitation only."

Sukhanov measured the fatuous mustache with a contemptuous look and unhurriedly reached into his pocket.

He had barely stepped inside when an ample woman stuffed into a tight dress of crimson velvet flew at him, opening her arms and crying shrilly, "Anatoly Pavlovich, the very man I was dying to see! Ah, do I have just the story for you!"

She was the wife of a famous theater critic; he had dined with them the other week. Tapping his chest with her plump index finger, she plunged into some involved tale, melting into debilitating giggles at every few words. Nodding mechanically, Sukhanov surveyed the place over her swaying shoulders. He had not been here for a while—in fact, not since . . . well, no need to be exact, he thought hastily, reining in his memory with the chilling sensation of the near-slip. Suffice it to say, it had been a long, a very long time, and everything looked quite different now.

The white-walled hall was welcomingly warm. A narrow red carpet ran across the shining floor in an appropriately solemn touch, unrolled, he was sure, just for the occasion, and the hum of manifold conversations splashed around long tables generously set with hors d'oeuvres. The crowd looked befittingly festive, and light danced playfully off every gesture, transforming a lifted champagne flute into liquid gold, setting a flock of sparks aflutter over an extended hand, causing tiny explosions with every turn of a woman's head. He saw countless dignitaries drifting about, and in the middle of the room he noticed Vasily, twirling a glass of wine and smiling his habitually thin smile as he bent toward an exceptionally bejeweled matron, whom Sukhanov recognized with a start as the Minister of Culture's wife. Ah, indeed, that boy will go far, very far, he thought once again with approval. Ksenya, needless to say, was not here yet; she always made a point of flaunting her thorough disregard for his position. But she was still young, only eighteen, and he was certain that, given her brilliant mind, she would in time—

The critic's wife leaned into him, oozing confidentiality.

"And so I say to him, 'It's all very well, Mark Abramovich, but your ending, my dear, your ending really doesn't work.' I mean, if you constantly hint at some terrible mystery, surely you should disclose it in the fifth act! And then, just imagine, he says to me, 'I don't think you understand my conception. By leaving things unexplained

I'm trying to convey the general absurdity of our existence.' Can you believe it? The general absurdity of our existence!"

As she collapsed in another outburst of helpless mirth, her breasts bounced up and down like two melons draped in taut crimson, her meaty earlobes flashed with amethysts the size of walnuts, and her second chin gave birth to a third. Muttering a halfhearted excuse, Sukhanov extricated himself from her voluminous grasp and quickly walked toward Vasily, and from halfway across the room her laughing shriek chased him still: "The absurdity of our existence, can you believe it, Anatoly Pavlovich?"

The Minister's wife bared her small, crowded teeth.

"Maria Nikolaevna, you look glamorous as always," said Sukhanov, and in a joking gesture of exaggerated politeness carried her hand to his lips.

"Like father, like son," she said in a languid drawl. "Both such charmers!"

At his side, Vasily smiled silkily. He had certainly grown into a handsome young man.

All around them conversations, wound up earlier in the evening, were slowly unwinding, traveling their preordained course toward the main event of the night. Moscow's artistic crème de la crème, ostensibly gathered to celebrate the eightieth birthday of one of their brightest stars, tacitly congratulated each other on their own success in life. Suddenly there was a rustle, a stir, glasses being raised first here, then there, as a chorus of *"Vashe zdorovie!"* spread across the hall, rolling through the crowd like exalted ripples originating somewhere at the heart of things and reaching wider and wider. Of course, the heart in question, the assembly's nerve center, had been apparent to Sukhanov's trained eye from the moment he had entered. In one of the more remote corners, casually surrounded by a few somberly clad youths with discreet bulges in their jackets, two men talked, interrupting each other amiably, laughing at each other's jokes, slapping each other on the back, all the while secretly watched by several hundred eyes. They had just drunk a toast to each other's health, these two—the guest of honor, the artist Pyotr Alekseevich Malinin, and the Minister of Culture. Anyone's importance could be measured visibly tonight by the degree of proximity to this innermost of circles, and imperceptibly, excitedly, the guests shifted closer and closer in dark, respectful waves of tailored suits and gowns, their crisp shirtfronts and low décolletages flashing like brilliant white foam on the crests.

It occurred to Sukhanov that the whole scene was oddly like a parody of Malinin's early work—one of those easily recognizable "Great Leader" paintings, with Lenin (or someone else, heavily mustachioed and currently unnameable) thundering from a far-off podium, on the unreachable horizon, and tides of workers and peasants spreading outward from it, initially shrunk by the perspective into mere symbols of class and righteous anger but presently growing larger, larger, until here they were, bigger than life, almost bursting out of the frame with their enraptured stares, half-opened mouths, clenched fists, ripped clothes. Understandably, such grim militant works had been tactfully omitted from the Soviet master's retrospective. Other, milder creations hung under the spotlights, presenting to the audience so-called Socialism with a Human Face—a slogan that was perhaps more familiar to Sukhanov than to anyone else here. Allowing himself a knowing smile, he took his most regretful leave of his most captivating company (in any case, it was useful to let the boy work on the woman a bit more) and leisurely made his way along the walls.

Birch trees bathed in the sunlight, bright and fresh as if grown to order, and broad blue rivers streamed merrily along emerald shores dotted with cows and smoking with factories. Sturdy girls beamed as they strode through the fields, proudly carrying sacks of potatoes; miners bent in grimy enthusiastic groups over newspapers announcing new railroad openings; and parades of gold-trimmed banners passed before the shining eyes of toddlers who were still too young to march but who already, wordlessly, gratefully, understood the future happiness of their existence. There were portraits here too, mostly of seamstresses, sailors, and peasants—in a word, the People—as well as several colorful illustrations of folktales, produced in Malinin's more whimsical moments and including the celebrated *Firebird,* displayed across the entrance, in the place of honor.

Sukhanov walked almost without pausing. The main quality uniting all these works, he felt privately, was the inherent ease with which they slid into oblivion the moment one's back was turned, so nondescript were they, so similar to a thousand other paintings. Malinin's genre scenes read like a page from a textbook, and Malinin's faces were drawn so precisely, so airlessly, that they seemed to lack one of the two requisite dimensions. Still, the old man was not altogether without talent, and there were three or four pieces, perhaps, that stood out from the rest. This one, for instance.

A pale-haired young woman in light blue emerged dreamily from the darker blue of the sky or possibly a lake, its colors melting gently into the colors of her dress. Her soft gaze was directed not at the viewer, but through him, beyond him, at something truly happy that only she could see, something that brought a tender shadow of a smile to her face. A different work this was, without a doubt— an intimate work. Sukhanov bent to read the label underneath: "*A Future Mother,* 1965. On loan from a private collection." Once again, he could not help wincing, even though he understood the inevitability of such a name—after all, he himself had played a role in establishing the tradition whereby portraits of family members were mildly frowned upon, tainted as they were with the sin of being "slightly bourgeois." Since the straightforward title *The Artist's Daughter* was thus out of the question, Pyotr Alekseevich had given them a choice.

"Either *A Future Mother* or *A Russian Beauty*," he had said. "Take your pick."

Like most Soviet art, the painting shied away from needless phys-iological detail (Sukhanov's mind automatically dealt out the term "sordid naturalism"), giving no obvious indications of its delicate subject: the woman's body, neither thin nor full, discreetly faded into the background. All the same, Sukhanov had found the title inexcus-ably crude. Surprisingly, it was Nina who had insisted on this choice. "Apart from the fact that calling my own portrait 'beauty' is in bad taste, beauty is really not what it's about," she had said as the two of them stood arguing in Sukhanov's study.

And indeed, she was right. Of course, the woman on the canvas was beautiful, for the likeness was considerable—and yet Sukhanov had always felt that the depiction failed to capture some vital quality of Nina's, some precious, elusive essence, uniquely hers, that imbued her with that cold, mysterious radiance he so admired. It was this quality that even in her awkward adolescence had earned her the nickname Mermaid, and made her eyes appear to change so unpre-dictably from gray to green to blue and her half-smile so hard to describe—the very same quality, perhaps, that, even now, made him look at her at times and wonder what her thoughts were. The thoughts of the painted Nina, on the other hand, were transparent. She had no obliqueness in her, no vagueness, no mystery as she sat there, young, healthy, content, listening to a new life, Vasily's life, stirring inside her. And ironically, it was precisely this simplicity, this clarity, this lack of depth, so typical of Malinin, that had endeared the portrait to Sukhanov. He had hung it in the study across from his desk and frequently glanced at it as he worked, especially—especially in the first few years. The vision of the unequivocally happy, unquestionably blue-eyed Nina never failed to reassure him, affirming over and over that everything had been justified, that his life was proceeding according to plan, that his choice had not been one irreparable, terrible—

Sukhanov briskly shook his head as if to rid himself of a persistent fly. In any case, he would certainly miss her for the next three months, he said to himself, and casting one last glance at the young woman floating in her blue cloud of joy, walked off in search of the original. He saw Nina from afar, standing with her father, smiling lightly at something the Minister had said. For an instant her eyes met his across the room, then slipped away. He headed toward her, but his progress was constantly halted by bothersome acquaintances entangling him in sticky cobwebs of anecdotes, compliments, and invitations. Then all at once there was a movement among the guests, a general reorganization, a snapping to order, a spreading hush; and a moment later the Minister himself appeared on a low podium in the back of the hall, a prudent glass of water in his hand.

Going to be a long one, Sukhanov thought without interest as he applauded.

"Dear comrades, I don't need to tell you why we have gathered here today," the Minister began when the place had fallen quiet. "Neither do I need to introduce to you our beloved Pyotr Alekseevich Malinin, one of the greatest artists of our century, two-time laureate of the Lenin Prize, member of the Academy of Arts of the USSR since 1947, the year of its creation, three-time winner of—"

As he spoke, he dipped his gaze repeatedly into a stack of paper. Feigning rapt attention, Sukhanov let himself drift away, basking in a wonderfully warm, mindless feeling of overall well-being. Everything in his life was well arranged, yes, everything was perfect, and most deservedly so—and thus he took it almost as his due when, after the important people had said all the necessary words and while the unimportant people were still holding forth, hopelessly trying to regain the attention of the merrily disintegrating room, the Minister emerged from the swiftly parting crowd and placed his hand on Sukhanov's shoulder.

"So, Tolya, how are things? Going well, I trust," he said jovially. "Lucky bastard, married to the most gorgeous woman in Moscow!"

Sukhanov brushed off the sudden distracting thought that the man reminded him of someone, and said something very pleasant and instantly forgettable about the Minister's wife. The Minister laughed, looked at him slyly, and asked, "You smoke?"

Sukhanov did not smoke.

"Naturally," he replied without a heartbeat of hesitation.

Leaving a trail of square-jawed youths behind them, the two walked outside, and immediately a cigarette materialized in Sukhanov's fingers, he knew not how. It was hastily followed by a lit match that originated somewhere in the darkness of the portico and dutifully flew up to his face, illuminating the proffering hand and the infinitely respectful smile of the doorman with the ridiculous mustache. The cringing recognition in the man's eyes pleased Sukhanov immensely. Cringe, my friend, cringe, he thought as he stood trying not to inhale the smoke, the Minister's hand still resting on his shoulder. Perhaps next time you will think twice before you bar the entrance to a man on the very best terms with the very best people—a man who is, in fact, the only son-in-law of the hero of the evening—and moreover, a voice inside him added with false modesty, a man who is himself something of a weight in the art world, pun most certainly intended.

For the past twelve years Anatoly Pavlovich Sukhanov had occupied the most influential, most enviable post of editor in chief at the country's leading art magazine, *Art of the World*.

The Minister had a funny manner of puffing out his cheeks as he exhaled his smoke.

"Masha was rather taken with your son," he said after a short, congenial silence. "A very nice young man. What is he doing, I forget?"

"He is at the Foreign Affairs Institute, graduating next spring," replied Sukhanov proudly. "Their number-one student. Takes to languages like a duck to water."

"Ah, is that so?" said the Minister, visibly impressed.

Assuredly, assuredly he resembled someone, especially when he blew out his cheeks in that fashion. . . . Suddenly worried that he was staring, Sukhanov glanced away, across the street—and it was then that he became aware of something distressing. He averted his eyes for an instant, then looked again. There was no mistake, none whatsoever.

"Listen, Tolya," the Minister was saying in the meantime, "I'm having a bit of a get-together at my dacha this Tuesday, nothing big, just me, Masha, and a few close friends. My daughter will be stopping by as well—a very pretty girl, by the way. So I thought maybe you and Vasily . . . Is something the matter?"

Sukhanov was craning his neck, staring up and down the quiet street.

"I don't know," he said in bewilderment. "My car . . . it's not where it's supposed to be. I told the fellow to wait for us over there."

"Yes, well, all chauffeurs drink," the Minister pronounced philosophically. "He'll turn up before the evening is over, I'm sure. Now, about Tuesday—"

But Sukhanov continued to blink and peer into the dimness.

"There must be some mistake," he kept muttering. "Volodya's been with us for a couple of years, and in all this time he's never . . . I simply can't think of a reason . . ."

Taking off his glasses, he rubbed the lenses with the underside of his jacket. Uncovered, his eyes looked indecently naked and lost. The Minister frowned slightly and tossed away his cigarette.

"Well, seeing as you are so preoccupied right now," he said some-what coldly, "we'll continue this conversation another time. So long, Tolya."

For a few minutes Sukhanov waited by the entrance, still staring, as if trying by sheer act of will to conjure the missing car from the dense shadows of the trees underneath which it rightfully should have been, by all the laws of his universe. Things like this never, almost never, happened to him, and when they did, they tended to upset him tremendously. As he stood there, a light drizzle began to fall, and soon the street was glistening unpleasantly. He turned to go inside, and the doorman leapt to throw the door open before him, but this time Sukhanov thought he saw the hint of a mocking smile on the man's mustachioed lips. Immediately he told himself it was only his imagination, but it nonetheless triggered a surge of sudden fear in him, as if some irreparable damage had been done—as if, in the very moment of his disturbing discovery, the Minister had begun to say something important, something absolutely vital, perhaps, and he, engrossed as he had been in his confusion, had missed it, missed it unforgivably, missed it forever . . .

But try as he might, the substance of the Minister's words escaped him, and the nagging little idea of the man's resemblance to someone kept getting mixed up with his thoughts and leading him astray, until, gradually, his panic abated. Even if there had been some unwanted rudeness on his part—and he was positive, almost positive there had been none—he would smooth it over later; right now he had a problem to resolve. If that fellow had really left to have a drink, they would fire him on the spot, he decided indignantly, and dodging conversations, set out to find Nina.

She had quit her father's side when the speeches had started, but Pyotr Alekseevich, to whom Sukhanov now paid hurried respects, said he had seen her only recently talking to Ksenya. Growing restless, Sukhanov dove into the crowd once again. A few paces away, a young girl with a boy's haircut blocked his way.

"Good evening, Anatoly Pavlovich," she said solemnly. Her voice was high and thin, almost childlike. "My name is Lina Gordon, I'm a journalist. I'm writing an article on the Malinin retrospective. Could you answer a couple of questions for me, please? As the editor of *Art of the World*, I'm sure you'll provide invaluable insight to my readers."

He looked at her incredulously. Her skinny neck stuck out of an absurdly cheap yellow dress, and her lips were pale and chapped. She was clutching an open pad.

"What . . . er . . . what newspaper did you say you were with?" he asked with an involuntary smile.

"I'm working for a Moscow State University magazine," she replied evenly, uncapping her pen. "So, do you like Malinin's paintings, Anatoly Pavlovich? Do you think they are good art?"

As he continued to study her, his amusement increased. Her raspberry-colored nail polish was peeling. She probably bit her nails, she was just the type.

"Ah, a university magazine," he said. "Naturally, you must mean a student publication. If you don't mind me asking, how old are you? Eighteen? Seventeen?"

The transparent tips of her awkwardly protruding, boyish ears brightened.

"My age is completely irrelevant here," she said. "I have an assignment from the magazine. Now, please, what do you think of Malinin's work?"

She was so earnest, so flushed with her own importance that he took pity on her.

"Oh, all right," he said, and cleared his throat. "I have only a minute, but in a nutshell, these canvases show the best of the Russian land, with all its grandeur, lyricism, and courage. Pyotr Alekseevich has an incredible gift for representing the true Russian people at their best moments, in such an open, thoughtful, direct way, which demonstrates most purely—"

She watched him with a brown-eyed, steady gaze; he found it mildly disconcerting that she took no notes. When he stopped talking, she shook her head.

"No, I don't believe you really think that," she said. "His paintings are so fake that everyone must see it, they are just afraid to say it. That trite portrait over there, for instance—obviously, there is not a grain of truth in it. Don't you agree?"

Taken aback by the certainty in her voice, he looked in the direction in which she was pointing. Then his eyes grew cold. The joke had all at once ceased to entertain him, and he remembered again his tippling chauffeur, the vague but unfortunate incident with the Minister, the tedious necessity to address the situation as soon as possible . . .

"I think the real question to ask, young lady, is how you came to be here," he said brusquely. "Only accredited journalists are permitted at this opening. A school assignment doesn't give you the right to accost people."

His tone clearly startled her. Her eyes narrowed and her mouth turned mean, making her look every bit the scrawny little adolescent that she was. She hesitated before answering, then said reluctantly, "Your daughter gave me an invitation. I'm in her class."

"Ah, my daughter! Of course, I should have known. I gave her an extra one and told her to bring along someone nice from her department." He regarded her angular face with distaste. "Well, charming to meet you, Lida."

"Lina," the girl corrected sullenly. Her pad, he noticed, was now closed.

"A piece of friendly advice," he said dryly. "Those artistic ideas of yours, I wouldn't advertise them so openly if I were you—you never know who might hear you. Oh, before we part, you haven't by any chance seen Ksenya?"

She jerked her chin toward the exit. He turned to go.

"I don't care who hears me," she threw at his back. "The times are changing."

He glanced at her over his shoulder, and his heart wavered. There she stood, so young, so defiant, so sad-looking in her ugly yellow dress two sizes too big, so infuriating in her self-righteousness, so pathetic in her desire to have the last word.

"The times are always changing, my dear Lida," he said, not unkindly. "But it would serve you well to remember that certain things always stay the same."

She might have said something in response, but he could no longer hear. Purposefully he strode across the room, to where he now saw Ksenya, dressed inappropriately in a pair of slacks, slouching by herself against the wall with that typical look of a casual observer on her face. His mood was turning more sour by the minute.

"I see you found a perfect use for your spare invitation," he said, sounding somewhat out of breath, as he stopped before her. "I've met your friend, and she is adorable. Has the highest opinion of your grandfather's work too."

Ksenya shrugged. "You don't have to like my friends," she said indifferently. "Most of them don't like you either."

Her heavy-lidded gray eyes seemed full of sleep. For some reason her answer made him feel neither angry nor offended but uncomfortable, as if he had missed the familiar door and walked into a strange room full of edgy objects and disturbing shadows.

"We can talk about your friends' feelings later," he said in what he hoped was a sufficiently stern voice. "Right now I'm looking for your mother. Have you seen her?"

"She's gone."

"Gone," he repeated. "Gone where?"

"She got one of her headaches and went home, about half an hour ago. She said it was nearly over anyway. Oh, I almost forgot, she took the car. She asked me to tell you."

He looked at his daughter without understanding.

"Why didn't she tell me herself?" he managed finally.

Ksenya shrugged again. "I guess she saw you talking to Mr. Big Shot and didn't want to disturb you. So, you boys had a good chat?"

Sukhanov had a sudden desire to clutch his head. Instead he nodded dully and stood thinking for a moment. The Minister and his wife had already departed.

Feeling a tiny throb in his left temple, the advent of a headache of his own, he slowly walked outside, leaving all the noise, light, and warmth behind him.

Two

It was raining in earnest now. Streetlamps swam through the liquid mist, their pale reflections drowning in an inverted world of running asphalt. The empty space before the Manège quivered in the wet darkness, and the gray monstrosity of the Hotel Moskva had melted away into a barely visible shimmer of lights. For a minute Sukhanov lingered in the shelter of the pseudo-Doric columns. He felt relieved that the mustachioed doorman was no longer there, having been replaced, he noticed, by another one, and a strange one at that—an older, slovenly man wearing a burgundy velveteen blazer. The new doorman was looking at him from the shadows. Probably amused to see me standing here, in my most formal attire, and without a chauffeur, Sukhanov thought with displeasure, and turning away, peered dejectedly through the wall of water.

Finding a taxi at this hour and in this weather would be almost impossible, and with a sigh he resigned himself to the inevitable; the metro station was, after all, very close, just beyond his field of vision.

He had not the slightest idea how much it cost. Pulling out his wallet, he ruffled through a stack of bills, gloomily groped for some coins, and fishing out a couple, dropped them into his coat pocket. The night breathed damply, heavily in his face, and the doorman, he saw, was still staring in his direction. Irritated, he squared his shoulders and descended into the rain.

"Anatoly, is that you?" asked a halting voice behind his back.

He froze. The voice—the voice was unmistakably familiar. Water ran down his collar, sending one particularly persistent little rivulet all the way down his spine. Slowly he turned and walked up the steps.

The doorman in the velveteen blazer moved into a shaft of light.

"Lev," said Sukhanov expressionlessly.

For the briefest of moments they regarded each other. Then, simultaneously, it must have occurred to both of them that, after so many years, something had to be done—an embrace, a kiss, some gesture of human warmth. . . . Stepping forward at the same time, they collided clumsily and, embarrassed, abbreviated their hug and shook hands instead, groping at each other's cuffs. Another drop of water, originating somewhere at Sukhanov's wrist, snaked icily down his arm.

"You've changed a lot," the fake doorman said. "Gained weight, become all solid. This tuxedo . . . And the glasses too . . . You never used to wear glasses."

"Yes, well, my eyes," Sukhanov said vaguely, and added after a pause, "None of us is getting any younger."

"No, it's not just the age, it's—"

The thought remained incomplete. A car splashed by, stirring red zigzags in its wake; they followed it with their eyes. When it passed, Marx Avenue reverted to shiny blackness. Sukhanov felt his initial shock subsiding into dull discomfort.

"And you, you haven't changed at all," he said.

In a strange way, he meant it, and not as a compliment. Of course, Lev Belkin displayed plenty of wear and tear for his fifty-three, or was it fifty-two, years—he seemed unkempt and unsettled, with all the telling signs of age and hard luck about him, and was dressed like an old circus clown; the dreadful velveteen blazer had brown leather patches at the elbows, and an absurd maroon bow tie sat askew at his throat. But Sukhanov knew wretchedness and disorder to be essentially the qualities of youth, which was why most worthwhile people eventually outlived them. Belkin had clearly chosen not to do so. To Sukhanov's eyes he looked just like the young man he had once known, only used, downtrodden, gone to seed. . . .

"I haven't changed, and yet you didn't recognize me," Belkin said.

"Well, you know what they say—if someone who knows you well doesn't recognize you, you'll end up rich," Sukhanov joked humorlessly.

"I'm afraid it's a bit late for that," the other man replied with a short laugh. "Not all of us are destined for riches."

"Oh, for God's sake!" Sukhanov said sharply. But immediately it occurred to him that, perhaps, Belkin had meant no offense and there had been no need to react with such hostility, no need at all. Belkin did not answer, and for an uneasy minute they watched the rain slash through Manezhnaya Square; and all the while Sukhanov searched for some friendly, casual words—yet none came to mind. It had simply been too long, and anything that could be said should have been said many years ago.

Presently a rectangle of brightness cut a patch out of the portico floor, and Sukhanov caught a glimpse of the real doorman in the vestibule, bending politely at the open door. The foyer yawned with an inviting warmth, and a well-known actor emerged, in the process of unfolding an enormous pink umbrella over his nineteen-year-old wife. The couple chirped "Good night" to Anatoly Pavlovich, stared at Belkin with unbridled curiosity, and ran to a Volga that had just pulled up. The girl was giggling, and Sukhanov distinctly heard her say *babochka*—"bow tie" or "butterfly"—but the night swallowed the rest of the sentence and he tried to convince himself she was discussing lepidoptery rather than Belkin's unfortunate neck decoration. Still, that was unpleasant, very unpleasant—the tittering, the gaping, and God only knew what they had thought. . . . He considered Belkin darkly, and a sense of oppression descended on him.

"So, Lev," he said, "how did I miss seeing you in there?"

"Oh," said Belkin, "I wasn't at the opening, I don't have an invitation. I was just—"

The door was being pushed open again, and in the widening gap Sukhanov saw the massive crimson bosom of the theater critic's wife, followed by her grasshopper of a husband. Suddenly frantic, he began to maneuver Belkin away from the entrance, down the steps, muttering as he did so, "People starting to leave . . . no reason to be in their way . . . might as well move . . ." Cold rain slapped his face as he rounded the corner; Belkin trotted after him obediently. Almost, almost, just a bit more—and finally, thank God, they were out of sight, pressed into the wall under the scanty protection of a narrow cornice. Mercifully, no one had seen—except for that long-haired what's-his-name with his pink umbrella and his adolescent bride, but no matter, he was not important enough. Trying to suppress a shudder of relief, Sukhanov wiped the water from his glasses.

"I mean to go when it's open to the public, of course," Belkin was saying, noticing nothing. "By the way, how was it?"

"Great. Very interesting works. A perfect space for displaying them too."

"Perfect, eh?" Belkin repeated, and squinted at him good-naturedly. "You used to say the Manège was better as a riding academy, that its architecture was suited for horses, not paintings—"

And then, without any warning, an incredible smile flashed across Belkin's face. It was his unforgettable trick of old, that smile, the sort that very few people ever possessed; it transformed his ordi-

narily woebegone features instantly, brilliantly, imbuing them with
rare humanity, with a kind of intense, radiant meaning. Smiling, he
lightly touched a button on Sukhanov's jacket.

"You also said that in a way it was appropriate, because most of
the artists who exhibited here were fit to be displayed only in a stable.
Do you remember, Tolya?"

It was astonishing, simply astonishing, that after all this time the
man could still smile like that—and it was suddenly disconcerting to
see how little his eyes had changed, how, in spite of the lines at the
corners, the pouches underneath, the eyelids that had grown heavy,
they could still dance in his face, they could still play with the same
dark, fiery, infectious life.

"I don't remember," Sukhanov replied stiffly. "I don't know . . .
Perhaps I said something like that once. In any event, they've redone
the place since—" He faltered and ended hurriedly, "It's completely
different now."

Belkin looked Sukhanov full in the face, then twisted his lips,
nodded, and released the button. The fire in his eyes dwindled away,
and the tired creases around his mouth became more pronounced.

"Funny," he said flatly, "it looks exactly the same to me. I visit
almost every exhibition, you know. Staying abreast of the new developments and all that. Not that there are any, but one keeps hoping."

"Yes," said Sukhanov, not knowing what else to say, and righted
his glasses.

The whole thing was awkward—awkward and unnecessary.
There was so little space under the cornice that with every motion
their shoulders nudged each other softly, and the dripping, splashing,
murky world kept creeping closer, invading their cramped refuge,
lapping at the edges of dryness, already seeping into Sukhanov's
beautifully polished shoes. He ached to be away, to be home, where it
was light, warm, and comfortable, to be drinking his nightly tea. . . .
The encounter was stretching to nightmarish proportions, and he

knew he needed to end it, end it now, this very instant—but strangely, he could do nothing, as if he were trapped in a tedious, helpless dream. A short-haired girl darted across their lengthening pause, and he thought he saw the edge of a yellow dress flash beneath the flapping fold of a flimsy coat, but she ran by so quickly he could not be sure. Belkin too watched her melt in the rain.

"So, is Nina here?" he asked when the water had erased the girl's steps.

"She got tired and went home early," Sukhanov said, and added, pointing across the street, "She took our car."

"Ah . . . A pity. I was hoping to see her. I bet she hasn't changed one bit."

"We all change," said Sukhanov. "None of us is getting any younger."

God, haven't I said that already, he thought miserably.

"And how is . . . er . . . Alla?" he asked, to prevent another silence.

"Oh, didn't you know? She left me a long time ago. She's married to a math teacher now. Has three kids. But she is doing quite well, thanks for asking."

"Sorry, I didn't know. . . . But apart from that . . . That is, how are you getting along in general?"

"Not too bad, thanks. Painting and all. And you?"

"Can't complain, can't complain . . ." He coughed, shifted his weight to the other foot. Their shoulders grazed again. "Well, it seems that the rain's almost over."

It was raining every bit as hard as before.

"Yes, certainly looks that way," agreed Belkin. "So, where are you off to now? I'm heading for the metro. Shall we walk together? I have an umbrella."

"I would, but . . . I need to go the other way," said Sukhanov with a vague gesture.

"Of course, I understand," Belkin said quietly. "Well, good-bye then, Anatoly. Good luck to you and everything."

He turned up the collar of his burgundy blazer, produced a disheveled umbrella from his pocket (ridiculous, who in the world keeps a wet umbrella in his pocket!), and without another glance stepped into the darkness. Sukhanov noticed that he stooped. Strange, he used to carry himself so straight, he thought involuntarily—and all at once, this stray little thought released in him some echo of the past, a solitary trembling note whose sound rose higher and higher in his chest, awakening inarticulate longings and, inseparable from them, a piercing, unfamiliar sorrow. He watched as Belkin trudged away into the downpour under his lopsided umbrella with one spoke sticking out, and he thought bitterly, Here we are, two aging fools, and our lives almost over. His throat tightened, and for a second he was afraid he would not be able to call out, to say anything at all. . . . Then the spasm passed.

"Leva, wait!" he shouted.

He feared at first that Belkin had not heard, that the rain had snatched away his words. Then Belkin turned. He was struggling with the umbrella, which had grown unruly.

"Listen, Leva, why did you come here tonight?"

"Oh, I was just passing by when the rain started, and I thought I'd wait it out!" Belkin yelled back.

Sukhanov could not see his eyes—he was too far, it was too dark.

"But . . . you have an umbrella!" he shouted again.

"Not a very useful one, as you can see."

"Oh yes, of course, I see! Well, so long now. Say hi to . . . I mean, take care of yourself!"

Belkin did not move. The umbrella flapped over his head like a demented bird. Several moments passed, dreary, endless as a lifetime. Then he muttered something under his breath and strode back, throwing up sprays of water with each heavy step. His face, as he stopped before Sukhanov, streamed with rain.

"All right, so that wasn't true," he said, scowling. "I came because I wanted to see you. You and Nina. I read about the opening, and I thought, What better chance will I have?"

Violently squashing the umbrella, he dropped it at his feet, then fumbled in his sagging pocket. A golden candy wrapper flew out, twirled in the wind, and drowned. Sukhanov observed his movements with strange anticipation. Finally Belkin extracted what looked like a glossy postcard and held it locked between his palms.

"I wanted to give you this," he said. "It's next Wednesday. Naturally, it's not going to be a big deal, nothing to write about in the papers. . . . Anyway, I realize now it was stupid of me, you can't possibly be interested, so—"

Wordlessly Sukhanov stretched out a slightly trembling hand. Belkin hesitated, then shrugged, and shoved the postcard at him. A jumble of multicolored letters leapt wildly, confusingly, in all directions, against a shocking neon-green background. Sukhanov took off his glasses, smeared rain all over the lenses, and tried again. The letters started to behave more predictably, and eventually, in a long minute or two, joined to form a few words—"L. B. Belkin (1932–). Moscow Through a Rainbow"—and, underneath, in smaller print, the address, the dates, the times . . .

And as Sukhanov looked in silence, he knew that his wrenching sorrow was giving way to some other, as yet unnamed, feeling, which was slowly unfurling its black, powerful wings inside his heart.

Belkin began to speak rapidly. "It's my first, you see. True, I've had a few things displayed here and there, but this one, it's all my own. Just a little gallery in the Arbat, but I'll have the whole place to myself. The name, of course, is idiotic—it's so cliché, it wasn't my idea, but I let them do it, because my work is all about color studies anyway, so I thought . . . Oh, hell, what am I talking about?"

Abruptly he stopped, pressing his fingertips to his temples. Then, in a different voice, quiet and oddly desperate, he said, "Listen, Tolya, I know we didn't remain friends, but it's been almost a quarter of a century, and . . . Well, it would make me really happy if you and Nina could come to the opening. It's on Wednesday, at seven o'clock, it's all written right here, in the corner, see?"

Sukhanov started as if emerging from a trance. He had a broad smile on his face.

"Of course," he said, twisting the card and smiling, smiling. "That is, I'll have to check my schedule, but I'll be glad if I can . . . Nina too, I'm sure . . . Most glad . . ."

Belkin looked at him closely, then averted his eyes.

"It would mean a lot to me," he said softly. "But I'll understand if you're busy, I know this is rather short notice. . . . Please say hi to Nina for me. Good night, Tolya."

"Good night, Leva," said Sukhanov, still smiling.

Belkin raised a hand in one last farewell and walked off, grappling with his glistening absurdity of an umbrella. Sukhanov remained where he was, crushing the card in his fingers, smiling the same frozen smile as he gazed into nothingness. In a short while the rain began to diminish, rarefy, slow down, until it reverted to the same innocuous drizzle with which it had started earlier—an hour or an eternity ago, depending on one's point of view. . . . Sukhanov blinked, shook the water off his shoes, buried the wet invitation in his pocket, and briskly set off in the opposite direction from the one in which his former best friend had disappeared.

He was halfway across Red Square when it occurred to him that he had forgotten to say congratulations.

THREE

The black face of the giant clock on the Spasskaya Tower swam ominously in the floodlit clouds; as its golden hand shivered and leapt to a new notch, the chimes announced a quarter to an hour. It had been years, if not decades, since Sukhanov had last found himself in Red Square so late at night, and the virtually deserted, brightly illuminated expanse made him feel uneasy. The greenish cobblestones, slippery from the rain, glistened coldly, and the cathedral of Vasily Blazhennyi rose before him like a many-headed, iridescent, scaly dragon from some tale with an unhappy ending. A youth in an oversized purple jacket appeared from nowhere and followed him for a while, his steps echoing loudly and menacingly in the surrounding stillness; then, just as abruptly, he was gone. Sukhanov nervously touched the lining of his breast pocket and walked faster. As he neared the end of the square, it seemed to him that someone tittered from the dense shadows. He reached the Bolshoi Moskvoretsky Bridge almost at a run.

There he stopped and leaned against the parapet to catch his breath. His legs were aching. Below, the Moscow River moved its slow, dense, brown waters, and from their depths emerged a flimsy upside-down city that existed only at night, created by a thousand shimmering intertwinings of streetlights, headlights, floodlights. The walls, the churches, the bell towers of the underwater city trembled with a desire to break free, to float away with the current, to leave the oppressing, crowded, dangerous Moscow far, far behind; but the night held them firmly, and they stayed forever tethered to their places by infinite golden chains of reflections. Other things were luckier in their flight—a dead branch, a billowing white scarf, a fleet of cigarette butts, a gasoline stain widening in the beam of light . . . Unable to tear his eyes away, Sukhanov looked at the rainbow-colored film spreading across the water. The invitation burned in his pocket, and that unnameable feeling was beating its great black wings in the hollow of his soul.

Suddenly the sounds of someone running banged along the pavement, growing closer. He swung around. The youth in the purple jacket stood behind him, grinning and breathing noisily. Sukhanov glanced up and down the bridge in desperation, but there was no one, no one at all; only cars flew in and out of the night, too quickly, too quickly . . . His heart pushed in his throat.

"Nice tie you have there, mister," the youth said conversationally. "What's the label?"

Sukhanov swallowed. "What do you mean, 'label'?"

"I mean, who made it?" the youth said. "It's got to be written on it."

Moving slowly as if underwater, Sukhanov lifted his favorite wine-red tie and read in a faltering voice, with a sense of nearing doom, "It's . . . er . . . Christian Dior."

"How nice for you," the youth said, clicking his tongue in appreciation.

"Listen, what do you want?" Sukhanov said hoarsely. "Do you want this tie? Take it."

"Nah, thanks, don't need it," said the youth, "not my style. How about two kopecks, though?"

"You want two kopecks?" Sukhanov repeated dully.

The youth nodded, and his eyes darted crazily in his pimpled face. Knowing that something unthinkable was about to befall him, Sukhanov reached a shaking hand into his pocket and held out a few coins. One single thought fluttered in him like a dying moth—why didn't I take the metro, why didn't I take the metro, why didn't I . . . The bridge was deserted, and he imagined himself flying, falling endlessly through the night, plunging toward a dark, cold death below, and this monster laughing, laughing above him. . . . The youth bent over his hand, so close that Sukhanov could smell the stale smoke on his breath.

"Let's see what you have here. Five, ten, another five . . . Aha, here we go!" He picked a small copper coin from Sukhanov's palm. "Well, thanks so much, mister. Got to go call my mom now. She always worries when I stay out late."

And with these words he turned and walked off, back toward Red Square. In an instant the bridge seemed filled with people. Two drunk girls stumbled along, singing over and over, "We wish you happiness," a line from a popular song; a middle-aged couple passed, arguing about a burnt teakettle; a group of six or seven little Asian men in suits trotted by, carrying a gigantic map of the city unfolded between them, taking countless pictures of the river, chattering in some birdlike tongue. Sukhanov stared about in astonishment, unable to comprehend what had just happened. Then, all at once, he understood, and a wave of laughter washed over him. That boy—that hooligan with the lunatic eyes—had simply needed change for a public phone.

And at that glorious moment of realization, all the misfortunes of the evening turned trivial in Sukhanov's mind, and even the whole

Belkin incident did not matter any longer. The beating of the black wings ceased in his heart. Oh, it was all quite obvious really, not worth another thought. Of course, the man had come for the sole purpose of humiliating him—him, Sukhanov, who had accomplished so much in life! Yes, he had come to fling his success in Sukhanov's face—but in truth, there was no success, just a measly little show that had arrived a lifetime too late and meant nothing. Still laughing, Sukhanov pulled the invitation out of his pocket. The glossy paper had hardened with dampness, but after a brief struggle he overcame its resistance, ripping it along the middle, then again, then again. . . . As he threw the pieces over the parapet and watched them spiral down into the lead-colored water, he felt perfectly at peace with himself. One shred fluttered in the air and landed on the railing; he saw three brightly colored letters, blue, indigo, and violet—the very tail of the rainbow. For an instant he looked at the letters with narrowed eyes, then shrugged and sent the shred into the dim, glimmering void with an adroit flick of his finger.

The rest happened with the magic facility of a dream. Immediately as he turned to go, a taxi approached with a welcoming green light burning behind its windshield. Incredibly, it pulled to a stop even before he had time to raise his hand, and then there he was, in the backseat, leaning forward to give the address.

After his brush with death, everything seemed impossibly amusing to him—the quickening flicker of shop signs beyond his window, the cab that, for some unfathomable reason, smelled of violets, the driver whom he could not see clearly in the shadows but whose funny straw-colored beard and old-fashioned glasses leapt in continuous jolts through the rearview mirror, and most of all, the stubborn solemnity with which the man kept assuring him that his street did not exist.

"Belinsky Street?" he was exclaiming. "Believe me, comrade, I know Moscow like my own hand"—every time he said that, he lifted a delicate, childlike hand off the wheel and wiggled his fingers—

"and there is no such street anywhere near the Tretyakovskaya Gallery."

"There most certainly is, I guarantee you," Sukhanov repeated. "I've lived on that street for the past twelve years, so I should know."

This argument would make the man fall quiet for a minute or two, but invariably he would start again, and his beard's reflection would flit about in agitation as the darkness inside the taxi breathlessly chased the darkness outside.

"Of course, it's your business, comrade. If you want to be taken to a place that does not exist, who am I to stop you? Why, I take people places all the time, and half of them end up somewhere they had no intention of going, but me, I never object, I—"

"Turn left here," Sukhanov interrupted. "The gray building on the right, you see?"

"This?" the driver said triumphantly. "I knew it! This here is no Belinsky Street. This is Voskresensky Passage. Let me back up to the sign and I'll show you, hold on."

Sukhanov smiled indulgently. The tires squealed. The square black letters on the white background spelled out "Belinsky Street," as, naturally, he knew they would. There was a momentary silence, and then a long, sorrowful sigh sounded in the dimness.

"I don't believe it!" the man wailed softly. "They've renamed this one too! And the old name was so much better. . . . Please accept my apologies. I've memorized the whole map of the city, you see, the street names, the intersections, everything, but my map is a bit out of date—it was printed before the Revolution—so this kind of thing is bound to happen from time to time."

"And does it happen often?" Sukhanov inquired innocently.

The man suppressed a sob. "Almost always," he confessed in a tragic whisper.

What a loon, thought Sukhanov, as he extracted a ten-ruble bill from his wallet.

"Perhaps you should buy yourself a new map with the change," he said generously, and chuckling under his breath, stepped out of the car, catching as he did so the last sparkle of the glasses and a farewell wave of the yellow beard bristling on the man's invisible chin.

Nina was standing in the illuminated doorway, her face tired and pale, her fingers drumming on the doorjamb.

"I saw the taxi from the window," she said. "I was getting worried—Ksenya and Vasily returned over an hour ago. . . . Oh, but your jacket is all wet!"

"The rain was nothing," said Sukhanov nonchalantly. "On the other hand, I did nearly get mugged."

Nina clutched the golden-edged blue robe at her throat.

"It's all my fault, isn't it?" she said. "I should have waited for you in the car."

A few minutes later Sukhanov, wrapped in a matching red robe, sat in the brightly lit kitchen, under a low-hanging orange lamp-shade, drinking cognac-laced tea and energetically devouring strawberry preserves. Around him, his family was gathered.

"And then I said to the man, 'You want my tie, eh? Well, I don't think so, I'm rather partial to it myself. Here, take these two kopecks instead, that's all you are good for,'" Sukhanov was saying with enjoyment between the sweet spoonfuls.

"But Tolya, he could have hurt you!" Nina exclaimed. "What if he had a knife?"

"He probably did," he said airily. "Ksenya, pass the sugar, please. . . . But when he saw I wouldn't make an easy victim, he just took his two kopecks and ran off."

"Father, you really are something," said Vasily, smiling.

"Yes, I wouldn't envy anyone who meets him one-on-one in a dark corner," said Ksenya.

"Wait a minute, that's hardly a compliment!" Sukhanov objected with a laugh.

In a short while, Vasily and Ksenya slipped away, and their doors closed in the far reaches of the corridor, his softly, hers with a bang. Nina and Sukhanov were left alone in the kitchen. He was in a wonderful mood.

"To be honest," he said, "I'm relieved this whole business wasn't Volodya's fault."

She glanced at him and moved her lips, but said nothing.

"He's a decent fellow, I would have been sad to let him go," he elaborated.

"I'm just glad everything ended well," she said, and pushed a plate of chocolate éclairs toward him. "Try these, they are really fresh. Valya bought them this evening."

For some time they drank their tea without speaking. Occasionally his or her spoon would graze the edge of a cup, and its silver click would fall like a pebble into a translucent pool of stillness, redefining it, making it cozier. The gentle light of the lamp wove a golden cocoon of tranquillity, perhaps even happiness, around them, closing them off protectively from the night, in whose shady courtyards and blind alleys unpleasant things were no doubt continuing to transpire this very moment—somewhere far, infinitely far away from the warm, sparkling, well-stocked kitchen of apartment fifteen, on the eighth floor of the nine-storied building number seven, Belinsky Street, in the heart of old Moscow. Indeed, at this instant, at nearly one o'clock in the morning on a chilly August night in the year 1985, just after the rain had washed over the roofs of the city, the familiar and delightful world of Anatoly Pavlovich Sukhanov existed quite independently of the world outside. The éclair melted deliciously on his tongue, and his tea was strong, just as he liked it. Row upon row of little jars containing concentrated tastes of the waning summer glittered evenly in cupboards all around him, and the air whispered of apples and cinnamon: Valya, their help who came in daily, had made his favorite apple pie only the day before, and the smells still lingered. A seemingly endless expanse of rooms unfolded behind his back, their comfortable dusk scintillating with the honeyed luster of parquet floors, damask wall upholstering, golden-flecked book bindings, crystal chandeliers opening like flowers in the high ceilings, many-antlered silver candelabra, and countless other precious possessions that the dim light hinted at tantalizingly, splendidly, as it seeped through the heavy velvet drapes. Somewhere in the recesses of his home, his two children were falling asleep, one a future diplomat, the other a future journalist, both equally gifted; and next to him, enclosed in the glowing circle of light, sat Nina, pale, disheveled, and so beautiful, her lips lightly traced with a glistening chocolate line. This was his world, and it was safe. The ebbing night had tried to meddle with him, to suck him into a dark, hidden, dangerous void— yet here he was at the end of the day, in his robe and slippers, eating his third pastry, and feeling content.

"You have some chocolate at the corner of your mouth, my love," he said. "Oh, and by the way, you'll never believe what happened just as I was . . . No, a bit higher . . . Now you've got it. . . . Yes, only imagine, as I was leaving the party, I ran into Belkin."

Nina set down her cup, missing the saucer. Some tea splashed out on the table.

"You saw Lev?" she said quietly.

"Lev Borisovich in person, the one and only," he replied with a wry smile.

The brown stain slowly devoured the tablecloth between them.

"What was he doing at the Manège?" she asked, her radiant green gaze fixed on his face with an unfamiliar, almost hopeful, expression. "Did he come to—"

"Oh, it was just a coincidence, nothing more," he said quickly. "He happened to be walking by when the rain began, and decided to wait it out under the portico. Practical things like umbrellas never occur to a man of his nature."

Her face suddenly remote, she looked down, noticed the stain, and started to dab at it assiduously with a dampened napkin. Sukhanov kept talking.

"He's become quite unpresentable, our Lev Borisovich has. Aged, unshaved, dressed in God knows what—some unimaginable bow-tie affair . . . I think he drinks. Of course, I would too if my life were such a dismal failure. But naturally, it was bound to come to this. Even his wife—"

"Do you want anything else?" she interrupted. "If you are done, I'll put everything away."

"Please," he said, and set down his last, unfinished, éclair. "Even his wife left him. Remember Alla? Frankly, I'm surprised she lasted as long as she did."

Nina continued to open and close cupboards in silence. Pleasantly full, he leaned back in his chair, delicately muffled a chocolate burp in his napkin, and hummed the duel aria from *Evgeny Onegin*. The table-cloth had a fetching pattern of wildflowers on it, he noticed absently. He was already beginning to feel a welcome advent of drowsiness when Nina sharply slammed the strawberry jar in its place. Startled, he glanced up, and found her looking at him. Her gray eyes were cold.

"His name is Vadim," she said.

"What was that, my love?"

"Our chauffeur. Our chauffeur's name is Vadim. Not Volodya. Not Vladislav. Not Vyacheslav. It's Vadim. He's worked for us for almost three years, and in all this time you haven't made an effort to remember his name."

Sukhanov sat up straight.

"So I did it again, didn't I?" he said amicably. "But my love, he has one of these names I always get wrong. You know how I am with names."

"Oh, it's not just names, Tolya, it's everything," she said, turning away. "In all my life, I've never met anyone with such a capacity to ignore and to forget."

The renewed kitchen silence ceased being comfortable. Frowning slightly, he rose to go.

"A courier came by while we were away," she said without looking in his direction, and dropped an avalanche of porcelain into the sink. "I put the envelope on your desk."

"I'll go and see," he said, and hesitated for a moment, then added with a somewhat ingratiating smile, "I simply don't know how I'm going to work without your portrait hovering over me, my love. I'm so used to its happy presence."

"I'm relieved it's gone," said Nina dryly. "It felt like a constant reproach to me."

"How do you mean?" he asked after a pause, but she said nothing else. The water was running noisily. With a suppressed sigh, he left the kitchen.

The large brown envelope contained three pages—two sheets of proofs, each in two pale columns of minuscule print, and a letter penned in sprawling handwriting, an intimate sign of particular respect. He skimmed it. *Dear Anatoly Pavlovich, would you be so kind as to check the enclosed for any possible additions or corrections. . . .*

The text, he already saw, was his own biography, to be included in an updated edition of *The Great Soviet Encyclopedia*, scheduled to appear early the next year. Feeling inexplicably nervous, he pulled closer his desk lamp, with its yellow shade perched on an elaborate bronze stand in the shape of a rearing Pegasus (a gift from his father-in-law), lifted a silver-handled magnifying glass from its embossed leather case ("To our highly esteemed Anatoly Pavlovich from his loyal colleagues, on the occasion of his fiftieth birthday"), and bent over the busy rows of facts.

"Born January 13, 1929, in Moscow. Demonstrated inordinate critical abilities early on. From 1947 to 1952, attended the Surikov Art Institute in order to acquire practical grounding for his theoretical studies. From 1952 to 1967, taught at the Moscow Higher Artistic and Technical Institute, during which period began to write his critically acclaimed works. In 1963, published his first article of major importance, 'Surrealism and Other Western "Isms" as Manifestations of Capitalist Insolvency' (reissued in monograph form in 1965), followed in 1964 by the equally significant *Contemporary Applications of the Socialist Realism Method to Landscape and Still Life*. Member of the Communist Party from 1964. Member of the USSR Union of Artists from 1965. In 1967, left his teaching job to head the Art Criticism Division of—"

Satisfied that his beginnings were covered in just the right manner, with no unnecessary, one might even say harmful, details, Sukhanov exhaled and read the rest less attentively, lightly nodding at each new landmark in his soaring career: a flock of articles, a host of distinctions, a couple more dizzying leaps through the ranks; two definitive textbooks, on the history and theory of Soviet art, in 1968 and 1970 (currently in their fourth and sixth editions, respectively); a critical study of Western art movements, in 1972; and finally, and most victoriously, his appointment as editor of *Art of the World* in 1973. A long paragraph was devoted to the summary of his work: "A. P. Sukhanov's studies achieve a brilliant synthesis of history and theory . . . invaluable for their practical applications to current developments . . . conclusive demonstration of impressionism, expressionism, and surrealism as movements in the service of capitalism . . . in his capacity as editor responsible for steering the field of Soviet art away from corrupting Western influences and toward true artistic principles . . ."

The last sentence, modestly rounding up the fireworks of praise, read simply: "At present lives in Moscow with his wife and two children."

And this, neatly compressed into the three and a half columns of fine print, was his life in its entirety—one man's conquering rise to prominence, with nothing to change and nothing to add, soon to be nestled side by side with greatness even greater than his in a massive compilation of Soviet accomplishment—the ultimate proof of having arrived.

At any other time, this brush with immortality would have engendered in Sukhanov a most contented glow of satisfaction, not unlike the delectably smooth warmth caused by a sip of the very best French cognac, and immediately he would have hurried to Nina, hoping for one of her rare smiles. But tonight she seemed in a strange, unapproachable mood, and his inability to share this triumph with her dampened his elation considerably. In addition, her accusation of forgetfulness bothered him, unfair though it was. Certainly, he was not very good at places, faces, names, for he did not care for the daily chaff of existence, and large numbers of people never became anything more to him than chance occupants of some random, briefly shared space—anonymous dwellers under the same roof, featureless crowds swimming past his car at red lights, blank-eyed students passing notes and peeling oranges in big auditoriums where he was occasionally asked to preside. It was likewise true that there were a number of things he had tried to forget on purpose, since he saw no reason to clutter his mind with facts and events that had long since outlived their usefulness. All the same, he was positive that everyone engaged in incidental editing of the past in order to survive—and that his memory, retaining everything vital, was just as good as the next man's.

Take his biography, for instance. Born in 1929, more than half a century ago—and yet his earliest recollection dated from shortly thereafter, when he could not have been more than two years old. A dirty gray carpet, a barefoot child playing listlessly with its shedding fibers in front of a window, beyond which there is an equally gray sky. Then an unexpected shaft of sunlight breaks through the clouds and penetrates the dusty room, and simultaneously two major shifts occur in the world. First, I realize that this foot with its splayed toes is mine, that this hand drawing a circle on the floor is also mine, that this playing child is, in fact, me—and second, and somehow more important, the carpet suddenly reveals its true color, and it's not gray at all, it's green, the deepest, purest, greenest green, the overwhelming color of my happiness. Yes, that is what I remember best—the colors, the fleeting shifts of shadows, certain ephemeral combinations of light and darkness; and when I lift my face to the window, the sunlight plays on my skin, alive and warm, and when I close my eyes, there are flashing red circles swimming lustrously behind my eyelids, and when I open my eyes again . . .

He opened his eyes, and was shocked to behold blackness instead of brightness behind the window and, reflected in the glass, the momentarily unrecognizable, vaguely unpleasant face of a middle-aged man with wide cheekbones, hair receding from a tall forehead, heavy jowls, small gray eyes swimming in two silver-rimmed holes of emptiness, and a thin mouth to which the lit windows in a building across the street imparted an illusory, horrible, golden-toothed smile. . . . Anatoly Pavlovich hastily took off his glasses. All at once it occurred to him that it was quite late, that it had been a very eventful day, that he was tired. Sighing, he slid the proofs neatly to the corner of his desk, pulled at a switch cord suspended between the bronze wings of Pegasus, and waded through familiar darkness to the bedroom where Nina was already sleeping, breathing in her soft, infinitely comforting way.

No sooner had he slipped into the night than he saw Belkin again, but this time there was nothing objectionable in his presence. Dressed in a tight maroon livery, Belkin stood immobile like a toy soldier in a corner of a hall set for a lavish dinner party but amusingly full of ribboned horses. The horses pranced about, having quiet, dignified conversations among themselves. One of them, covered with an embroidered red cloth with little golden bells around the edges, trotted toward Sukhanov and neighed solemnly, "My daughter is a very pretty girl," and he was just about to laugh in the horse's face, when Belkin jumped, grabbed hold of the tablecloth on the longest table, and pulled, and all the plates and silverware and goblets cascaded onto the floor with an earsplitting crash. Scandalized by such uncivilized behavior, Sukhanov sat up abruptly—and realized that Nina's soft breathing had stopped, and that she too was awake, leaning on her elbow in the dark next to him, listening intently. Tinkles of broken glass were still falling somewhere overhead, and now came a woman's muffled scream followed by a stampede of frantic footsteps. Then all was silent.

"What's going on?" he whispered.

"The woman upstairs has a sick father," Nina whispered back. "He must be having a bad night."

They listened for a while longer, but all seemed quiet, and Nina laid her head back onto her pillow; soon her breathing grew even again. The phosphorescent clock by the bed showed a few minutes past four. Feeling a bit unsettled, Sukhanov closed his eyes as well, wishing he could return to his curious dream about the talking horse—and it was precisely then that the day played one last trick on Anatoly Pavlovich. His memory stirred, reshuffled itself—and he knew without the slightest doubt that at the moment when he had stopped paying attention, the Minister of Culture had been in the process of inviting him to one of his famed dacha gatherings, and that there had even been some hint of an incredible, celestial combination involving the Minister's daughter and his own Vasily. Sukhanov moaned. Then, as if to console him, his memory obediently served up the image he had vainly sought to capture at the party—a fat, pompous hamster from a popular children's cartoon, its cheeks swollen with stolen grain. The resemblance was indeed uncanny.

Four

On a brightly illuminated square, before gingerbread houses with red roofs and golden shutters, Swanilda and her friends threw their legs up in the air in a flurry of lace and enthusiasm. Sukhanov felt distracted. He was sitting so close he could hear the tentative creaks of the floorboards and the soft slaps of the dancers' feet, could see that a braided wig on one of the women had slipped to the side, could almost guess at the multicogged machinery concealed in the wings, at any moment ready to set the silver foil of the moon gliding across a painted sky or wafts of smoke puffing cozily from two-dimensional chimneys. His box, draped in crimson velvet, sealed with an embroidered coat of arms, and almost hanging over the stage, was a clear mark of privilege, and yet, ironically, this very proximity revealed the dance to be replete with sweaty effort, robbing it of the magical illusion necessary for his enjoyment—so much so that he found himself envying the nobodies in the top gallery for whom the ballet must have seemed one blurry, whirling extravaganza of music, color, and light.

During the second intermission, Vasily roamed the sparkling cavity of the theater with his binoculars, announced that he saw an acquaintance, and slipped out. Sukhanov was left alone with his mother. He had meant for this to be a full family outing, but Nina still complained of a headache, and Ksenya had declared a particular dislike for *Coppelia*. "This is a perfect illustration of the difference between the French and the Germans," she had said. "Delibes takes Hoffmann's sinister tale of love and insanity and turns it into a story of a village Don Juan who is courting two women at once. Read it, and you'll see what I mean." She had then tossed a weighty volume onto his desk, upsetting his papers and causing a sheet of his biography to flutter to the floor; but before he had had time to scold her, Vasily had asked whether he could borrow his cuff links, Valya had come knocking on the door with an invitation to tea, the chauffeur had called from downstairs to report that the car was ready—and now here he was, confined in the mothball-permeated, cherry-colored plushness of the box with his mother, making polite little noises of attention in her direction.

"I think the costumes and the sets are lovely," she replied in answer to his question, glancing at him in her quick, habitually frightened manner. "Only I can't quite figure out . . . If Coppelia is the boy's fiancée, then who is this other girl?"

"No, Mother, it's Swanilda who is the fiancée," he said, swallowing a sigh. "Swanilda is the village girl, and Coppelia . . ." Ruffling the program, he read the mildly ridiculous synopsis to her once again. "'And in the end,'" he finished patiently, "'the village celebrates its new church bell, and Franz and Dr. Coppelius each get a bag of gold.'"

Nadezhda Sergeevna nervously readjusted her ill-fitting purple dress.

"But I thought Dr. Coppelius was a negative character," she said with another frightened look at her son.

Before he could answer, the lights began to dim, the yellow tassels on the curtain quivered and started to slide, a burst of music erupted, and Vasily tiptoed back to his seat, stepping on his neighbors' feet and murmuring apologies. Sukhanov resigned himself to another stretch of melodious boredom. A little girl directly behind him, the daughter of someone in the Bolshoi's top administration, was unwrapping a lollipop, noisily, endlessly, infuriatingly, and her mother kept imploring her to stop, in a loud, tragic whisper; there were always too many children at matinees. Mercifully, the performance ended quickly.

As the three of them emerged from the shadowy forest of the Bolshoi's columned lobby, his mother leaning heavily on his arm, the slanting afternoon sun that set fire to pools of yesterday's rainwater disoriented Sukhanov for a moment. They had not yet descended the steps when Vasily said he had to meet some friends. It seemed to Sukhanov that his son's eyes were cold and his parting abrupt; but of course, his perceptions might have been colored by the previous night's realization that, through an accidental blunder on his part, he had deprived the boy of a potentially brilliant twist of fate. He had tried to forget that unlucky brush with august favor, but a faintly nauseating feeling, strangely akin to a feeling of guilt, kept stirring inside him, and it was almost with relief that he watched Vasily run down the staircase and vanish in the crowd of theatergoers. Most likely, it was the same feeling of guilt that prompted him, in the very next breath, to accept his mother's offer of tea—for it had been her invitation to Malinin's opening that he had given to Ksenya, thinking Nadezhda Sergeevna a bit unpresentable for an event of such importance.

In truth, Sukhanov rarely enjoyed his mother's company. Apart from her grim button-down dresses, her long gray hair pulled back in a fastidious bun, her eternal air of watchful uncertainty accompanied by fluttering gestures and startled looks, and the cloyingly sweet smell of Krasnyi Oktyabr, a perfume she had used all her life—in short, apart from the things one gleaned within the first half-hour of being in her presence—there seemed to be nothing material about her. She used to work in one of those ubiquitous patriotic organizations with a conspiratorial acronym for a name that had mushroomed in the first days of the Revolution, but which had, unlike most others, survived the tossings of history and continued to exist in some forgotten corner of Moscow. She had spent thirty years there as an accountant, although she had no formal education and no particular acuity for numbers. Sukhanov had always found it difficult to imagine her bent for hours over some massive desk in a poorly lit office with a rain-stained view of a littered courtyard and a few dying plants on the windowsills, writing down columns of meaningless arithmetic; but at least her job, vapid as it had been, had offered her a peg on which to hang her days, her weeks, her years. Ever since her retirement two decades earlier, her life had lost what little shape it had. He had never seen her with a book, walking made her tired, and the arts left her indifferent; he had no doubt it was only her misplaced sense of duty that made her timorously, with neither enjoyment nor understanding, accompany him every few months on some cultural outing. She had no acquaintances that he knew of, and no living relatives except himself. Her two-room apartment, in an old Arbat building with no elevator, invariably made him feel that her private clock had stopped many years before, as if the very notions of past and future had long since lost their relevance here. Everything was spotless, precisely placed, and absolutely unchanged from his previous visit, all his previous visits—from the time, in fact, when she had first moved here, in 1964. Purple bouquets of artificial flowers bristled pompously in black vases on her bureaus, whose surfaces were covered with yellowing doilies; a small reproduction of Shishkin's *Pine Forest* decorated the wall above her drab green couch with its primly arranged profusion of lacy pillows; the same

aluminum-encased clock that showed a red-lettered date in the narrow slot in its base stood on top of the old-fashioned television set
that she stubbornly refused to relinquish in favor of a newer model.
Even the air in the apartment did not play or move but simply hung,
and Sukhanov involuntarily began to breathe deeper and talk louder
the moment he walked inside, as if trying to drown out a persistent
feeling of sadness.

"Just one more, Tolya, eat one more," she pleaded, pushing at
him a plate piled with sugarcoated confections he abhorred. "Are
you sure? Well, at least take a few home to the kids, I have plenty.
Here, why don't I wrap them up for you, come to the kitchen."

"Mother, please," he protested, "the kids are no longer kids, they
don't need—"

But her mincing steps were already pattering down the corridor.
Sighing, he followed her from the living room, where she always
served him tea out of some dim notion of good manners. She was
waiting for him on the threshold of her tiny kitchen, looking back
with an unexpected sly smile.

"Come on in," she said, beckoning. "I want to show you something."

Mildly surprised by this departure from routine, he stepped
inside, dipping his head under a low arch—and saw it right away. On
top of a squatting cupboard by the window, next to a tower of boxes
containing the unpalatable sugared treats, stood a round cage. A
small yellow bird on a miniature swing cheerfully moved its short tail
up and down, and neatly deposited a compact white drop on a crumpled newspaper below.

"You've got yourself a canary," he said, trying to keep the disgust
out of his voice.

"Yes, isn't she sweet," said Nadezhda Sergeevna, pressing her
hands together. "I've named her Malvina."

"How nice. Where did you get it?"

"Oh, from an acquaintance. You do think the name suits her, don't you?"

"What acquaintance?" he asked, his surprise deepening.

She mumbled vaguely about someone's cousin staying with relatives on a visit, and then, clearly considering the matter closed, began to sigh over her acquisition, imploring him to look, just look at this dainty beak, the color of these feathers, these bright beady eyes, so pretty, so intelligent. . . . Growing bored, Sukhanov stared outside. An old man was hobbling along the pavement, once in a while bending to pick something up, a cigarette butt most likely; a homeless dog darted from one courtyard to another; and over at the corner he saw—with another inexplicable tremor of guilt, though weaker this time—Vadim dozing over a newspaper, behind a lowered window of the Volga. His mother kept talking. For some reason the bird did not sing, although she was sure it would in time, it just needed to feel welcome. . . . A new smell, a slightly acrid smell of fowl droppings, was stealthily seeping into the familiar smells of shortbread cookies and *tvorog*.

Stifling a yawn, Sukhanov began to take his leave.

"But Tolya, you do like her, don't you?" Nadezhda Sergeevna asked from the doorway, smiling anxiously.

"As long as it makes you happy," he said absently, as always searching for an elevator button, as always remembering a moment later. "Frankly, I don't really care for birds myself."

"Well, I don't know why you wouldn't," she said in a petulant voice. "You did when you were a child."

He looked at her with immediate interest. She had never told him any stories about his childhood, even on those rare occasions when he had pleaded with her for a word, a family anecdote, a particular gesture or expression he might have used when he was little— anything at all to imbue with life a few black-and-white prewar snapshots of a skinny boy posing expressionlessly, unnaturally, between the gray covers of her photo album.

"I used to like birds?" he asked in amusement.

A frightened shadow flitted across her face, as if she had said more than she should have.

"You and every other child your age," she muttered with that little grimace of nervousness he knew so well. "Good night, Tolya."

"Good night, Mother," he said with a sigh. "The tea was delicious."

Pressing the shapeless package of sweets to his chest, he descended the stairs. For the duration of all six flights he could hear her fumbling tremulously with the lock; then the heavy front door slid closed behind him with a muted bang, and he was pushed into the softly glowing evening.

It was warm, warmer than the day before, and the sun, about to glide below the stubble of antennas on the neighboring roofs, suffused the air, the trees, the peeling stucco façades with a vespertine lucidity, imparting to the old quarter of Moscow that precious quality of rosy precision occasionally found in faintly colored nineteenth-century photographs of city vistas. Sukhanov walked past the houses with yawning gateways, which, in their depths, after one's gaze had traveled through a sour-smelling, graffiti-covered, slightly menacing dusk, miraculously revealed flashes of cool green leafiness swaying on a light breeze in small, secret gardens. A couple of buildings down, the swift movement of a hairy hand pushed open a window. As its frame swung out, the sun shot through the glass in a fiery orange zigzag, and out into the street spilled the zesty smell of roasted chicken and the rich honey of some classic romance; the performer's old-fashioned tenor sang caressingly of a solitary sail gliding through the blue mist of the sea. And suddenly Anatoly Pavlovich felt an odd, poignant tug at his heart, as if at that moment all these colors, smells, and sounds of a Moscow evening came together in just this way solely in order to re-create some long-forgotten combination—that of another quiet Arbat street lit by another nearing sunset, seen by a child peering out of the open window of a cramped kitchen where another chicken, a remote ancestor of this one, had been roasting in an oven, while somewhere in the dim heart of the apartment a phonograph had whined soulfully, swelling with the very same romance by Varlamov. . . .

He slowed down, looked around him again, with different eyes this time, and thought how strange it was that he came here so rarely, only a few times a year, on these reluctant, vaguely embarrassing tea-drinking visits—and yet it had been just a few crooked, rambling, wonderful streets from this very spot that he had spent so much of his life; and all these courtyards, all these boarded-up churches, the stucco decorations of the façades, the darkening alleys he was now passing with the mild apprehension of a middle-aged man—all of this he must have once known with the most intimate knowledge of scraped knees and cut-up palms, the knowledge of a lively, inquisitive, troublesome boy. Former street names, learned from an old neighbor, rose to his lips like a charming tune from the past— Filippovsky Lane, Malyi Afanasievsky, Bolshoi Afanasievsky . . . And when, at the corner, the houses finally fell apart, revealing the wide beginnings of Gogolevsky Boulevard, and Vadim appeared from under the newspaper, yawning as he scrambled to wakefulness, Sukhanov surprised himself.

"Drive down the boulevard and meet me at its lower end, by the metro, will you?" he said airily. "The evening is so nice, I'd like to take a little walk."

Aware of his Volga pulling out into the street immediately behind him, he crossed with an unaccustomed recklessness, at a yellow light, and entered the shade of the trees surrounding a statue of Gogol. The author of *Dead Souls* was, as usual, stiffly striding forward with a sarcastic half-smile on his lips. Sukhanov hesitated; but the reddening sun dappled the ground so alluringly and the leaves rustled so lightly that he shrugged and sat down on the nearest bench—only for a minute, he told himself as he gazed about him, pleasantly stirred by the proximity of his earliest years. All the other benches were occupied, mostly by embracing couples, with a sprinkle of solitary women here and there; one of them, with the prim face of a provincial schoolteacher, was tossing crumbs at an undulating sea of pigeons. A bit farther down the boulevard, a pack of small children played noisily, climbing over a wooden mushroom, falling off, laughing, climbing again. I might have come here as a toddler, he thought sentimentally.

The other end of the bench dipped heavily, and he emerged from his sun-drenched reverie to find an individual of indeterminate age and highly disreputable appearance tilting toward him with a loose, unfocused grin.

"Guess what I have inside my head?" the character whispered with a conspiratorial wink.

Sukhanov surveyed the man's gleaming eyes, shaved head, inflamed cheeks, gapped yellow grin, and the stained salmon-colored scarf wrapped around his neck, then turned away in prohibitive silence.

"What, too proud to talk to me?" the man said accusingly behind his back, louder this time. "Why don't you answer my question? What do I have inside my head?"

A nearby couple looked up with curiosity. Wincing, Sukhanov turned back.

"I have not the slightest idea," he said in an icy tone.

The man roared in drunken triumph. "No one ever guesses!" he bellowed right into Sukhanov's face. Surprisingly, there was no alcohol on his breath. "But I like you, so I'll tell you anyway. I have an inflated balloon inside my head, that's what I have, yeah, and it feels great! Of course, you're probably just as ungrateful as the rest of them, but I sense great affinity between us, so I'm going to tell you how I did it."

Sukhanov regarded the man with loathing—and then a solution occurred to him, so simple and mischievous he almost laughed with the malicious pleasure of a boy.

"Why don't you go and tell that lady over there instead?" he said quietly, nodding at the stern schoolteacher who was still feeding her pigeons. "I'm sure she'll be happy to know."

The madman swung around and studied the woman, chewing thoughtfully at one end of his scarf. After a long minute he broke into an ecstatic smile, heaved himself up, and murmuring under his breath, headed toward her with the unsteady jerks of a cotton doll. On reaching the gray sea of birds that spilled away from her bench in shifting, cooing waves, he appeared briefly confounded, then raised his arms high over his head, yelled something, and plunged forward stumbling. The woman shrieked, and a hundred pigeons took off at once, tearing the air, erasing the trees and the roofs, obliterating even the confidently smirking, striding Gogol—and forgetting everything else, Sukhanov stared, stared at their flight, stared at their wings. . . .

The birds flew in rustling, sparkling, ever-widening circles above his head, their hundreds of wings lifting and falling in reverberant staccato, glowing with rosy translucence against the sunset—and when, after many pounding heartbeats, they began to descend to the ground, one after another, like so many falling petals, he saw a different statue revealed in the same place. This too is a Gogol, but one sitting heavily slumped forward, an ill, lonely, heartbroken man—the very same Gogol, indeed, whose mournful aspect will be eventually declared to "misrepresent Soviet reality" and who will then, in the year 1952, be removed, replaced, abandoned in some unfrequented nook of the city. And here, barely reaching the sad man's feet on the pedestal, I stand with my head tipped back—a three-year-old who has just chased a flock of pigeons and is now watching their circling flight in open-mouthed fascination. Yes, I demand to be brought here day after day for this very reason, for I never tire of the excitement of breaking into a sudden run and startling these wonderful creatures with their puffed-up chests and iridescent throats and hoarse calls, setting them aflutter again and again, and then breathlessly staring after them, trying to catch the precise, brilliant moment when the sun bursts goldenly through the chinks in their flapping wings—until one day a face, a man's face, a giant's face with laughing eyes the color of pigeons' wings, materializes out of the birds' flickering and fluttering. The face moves closer and closer, until it is level with mine, and then I hear a voice—a voice that I somehow know already, a voice I have always known.

"So you like birds, Tolya, do you? Come then, I want to show you something."

My hand timidly finds its way into the giant's hand, and we walk—walk along the tree-lined Gogolevsky Boulevard, past kiosks selling tepid lemonade, past noisy children climbing a wooden mushroom that I find boring, past yellow-and-white mansions flecked with the sun, then through low gates of cast iron, and up an imposing marble staircase—and finally I stand in a long hall with dimness in the corners, and high above me, almost touching the ceiling, revealed in a majestic sweep of light, trembles an enormous creature with dark metal veins running through its spreading, transparent wings.

"An inventor made this," the giant tells me. "These are artificial wings for a man, you see, so he can put them on and fly. Would you like to fly, Tolya?"

I imagine myself rising, rising with the beautiful, graceful creatures over that unhappy man of stone, spiraling higher into the glowing sky, and, overwhelmed, I nod quickly, repeatedly, and my eyes must be shining, because the man who is with me smiles at me—but already I see that the creature under the ceiling looks clumsy, gigantic, unyielding, not at all like the birds I know, and my certainty wavers.

"I don't like it, it's ugly," I say disappointedly. The man laughs and ruffles my hair and takes me away; and as we walk outside, into the noise and the sunlight and the smells of hot pastries, he says to me, "This flying machine is an important step toward the dream, Tolya, but it's not the dream itself. You are right, man hopes to fly without any machines one day, soaring up and up with his will alone, free as a bird—and that day, if it ever comes, will be humanity's most glorious triumph."

"When I grow up, I want to fly without machines," I tell him, and as I look up, I see the most brilliant smile trembling under the mustache on his joyful, his dear face, seconds before the street, the light, the man himself begin to fade out like the last scene in a silent film. . . .

His eyes closed, Anatoly Pavlovich sat on the bench, taking shallow breaths, feeling as if a flock of birds had just traveled singing through his mind. In what murky subliminal cavern had it been lying dormant all these years, this priceless burst of a memory, only to yield itself in all its vivid colors at the lightest touch of fate? True, a factual basis for the discovery had been there for a long while. Once, in his reading, he had chanced across a curious tidbit about Vladimir Tatlin, an avant-garde artist who in middle age had become obsessed with flight and had spent years building models, and whose flying glider had been exhibited in 1932 at the State Museum of Fine Arts, now the Pushkin Museum, not ten minutes away from here. Sukhanov had carried that irrelevant scrap of information with him for many years, probably because the glider's name, *Letatlin,* had amused him with its ingenious merger of inventor and invention, of Tatlin and *letat',* "to fly"; yet it had remained only a piece of textbook knowledge—until now, when a lucky convergence of words, shades, and gestures succeeded in tearing one magically prolonged glimpse of the past from the steely grip of oblivion and ensconcing it in his soul, quivering and alive.

Naturally, he did not doubt that the vision was faulty in places and that his later knowledge superimposed itself now and again over the lacunae of memory. For one thing, the man of his recollection sported a mustache, looking, in fact, exactly like the dashing suitor offering a bouquet of roses in a black-and-white photograph over Nadezhda Sergeevna's bed; and even though his mother had told him that Pavel Sukhanov had shaved his mustache once and for all on the day of their wedding, the face bending over him stubbornly refused to shed it. And of course, he did not really believe he had succeeded in reproducing his father's actual words, for the phrasing was suspiciously sophisticated and would not have been understood, much less remembered, by a three-year-old. All the same, he knew the essence of the encounter had been captured. Tatlin's glider rose in his mind's eye with perfect clarity, the general meaning of the conversation was intact—and most important, he was sure, absolutely sure, of the wonderful smile that had lit up the man's face when the little boy had said, "I want to fly."

Sukhanov had been too young to salvage much of value from the few years he had shared with his father. In a meager collection of his childhood mementos, no more than snapshots really, the man faded in and out of sight, crossing a hallway, gulping scalding tea over a counter, bending to tie his shoelaces, saying a rushed good-bye—always stepping into a frame only to step out of it an instant later. The gift he had received this summer evening was thus made all the more precious, for not only was it his earliest memory of Pavel Sukhanov—it was also one of the brightest, possessing as it did genuine life and warmth.

Sukhanov stood up, dusted his pants, and smiling a secret little smile, absently floated down the boulevard, through the city that was being washed away by darkness. Only a few paces later, he encountered Vadim, who was almost running toward him. He shrugged, brushing away the chauffeur's questions—of course he was all right, it had been only a minute or two, had it not? Just as absently he climbed into the backseat of the suddenly manifested car, and a moment later, when they came to an abrupt stop, was surprised to see his own building looming above him.

He had already taken a few steps toward the door when something occurred to him, and returning, he rapped on the front window.

"Listen, how old is your daughter?" he asked. "Eight, isn't she?"

"She turned eleven last week," Vadim replied with a startled glance.

"Simply incredible how time flies," murmured Sukhanov. "But never mind, she'll still have a sweet tooth. Here, why don't you take these for her, she'll like them. . . ."

And thrusting the crumpled package of crumbling sweets at the perplexed chauffeur, he smiled the same secret, dreamy smile, and was off.

Five

On the landing Sukhanov met Valya, who was just leaving for the day. Married to the caretaker of their apartment house, she lived somewhere in the building's nether regions.

"They're waiting for you with supper, Anatoly Pavlovich," she said, and smiled shyly, revealing a gap between her front teeth. "I've made my *vareniki* with cherries you like so much, this being Sunday and all."

Indeed, the whole apartment was seasoned with sweet, rich smells; the woman could certainly cook. Sukhanov ate in silence. He considered telling his family about the small mnemonic miracle that had befallen him earlier that evening, but Nina wore a pained look on her face and from time to time massaged her temples, Ksenya distractedly rolled a ball of bread around the rim of her plate, and Vasily was in the middle of a story about some diplomat he knew. Not for the first time, Sukhanov noticed that his son did not look as young as a twenty-year-old should and that his light blue eyes were flat and unfathomable like those oval pools of cold paint one saw in place of eyes on Modigliani's faces. And unexpectedly, disjointedly, he wondered how well his children actually knew him, and how they would remember him when he was gone—whether in their minds he would amount to more than a dry encyclopedia article and a handful of snapshots to illustrate it: Anatoly Pavlovich at a lectern holding forth on the demise of Western art, Anatoly Pavlovich working at his desk, with the clickety-clack of his typewriter ricocheting off the study walls and the invisible sign "Do Not Disturb" on his closed door, Anatoly Pavlovich at this or that party, sporting this or that tasteful tie, conversing with this or that famous personage . . .

But immediately he scoffed at the notion. While it was true, perhaps, that he did not often talk to Ksenya and Vasily about his or their lives and that their family map shone with uncharted white spots of terra incognita, entire regions where he had never thought it wise or necessary to venture, hadn't they shared so many pleasant times over the past two decades—so many leisurely vacations by the sea, Black and Baltic, so many lovely theater evenings, so many content suppers at home like the one tonight—all of them moments of warmth and wordless understanding? Yes, after all these years they were simply bound to know one another with a knowledge of love, truer, deeper, more perfect than any other kind of knowledge. . . . Sukhanov swallowed a small sigh and, remembering he had an important article to finish by Thursday, abandoned the last bite on his plate and left for the study.

As soon as he crossed the threshold, he felt that something had changed in the room in his absence, as if the very air had become suffused with a different meaning; but it was not until he turned on the lamp that he realized what had happened. The empty space on the wall across from his desk, the space awaiting the return of Nina's portrait, was no longer empty—a large oil painting now hung in its place. He looked at it, and his heart beat unsteadily.

A raven-haired girl sat by dark moonlit waters. The luminous curve of her nude body was misty as a dream, even slightly transparent, so that, if one looked very closely, one could just make out pale shapes of water lilies visible through her honey-colored, unearthly flesh. An indistinct silhouette of a youth, perhaps an admiring shepherd, was crouching in the rushes behind her, but she took no notice of him. She was gazing away, over the waters, to a horizon where a magnificent white swan was floating, slowly, majestically, triumphantly, moving closer and closer. Zeus and Leda, the seducer and the seduced . . . The whole thing was beautiful but at the same time oppressive, and one was tormented by the inability to see the expression on Leda's face, for it was turned away, affording only the gentlest hint of a profile, the tender angularity of a cheekbone, the barest outline of full lips—not nearly enough to see whether she felt exultant at the god's imminent approach, or whether she was afraid. In the lower left corner was a date, 1957, and next to it sprawled a familiar, proud signature.

Sukhanov took off his glasses, extracted a handkerchief from his pocket, rubbed the lenses, folded the handkerchief away, put the glasses back on, cleared his throat, and called for Nina. She came unhurriedly and stopped in the doorway, her bare arms crossed, turquoise bracelets clicking faintly on her wrists.

"What is this?" he asked, frowning ever so slightly, tapping his fountain pen against the proofs of his biography.

"Oh, don't you remember?" she said, shrugging. "Lev gave it to us on our wedding day. I thought you'd remember."

"I do remember," he replied dryly. "What I mean is, why is it here?"

"I just thought the wall looked too bare as it was," she said. "And then our last night's conversation about Lev, and your going to see *Swan Lake,* reminded me that we had this somewhere. It goes well with the overall color scheme, don't you think?"

"We didn't see *Swan Lake,*" he said, trying to keep his voice even. "We saw *Coppelia.*"

"Did you really? I was sure it was *Swan Lake*. In any case, you can take it down if it bothers you," she said with the same air of indifference, and gliding out into the shadows of the hallway, softly closed the door, her bracelets jingling.

Unwilling to admit that the painting's presence did unnerve him, Sukhanov resolutely turned to the article he was writing. But the specter of his reflection in the window again distracted him, the spectacles sparkling blindly in a skull-like face; the swan kept glancing at him with its malevolent golden eye; and his thoughts refused to follow their prescribed direction, swooping instead like a flock of pigeons over old Moscow, with all its abandoned houses, all its crushed church domes, all its forgotten faces from the past. . . . When he heard a ghostly radio somewhere outside transmitting the chiming of the clock in Red Square, he counted and, at the eleventh stroke, stood up heavily.

Passing along winding corridors whose parquet floors were slippery with many layers of polish, he imagined a barely perceptible musical rhythm pulsating like a prolonged moan behind the door to Ksenya's room, and a moment later caught a snippet of a telephone conversation, Vasily's indignant voice saying to an invisible someone, "I don't understand how he could . . ." and then fading away, muffled by darkened distances. When he entered the bedroom, he found Nina already in bed, propped up against a pillow with a thick book, her pale face gleaming with the silvery pollen of some precious night cream.

"What are you reading, my love?" he asked, feeling oddly like someone seeking reconciliation after a quarrel.

"Van Gogh's letters to his brother," she replied without looking up.

"Maybe you should try some clever detective story instead," he offered with a tentative smile. "I could recommend one or two."

But she said nothing, and with an inexplicable sinking of spirits, he wormed his way under the blanket on his side of their enormous bed. For a few minutes he leafed through a novel he had picked up from his nightstand, but the words meant nothing, all the characters seemed to have the same name, and he could not find the place where he had stopped previously. Giving up, he lay back in the crispy stillness of the sheets, lit on one side by Nina's pink lampshade, and listened to a car honking a few streets away, a dog barking listlessly in the courtyard, his wife turning the pages of her book . . .

"The light bothers me," he said finally.

She nodded, placed her velvet bookmark between the pages, clicked off the lamp, and slid into the darkness, her back toward him. He remained still, waiting for her breathing to acquire the nebulous weightlessness of dreams; but time passed, and he sensed that she was still awake.

"An amazing thing happened to me today," he whispered. "I remembered something wonderful from my childhood. May I tell you?"

But there was no answer; she must have been asleep after all. For a long while he struggled with the night in a vain attempt to follow her, employing every trick he knew—studying his measured heartbeats, counting backward, drawing complicated figures behind his closed eyelids, picturing a trotting line of sheep, camels, elephants juggling multicolored balls with their trunks—yet sleep continued to elude him. After an hour of torture, his head swimming with garlands of figures and caravans of beasts, he climbed out of bed and, his feet somehow condensing into slippers, walked back to the study to do more work.

A yellow rectangle of light from a streetlamp on the corner of Belinsky Street sliced through the window and fell directly onto Belkin's painting, making it glow in the obscurity of the room with a strange, almost three-dimensional intensity. Casting an involuntary glance on it, he noticed with surprise that Leda no longer had her flowing black tresses: a blonde now sat by the lake, her short hair resting in a perfectly curled wave on the elongated nape of her neck.

At the sound of his footsteps, she turned, and with a painful start he recognized Nina—Nina enveloped by the sweet, sinful aromas of the lilies, lulled by the lazy lapping of the waters, her fifty-two-year-old body still glorious, still gleaming—a perfect middle-aged Leda awaiting her feathered god.

She looked at him without recognition and then indifferently moved her eyes away, to an unseen horizon on which the white question mark of the swan's neck was about to materialize in a few casual brushstrokes. Frozen in the middle of the room, he felt helpless and suddenly aged in his old-man polka-dot pajamas, dreading the inevitable divine seduction yet unable to turn away—but something else happened as he watched. A ripple ran through Nina's flesh, and it paled to a shade lighter than moonlight: her back was sprouting a pair of beautiful swan wings. In a dazzling flash of whiteness, she rose to her feet—and as she did so, he heard a rustle at the window behind him. He swung around and felt terribly disoriented for one dizzying moment. Then, at once, he understood.

The painting on the wall was not a painting at all, but a simple mirror whose frame neatly contained the reflection of the window; and there, only a few steps away, standing on the windowsill, was the real Nina, winged and naked, cautiously trying the temperature of the sky with her big toe, that little gesture of hers he knew so well (she disliked cold water). With a startled cry, he rushed toward her, to prevent, to stop, to catch . . . He was too late. Already, with that maddening fluid grace she possessed, she glided into the black translucence of the night, leaving behind a solitary feather fluttering slowly to the floor—and although he wanted to shout, to protest, to implore, no words came to him, none at all, and silently, knowing she would never return, he watched as she flew farther and farther away, melting amidst the cold stars above the fairy-tale city of Moscow. . . .

When she was gone, he collapsed into his chair in despair. The rearing Pegasus underneath the lampshade regarded him with sympathy out of the corner of its bronze eye and then, unexpectedly, tore its mouth wide open and neighed, loudly, violently, in an operatic bass, "Damnation, damnation to her!" Embarrassed, Sukhanov mumbled, "Well, I wouldn't put it quite like that," and began to fumble with the lamp switch, trying to make it stop. But the sound would not cease—and he saw that their bedroom was once again lit with a pink glow, Nina's side of the bed was empty, the balcony door stood ajar, and from somewhere outside there flowed into the room a powerful voice singing, "Damnation, damnation to her for all of eternity!"

Unhappily Sukhanov scrambled out of bed. His slippers were nowhere to be found, and cursing inaudibly, he walked out onto the balcony barefoot. Nina was leaning over the railings. The predawn breeze swelled her apricot-colored nightgown, filling it with gentle brightness, so that she appeared trapped in a glowing cocoon of orange air. She barely glanced at him, but he saw that she looked worried.

The operatic chant clearly issued from the apartment directly below.

"What the hell is this? Who's making all that noise?" he asked in a whisper.

"Ivan Svechkin," Nina whispered back. "You know, the composer who lives downstairs. He writes children's songs. 'That Happy Day in April When Our Ilyich Was Born' is one of his."

"Well, this sounds like a church chant," he said with irritation. "I suppose he has a good reason for treating his neighbors to a nice bit of liturgy in the middle of the night?"

There were signs of sleepy stirrings on all four sides of the courtyard—windows lit, shadows peering from behind curtains, balcony doors slamming.

"I've heard he has a very unhappy marriage," said Nina quietly. "His wife is twenty years younger, and he gets jealous, can't stand to have her out of his sight. . . . He must be having some kind of nervous breakdown."

They fell into an uneasy silence, listening. The rhythmical liturgy went on and on: "Damnation, damnation to her, damnation to her for all of eternity!" And as the minutes passed, it began to seem to Sukhanov that their warily expectant courtyard was being gradually transformed into the interior of a great, roofless, solemn church. The Big Dipper swung like an incense holder, spraying drops of stars into the skies above; gilded squares of lit windows all around them turned into jeweled icons, encircled by candle flames, glimmering with blackened lacquer on ancient stone walls—and for an instant he even imagined that the spirit of some fallen angel was truly being cast out by communal condemnation into the chilly August nothingness. . . .

Then a police siren exploded nearby. Someone must have called to complain about public disturbance tinged with religious propaganda. The illusion of the church vanished. Windows went out one by one, and clicking, shutting, banging noises echoed and reechoed through the courtyard. The singing wavered, then stopped abruptly in the depths of the apartment below, and they heard the faint sound of a woman weeping. Nina winced and walked back inside; he followed, closing the balcony door behind him. The crying grew indiscernible.

"I hope I can fall asleep after all this," he said. "What time is it?"

"Five past four," she replied, sliding back under the covers, and added with a sigh, "How sad that must be. . . . Poor girl!"

"Your poor girl probably cheats on him left and right," he said unpleasantly. "Where there's smoke, there's fire."

She looked at him with silent reproach and switched off the light.

He was about to retire as well, when some odd association reminded him he had a small matter to attend to. Murmuring that he would be back in a moment, he made his way to the study (in the process tripping over his slippers, which for some reason lay sprawled just past the threshold). The painting on the wall was illuminated, as before, by the yellow light of the streetlamp, but gazing at the swan sat the tremulous black-haired Leda—not in the least like the serene blonde Nina, of course.

His arms around the frame, Sukhanov carefully began to push it upward, maneuvering to slide the painting off its hook. When it was freed, he carried the heavy canvas out into the hallway, tiptoed past the bedroom, past the arched entryway to the living room, past the velvet magnificence of the dining room, past the doors that led into his children's mysterious lives, and onward, through the kitchen, and to a cramped closet. There he released his burden and, smiling with satisfaction, watched as Leda slid along the wall and settled in the shadows, looking rather forlorn among all the mops and shoes and discarded stuffed animals and who knew what other neglected, unloved things that crowded inside this dim space with its damp smell of oblivion. But as his eyes lingered on the painted girl's slim waist, narrow shoulders, stretched-out neck, her whole long-legged, warm, softly gleaming shape, he felt an unwanted trembling in his chest, as if in an unguarded moment or a careless dream some particle of his soul had accidentally caught a whiff of a real, if fleeting, resemblance—or perhaps not so much an actual resemblance as an overall familiarity, a certain congruence of moods, a spiritual likeness to something, to someone . . .

And then, all at once, a monstrous birth took place in his innermost, darkest depths. He sensed a repulsive, slimy, impossible creature stirring, stretching, rising sluggishly from its murky abyss, already twisting his insides, almost ready to trespass into his mind, to poke its ugly snout onto the surface of his thoughts—and he feared that once the snout broke through, the poisonous words of his premonition would be released, and there would be no taking them back, and he would have to face the possibility that all these many years ago Lev Belkin had . . . had . . .

"What nonsense," said Sukhanov promptly, perhaps a bit louder than was advisable in the sleeping house, and slammed the closet door shut.

The floor reverberated with his decisive steps as he marched back to the study. There he threw open a cabinet, rummaged through its obscure contents, and finally unearthed a small still life, already framed. Forcefully humming the duel aria from *Onegin*, he installed it on the orphaned wall and stepped back to consider. His father-in-law's perfectly round, red apples shone in an abundant pile on a yellow ceramic dish. The overall effect rather pleased him—and even more important, the bright cheerfulness of the composition turned out to be conducive to his productivity, as he discovered the very next day, when, the unpleasantly turbulent night shrugged away, the disappearance of Leda left without comment, the city stretching cloudy and still below his window, he sat at his desk, sipping his morning coffee, wrapped comfortably in his robe, and mused over the article.

S I X

The article presented a curious problem.

Sukhanov felt for a bookmark in a tattered volume on his desk, opened it, and reread the underlined conclusion to a chapter: "Surrealism can thus be rightfully called a betrayer of the people, locked as it is in deadly opposition to all humanistic values and traditions. It cherishes madness and cultivates decadent indifference toward social good. Its sickening visions strive to drive a healthy man into the realm of fantasy, distracting him from the noble goal of combating world capitalism. Therefore, as a movement it has nothing of value to offer to the mature artistic perceptions of the Soviet people. Moreover, some of its more harmful elements, such as its obsessions with horror and pornography, represented most fully in the work of Salvador Dalí . . ."

He shut the book and regarded the distinguished gray of the cover, on which the indented letters of the author's name—his own—glittered dully with fading golden print. Then, frowning thoughtfully, he pushed the volume aside. Though published in 1965, his monograph on Western art served him still as an inexhaustible source of assertions that could be reused on most occasions, with only minor rephrasing and retouching; this time, however, he felt certain that something else—something, in fact, quite different—was expected.

As a rule, Sukhanov no longer wrote any articles himself: at his level of importance, creation had by necessity sunk to the bottom of his list of priorities. He was content with regulating the general flow of things—supervising the obsequiously smooth workings of his staff, distributing a monthly set of preselected themes among a trusted handful of critics, then poring through their texts to weed out a few chance occurrences of names better left unmentioned or to nudge two or three carelessly straying phrases back into the herd. He prepared each glossy, pleasantly substantial issue of *Art of the World* according to the same simple yet unfailing recipe: Take a doughy theoretical discourse on the methods and principles of Revolutionary art, stuff it with two or three well-seasoned essays portraying Repin and Fedotov as precursors of socialist realism and Levitan as an enemy of tsarism, mix in a sugarcoated biography of a famous Soviet master in the vein of Malinin and a spicy discovery of some unjustly ignored genius of the Italian Renaissance who was vilely persecuted by the Church, whisk in, for a bit of exotic flavor, an interview with this or that diamond-in-the-rough from a remote Asian republic (whose artistic development was clearly born of the wonders of Soviet education), and finally, generously pepper the whole with quotations from Marx and Lenin. Above all, Sukhanov was famous for his skillful omissions. While he would occasionally allow a cautious account of some contemporary Polish or Bulgarian artist (who invariably celebrated in his canvases the wonderful friendship blossoming between his and the Soviet people), Western art of the present century wandered through the pages of the magazine like a mildly embarrassing hallucination—a mute, befuddled, miserable ghost who was ridiculed, kicked, and exorcised, but whose name was never pronounced and whose face was never revealed.

This state of affairs had existed unchanged for years, from the day Sukhanov had first assumed the reins—and until a routine staff meeting one month ago. At that meeting, Sergei Nikolaevich Pugovichkin, the assistant editor in chief and Sukhanov's second-in-command, had let slip a disturbing rumor that had somehow filtered through the ranks. It appeared that somewhere in the celestial above, certain nebulous changes had been transpiring ever since the ascension of the new Party leader in March, and among other things, a Very Important Someone (who, naturally, remained unnamed) had been overheard expressing the hope that *Art of the World* might begin dedicating at least one article per issue to a "prominent Western artist," starting, for instance, with Salvador Dalí—for, as that enigmatic personage had been reputed to observe, "Dalí's as good as anyone, and one must start somewhere." Trying not to betray the shock he had felt at the idea of Dalí's melting clocks making an appearance in the pages of his magazine, Sukhanov had shrugged nonchalantly and announced that he might as well tackle the subject himself. He was, after all, universally acknowledged as the foremost expert in the field.

This, then, was the article in question. The problem lay in the fact that the more specific he became about Dalí's life—the more he occupied himself with dates of exhibitions, titles of paintings, and places of residence—the harder it was to sustain that pure pitch of abstract condemnation he had always felt compelled to cultivate when writing about surrealism. As the voice of authority, Anatoly Pavlovich Sukhanov was unmerciful, unwavering, unforgiving—and exceedingly vague. Viewing his entrusted task as not so much educational but ritualistic in spirit—a task of juxtaposing good and evil, day and night, East and West—he had for years presided over the

roasting of the surrealist specter on a spit of righteous class indignation as the drums beat louder and louder, the dance around the fire
grew more and more exuberant, and the victim became increasingly
obscured by clouds of billowing smoke. Yet now, unbelievably, he
was being asked to describe the curl of the victim's mustache, the
occupations of his parents, and the colors of his palette. It was little
wonder that for the past few weeks Sukhanov had felt ill at ease
whenever he had thought about the subject.

Now, however, as he shut his monograph, stirred sugar into a fresh
cup of coffee, and stared at the shiny abundance of Malinin's red
apples on the wall, he chanced to recall an amusing anecdote from
Dalí's life that might just provide the angle he needed. Encouraged, he
began to bang out hasty paragraphs on his unwieldy typewriter, and
was already nearing the end of the third page when Nina's voice
sounded across the corridor: "Tolya, don't you have a staff meeting at
twelve? Vadim will be here in less than half an hour!"

He glanced at the clock on his desk and completed his sentence
with an exclamatory punch. Continuing to trace every possible per-
mutation of the thought in his mind, he stepped in and out of the
shower, combed his hair, buttoned his shirt, overcame the resistance
of newly pressed pants, and finally, struggling with his right cuff
link and simultaneously debating the prudence of introducing the
word "pathological" into the discussion, drifted toward a bedroom
closet, pushed its door open with his elbow—and was brought to an
abrupt stop.

There, on the top shelves, lay his neatly folded sets of beige and
blue pajamas; here, on the bottom shelves, towered pale stacks of cotton handkerchiefs, embroidered with discreet indigo initials and permeated with faint cologne smells, and dark stacks of socks, flashing
diamonds and zigzags; underneath, in the hazelwood cavities of three
open drawers, glistened the shiny coils of his numerous belts. But the
inside of the door—the inside of the door was empty, unexpectedly

empty, and the little metal hooks, bereft of their entrusted weight, sparkled conspicuously all along the tie rack. His ties were gone; gone also were his three or four velvet bow ties (perfectly respectable specimens, black, white, and crimson, worn exclusively on Bolshoi Theater evenings). Only two orphaned pairs of suspenders dangled sadly in the void that the day before had been ordered into vertical silk stripes of so many noble colors.

Sukhanov stood for a minute contemplating the closet. When his vexation had ripened sufficiently, he walked to the living room. Nina was curled up in an armchair by the window, eating a sliced peach and gazing vacantly at the gray skies sliding over the roofs. A book lay forgotten beside her.

"Next time you decide to take my ties to the cleaners, my dear," he said in consternation, "it might be useful to leave me one or two. I do have an office to go to."

She looked up. Her lips were bright with the juice of the fruit, and her eyes were vague.

"Ties?" she said. "I haven't taken any of your ties."

In a moment they were confronting the emptiness together.

"How very strange," Nina said after a puzzled pause. "When was the last time—"

He had last put on a tie the previous morning, while dressing for *Coppelia,* and had not opened the closet since. (Upon his return, he had tossed the used tie onto the back of a chair, where its subdued blue pendulum had swung for a few beats before coming to a stop, and where it hung now in rumpled solitude.) The mysterious removal of his property must have taken place between his and Vasily's departure for the Bolshoi and his arrival home at seven that evening. Nina seemed just as perplexed as he was, and Vasily flatly denied any knowledge of the matter. Ksenya had already left for *Komsomolskaya Pravda,* where she was interning for the summer;

but naturally, as Nina pointed out, she had no reason to venture into his closet, and practical jokes were simply not in her nature.

Sukhanov was beginning to feel incensed.

"It doesn't make sense," he said. "And in any case, you were in bed with a headache all day, so no one could have sneaked into the bedroom without you seeing them!"

It seemed to him that a silvery shadow flickered swiftly through her eyes, but it must have been a trick of light, for just then a tentative tentacle of sunshine, the first of the day, probed the bedroom, playfully touching the closet's bronze doorknobs and glittering off the belt buckles. Nina busied herself with verifying the obvious once again—checking among the socks, between the pajamas, under the handkerchiefs.

"I'm sure we'll find them," she was saying as she sifted through the clothes. "Perhaps you moved them somewhere yourself? Because there was no one here except me and Ksenya, and—"

"Well, I'll be damned!" Sukhanov said suddenly. "Of course, it's that woman!"

Nina straightened and regarded him blankly.

"Well, she was here as well, wasn't she?" he said. His mouth had grown tight. "I knew we never should have let her into the house, she's nothing but the wife of a drunk. I bet she pinches things here and there, and he sells them on the black market!"

"Please tell me you aren't talking about Valya," said Nina slowly.

Breathing with an effort but looking ominously collected, he scooped up his lone surviving tie, strode into the entrance hall, stiffly stomped his feet into a pair of shoes, and began to unlock the front door. Nina flew after him but slipped on the parquet floor, shedding a feathered slipper, which flipped over in the air like a small wounded bird. He was already crossing the threshold when she grabbed hold of his arm.

"Please, Tolya"—she spoke in a rush—"there must be some explanation, I beg you, don't do this, she's worked for us for ten years, and I don't know a more honest—"

A telephone exploded shrilly in the hallway, and simultaneously something heavy crashed onto the floor above their heads. Startled, Nina turned around. Freed of her imploring touch, Sukhanov marched onto the landing, slammed the door behind him, and not waiting for the elevator, which had just come to a grating halt somewhere in the bowels of the house, descended the stairs.

The stairwell split the gray monstrosity of the building in half, laying it open like an enormous, overripe fruit, with the imposing leather-padded, nail-studded doors, two on each floor, embedded in its yawning pulp like dark seeds, every one of them containing its own luxurious blossom of success. Here, on the seventh floor, across from the unhinged composer, resided a corpulent opera singer from Tbilisi who had left the stage years before but still treated her numerous guests to tremulous arias accompanied by the velvety barking of her three fat, indolent basset hounds; whenever she gave one of her homespun concerts, some mysterious arrangement of pipes would carry the disembodied barking and trilling through walls and floors and carefully deposit their echoes in Sukhanov's study, annoying him to no end. On the sixth floor, below the composer, lived a high-ranking Party official, a jovial fellow with an amazing profusion of warts on his chin and a plump wife who looked like his sister, and on the fifth, the elevator sometimes dropped off a sad little man in tortoiseshell glasses who resembled a poor relative from the provinces but whom Sukhanov knew to be one of the foremost classics of Soviet literature, the author of the celebrated trilogy *We the Miners*.

After that, more than thrice removed from his own eighth-floor domain, the inhabitants grew anonymous. As he reached the fourth floor, he heard children's cries seeping out from under a door, and on the third, after a particularly long flight of stairs, punctuated by the comma of an orange peel spilling out of the trash chute, he leaned against the railing to steady his trembling legs and thought he detected the sweet fragrance of lilies and the light tinkling of a piano in the depths of apartment number five. The fleeting combination of sounds and smells reminded him that once, in a predawn hour, coming home from a New Year's Eve party, he had encountered a tantalizingly reticent, elegantly perfumed woman with features of Nefertiti, pearls swaying fluidly in her ears, stepping out of the lobby and disappearing into a chauffeured automobile as gray as the sky— but before he had time to glance curiously at the door, the wintry recollection turned and escaped him, and his thoughts, in chasing after it, inadvertently stumbled upon a vision of another chauffeured car, another perfumed woman.

He found himself thinking of the past Saturday evening, of his father-in-law's retrospective at the Manège. And then, as if merely waiting for their chance to intrude, a multitude of unnecessary, uncivilized associations crowded his mind—the offended Minister, the unbearable encounter with Belkin, the indignity of the near-mugging, the loss of the blue-eyed Nina presiding tranquilly over his work, the subsequent invasion of his sanctuary by the shameless swan-loving nude at the head of a flock of disturbing dreams and irrelevant suspicions . . . No matter, the nude was gone, he reminded himself quickly—and in any case, these were all minor occurrences, to be forgotten in another day or two—and certainly no reason for him to be standing here, on an unfamiliar landing, feeling as unsettled as he did, no reason at all. And murmuring angrily (What nerve the woman has, can you believe it, stealing like that!), he purposefully walked down the remaining flights—was that a plate breaking in apartment three?—and arrived in the lobby, with the sun, now fully out, splashing brilliantly on the marble floors.

Here he hesitated, not knowing where the caretaker lived; but the concierge was already rising from behind the desk with a cloyingly respectful, insincere smile, and, suddenly embarrassed, Sukhanov nodded coldly and hastened down another staircase, markedly narrower and darker, which disappeared into the obscure strata of the building. Before he knew it, he was staggering through the uncharted territory of the basement, crisscrossed with low-ceilinged, cramped, poorly lit corridors. The smells of cabbage stew and detergent clung to walls the color of sickness; an ill-looking striped cat slunk past him, its invisible tail bristling; shapeless objects cringed in the corners, briefly suggesting rags, pails, brooms, a rolled-up poster, a three-legged chair, a doll with a missing arm, then sinking back into the shadows. . . . After the sparkling expanse of the lobby, the building's faintly unclean, unsavory underside jarred his senses, and he felt a dull oppression descending on him, as if all nine stories of human existence above were weighing heavily on his spirit.

A metal door stood ajar at the end of the hallway. When his first knock went unanswered, he knocked again, louder this time, and hearing some remote rumble in response, walked in—and stopped, assailed by a sharp, multilayered, terrible smell. A mammoth pile of garbage towered in the murkiness above him. He took an involuntary step back, and as his foot sank into something pulpy—an apple core, perhaps, or a banana peel, he did not want to look closely— the gigantic body quivered, shedding a fish head with oily eyes, a soiled paper bag, a swarm of potato skins, creeping a little closer to his immaculate shoes, an inch, another inch, seemingly on the verge of disintegrating completely, of swallowing him up in its noxious horror. . . .

He stood still for one long, stupefying moment, then, seized with panic, flew outside, threw the door shut behind him, and pressing his hands to his temples, thought confusedly, What is this, how can this be, in my own house . . . And all at once the idea of confronting Valya began to seem disgusting, indecorous, mean, as if it too belonged to this underground world of rotting, malodorous refuse;

and he was overpowered by a squeamish desire to leave, leave immediately, return to the light, to the air, to his familiar reality. Almost
running now, he turned the corner and stumbled against the wall,
and the wall, strangely yielding to his touch, let out a wail and leapt
off into the darkness. He stared after it, instinctively groping for his
heart in the folds of his jacket. Then, seeing nothing but the cat he
had encountered earlier in this labyrinth of corridors, he swore nervously and resumed walking, more slowly now, when a door he had
not noticed opened in front of him, and there was Valya, her hands
glistening wet, peering into the gloom with her slightly cross-eyed,
amiable look.

"Why, it's you, Anatoly Pavlovich!" she said in surprise. "I thought
I heard Marusya cry out just now. Marusya is my cat."

"I saw it," he said, taken aback by her sudden appearance. "I also
saw a room full of garbage."

"Oh, that's our trash chute dump," Valya explained. "Kolya keeps
it locked, only he forgets sometimes. I'll tell him."

"Yes, please see to it. It's most . . . most unhygienic, you know."

A short silence hung between them. Then Valya smiled in her shy,
dimpled way.

"I was going to come up in half an hour as usual," she said, and
wiped her hands on her apron, "but I'll be glad to start earlier if you
need me now, Anatoly Pavlovich."

He looked at her, the big, homely woman in an unbecomingly
tight blouse, her hair untidy, her round, kind face anxious with a
desire to be useful, and his conviction of her guilt faltered. "Just give
me a second to check on a couple of things, and I'll be ready to go,"
she was saying, ushering him into a tiny hallway crowded with bundles of freshly washed laundry. A little girl of about six, so blonde
her eyebrows and eyelashes were invisible, emerged from somewhere
and regarded him seriously for an instant, then wandered off. A telephone started to ring, and a sharp smell of burning porridge began

to spread through the apartment. Valya shouted to someone named Stepasha to switch off the stove and to Annechka to answer the phone, then turned back to Sukhanov with a flustered smile.

"I'll just be a second," she repeated. "I have my hands full with these children."

Mechanically his eyes fell on her hands, large, carrot-colored, almost manly, hanging loosely by her sides like two independent creatures briefly asleep—and suddenly an unexpected vision of these hands greedily handling his ties, his lovely silk specimens collected like rare butterflies on his infrequent European sojourns, made his insides dissolve in irrational fury.

"Actually, Valentina Aleksandrovna," he said shakily, "don't bother coming up today. Or tomorrow. Or at all. In fact, I came to inform you that you are dismissed."

The burnt smell and the hurt look in her eyes were the last things he remembered clearly. The ensuing scene was brief and revolting. Trying to keep his voice steady, he told her that the black-market proceeds from her loot would no doubt exceed tenfold what they owed her for the month of August, but of course she was free to keep the difference, they would not prosecute.

She stood still, pulling on her apron, blinking rapidly, her kind face crumpling.

"What . . . What do you mean?" she said finally, and her words were moist and heavy, almost trailing into sobs. "Do you think I *stole* something from you? . . . Dear God, how could you . . . I would never . . . And for you to come here and talk to me like that . . . How could you . . . You call yourself an educated man . . ."

The little girl came into the corridor, looked at her crying mother without emotion, and announced that some lady urgently wanted her on the phone. Cringing, Sukhanov escaped into the dimness of the basement, nearly tripped over the mangy cat once again, and rushed up the stairs, taking two steps at a time and bursting into the lobby so abruptly that he startled the concierge out of a nap.

When, hours later, Vadim delivered Sukhanov to his front entrance, the mellow August dusk had already suffused Belinsky Street. The staff meeting had been unpleasant, full of inexplicable lacunae of small silences and awkward glances exchanged on the periphery of his vision, and he was feeling exhausted, tense, and hungry. Tilting his head back in some trepidation, he was relieved to see that the kitchen windows were bright and welcoming as usual, with signs of shadowy activity transpiring behind the cheerfully checkered curtains, and for the whole duration of his slow ascent along the building's vertebrae in the creaking elevator he indulged in the hope that in his absence his ties had been found, Valya reinstated with due apologies (Nina always knew how to handle such matters), and now another delicious supper awaited him, still smoking, under the merry orange lampshade, on the table scintillating with glasses of wine and surrounded by his understanding, caring family.

As soon as he stepped inside, however, he was met by a charred smell and the resentful banging of cupboards, and instantly his vision of a cozy domestic evening put its tail between its legs and scurried into a corner, to remain there, cowering unhappily, throughout a strained, tasteless meal. Glaring at him over a bowl of burnt rice, Ksenya announced that both she and her mother had spent the afternoon begging Valya to forget the incident, but Valya had only shaken her head and cried, and even a discreetly proffered envelope containing thrice her monthly wages had proved of no avail. He kept prudently quiet for a while, aware, even without looking up, of Nina's wordless presence at the other end of the table, of her lowered face, which seemed not so much stern or upset as infinitely tired,

with deep lines tugging at the edges of her pale mouth; but when
Ksenya repeated, for the third time, that she was sure of Valya's inno-
cence, he could no longer contain himself.

"If you are so sure she didn't do it," he said bitingly, "I suppose
you can enlighten us as to who did?"

"All I'm saying is, you mustn't jump to conclusions like that," she
said with less assurance. "You can't just go around accusing people
of stealing without considering every other possibility first!"

"Oh, but I did," said Sukhanov, allowing himself a dry smile. "I
considered the possibility that a little green man was flying past our
bedroom window and took a liking to my ties. Frankly, this seemed
unlikely."

Ksenya started to reply, but Vasily interrupted her.

"Oh, for heaven's sake," he said in a bored tone. "I think Father
was perfectly in the right, we'll just hire someone else. Honestly, must
we spend our whole evening talking about some janitor's wife?"

"Vasily!" Nina exclaimed in a shocked voice.

Wishing his son would have found some other way to express his
solidarity, Sukhanov hastily looked down at his plate and in feigned
concentration probed a beef cutlet whose middle shone with a suspect pink. Of course, Nina had never shown much culinary promise,
but this was rather worse than he would have expected, reminding
him, in fact, of the miserable fare of his early childhood—the many
barely edible meals that his mother had set out before him day after
day in a corner of their crowded Arbat kitchen. Actually, the kitchen
had been quite spacious once, but now an invisible line divided it in
two, and each half was crammed to the full with a herd of mis-
matched chairs stumbling around a limping table. The Sukhanovs
shared their table with Zoya Vladimirovna Vienberg, a dowdy music
teacher of indeterminate years with a shadow of a mustache above
her upper lip, and an old soft-spoken couple who always dressed
rather formally for supper and sat picking at their food like birds,

smiling sadly at each other. The wife had a pink and wrinkled face, like an apple left out in the frost, and bluish hair; its color fascinated me to no end, and I would often stare at the tight, shiny curls for a full minute at a time, until my mother would reprimand me for my rudeness in a dramatic whisper.

The other table, situated advantageously next to the stove, belonged to the Morozov family, consisting of a husband, a wife, the husband's unmarried sister, and two sons, indifferent brutes three and five years my senior. The sister, Pelageya Morozova, an indolent, slightly overweight young woman with sleepy eyes, a bright red mouth, and an alluring mole above her upper lip (in another few years she would start passing, smiling coyly, heavy breasts swinging, through many of my adolescent fantasies), prepared all their meals, and was so much better at it than my mother that tasteless clumps of porridge or sticky macaroni would often wedge themselves in my throat as I listened to the appetizing hiss of chicken from Pelageya's pan and, tortured by the loud, satisfied guffaws of the Morozov boys, agonizingly imagined the succulent taste of the meat in their mouths.

The only thing that made these measly repasts in any way bearable was an ever-present hope that tonight, against all expectations, my father would return home early. Hearing the jingle of a doorbell in the hallway, the obnoxious Morozovs would instantly lower their voices, for he inspired even them with respect. Shouting, "Papa, Papa!" I would leap from my seat and fly to let him in. In a minute, my hand in his, he would enter the kitchen, smiling broadly, sit down at the table with us, ask me how I liked school, gently tease the poor unattractive music teacher, who never failed to blush dark red in his presence, say something kind to the old man and his wife, and then take my mother's face in his hands in that casually warm, special way he had—and his strong, confident, handsome presence would lend a sense of completion to my fragmented, boisterous, inconsequential day.

Of course, all through that year of 1936—my first uninterrupted year of consciousness—my father almost always remained at his mysterious job until late into the night, and for days at a time my only glimpse of him would be that of a tall, square-shouldered figure silhouetted in the doorway of our room against the sickly yellow gleam of a corridor lightbulb, only to step inside and dissolve in dense shadow in the next moment, whereupon I would lie, half submerged in disjointed dreams full of the most brilliant, glowing colors, and hear through the blanket's thick woolen layer the rustling of clothes being shed, the solitary complaint of a mattress, and the muffled, indecipherable whispers of my parents quickly fading in the darkness beyond. Yet every evening at supper I would be full of hope once more. Deep in my heart I believed that if I wanted it hard enough, if I concentrated on it with my whole being, I could make it happen, I could summon my father to appear, I could will the wonderful sound of his arrival out of nothingness—and closing my eyes, forgetting the plate of burnt rice and undercooked cutlets before me, I would make the doorbell jingle in my mind over and over until finally something would yield in the fabric of the universe, and the long-awaited ring would truly fill the kitchen, and I would rush off shouting—

"Papa! Papa, shall I get it?"

He opened his eyes. The doorbell sounded again.

"Shall I get it?" Ksenya repeated impatiently.

"No, I . . . I'll see who it is myself," replied Anatoly Pavlovich in a slightly unsteady voice, and slowly rose from the table.

Seven

On the landing before their door stood a stranger. His pleasant middle-aged face sported a neat little beard, and his blue eyes shone with a mild, harmless, nearsighted friendliness behind his glasses. The glasses, with their delicate metal-rimmed frames and round lenses, resembled a turn-of-the-century pince-nez; combined with the soft brown hat on his head and the small bulging suitcase at his feet, they made him look altogether as if he had just walked out of a Chekhov tale about some kindly small-town pharmacist on a nice family visit.

At the sight of Sukhanov, the man swiftly took off his hat.

"*Dobryi vecher!*" he said in a voice brimming with emotion, twisting the hat in his hands.

"Good evening," Sukhanov replied coldly. "How can I—"

"Oh dear, I've caught you in the middle of supper, haven't I?" the man exclaimed, and pressed the hat to his heart. "How awkward, I so hate to be in the way. Oh, but please don't worry about me, I've already eaten, honestly I have. Heavens, just to think that finally, after all these years . . . No, no, no help necessary, allow me . . ."

And cramming his hat back onto his head, he picked up his suitcase with a grunt and began to maneuver it past Sukhanov, bumping him painfully on the leg in the process. What does he have in there, bricks? Sukhanov thought with irritation, and stepping to the side, blocked the stranger's way.

"Just a minute," he said peremptorily. "I'm afraid there's been a mistake."

The man let go of his suitcase and looked up in dismay.

"Oh no, did I confuse the days again?" he moaned. "I'm sure I did, it must not yet be Monday, and of course you were expecting me on Monday, and here I am, inconveniencing you most terribly, and I can't tell you how sorry—"

"Comrade, it's not the *day,* it's the *apartment* you got wrong," interrupted Sukhanov. "This here is number fifteen. Who is it you're trying to find?"

The man's face worked its way from dismay to relief to deep confusion.

"Number fifteen, yes, that's right, but . . . I don't understand. . . . You *were* expecting me, weren't you?" he mumbled, peering anxiously into Sukhanov's eyes. "You did get my letter, of course, so you knew . . . unless . . . No, no, that's impossible, I remember sealing it and putting it in my pocket. . . . Oh heavens, but did I actually . . ."

Beginning to tire of this nonsense, Sukhanov placed his hand firmly on the intruder's elbow and was just about to prompt him back onto the landing, when the man let out a sigh.

"I shouldn't have hoped you'd recognize me," he said dejectedly.

Momentarily uneasy, Sukhanov regarded the fellow's worried, gentle face, the outmoded glasses, the blond beard. . . . Then, relieved, he shook his head.

"Naturally, it was many years ago, and under such painful circumstances," the man whispered as if to himself, and then added hurriedly, with a most heartfelt smile, "Really, I understand, I'm not in the least offended. I'm Fyodor. Fyodor Dalevich."

Some vague recollection poked its muzzle onto the surface of Sukhanov's mind, but he was too slow to catch it and it quickly dove back into the murky past.

"I'm sorry, but I'm afraid I'm not quite . . ." he murmured, attempting to smile back.

The man looked at him closely across the ensuing silence, and all of a sudden his beard started to quiver and his spectacles commenced to slide off his nose. Gasping with laughter, he threw himself at Sukhanov and crushed his sides in a vigorous embrace.

"Ah, Tolya, Tolya, you really had me going there for a minute!" he cried into Sukhanov's shoulder.

What the hell, thought Sukhanov, struggling to extricate his chin from the hollow of the stranger's back—and at that precise moment Nina walked into the hallway, a cup of tea forgotten in her hand.

"Was that anyone—" she began, and stopped abruptly.

At the sound of her voice, the man released Sukhanov and dashed toward her, tearing off his hat once again and exclaiming warmly, "And this must be the lovely Nina Petrovna! Such a pleasure to meet you. Nadezhda Sergeevna has told me so many things about you."

"Nadezhda Sergeevna," Sukhanov repeated dully.

As the man enthusiastically reached for Nina's hands, he dropped his hat. Smiling a puzzled smile, she tried to help him catch it and, with the predictability of a slapstick routine, accidentally let the cup slip out of her grasp. The porcelain hit the parquet and shattered into a hundred white and golden shards, splashing tea onto Sukhanov's pants.

"Would you . . . would you excuse me . . ." he then said faintly. "I'll only be a minute, I . . . Nina, why don't you offer our guest some tea or something, I just have to . . ."

And leaving Nina and the profusely apologetic visitor to collect the remains of the cup, Sukhanov ran down a corridor, which seemed strangely unfamiliar, with lurid red roses leaping into his face off ugly wallpaper, and darted into his study as if being chased. Slamming the door behind him, he pressed a shaking hand to his forehead, then took a few steadying breaths and dialed his mother's number.

She answered on the seventh ring; he was counting.

"Mother, listen, something completely absurd has just—"

The connection was bad, full of fuzziness and booming echoes, with occasional snippets of shadowy conversations crossing over from some parallel dimension.

"Tolya, is that you? Tolya, speak louder!" Nadezhda Sergeevna was saying from an immeasurable distance. "You what? . . . Who? . . . Ah, Fyodor! Well, I'm so glad he's finally with you. I'm sure you'll like him, he is such a nice young man. So thoughtful of him to give me my Malvina."

"Malvina? That silly canary?" Sukhanov shouted against the noise. "You got your canary from that man? Just who the devil is he?"

His mother's voice dipped into a static-filled chasm, replaced by a rich baritone that said, very close to his ear, "And don't forget to make sure your boots have no leaks." Then Nadezhda Sergeevna hazily surfaced again.

". . . and no need to swear," she said disapprovingly. "I should think that after all these years you'd be glad to see your cousin again."

"What on earth do you mean, cousin?" he cried. "I don't have any cousins!"

Dipping in and out of the fog, Nadezhda Sergeevna talked rapidly.

"Don't you remember . . . Irochka, I called her . . . grandmother's cousin's only daughter . . . used to live in Moscow, and once we even . . . Surely you remember how . . . But then they moved to . . . She died a few . . . her husband also, and Fyodor is their only . . . an educated man . . . at a museum there, and now he is writing . . . Very interesting, he's told me all about . . . I'm sure you'll be glad to get to know him during his stay, he's such a nice . . ."

"What was that last thing?" Sukhanov gasped. "Did you just say that this Dalevich fellow will be *staying with us?*"

There was another unnatural, creaking stillness, and then the same baritone announced heatedly, "No, listen, it's better to dig for fresh worms once we get there."

". . . shouldn't mind too much, since it's only for a week or two," his mother's voice returned from afar. "Well, give my regards to Fyodor. *Spokoinoi nochi,* Tolya."

"A *week or two?*" he shouted in disbelief. "Mother, wait, what do you expect me to—"

The line went dead. Seething, he dialed her number again, and got a busy signal.

When Sukhanov returned to the kitchen, he found his dubious new cousin presiding at the table in his place, heartily devouring the inedible cutlets and between bites drawing sinuous shapes on a napkin. Nina and Ksenya were following the quick movements of his hand with interest; Vasily sat frowning, tapping his spoon against a saucer. "Most people think that the window carvings are purely ornamental," Dalevich was saying, "but in fact, many of them are symbolic designs going back to pagan times. This one, for instance, is believed to bring good luck and prosperity, and this one, to ward off—"

Noticing Sukhanov on the threshold, he hastily put down the pen.

"Your family has been most kind in indulging me," he said with a flustered smile. "Northern architecture is one of my favorite subjects and I could bore you all for hours, but I really should be going now. Tolya, I can't tell you how sorry I am for barging in on you like this. It appears that you never did receive my letter. I simply can't imagine how . . . But no matter, I won't burden you any longer, you've been too patient with me as it is. Nina Petrovna, thank you for the most delicious supper. Now, where did I put my hat?"

Sukhanov had to restrain himself from laughing with relief.

"Oh, no bother at all, Fyodor!" he said expansively. "It's always nice to see family. In fact, if you are staying in Moscow for the next few days, why don't you drop by again sometime——"

"But Fyodor Mikhailovich," said Ksenya, "where exactly are you going?"

Dalevich had already stood and was fussing with a lock on his suitcase.

"Please don't worry about me," he said earnestly. "I have an acquaintance or two in Moscow, they'll find a corner to spare. Here, Tolya, before I go, I brought you a little something—just a souvenir from the Russian North, nothing special."

And he pulled an elaborate lace tablecloth out of his suitcase.

"But it's lovely!" Nina exclaimed.

"Yes, very pretty," Sukhanov said uncomfortably. "You really shouldn't have. If you need my help getting in touch with your friends, I could——"

"Surely you see that we can't let him leave," Nina interrupted with a withering look at her husband. "Fyodor Mikhailovich, it's already past nine o'clock, so why don't you just stay with us tonight, and we'll figure out what to do tomorrow."

"Oh, that's so terribly nice of you," Dalevich mumbled in visible confusion. "I wouldn't like to presume, and I do feel awful about that letter. . . . But perhaps, if you had a couch somewhere . . ."

"You can have my room," Ksenya said impulsively.

Dalevich's words stumbled once or twice and sank under the weight of his gratitude. A brief silence fell. Then Vasily emphatically put down his cup and rose, scraping his chair against the floor with a long, nasty sound.

"How touching," he said with a disdainful smile. "Long-lost relatives reunited and all that. I suppose this is the moment when I offer my room as well, and then we all sit arguing about it for another hour, wallowing in the pleasant glow of familial kindness."

"Vasily!" Nina said sharply.

And then Sukhanov felt that the day was running circles around him, and that all of this—Vasily's derisive remark, Nina's chastising reply, the hollow sensation in his stomach after the unsatisfactory meal, the strange yellow-bearded man apologizing effusively, the burnt smell lingering in the air—all of this had happened before, had, in fact, happened repeatedly, and he was forever trapped in a nightmarish cycle of domestic disasters. Bleakly, without interfering, he watched his son leave the kitchen, as if hoping that with his departure the vicious circle would somehow break and normal life would return. When a door slammed a corridor away, Sukhanov sighed, shook off his immobility, and excusing himself, walked out as well. Growing fainter behind him, Dalevich's voice was imploring Nina not to be angry, the young man's feelings were understandable, it was all really his, Dalevich's, fault, he should never have imposed like this, he could not tell her how sorry . . . Sukhanov had a sudden urge to spit.

Before Vasily's room, he hesitated, then thought better of it, and proceeded into the dining room to pour himself a brandy. Its prickling warmth comforted him a little, and when Nina's steps sounded in the hallway, he hastened to intercept her. She went into the bedroom, and he followed her meekly. The darkness, aromatic with the memories of her creams, briefly caressed his skin like a cool, soothing hand. A moment later she switched on the light; in the pink glow of the lamp, her face was chilly.

"Look, I honestly had no idea he was coming," he said, trying to catch her gaze. "In fact, I'm not even sure who he is, exactly, some thrice removed cousin or something, I don't think I've ever met him."

"He remembers meeting *you,*" she remarked as she busied herself with extracting stacks of fresh linens from a closet. "He says you made a big impression on him when he was a child."

"I'm sure he does," he said, shrugging. "Anyone would if it got them room and board. Anyway, I know it's very inconvenient, but it's only for one night, and first thing tomorrow morning . . . My love, what are you . . . Why are you doing this?"

Nina was tearing the sheets off their bed.

"We are giving Fyodor the bedroom," she said matter-of-factly. "It's the least we can do after Vasily's inexcusable behavior, don't you think?"

He watched her methodically tuck the starched edges of a new sheet under the mattress corners. "So where are *we* to sleep?" he asked.

"I thought I'd take the living room couch, and you can have the one in your study, it's comfortable enough," she replied evenly. "I'll bring you your linens. You may want to grab a blanket too, the nights are getting cold."

"I've noticed," he said with bitterness, and turned to go. In the doorway he paused to cast a furtive glance back at her. Today she wore no sparkling earrings, no clinking bracelets, and her features, bereft of the glossy glamour that makeup lent them, seemed soft and hazy, as if glimpsed imprecisely through a light curtain of rain. Suddenly, prompted by an oddly urgent impulse, he swore to himself that if she looked up, if only for an instant, he would reenter the pink stuffiness of the room—and talk to her, really talk to her, for the first time in who knew how long. He would confess what he had felt when he had seen Belkin walk away in the downpour; he would share with her the happy childhood memory of his father and the upsetting dream about her flying away; he would take her in his arms and tell her that she still looked beautiful, in spite of those resentful lines

tugging at her mouth. . . . For a long moment he waited, but she did
not look up.

He nodded curtly and left.

In the middle of the night, having grown at once aware of a rapidly
solidifying cramp in his lower back, Sukhanov rose and headed for
the bathroom. Barely awake, he moved through the darkness, automatically went through the motions of emptying his bladder, sleep-
walked his way back through his familiar kingdom, and unthinkingly
pushed open the bedroom door. Here he stopped, first blinded by
unexpected light and then befuddled by the sight of his conjugal bed
empty and the figure of a man in a robe hunched over in the armchair
in the corner, scribbling busily on his knee. And then, for just one
instant, before the man lifted his head, Sukhanov was seized by a
powerful, disorienting feeling, not unlike vertigo, as if he had been
snatched out of his state of semiwakefulness only to be hurled, his
mind dizzy, into a darker, deeper vortex of dreaming. But the moment
passed, and the world righted itself. His tottering step back was
checked by the solidity of a half-unpacked suitcase; the seated man
looked up, revealing the old-fashioned glasses, blond beard, and
amiably questioning smile of Fyodor Dalevich; and already, feeling
perfectly clearheaded, Sukhanov heard himself apologizing gruffly
for walking through the wrong door, misled as he had been by the
force of habit.

The insignificant incident over, he returned to the study; but the
couch, far from comfortable at the best of times, now positively bristled with springs and angularities, and the accidental vision of a man
sitting in an armchair with a notebook on his knee tormented him
with the nagging persistence of a well-known name or connection
that inexplicably escapes one's memory at the precise instant of

alighting on one's lips and then haunts one for long, helpless hours. Restless minutes followed one after another into the predawn hush, and still he lay tossing. Then the same shadowy radio he had heard the night before carried through an open window the echo of the Red Square clock striking four times—and astonishingly, he had it. As the sought piece of the puzzle slid into its place in the past with a satisfying, liberating click, there surfaced before him the gentle face of an old man from the communal Arbat apartment on whom an unhappy little boy had once been persuaded to play a senseless, cruel prank.

It happened in the spring of 1937, some three months after Pavel Sukhanov had left Moscow. The mystery enveloping his father's job had lifted from young Anatoly's mind one day shortly after his eighth birthday. On that January day, when the whole world was particularly white and cold and every word seemed to hang in the air a bit longer, as if frozen, his smiling but curiously red-eyed mother sat him down and explained that a new factory near Gorky needed the help of a talented engineer with an unparalleled knowledge of building airplanes. It would only be for a little while, she said; and even though his eyes glistened, he nodded with the seriousness of an adult and felt proud of his father's importance to the country.

But after his father had gone, with a handshake so strong that for days afterward he could recall its grip in his fingers, things started to change—imperceptibly at first, then faster. Nadezhda Sukhanova now wandered through life without animation, leaving dirty plates in the sink and forgetting to turn off the lights in the shared bathroom, and Anatoly's school days, with no one to ask about them, chased one another into bleak oblivion. Then gradually, as the winter melted into spring and his evenings were slowly drained of all hope of his father's speedy return, the presence of the Morozovs began to make itself felt in the rambling six-room apartment. The head of the family, Anton Morozov, a burly thirty-three-year-old

man with hairy arms and a face resembling a slab of beef, left obnoxious cigarette stubs in the music teacher's teacups, and was once
heard to inquire in a conspicuously loud voice, his eyes narrowed
shrewdly, why the old couple who sat at the Sukhanovs' table were
occupying two rooms between them when one would suffice just as
well. Morozov's sister Pelageya, when hanging lines of stockings and
camisoles to dry, took to casually usurping the other half of the
kitchen, and a few times at supper, his wife, Galka, sharply berated
the nervously perspiring Zoya Vienberg for the weekly singing lessons she gave, threatening to complain to the authorities about the
noise.

In late March, when the icicles started to break off the roofs,
smashing onto the pavement below with precise crystal explosions,
and there was still no sign of Pavel Sukhanov, the Morozov boys
seemed to notice Anatoly's existence for the first time. The younger
of the two viciously tripped him in the hallway and, as he sat up, surprised and hurt, hugging his scraped knee, snickered coldly and told
him to run and cry in his mother's lap; and a week later, the older
boy got hold of a nice red notebook in which Anatoly had been laboriously drawing the unsteady round letters of his homework and,
grinning with pleasure, fed it page by page into a trash chute before
Anatoly's eyes. Their shouting and guffawing disturbed him almost
nightly, populating his dreams with wide-mouthed, red-faced, thick-
armed, terrifying bullies. And when one day the two cornered him
in the yard and, nudging each other, told him about the old man's
manuscript, it was in the hope of shaking off his nightmares, of
showing them that he was not to be ridiculed—that, indeed, he could
be one of them—that Anatoly swallowed and, his eyes bright, said
quickly, "Sure, I'll do it."

In spite of seeing him and his blue-haired wife daily at the kitchen
table, I knew almost nothing about the old man. His name was

Gradsky; he seemed to be in his late sixties; his hands were delicate, frail, and yellow, like ancient papyrus. Anton Morozov derisively called him "the Professor." Apart from quiet greetings spoken into his meticulously trimmed beard, he said very little, and I never heard him talk about himself, but the Morozov boys claimed to have found out quite a bit about him—including the interesting fact that every night, after his wife retired to the neighboring bedroom, the light continued to seep out for hours from underneath the door to his tiny study. Once, when the door had stood briefly ajar, they had caught a glimpse of him dozing over a thick stack of papers on his desk. He was writing some book, they said to me; they had overheard him referring to it as the work of his life. If I returned successful from my mission, they told me smiling, they would fold the pages into boats and set them traveling with the merry blue waters of melting April snows down the widest streets of Moscow.

"Great," I said to them, my throat dry.

That night my soul wept with loneliness as I lay awake, adapting my shallow, anxious breathing to my mother's measured breaths and delaying, delaying for as long as I could. When the predawn dampness crept in through the cracks in the windowpanes, I rose and tiptoed barefoot along the creaking corridor. The stillness rippled with the great whistling snores of Anton Morozov. No light marked the thresholds. When I reached the next-to-last door, I stopped and hesitated, feeling all the while the expectant malice of the Morozov boys at my back, thinking especially of the slanting eyes and the slow grin of Sashka, the older one. Then the cuckoo, sounding peevish, announced four o'clock from its perch in the kitchen, and, my heart leaping wildly through my rib cage, I pushed the door open. As I stole in, the hinges issued a sharp little squeak.

If I had ever entered Gradsky's study before, I had been too young to remember. The darkness, suffused with a pale gray light falling through the narrow rectangle of the room's solitary window, rarefied here and condensed there into deeper pockets of shade in patterns unfamiliar to me. I guessed at a bookcase, a desk, the silhouette of a stocky lamp. Navigating stealthily around invisible edges, I crossed the room to the desk, groped for the lamp's cord, and pulled. A green-shaded light flooded the world, immediately blinding me, but after a few blinks I saw the peeling wood surface strewn with stacks of paper covered in neat, minuscule handwriting—and an instant later, something else, which made my heart shoot up into my throat. I had, of course, expected the study to be empty, but there, in an armchair in the corner, a man in a heavy robe sat hunched over, a notebook reposing on his knee. For one wild, panic-filled second, I imagined myself gathering the scattered pages, then dashing, his cries ignored, through the slumbering apartment to the safety of my room, and once there, tearing open the windows and throwing the whole armload of papers into the fading night, to watch them twirl like hundreds of white birds against the brightening skies and then slowly flutter down, down, from the fifth floor to the yard below, to the torrents of melting snows that would wash them away forever. . . . But in another erratic heartbeat I remembered the heavy tape that still ran around the windowpanes, binding them shut to keep out the winter drafts, and my thoughts darted in confusion—and already the old man in the armchair was stirring, lifting his head, revealing his neat silver beard, his flashing glasses. . . . Squinting with surprise, he regarded me in silence. I stood before him, lost and frightened, thinking of the hurt expression that would settle on my mother's face when she found out what I had tried to do. Then, unexpectedly, he smiled.

"Oh, it's you, Tolya," he said. "Can't sleep, can you? Well, in truth, neither can I. I was just resting my eyes. Nice of you to visit me."

I remembered the respectful words my father had always found for him, and grew suddenly ashamed of myself. At the same time I disliked the old man intensely, both for the feeling that rose in me and for the kindness with which he spoke; and the strangeness of his room, which I now saw clearly for the first time, made me feel uneasy. It was small and stuffy, this room, with a disproportionately high ceiling and an unusual smell of leather, mold, and dust permeating the air; and although its scanty furnishings were no different from any others in the apartment, many disturbingly foreign things caught my eye. There were towers of books on the floor, the volumes thick and brown and etched, unlike any I had ever seen at the school library, and more books with gilded spines organized in grave processions behind the glass doors of a bookcase; a magazine lying on the desk, its cover bearing a long-haired woman with a fantastically coiled fishtail and glittering with golden letters, some familiar and others odd and curly-looking; a round convex glass that made a few words on the page beneath it swim up to its surface enlarged and distorted; and next to it, strangest of all, a small transparent dome whose depths blossomed with multitudes of tiny flowers, white, crimson, and purple, their artificial petals so delicate, so lovely . . .

"It's a paperweight. Made of Venetian glass," the kind voice said above me. The old man, unnoticed, had risen from his armchair. "A little trinket from a trip I made when I was young. You can take it if you like."

It felt cold and smooth to the touch, and when I lifted it to the lamp, the light filled it with an enchanting, flickering, rosy glow, like that of a distant fire. Then I thought of the narrowing eyes of Sashka Morozov and, hastily shaking my head, set the weight down, on top of a stack of pages.

"Is this the book you are writing?" I asked sullenly, to say something. "What is it about?"

"Ah, so you've heard about my book," he said smiling. "Well, you see, it concerns the aesthetic principles of the Italian Renaissance. . . .

But I suppose that doesn't tell you very much. To put it simply, it's about art—art and beauty. Do you like art, Tolya?"

I remembered a teacher who had once read us a snappy Mayakovsky rhyme about pineapples and quails, and how I had not known what it meant until she explained about the fat, overdressed men who had exploited the masses just so they could eat such delicacies and surround themselves with beautiful things. I thought also of the posters in my school—the red-and-black ones lining the hallways, with powerful youths who held enormous hammers in their hands and looked not unlike Anton Morozov, and the others hanging in the cafeteria, depicting nasty bugs and admonishing us to wash our hands before eating. The Professor's glasses sparkled patiently as he waited for my reply.

"Beauty is for the bourgeois," I said disdainfully.

He smiled again, cheerlessly this time.

"You think so?" he said, and picked up the magazine with the gold-lettered cover, leafed through it, found the paragraph he sought, and read, aloud but in a quiet, thoughtful voice, as if talking to himself: "'We believe that life without Beauty is impossible, that we must attain a free and brilliant art for our descendants, one that is illumined by the sun and induced by tireless search; we believe that we must preserve for them the Eternal values forged by many generations. . . . Art is eternal, for it is founded on that which cannot be rejected. Art is whole, for its single source is the soul. Art is free, for it is created by the free impulse of creation. . . .'"

Not understanding, I stared at him with hostility. When a yawn came, I did not bother to suppress it as my mother had taught me. He glanced at me as if only now remembering my presence and, with a short, embarrassed laugh, set the magazine down.

"I apologize," he said quickly. "I just wanted to hear these words spoken. Wonderful publication this was, *The World of Art*. . . . No matter. Before you go, Tolya, may I show you something? See if you think it's beautiful."

I might have refused, but without waiting for my reply, he had already pulled a tall volume off a shelf. He opened it at a bookmark, then laid it on the desk and carefully lifted the diaphanous sheet that covered the page. A whiff of mildew fleetingly brushed my cheek. This was to be my last coherent impression before I let my eyes fall to the page.

In anyone's life there can be only a few such moments—moments when a long, ringing hush fills your hearing, the world stands still as if under a magic spell, and thoughts and feelings course freely through your being, traversing the whole of eternity in the duration of a minute, so that when time resumes and you return from whatever nameless, dazzling void you briefly inhabited, you find yourself changed, changed irrevocably, and from then on, whether you want it or not, your life flows in a different direction. This was such a moment for me. Had I been thirteen or fourteen, perhaps none of this would have happened—perhaps I would have looked obediently where the old man was pointing and, with the indiscriminate thrill of an adolescent, would have seen merely a picture of a naked woman who, in covering herself with her impossibly long tresses, still left enough exposed to attract a prurient gaze.

But I was only eight, and I did not see a naked woman. Instead I saw tender ripples of the palest silvery gray, and a green so lush, so full of golden hints it felt like trapped sunshine, and glowing, translucent whites, and the brightest coppery sheen, and a pink that was not pink at all but in truth had no name fitting enough to describe it, so pearly and iridescent it was, more precious than the inside spiral of a seashell—yes, I saw all the brilliant, deep, lucid colors that had visited me before in my dreams, now released for the first time and given the most perfect, most radiant form. Entranced, I watched, for a suspended, breathless span of my private eternity, as the shades and the textures flowed smoothly into one another, creating harmony, creating glory, creating beauty. . . .

The old man was talking above my head about some man named Botticelli, some woman named Venus, some place named Florence. I heard nothing.

"Do you have any more you can show me?" I said when I could speak.

He fell silent and looked into my face, closer than before.

"Oh yes, plenty more," he then said gently. "But tonight may not be . . . Oh dear, this watch can't possibly be correct! Past four in the morning, is it really? Why don't you come by again tomorrow, Tolya . . . er . . . at a slightly earlier time, perhaps?"

It was almost light when I finally fell asleep. The torments I was bound to suffer at the hands of the Morozov boys did not force themselves into my dreams even once—I dreamt instead of a glowing, bright-eyed goddess being born amidst a heavenly swirl of shapes and colors. The next morning, I woke up with a smile of absolute happiness upon my lips, knowing that a new, different life lay before me.

Eight

On Tuesday morning, Sukhanov woke up late and was surprised to find himself smiling; he must have had an especially pleasant dream. Casting around his memory for its fading shimmer, he emerged yawning into the hallway and was surprised again, even more pleasantly, by the delicious smell of fried onions zestfully seasoning the whole apartment. Thinking that his life without Valya's culinary talents might turn out to be acceptable after all, he sleepily followed his nose into the kitchen—and upon entering, was shocked to see Dalevich bending over the stove, wearing Nina's apron and flourishing a spatula.

"You've got to try this," said Ksenya, speaking with her mouth full. "The best omelet I've had in my life!"

Conscious of the ridiculous figure he cut standing in a wide shaft of sunlight, dressed in polka-dot pajamas that betrayed the rotundity of his stomach, with an undulating weave of the sofa's pattern printed across his cheek, Sukhanov announced that he was not really hungry (Nina's eyebrows rose slightly), not to mention that he needed to return to work without further ado—and would Ksenya be so kind as to bring him some coffee when it was ready? Then, murmuring unintelligible apologies to Dalevich, he retreated, past his son's door, which was still demonstratively shut, back to the study. By the time he established himself at his desk, the last traces of his blithe morning mood had melted away like a desert mirage, and a long caravan of tedious, unhappy thoughts plodded across his mind. There was the matter of the room that needed to be arranged for that nuisance of a relative, and Vasily, whose slippery gaze and scoffing remarks had started to trouble him in earnest, and of course, the problem at hand—this insufferable essay on Dalí that had been foisted upon him with so little ceremony.

The essay, at least, was resolving itself, he concluded after reviewing the text from the previous day. He had begun his narrative with a providentially remembered anecdote, which, being not only amusing but also undeniably metaphorical, spared him the unpleasantness of resorting to such harsh words as, for instance, "abnormal." Once, during an arranged breakfast with a prominent Soviet poet, Dalí had commented in passing on the stunning beauty of an atomic mushroom cloud rising in purple ripeness into the skies. Justifiably outraged by such lack of humanity, the Soviet celebrity, at a loss for a fitting repartee, promptly spat in Dalí's coffee. The artist remained unruffled. "I've tasted coffee with cream and sugar, with milk and various liqueurs," he observed thoughtfully, "but never before with spittle"—and savoring the moment, he slowly carried the cup to his mustachioed lips.

Setting the emptied cup back into its porcelain nest, Sukhanov fed a blank page into his ancient typewriter. Strangely, in spite of the auspicious beginning, he felt singularly uninspired and for a while sat without typing, lightly tapping his index finger against the space bar and looking at his shelves. He knew the contents of his work library down to the spine. Starting with the subdued yet foreboding drumroll of a short essay collection by Marx and Engels, it continued with the tremulous flutelike notes of Plekhanov and Lunacharsky, then, with a wide, powerful sweep, moved into the avalanchine brasses of the maroon-clad marching band of Lenin's *Complete Works,* and finally, passing through an unwavering chorus of the next sixty years of Soviet criticism (his own specimens proudly present in the multi-colored glory of all their editions), disintegrated rather incongruously into a random assortment of art books, with the chaotic wheeze and rattle of surrealist castanets, gongs, and cymbals all but drowning out the Renaissance violins. (The surrealist gathering included a perplex-ing brochure, published in New York, entitled "Safe Surrealist Games for Your Home," and a catalogue whose cover pictured a man in a bowler hat with a bird in place of his face.)

He sat gazing at the books for many empty minutes, ostensibly debating the choice of a quotation suitable as commentary on the Dalí episode, in reality letting his thoughts wander somewhere far, far away; but eventually the shelves swam back into focus, and sigh-ing, he reached for the most dog-eared volume of Lenin's *Works.* It fell open predictably in just the place he sought, so often had he made use of these few thickly underlined paragraphs. Barely consult-ing the page, he began to type: "As Vladimir Ilyich Lenin said in his famous 1920 speech at the Third Congress of the Russian Commu-nist Youth Union, 'For us morality, taken apart from the human soci-ety, does not exist; it is a fraud. For us morality is subordinate to the interests of class struggle of the proletariat. Morality serves for the human society to ascend higher, to get rid of the exploitation of labor.'" He paused to consider, then went on, much more haltingly: "Without doubt, the same truth applies to art. Any art devoid of its underlying human principle can only lead to moral chaos, and . . ."

Each word dragged itself with an effort, like a half-dead prisoner burdened with lead weights at his ankles, and the world around

seemed to conspire to make Sukhanov distracted and uncomfortable. The sun, rising higher, merrily danced off the bronze Pegasus at
his elbow, tossing handfuls of annoying little flashes into his eyes.
The customary piece of toast that Nina brought in at eleven o'clock
tasted vaguely of herring. The robe he wore felt stifling and unclean,
but he was forced to perspire in helpless irritation since his clothes
were trapped in the bedroom closet and he did not want to risk
another awkward encounter with Dalevich. The telephone kept ringing with muffled persistence in the distant reaches of the apartment,
making him lose what little concentration he could muster. After a
mostly fruitless hour punctuated by sporadic bursts of typing, he
pulled the page out of the typewriter and considered his single paragraph with a displeased frown. For a moment his pen hung poised
over the lines like a bird of prey ready to swoop down for the kill;
then, descending swiftly, it moved across the paper with such violence that a few sharp tears appeared in the text.

The new version was markedly shorter.

"In the well-known words of V. I. Lenin," it read now, " 'Morality,
taken apart from the human society, does not exist [tear]. . . . Morality serves for the human society to ascend higher [larger tear]. . . .' In
certain ways, these words may apply to art."

Here the paragraph ended, clearly leading nowhere. After some
thought, Sukhanov crumpled the page and tossed it away, sending
after it the three pages from the previous day. He missed the wastebasket every time. He then rolled a new sheet into the typewriter and
banged out angrily: "Salvador Dalí was born in 1904 in a small Spanish town. The artist's father was . . ." At which point he stopped, and
stared at nothing.

When, another futile hour later, an apologetic knock sounded on
his door, he was glad for the interruption. It was his cousin, inviting
him to dinner.

"I've taken the liberty to roast a small chicken," said Fyodor Mikhailovich with a self-deprecating shrug, looking more than ever like a pleasant gentleman from the turn of the century.

At dinner, Vasily was absent again; he had apparently left sometime before, to spend the day at a friend's dacha. "Ah yes, those last joys of summer," said Sukhanov with a short laugh, addressing no one in particular. Nina had wanted to set the table in the dining room, since they had a guest, but Dalevich had implored her not to do anything special on his account. "Please don't pay any heed to my presence," he had begged in a heartfelt voice. In truth, it was rather hard to ignore his presence, as the man dominated all conversation. A curator of some northern folk museum, he had come to Moscow, it seemed, for the purpose of researching a book on icons, and now, his beard bristling, his glasses dancing, spoke with an endless, tiresome enthusiasm about egg yolk and cinnabar and what it must have meant for an artist to extract the colors for his masterpieces with his own hands from the world around him, from the earth upon which he had walked. . . .

Sukhanov soon grew restless. "So, Fyodor," he interrupted with a thin smile, "what do you think, did Rublev really exist, or is this just another myth of art history?"

Dalevich looked startled. Then he laughed.

"The only reason people doubt the existence of Rublev—or Shakespeare, for that matter," he said, raising a gnawed chicken leg for emphasis, "is that it's hard for ordinary minds like ours to imagine a genius of such magnitude. It makes us feel safer, wouldn't you agree, to split a giant into several more manageable, only moderately oversized figures. And yet, however much it may dwarf us, I'm certain that the giants did live." He paused for a discreet nibble on the chicken leg, then said mildly, "I hear, Tolya, you are writing a book as well?"

Sukhanov ceased smiling.

"An article," he said stiffly. "About Dalí. The surrealist."

"Ah, but how fascinating!" Fyodor Mikhailovich exclaimed with delight. "So what's your opinion of him, if I may ask?"

Avoiding references to either capitalism or socialism, Sukhanov carefully discoursed on the harmful irrationality of surrealist works, which set out to pervert the sacred purpose of art—that of leading mankind to new triumphs, to the greater and fuller realization of its potential. Fyodor Mikhailovich nodded with polite interest.

"Naturally, your article must express the official viewpoint of your magazine," he said when Sukhanov finished. "I was more curious to find out what you yourself thought about Dalí. Do you like his paintings, Tolya? Do you think they are good art?"

Ksenya tried to suppress a snicker and failed—and once again, Sukhanov had the strange, disorienting feeling that his life had made yet another circle, that someone had asked him these very questions before.

He looked at his cousin with barely hidden hostility.

"Is it so inconceivable that my own viewpoint actually coincides with that of my magazine?" he said sharply. "What do *you* think about Dalí? You like him, I take it?"

"No, I can't say I do," said Fyodor Mikhailovich thoughtfully. "True, the man once had undeniable talent. His early visions are haunting, don't you find—those pulpy, dripping clocks, those burning giraffes, Venus de Milo with drawers carved all along her body—great, dark metaphors for our nightmarish century. Unfortunately, after these first brilliant steps, he stopped striving and began to repeat himself—more clocks, more giraffes, more drawers, all those sleek juxtapositions of random objects that seem striking for a moment but are devoid of any real meaning, all those amusing tricks for the eye, like Raphael's Madonna fitted into an ear, you know it? He managed to trivialize himself completely. True art, in my modest opinion, must uphold a harmonious balance between form and content, and content is precisely what he's lost. The man is nothing but a trickster now. A pity, really. He allowed the surrealist form he once invented to overtake him and thus failed to live up to the demands of his own gift, becoming just another small man cursed with a great talent. . . . Nina Petrovna, are you all right?"

Nina slowly moved her eyes away from her husband's face.

"I'm sorry, I was just thinking about something," she said quietly. "Would anyone like more chicken?"

Late in the evening, Sukhanov went for a walk. Walks were not in his habit, but as the day dragged on sluggishly, moving through the customary time markers of work, dinner, work, supper, its cumulative effect made him long to step outside the confines of the familiar setting, if only for a quick turn around the neighborhood. For the first time in years, being inside the four walls of his home imparted no sense of well-heeled security; rather, it made him feel claustrophobic and helpless, as if he were a minor character in some minimalist novel, sent to travel the corridor between the kitchen and the study forever and ever by a cruel, uncaring author, while he, powerless to break out of the hateful paragraph, dreamt perhaps of being magically transported from a bedroom yawn to a small rented boat on a public park's pond, with the first summer sunlight warming his face and a girl in a flowing green scarf nibbling on an ice cream cone, and laughing, and looking into his eyes. . . . Of course, the boat had long since carried the girl away into the mists of the past, thought Sukhanov with an odd pang of regret as he stopped to watch a leaf fluttering through the air. The woman she had become still wore flowing scarves from time to time, but she did not laugh very much and hardly ever looked into his eyes. But perhaps this was as things were supposed to be when one ceased to be young, and it was simply the advent of autumn, both in the world around him and in his own life, that caused him to indulge in such melancholy reflections.

The leaf touched the ground; he walked away, shrugging.

At ten o'clock, the streets of the Zamoskvorechie were quiet and dark, with only an occasional streetlamp depriving the night of a peeling façade, a solitary branch glowing with emerald fire in the depths of an invisible tree, or strikingly, a bright flowering of domes above the low rooftops. The rarefied jingling of a late trolley reached him from Bolshaya Polyanka Street, a courtyard away; a solitary guitar twang fell from a window open somewhere above his head. Another gloomy, poorly lit street, empty save for the ghosts of portly merchants who had inhabited this quarter of Moscow in centuries past and who now hurried obliviously, crossing themselves, in and out of a dilapidated church, led him to the Tretyakovskaya Gallery, which sat in the middle of its illuminated yard like a multilayered cake on a platter. The day's foreign crowds had all washed away until morning, leaving unfamiliar-looking soda bottles, crumpled ticket stubs, and cigarette butts in their wake. Now only rare intertwined couples strolled through the echoing night, heads close together, quarreling or giggling, perfectly indifferent to the fact that just a few walls away hung the highest accomplishment of Russian art—*The Trinity* by Andrei Rublev, the legendary fifteenth-century icon painter who might or might not have existed.

Sukhanov too walked without pausing. For twelve long years, he had lived mere minutes from here—could, in fact, see the glint of the gallery's roof from his kitchen windows—yet in all that time he had been inside only on two or three obligatory visits with his then preadolescent children. Apart from Ksenya's bright-eyed fascination with Vrubel's Demon and Vasily's tepid curiosity about the dress of eighteenth-century courtiers, they had remained on the whole uninterested. "Why do they put everything under glass?" Ksenya had whined in every room. "I can see nothing but my own reflection!"

Underneath this innocuous layer of infrequent memories lay another, deeper deposit, dating from the years when he and Nina, still young, still childless, had lived on the other side of the river, and every day Nina had passed through the halls of the Tretyakovka as one of its many anonymous curators. Briefly Sukhanov wondered whether she still came here from time to time; if she did, she never mentioned it. Then, unwilling to probe any further into this particular pocket of darkness, as if afraid of all the bats that might fly screeching into his face out of the void, he forced his thoughts away. Past the museum, a short, crooked alley swallowed him into its ill-smelling shadow and, before he had time to suck in his breath, spat him out into the sudden lights of a square, with a red M swimming through a pinkish haze and two or three neon signs with gaping holes of burnt-out letters flickering in the dimness beyond. The ice cream kiosk, he saw, had closed for the day only minutes earlier. A short-haired girl in a yellow dress, hurrying toward the metro, was just beginning to strip her Eskimo of its wrapper. Sukhanov watched her absently. When she vanished down the staircase leading underground, he turned to go back home.

He was already nearing his building when a taxi pulled up a few paces away. Its door swung open, and a tall, slim youth in a sleek blazer spilled out into the night, chased by the contentious voice of the driver. The words traveled shrilly down quiet Belinsky Street: "Hey, golden boy, and what about these wine stains on my seat?" The passenger shrugged with a loose haughtiness of inebriation and sent a negligent bill flying through the taxi's window.

"Buy yourself a new car with the change, why don't you?" he said, walking away.

The man was Vasily.

Displeased, Sukhanov stopped and watched him weave unsteadily in and out of pale strips of light—but as he watched, he began to smile, and as he smiled, he unexpectedly found his recent feeling toward his son changing, lightening, shifting from that of wary bemusement to that of an amiable, generous, fatherly tolerance. Surprising himself, he called out, and Vasily turned and haltingly waded toward him, careful to circumnavigate every dense concentration of shadow on the pavement.

"Doesn't anyone clean the streets anymore?" he queried garrulously. "I swear, that janitor does nothing but drink. . . . Papa, is that you?"

Chuckling with amusement, Sukhanov guided him to a bench, which materialized obligingly five steps away, sat down himself, and feeling more and more expansive by the minute, accepted a sip from a half-empty bottle of wine the boy extracted, after some fumbling, from an inner pocket of his blazer. He had braced himself for a cheap, pungent taste, but discovered the wine to be truly excellent, velvety and rich, lingering on the tip of his tongue with a nobly understated sweetness. Gently he wrested the bottle away from Vasily and, curious, turned it this way and that, trying to discern the label through the darkness, until the red-and-golden letters flashed on the distinctive black background.

"But this is Kindzmarauli," he said, surprised. "Must have been some party!"

He took another sip, savoring it this time, letting his memory drift to his own youth, to that unforgettable trip to the sea he had taken with Nina the summer after their wedding, to the nights filled with overripe peaches and stars falling like rain and the cheap wines of Georgia, sold by the barrel in small mountain settlements—nothing like this one, of course, and yet sharing with it the same sunshine, the same air, the same undercurrent of happiness, enough for the present superior taste, by dint of relatedness, to reawaken in his being echoes of a thousand trifles that had once made him feel so alive. Suddenly the desire to reminisce overwhelmed him. Putting his arm around Vasily's shoulders, he imagined himself talking about so many things, telling so many stories—about a small boy chasing pigeons, and a brilliant engineer in love with his country, and an old man nicknamed the Professor who, unbeknownst to himself, had possessed something very akin to magic—all the things that he had never had time or inclination to share with his children, all the barely expressible and deeply personal things that lived, poignant, precious, endlessly important, beyond the common property of dull biographical facts. He thought how much he would have given to talk like this with his own father, and how unique this moment was, with the two of them sitting side by side, passing wine to each other in an eloquent silence of true intimacy, separated from the whole universe by this hour of understanding, with the solemn August night lying expectantly at their feet and the city watching over them with its hundreds of lit windows, and how, years and years from now, Vasily would still remember the words that he was just about to—

"Yes, not too bad," Vasily said. "You should have seen the man's digs!"

It took Sukhanov a long minute to recall the comment he had made just before boarding his present train of thought. Mechanically, he said, "Ah yes, the party. What man? Weren't you at Olga's dacha? And by the way, I meant to ask you—"

Olga was a charming girl involved with Vasily in a romance that had lasted for several lukewarm years now, and it occurred to Sukhanov that the subject might serve as a suitable introduction to a momentous discourse on youth, happiness, and other matters distilled by his lifelong wisdom.

"Of course I wasn't at Olga's," said Vasily in a surprised voice. "Didn't you know where I went? Remember that little get-together planned by the Minister of Culture?"

"The Minister of Culture?" Sukhanov repeated blankly.

"Yes, he invited both of us to come to his dacha tonight, remember?" said Vasily offhandedly.

A dog began to bark hoarsely a few streets away. Sukhanov looked at his son in deepening silence. The boy's eyes had narrowed, and he did not seem half as tipsy as before.

"Oh, that's right, you forgot to tell me about it!" he said with a cold smile. "Slipped your mind, did it? But I happened to see the Minister's wife at that matinee at the Bolshoi, and she mentioned it to me. As a matter of fact, she wanted to make sure we'd be there. I told her you were rather busy nowadays, but as for me, I'd be delighted."

"Vasily," said Sukhanov slowly. "You must understand, it wasn't an intentional . . . I didn't . . . I just wasn't sure we were invited, you see. I wish you had told me, I myself would have liked to . . . Ah, forget it. That was lucky, you running into the woman."

"Well, I wouldn't exactly call it luck," said Vasily. "I overheard she was going to be at the theater. Why else, do you think, would I agree to suffer through three hours of boredom? I mean, no offense, but Grandma isn't exactly a bundle of laughs, and I find *Coppelia* greatly overrated."

"Oh," said Sukhanov. "Oh, I see. Well, I'm glad it worked out. Many interesting people at the party, I suppose . . . By the way, did you meet their daughter? I hear she is pretty."

"No, not particularly, unless, of course, your preferences run to tiny eyes and a general absence of neck. Which, personally, I'm willing to live with if they belong to a minister's offspring. We hit it off rather well, I believe. I'm taking her out to dinner. Another sip?"

"No, thank you," said Sukhanov cheerlessly. For some reason, he failed to feel happy for his son. Instead, he found himself strangely rattled by the conversation, so different from the one he had pictured. "And what about Olga?"

"Oh well, I figure we both need a change of scenery," said Vasily with a shrug.

It was drawing closer to midnight; the lights were starting to go out in the houses around them, and the bench had turned cold. A leaf fell into Sukhanov's lap; he picked it up and twirled it in his fingers. The dog, now barking only a street away, was joined by another, and their howling made him edgy and sad at the same time, as if he had lost something vital.

"Were you ever even in love with her?" he asked quietly.

Vasily looked vastly amused.

"I don't believe it," he drawled. "You, of all people, are going to lecture me about love?"

"What is that supposed to mean?" said Anatoly Pavlovich, straightening with slow dignity. "Your mother and I married for love!"

"But it sure was nice that she wasn't the daughter of a bus driver, right?" Vasily replied, smiling. "I mean, how fortunate that her famous father was just the person to help you start your wonderful little career in art criticism. Talk of lucky coincidences!"

And that was when Sukhanov looked at his son—and saw a grown man whom he did not recognize. The man had light blue eyes and dark blond hair. The man was wearing a perfectly tailored blazer and drinking expensive wine. The man looked altogether like someone he had once known, but the man was an impostor. Had to be.

Sukhanov began to stand up.

"Let's go home, I'm getting cold," he said expressionlessly. "And by the way, Fyodor is staying with us for one more night. I expect you to be polite."

"Do you know what your trouble is?" said the man on the bench, not attempting to move. "You do everything halfway. So you married up, so you sold out, wrote ideological nonsense you didn't believe in, fine and good—but what did you get for it? A comfortable apartment in the Zamoskvorechie, a nice dacha, and a cushy little job at some magazine! Honestly, Father, was that the extent of your ambition, was it even worth all the sacrifice, to become an important man in such a small world? Do you realize how high you could have risen with Grandpa's connections if only you had wanted to? But then again, maybe you couldn't have, maybe you simply didn't have it in you, maybe—"

Anatoly Pavlovich turned and walked away with heavy steps, feeling his age in his shoulders and knees. In another moment, the empty bottle clanged dully as it rolled under the bench, and Vasily followed him, still talking—talking about his own plans, his influential grandfather, some place in the Crimea, the Minister, the Minister's overweight daughter . . . Sukhanov was no longer listening. When the elevator arrived, boxlike and lurching, and the smiling concierge swung open its iron gate, he waited for his son to pass inside the dismally mirrored coffin and then announced he was going to take the stairs instead.

"Good for one's health," he explained to the concierge.

"So I've heard," replied the concierge enthusiastically. "They say every step up adds a second to a man's life!"

For a moment Sukhanov wondered whether he wanted these extra seconds, these tiny units of life, pulsing with animation, stored in his body for future usage. Then he nodded and began to climb. On the third landing, he heard a plate smashing onto the floor in the apartment belonging to the mysterious woman with Nefertiti's profile. As he continued to ascend, he thought that an altogether unusual amount of porcelain was being broken nowadays in building number seven, Belinsky Street, in the city of Moscow.

Nine

It happened the way he had always imagined—an explosion of ruthless knocks on the front door ripping through the stillness of sleep. The first volley merged with his dream, which immediately turned noisy and violent, with him dashing through grimy, bullet-riddled corridors, pursued by a mob of men with hairy arms and faces like slabs of beef; but when another salvo of raps slit his nightmare wide open, Sukhanov sat up and listened, his skin tightening with a sense of unreality. All was quiet about him, yet the silence rang with that menacing hollowness that follows upon a loud, sharp sound.

He rose and, struggling with his robe (which, clownishly, ridiculously, frighteningly, had grown a third sleeve and kept escaping him), traversed the predawn darkness as if in slow motion; the thuds of his slippers fell upon the floor like his own uneven heartbeats. In the entrance hall, he tripped against the ghosts of two umbrellas forgotten by the wall and, swearing, was just about to flip the light switch when the shadows exploded with knocking once again, unbearably close now. No longer able to pretend it had been a dream, he stood staring, staring at the front door, without moving, almost without breathing, feeling suddenly afraid and alone—as afraid and alone as he had felt forty-eight years ago, on the night when those polished black shoes had invaded their Arbat existence for the third, and final, time.

The first time he barely noticed, lost as he was in his new world. His routine of classes, holidays, meals in the months following his attempt to steal Gradsky's manuscript had become a mere backdrop to the radiant, unearthly discoveries that awaited him almost nightly in the Professor's dusty, cramped room, where the shouts of boys chasing one another in the yard and the familiar smells of meat pies and hot asphalt never penetrated and where, in the green glow of the lampshade, the precious gilded books slowly released their unforgettable fragrance, that scent of brittle paper and mustiness that for Anatoly would forever be the scent of previously unimaginable beauty. He moved through the summer of 1937 in a haze of secret excitement, inaudibly intoning the sonorous names of men who had walked the streets of strange watery and golden cities in centuries past and yet seemed to him more real than the flesh-and-blood inhabitants of his apartment—shadowy, inconsequential presences with whom he held shadowy conversations or who on occasion subjected him to somewhat less shadowy beatings.

Afterward, all he could recall of the poor unlovely Zoya Vienberg in those final weeks was the nearsighted, trembling fussiness with which she had spent the last day before the new school year sorting her dull brown folders, stuffed to the point of bursting with sheet music, on their kitchen table between meals, and the hysterical note that had stolen into her voice once or twice when she had addressed Galka Morozova. Then, one afternoon in October, Anatoly returned from school to find Zoya Vladimirovna's door branded with a formidable-looking seal, and his mother and the Gradsky couple oddly reluctant to reply when Anton Morozov proclaimed indignantly that he was not surprised—that, in fact, he had sus- pected something like this all along. The music teacher never came back, and in another few weeks Morozov's sister Pelageya matter-of- factly moved into the unoccupied room.

I hardly wondered about it at first, for the woman's absence was never discussed and our life remained largely the same. But as the autumn deepened, I noticed that some change, slow and painful like corrosion, was eating away at the happiness of my evenings with the Professor. He appeared distracted or uninterested, and would often pause in the middle of a sentence, forgetting to turn the page and lis- tening intently—whether to the dry cough of his ailing wife behind the wall or to some other sound he expected to hear, I was not sure; and gradually, as the cold crept through the cracks of our old ram- bling building, a sense of unease furtively worked its way into my heart. And then one night, shortly before my ninth birthday, I woke up in the chilly December darkness to a silence that had ceased to be silent, that was filling with the muted sounds of stolidly shod feet trampling through our apartment, through our life.

In the morning, there was a tossing whirlwind of snow outside the windows, and the Professor ran out without a hat and was gone all day. My mother spent the afternoon frantically pleading with remote telephone operators, and then suddenly broke down crying and, clutching my shoulders, told me, in a voice I had never heard before, that my father might be staying in Gorky for a while longer and that I was the only thing she had left. And later that day, Anton Morozov stopped me in the corridor and, towering over me like some hirsute, sour-smelling mountain, asked me whether I knew that Tatyana Gradskaya's family had all been vicious tsarists and that, before Lenin had set things right, our apartment had actually belonged to the Gradsky couple.

I had not known, and the idea of two people once owning the whole vast unfolding of space where so many lives, including my own, were now concentrated shocked me deeply. I thought of a twisted stump in our ceiling that must have once held a crystal chandelier of the kind I had seen in one of the Professor's books, and of a large pale patch that I had noticed on the wallpaper in the Morozovs' room and which, I now recalled the Professor telling me, marked the place where a piano used to stand. I imagined the blue-haired, quiet little woman and the soft-spoken, kindly old man, whom I had thought I knew so well, waltzing through all that magnificent expanse sparkling with the glass and silver and lacquer of a thousand marvelous, elegant, foreign things—and I felt bitter, I felt betrayed.

Beauty did, after all, belong to the bourgeois.

That night, when the front door opened and closed and the unrecognizable steps of an ancient man scuffled across my hearing, I followed him into his study and told him I would visit him no longer.

The Professor's face was erased by grief; his room lay in ruins about him.

"Yes, it's best, I think," he said flatly, avoiding my eyes. "I myself was about to suggest . . ." Taking off his glasses, he began to rub the lenses with the underside of his jacket, meticulously, needlessly, endlessly. When he spoke again, his voice had aged many years. "Well, Tolya, I have enjoyed our friendship. You know, I was going to make you a present on your birthday—that Botticelli album, actually. You can take it now if you like. I meant to write an inscription, but I'm not sure whether . . ."

It was strange to see him like this, and I hesitated for a long moment.

"I'll take it," I finally said, "but I don't need the inscription."

He nodded without surprise, and finding the volume in the chaos of books on the floor, dusted it lightly and handed it to me.

"She's done nothing wrong, you know," he said, attempting a smile. "It's all just a temporary mistake, I'm sure. . . . Maybe, once she comes back, you and I could resume our delightful art evenings? I would like to think so, Tolya. Well, so long now. Be happy."

Suddenly uncomfortable, I mumbled, "Thanks," and left, pretending not to notice his outstretched, embarrassingly trembling hand. As I was closing the door behind me, a rising clump in my throat made me turn and cast a glance back. The Professor was still standing uncertainly amid his mistreated books, his face expressionless in the green glare of the lamp, his unseeing eyes gazing at the empty surface of the desk, where, only the day before, his nearly completed manuscript, the work of his life, had been stacked in neat piles, chapter by chapter.

They took him away two nights later. I was lying awake, and heard the pounding and Morozov's voice muttering a hurried explanation in the hallway and more voices and heavy steps. Seized with some madness, I crawled through the darkness and, cracking open our door, looked out—for one instant only, because immediately my mother, who must have been lying awake as well, screamed at me in a furious, panicking whisper, and obeying, I drew away.

For a long time we waited, huddling together, she and I, listening to the faraway, barely discernible sounds of papers torn and spirits broken, until more steps, some sharply heeled, others soft and scuffling, traveled from end to end of our apartment, and the front door slammed once again, leaving behind a wary hush.

"It's over," my mother whispered in a collapsing voice, but I felt no relief, neither then, nor the next day, nor the day after that—for that momentary glimpse I had had of the broad leather backs and polished black shoes receding into the dimness of our corridor had been enough to inspire me with a numbing, lonely terror that would last for weeks. Night after night I would lie awake, touching the edge of the Botticelli album under my pillow and imagining with a halting heart that soon, soon, any day now, they would learn that I too was different, that I too deserved their righteous anger, that I too had been tainted by enemies of the people—and they would return once more, this time for me. Finally, one evening in February, unable to sustain this wordless, guilty fear any longer, I stole outside with the damning book hidden under my coat, ran down our street, ducked into a courtyard a few houses away, and there, in a murky, quiet corner, cringing under the accusing glare of a few lit windows behind which other boys were surely doing their homework or building nice toy planes with their fathers, I buried my dangerous treasure in a giant drift of snow and darted away.

With the advent of spring, a semblance of normality returned to my life. A new resident, a jocular construction worker who knew amazing card tricks, moved into the Professor's study, my mother began to talk again about my father's return and smile her wan, anxious smile, and the Morozov boys grew bored with tormenting me.

"Want to see something funny?" Sashka said to me one day. "In a courtyard down the street, the snow is turning all sorts of crazy colors!"

And so I went and stood in a crowd of children and with them laughed at the golden green and the pearly pink and the brightest copper rivulets of the melting snowdrift. And as I laughed, the last remnants of my secret dread lifted from me, for at that moment I saw that I was finally safe, that I was one of them now, that I could simply forget all about those brilliantly tinted revelations in the darkly glowing room of the treacherous old man who had possessed so many dusty wonders. And yet, somewhere deep, deep inside me, the memory of the rainbow-colored marvels must have survived—and so did the fear, because for the next three years, until the beginning of the war, I would awaken every so often gasping from a nightmare in which I flew down bullet-riddled corridors pursued by a mob of Anton Morozov doubles in shining black shoes; and every time it happened, I would get out of bed, tiptoe to the front door, and stand there for a long while in a grip of clinging, cold fear, listening to the soundless void on the other side and imagining a volley of ruthless knocks that could shatter the drafty darkness at any moment. . . .

The knocking shook the door again, more impatient this time. With dizzying speed Sukhanov traversed forty-eight years of his life in the opposite direction and emerged onto the surface of reality.

"Who is it?" he asked, his voice shaken.

The answer came promptly.

"Militia, open up!"

Though far removed from the inarticulate, sinister, almost surreal menace of his nightmares, the words were nonetheless extremely disturbing, and he found himself clammy with apprehension as he fiddled with the locks. The landing was dim, full of wavering shadow; the bulb over the elevator gate had begun to flicker some days earlier. In the uncertain light he saw three figures looming before him—two uniformed militiamen and, behind them, a large woman of fifty-odd years in an unbecomingly flimsy tangerine kimono, her head blooming with a profusion of pink curlers. With a start Sukhanov recognized Tamara Bubuladze, the celebrated Amneris from the floor below.

For a moment an uneasy silence hung between them, disturbed only by rare, drowsy barks of Bubuladze's basset hounds reaching them mutedly from the stairwell. Then the older of the militiamen, with a potato-like nose, turned to the singer.

"Seems quiet enough to me, Madame Bubuladze," he said doubtfully, "and this man here doesn't quite . . . Are you sure this is the apartment?"

"Of course I'm sure!" the woman cried, glaring at Sukhanov. "Sounds carry from their place to mine perfectly well. Shameless, positively shameless, and at his age! . . . Ah, and this must be one of the hussies!"

Turning, Sukhanov saw Ksenya's nightgown gleaming faintly in the hallway behind him.

"This hussy," he said, "is my daughter. What exactly—"

"Anyone else with you?" interrupted the younger militiaman, his cheeks red as tomatoes.

"My wife, my son, and my cousin," said Sukhanov dryly. "Now, can someone please tell me why I was dragged out of bed at . . . What time is it, anyway?"

Signs of confused stirring were spreading through the apartment: bedsprings creaking, an irritated yawn, the clicking of Nina's slippers crossing invisible space, a lamp switched on somewhere.

"Just past four," said the potato nose in a deflated voice. "It appears there's been a mistake. This lady called us about . . . er . . . a noisy party . . ."

"An *orgy*," said the opera singer vehemently. "I called you about an orgy, and no need to mince words. An orgy is precisely what I heard."

"Yes, well," said the tomato cheeks cautiously, "but it obviously wasn't these people here, was it now, Madame Bubuladze? Seems they were all asleep. Maybe you just had a . . . a bad dream? Why don't we take you back to your—"

"That," said the woman, "was no dream. I'm not crazy, I can still tell a dream from reality, thank you very much."

"If it's all the same to you, Tamara Eduardovna," Sukhanov interjected pointedly, "I'd like to get back to bed sometime tonight. If you comrades want to come in and make sure—"

The vegetables exchanged quick looks.

"No, no, that's not necessary," said the potato wearily. "Sorry for the disturbance."

As he shut the door, Sukhanov caught one last glimpse of the heaving, boulderlike breasts and heard the once famous mezzo-soprano shriek, "And *I* say, such behavior must not be—" The door's heavy padding sliced the edge off the sound just as it rose to its highest note of indignation.

He appeared disgruntled as he explained the incident to a perplexed Nina before retiring to his couch—but in truth, he found it rather amusing (especially as its comic absurdity had rescued him from a further onslaught of dark recollections), and it was with unfeigned laughter that he emerged for breakfast the next day. The whole family, it seemed, had already dispersed on their morning errands; Dalevich alone sat in the kitchen, cutting an apple into thin, precise slices and feeding them delicately to his beard.

"What a night!" he said, smiling. "Is it always so exciting around here? I see what they mean about life in the big city."

"I'd say the past few days have been somewhat more eventful than usual," Sukhanov replied with a chuckle. "That woman clearly has a loose screw. I hope you were able to fall asleep again."

"To be honest, I didn't try," said Dalevich. "I spent the rest of the night working on my book. I prefer writing at night anyway. My ideas flow better when it's dark and quiet."

"Excellent pancakes," observed Sukhanov. "Did Nina make them? . . . Ah, I suspected as much. . . . Speaking of your book, Fedya, I've been thinking about, how did you put it, this 'harmonious balance between form and content' that you say characterizes all true art, and I'm curious about something. In terms of form, the old Russian icons are, you must agree, quite primitive—all those stilted processions of Byzantine saints with unnaturally small faces, short arms, trite golden locks, and eyes the size of saucers, tacked onto flat backgrounds. With their form so imperfect, how can you regard your icons as great art?"

"My dear Tolya," Dalevich replied, "I can't believe that an experienced critic like yourself would stumble into the common pitfall of confusing 'perfect form' with a form that is merely flawless in its execution. Of course, in its technical aspects, the manner of icon painting is medieval and therefore by necessity flawed. And yet, I insist, it *is* perfect—insofar as by 'perfect' I mean simply the form most suitable to its subject. What better way is there to portray man's unearthly aspirations, I ask you, than by ignoring irrelevant flesh with its trappings of chiaroscuro and perspective, and presenting instead these floating, pure colors, these insubstantial bodies, these luminous faces, these enormous, mournful eyes? These works create an impression of a door in our dim, mundane lives, opening for a moment to reveal an ethereal glimpse of heaven, a golden flash of God's paradise. The effect becomes far less wondrous if one dilutes such stark, glowing purity with even the smallest dose of your accurately rendered reality. Compare, for instance, Rublev's Trinity with that of Simon Ushakov, painted some two hundred fifty years later, on the threshold of a new, material age. Instead of Rublev's single chalice, Ushakov places *eleven* objects on the table before the angels, thereby inadvertently reducing them from Holy Trinity to some sort of picnicking trio! Realistic form is hardly suited for works of spiritual content, wouldn't you say?"

"Spiritual content?" Sukhanov repeated with derision. "Is that what you call spirit, then—a dark tangle of superstitious clichés robed in centuries of random symbols and served up on an elaborately jeweled platter for peasants' consumption?"

"And what do *you* call spirit, if I may ask—now that you've so neatly disposed of every world religion, and all in a dozen words?" said Dalevich, smiling.

"The eternal human striving to attain new heights," said Sukhanov without hesitation.

"By which you mean, no doubt, various cultural developments ultimately designed to facilitate the advent of bigger factories and happier family units?" asked Dalevich amiably. "That is, after all, what you people preach—useful art in service of a Great Tomorrow? And by the way, have you ever considered that your socialist realism and my religious painting have much in common—indeed, the one may be said to be a logical, if sadly impoverished, continuation of the other. Both have deep communal roots, and both serve a noble purpose—the good of the people or the salvation of all mankind, as the case may be. In both, too, the painter is an anonymous teacher of sorts, a compassionate man with a holy mission to educate, to enlighten, to show the way—a very Russian idea of the artist in general, don't you find, so unlike the Western type of a solitary dreamer engaged in a private game of self-glorification. And of course, both socialist realism and icon painting are concerned with an ideal, visionary future, except that yours is strictly material, an earthly paradise of your own devising, so to speak, while mine—"

"What in the devil's name does socialist realism have to do with it?" interrupted Sukhanov. "I'm talking about *art*! Art is not about some common purpose or noble mission. It's an expression of an artist's soul, his individual, titanic struggle to rise above the ordinary, to speak a word unheard before, to extract an unexpected, mysterious, radiant nugget of beauty from the many obscure layers of our existence, to glimpse a bit of the infinite in everyday life—and truly great art comes to us like an ecstatic revelation, it sets our whole being on fire! And your medieval wall-painters were nothing but practitioners of applied arts, obedient illustrators of a few stale, commonplace truths about a small man's eternity. Crushed by the weight of their own credo 'Blessed are the poor in spirit,' they never took risks, never overstepped their boundaries, never tried to set vibrating some new, previously untouched chord in our souls—"

He stopped, short of breath, surprised by the sudden passion that had made his voice ring, caught off guard by an overwhelming desire that, awakening all at once, claimed his whole being—a desire to break the silence of so many years, to release his innermost thoughts on the subject once closest to his heart—and to be understood. His cousin, he noticed, was looking at him with something nearing astonishment, a slice of apple forgotten on its way to his beard. A broadening hush slowly ate into the air like a spreading stain into a piece of cloth. Finally Dalevich blinked, put the slice of apple back on the saucer, and clapped with weighty, theatrical cheer.

"Bravo, Tolya!" he exclaimed. "Spoken like an artist, not a critic—and certainly not a critic from *Art of the World*! Still, for all your eloquence, I could never share your disdain for, what do you call them, 'boundaries.' I agree that art should be about striving, but I believe it is precisely by striving *within* its boundaries that art can achieve its highest peaks. An artist of true genius is not one who wholly dismisses old traditions and plunges us headfirst into an unknown, disorienting, possibly meaningless paradigm, but rather one who, working from within a predetermined framework, subtly manages to push away our blinders an inch or two, to reflect our faces in a mildly distorted mirror, to find a second bottom in the most familiar things or a second meaning in the most exhausted words—in short, to wipe the accumulations of dust from our world—and who by doing so allows us to rise with him to a higher plane of existence. That is why Chagall, with his deceptively simple, childlike universe of flying fiddlers, green-faced lovers, and mysteriously smiling cows, will always be greater than Kandinsky, with his icy swirls of color and elegant abstract compositions, for all the brilliant innovations of the latter."

"A dubious argument," said Sukhanov thoughtfully. "Isn't it paradoxical to argue that artists who make tiny steps are greater than those who make giant strides?"

"Personally, I find paradoxes refreshing, especially when . . . Heavens, is it really ten o'clock? I'm afraid, Tolya, we'll have to continue our discussion some other time—I have to pay a visit to an acquaintance, he's helping me with my research. . . . Or better yet, why don't you come with me? Oleg has a splendid collection of icons. Come, you two can talk about medieval art to your hearts' content. What do you say, eh?"

Sukhanov had planned to spend all day at his desk, as the ill-fated Dalí article was due the next morning and he had written nothing beyond the first sentence.

"Ah, why not," he said lightly, brushing crumbs off his lap. "I have some time to kill."

Summer seemed to have tiptoed out of Moscow while no one was looking. In the gray, diffused light of a gloomy autumnal day, the streets of the Zamoskvorechie were drab and unwelcoming. The wind drove along the pavements a procession of yellowing leaves and, mixed in among them, ice cream wrappers and an occasional newspaper page.

Dalevich trotted alongside Sukhanov, talking in his mild, persuasive voice. "One could go even further," he was saying, "and argue that repression ultimately benefits the arts. By the way, your Dalí held precisely that view. Take a man with a mustache, for instance—nothing interesting under ordinary circumstances, wouldn't you agree?"

"Er . . . yes," said Sukhanov, not listening. A stray playbill leapt out of nowhere and flattened itself against his trouser leg. He bent to pick it up, scanned it without curiosity (*Dead Souls,* at the Malyi Theater—a mangled remnant of someone's long-past evening from the last theater season), then released it. The bill danced frenziedly across the road.

"Yes, but if some tyrant bans all facial hair, an ingenious person might contrive to grow a secret mustache, say, around his ankle, and that *would* be interesting, no? So in a way, you see, imposing limits on creativity may actually stimulate the appearance of better, or at least more innovative, art. Of course, in Russia, boundaries and rules— whether set by the Church, the tsar, or the Party—have always been an integral part of any artistic endeavor, and this may account—"

"Are we getting close now?" Sukhanov interrupted. For the past few minutes he had been asking himself with growing befuddlement why on earth he had agreed to visit a total stranger—an icon collector, of all things—on this busy, this extremely busy day.

"Almost there," said Dalevich brightly. "Just through this gateway and across the yard. Anyway, as I was saying, this may account in part for the astonishing regularity with which our land has given birth to geniuses. Although, to be honest, the last five or six decades—"

A low archway in a nondescript wall led them from the bustle of Bolshaya Ordynka onto a narrow path twittering with invisible birds. A peeling one-story house, almost a shed, stretched on their right; on their left rose a toylike church, half concealed by tall purple-headed wildflowers swaying in the wind. Sukhanov paused in surprise. He had hurried with crowds on the other side of the wall scores of times and yet had never suspected the existence of this quiet little nook, shady, damp, and melancholy like some tenderly heartrending watercolor by Levitan—but of course, Moscow was full of such forgotten, crumbling corners, exiled reminders of a different life.

The church had a single darkened dome with no cross on it.

"How very old it is," Sukhanov said, looking at the carvings of strange beasts covering the once white walls. "Fourteenth century, perhaps?"

Dalevich gently took his elbow and guided him along the path into an unkempt yard encircled by more low, peeling houses.

"Actually, no, it's quite new," he said readily. "Designed in a pseudo-Russian style by one Aleksei Shchusev, at the turn of the century. This used to be a convent, founded by the Grand Duchess Elizaveta Fyodorovna in 1908, if I'm not mistaken. Naturally, soon after the Revolution the convent was closed, the royal benefactress thrown alive down a mineshaft—and then, in a nice twist, Shchusev went on to build the Lenin Mausoleum and the ever-so-charming Hotel Moskva. The history of architecture—like any other history, I suppose—is simply full of these little ironies, don't you find? Ah, and that over there is Oleg's house, he rents a . . . Tolya?"

Sukhanov had stopped a few paces away with a wondering look on his face.

"So peaceful here," he said with an apologetic half-smile. "I just wanted . . . Listen for a moment."

Overcast stillness reigned about them, yet it was not altogether quiet. Dusty sparrows chirruped in the dense undergrowth; a young woman, her head covered with a somber kerchief, walked hurriedly across the yard, raising small, timid sounds in her wake—a pebble rolling, a door creaking on its hinges, a splash when her foot slipped into a pool of rainwater; and if one listened very closely, one could almost hear the purple flowers rustling against the church walls. In the early, aromatic days of summer, there would be many butterflies, yellow, white, and orange, spiraling like sunspots over these weeds, which, Sukhanov somehow knew, were called *ivanchai*—Ivan's *chai*, Ivan's tea—an odd, lyrical name that came back to him all at once from a remote childhood lesson, bringing with it a host of other soft-hued recollections of his fourteenth, his fifteenth years: the flowers he had pressed patiently between book pages for botany class; the birds calling to one another high in the trees during his solitary runs through the woods, with his head upturned to drink in the sun-dappled colors of the sky; the comforting, sweet, slightly decaying smells of the earth meeting him as he had fallen exhausted and newly rich into the grass. . . . Yes, this yard smelled a bit like that, of dying flowers and rain and past summers, and it was strange to think that only a stone's throw away, on the other side of this wall, a monstrous city unfolded its hectic streets, rumbling with buses, crowded with people, littered with ticket stubs and candy wrappers and other chaff of tired, ephemeral enjoyments—for here, all around him, were the sounds and scents and colors not of the capital but of some small provincial town miles and ages away, a town that was dreary, neglected, yet somehow dear . . . A town, in fact, very much like Inza in the Ulyanovsk region, three crammed, malodorous, frightening train rides from Moscow, where my mother and I spent two years in wartime evacuation.

We lived in a drafty one-story house on the outskirts, taken in by a taciturn aunt of some chance family acquaintance. I shared a corner with the woman's two sons, and every morning the three of us would stumble together through darkness and snow to a school on the other side of town. And it was there, in the early winter of 1942, that I met Oleg Romanov, a onetime pupil of Chagall and now an unprepossessing teacher of drawing—and in the course of one lesson, while my bored schoolmates passed notes and hand-rolled cigarettes across the freezing classroom, I unexpectedly had a glimpse of the truth.

I had long since decided that art was a dangerous, shameful secret of my half-forgotten early childhood, woven out of decadent dreams and seductive songs by demigods from magical far-off countries in centuries past, preserved for a brief while by devious betrayers of the state, then washed away forever with the melting Arbat snows. Now I saw that I had been mistaken. Art was not a private embarrassment or a wicked foreign enchantment. Even more amazing, art was not dead. It continued to live, today, now, in this sorry little town that had some two hundred houses and not a single paved street—and it was brought into existence on an average day by a modest man called Oleg Romanov—a man with a funny lisp and nearsighted eyes—a man who was not very different from other men I knew and yet who somehow, out of nothing, out of the cold, grave, broken world about him, could summon to life those misty, shining landscapes of unfolding vistas, so uniquely his own. . . .

For several nights I barely slept, weighing my discovery and all its implications in my reeling soul. Then, at a lesson two or three weeks later, after I had spent a torturous hour struggling to draw an increasingly tricky cup, Romanov called me aside.

"You show potential, Sukhanov," he said almost reluctantly. "An interesting effort—trying to depict both the outside of the cup and its contents with one image. I can give you private art lessons if you like."

That was another revelation: Art, that glowing, elusive miracle, that sublime universe populated by divinities, could be taught—and an awkward sketch of a teacup could somehow hold the key to a priceless apprenticeship. It would be a lot of work, of course, Romanov said sternly. I would have to start noticing the world around me, learn its smells, its colors, its sounds, the shapes and textures of its creatures, from a deceptively plain sparrow and a common yellow butterfly to man, the glory of creation; I would wrest the secrets of dyes from the earth at my feet, memorize the tints of sunset and the shadows of rain, distinguish between the many shades of white, read a rainbow like a poem—and one day, after much effort, many sleepless nights, and mounds of broken pencils and matted brushes, I might finally arrive at . . . at . . .

"I'm afraid we are running late," said the soft voice of Fyodor Dalevich.

And as Sukhanov emerged from his impossibly vivid daydream and met his cousin's politely questioning eyes, he felt something new, something dark, stir inside him. And that something was dread, numbing, overpowering dread—for as he stood in the middle of the yard belonging to his evacuation years and listened to the echo of memories fading in the depths of his being, he understood precisely toward what future abyss his recollections were pushing him, mercilessly, inexorably . . .

"Forgotten something?" Dalevich inquired with a helpful smile.

"On the contrary," Sukhanov stuttered, "I've just remembered I . . . There is something I must do. Please apologize to your friend— tell him some other time, perhaps. . . ."

He turned to walk away.

"Of course, I understand," Dalevich called out after him. "Although I was hoping we could finish our discussion. I meant to tell you about this article I've written—"

Sukhanov glanced back at the quiet, overgrown yard, at the darkened windows, at the flaking paint on the low buildings, in one of which someone named Oleg was at this very moment awaiting his arrival. . . .

"Some other time, perhaps," he repeated flatly.

Then briskly, without another look, he strode toward his present.

Tεn

The clock on Sukhanov's desk showed ten past six when Nina cracked open his door and, without entering, told him that she was leaving to meet a friend for a play and would be home late.

"Don't wait for me with supper," she said, adjusting the clasp of her bracelet, which kept snapping open.

He noticed that she wore unfamiliar earrings, delicate silver spirals, which, dangling gently along her neck, made her face look thinner and somehow younger. Her lipstick seemed new as well, a girlish pink instead of her usual muted peach.

"A play?" he said. "I didn't know you were going to see a play."

"*The Cherry Orchard,* at the Malyi," she explained quickly. The bracelet would not stay closed. "Liusya called yesterday, she has a spare ticket."

Mechanically he recalled the stray playbill that the wind had delivered into his hands.

"It's supposed to rain later tonight," he said. "Of course, you are taking the car?"

"No, Vadim asked for an evening off. Don't worry, I'll be fine."

"You should get a taxi back," he suggested, and added, after the briefest hesitation, "Have I seen those earrings before?"

"A hundred times," she replied with impatience. "I must go, I'm running late."

She vanished in a gleaming whirl of white and gray silk, leaving a faint smell of lily of the valley behind her, and he heard her high heels hastily traversing the evening silence before being erased by the bang of the front door. For a moment he debated leaning over the balcony and following her sonorous progress down the darkening street, but the paralyzing dread he had experienced in the yard of the decrepit convent still hovered somewhere in the vicinity of his heart, and, oddly reluctant to move, he turned back to his desk instead and busied himself with the stiff workings of the typewriter.

It was nearly eleven when, under the disapproving eye of the bronze Pegasus, he typed the last sentence of his meandering, rather inconclusive conclusion and, having wrested the page from the jaws of the antiquated contraption, added it to a thin stack of paper, vengefully stabbed the whole with a bent paper clip, and leaned back, considering. The article, he knew, said shamefully little, barely straying beyond a meager smattering of facts. *Salvador Dalí was born in 1904 in a small Spanish town. The artist's father was . . .* Feeling suddenly in need of fresh air, Sukhanov rose, erased the light with a flick of the wrist, pushed open the balcony door, and stepped outside, into the pale, cool night.

It had indeed begun to drizzle a while ago. The roofs and the church domes glistened, and the city rustled and splashed in a soft, newly autumnal rhythm, rising and falling with the wet sounds of infrequent cars sliding down the streets, a distant chorus of young, tipsy voices bellowing nonsensical rhymes to the tune of the "Ode to Joy," and the regular tapping of a walking stick belonging to a shrunken old man who every night shuffled slowly along Belinsky Street, before him a giant black dog on a straining leash. A thinning wraith of cigarette smoke drifted from somewhere above, and from below, meeting it in midair, floated a scrap of quiet conversation; Sukhanov heard a woman's voice saying sadly, "We'll have such a harvest of apples this year—and no one to eat them. . . ." And all at once, as he stood listening and watching, breathing deeply, the night seemed to him so full of hidden movement, so poignantly alive, so unlike the habitually stuffy stillness hanging, thick and immobile, in the room at his back, that he felt startled, just as he might if, leafing through the sixth edition of his textbook on Soviet art theory, he discovered a poem printed discreetly between two authoritative paragraphs—some short verse with no apparent sense and yet full of lilting grace, gray and gentle like rain itself. . . .

And in that lucid moment of surprise, a realization that for the last few days had lurked in the shadowy recesses of his thoughts forced its way to the surface. Something was happening to him—something strange, something, in fact, extremely unsettling—something that he was unable to explain, much less stop or control.

He was being assailed by his past.

Anatoly Pavlovich had always made a habit of gluing shut the pages of passing years, leaving at hand only some brief paragraphs for basic reference and a few heavily edited sunny patches for sentimental indulgence. Yet of late, memories were welling up in his soul, unbidden and relentless—and if at first he had found them to be pleasantly nostalgic sojourns into the pastel-tinted landscapes of his early childhood, now they were beginning to grow bleaker, harsher, more disturbing, disrupting the tranquillity of his mind, of his life, bringing him closer and closer to the forbidden edge of a personal darkness he had not leaned over in decades. This morning, in the

yard, he had caught himself on the verge of reliving the horror of
that day in November of 1943—that single moment of suspended
belief followed by an immensity of pain that had swept through
his soul, wiping it clean, and afterward, that persistent sensation of
being lost, wordless, adrift, in a fog teeming with grotesquely sympathetic strangers. The mere possibility of drawing near that memory
produced a chilly numbness in the back of his head, and he knew he
could not, must not, let it torment him, not now, not after all these
years . . .

Again he forced his thoughts away with a trembling sensation of
stepping, just in time, from the brink of the abyss. The night pattered
and glimmered before him. He touched his hand to his forehead,
then, suppressing a shudder, moved to go back inside, when another
waft of smoke drifted from above and something solid hit him
squarely on the head and, bouncing off the banister, plummeted into
the bushes. Incredulous, he followed it with his eyes: it was a loaf of
bread. Then, craning his neck as far as his stoutness allowed, he
looked up and found himself confronted with an unfamiliar old man
in a red ski cap, hanging over the railing of the top, ninth-floor, balcony. The old man's body was invisible from that angle, and his small
round face, with its beady black eyes, wrinkled yellowish skin, and
snub nose, bore a remarkable resemblance to an aging marmoset.
Sukhanov had an uncanny impression of a withering balloon with
monkey features drawn on it and a cigarette glued to its surface,
floating in the smoky fog.

The man winked, and the impression was gone.

"Good news, comrade," the man whispered conspiratorially. "I've
just spoken to Lenin, and he wants me to tell you that everything's
going according to plan. It will start at four in the morning, on the
dot. Be prepared."

"I beg your pardon?" Sukhanov said frostily. "Are you talking
to me?"

The old man beamed at him with sly benevolence. "Just continue following the instructions," he whispered brightly. "And beware of our enemies. Our enemies are everywhere. Always watch your back."

At that moment the ceiling of Sukhanov's study shook with an onrush of thumping steps, and a woman's shrill exclamation escaped into the night: "Papa, why aren't you in bed? Have you taken your medicine?" The apparition cast a furtive glance over his invisible shoulder, then turned back to Sukhanov, flashed him a toothless smile, dropping his cigarette in passing, and vanished abruptly, as if someone had jerked the string tied to the balloon. An instant later the balcony door above banged shut, muting the sounds of an ensuing struggle.

Eight floors below, a red flicker of the cigarette flared up and went out.

Wiping the drizzle off his face, Sukhanov walked inside and bolted the door behind him with an unsteady hand, muttering, "Honestly, has everyone in this building gone insane?" After the luminous softness of the night, the darkness of the room blinded him unpleasantly. He moved to switch on the lamp—and immediately a multitude of shadows leapt away from him like a herd of frightened, misshapen beasts. For a minute, before his eyes adjusted to the light, he had a jarring sensation of actual creatures, insubstantial, colorless, weightless like dust balls, huddling in hidden corners and watching him stealthily—from under the sofa, from behind the door, from over the rim of the wastebasket . . .

He blinked, rubbed his temples. It was at once clear to him that he was not getting enough rest, that the disturbances of the past few days were turning his thoughts hazy and uncertain like a watercolor forgotten in the rain; and he suddenly longed to retire with a light book and let himself drift into dreamless sleep on the wave of some author's inconsequential rambling. It took him a moment to recall what novel he was reading—a poor translation of an absurd Western title published in the difficult-to-obtain, subscription-only series Science Fiction, with a paranoid, unlikable hero who was constantly being tossed in and out of strangers' bodies; all in all, just the sort of vapid reading he favored after a long, exhausting day of mental acrobatics. On the heels of that thought, however, came the realization that the volume still lay where he had abandoned it a few days before—on the nightstand in the bedroom.

Slipping into the corridor, he irresolutely considered a thin strip of light seeping from under the closed bedroom door. He had been too busy to talk to Dalevich after their failed morning walk, and at this hour, the prospect of explaining himself to an overly polite man he hardly knew, likely to be attired in his pajamas and possibly half asleep, seemed an altogether awkward proposition. Sighing with annoyance, he tiptoed back, casting a glance into the faintly sparkling cavern of the unlit living room and noting Nina's folded linens stacked neatly at the foot of the sofa. Plays certainly ran quite long these days, didn't they. . . . Shutting the study door with a bit more force than he intended, he looked about his shelves with a frown— and then his eyes fell on a thick red book with golden lettering on its spine, lying half drowned amid the papers on his desk.

This was, of course, the collection of E. T. A. Hoffmann's novellas that Ksenya had tossed at him on the morning of the Bolshoi performance. He had forgotten all about it. The ballet *Coppelia,* she had said, was based on Hoffmann's story "The Sandman"; she had wanted him to read it. For her age, Ksenya was extremely well read and opinionated, uncomfortably so at times; indeed, of late, her air of intellectual arrogance made it increasingly difficult for him to talk to her, especially as she made no secret of her absolute disdain for his work. A few years ago, she had gone through a period of fascination with Greek mythology and out of some footnote had mined a nickname for him, which, irritatingly, had survived all the subsequent upheavals of her adolescence. She called him Cerberus to this day. As she had pointed out on one occasion, the original Cerberus, that monstrous three-headed dog guarding the kingdom of the dead, devoured not only the spirits of the dead who tried to escape into the light of day but also the living who attempted to descend into the underworld.

"A fitting metaphor for Soviet art, the sad fate of any artist who still has some living spirit left in him, and the role of a critic in bringing that fate about, don't you think?" she had said to him without smiling—his own daughter, at that time barely fifteen years old. . . . It was ironic, he thought, choking on a quick, bitter laugh, that of his two children, one rejected what he did so completely, while the other—the other, in accepting it, was willing to go to lengths that he himself would consider amoral. Musing, he picked up the Hoffmann volume and weighed it in his hand. Reading the story would at least give him something to discuss with Ksenya over breakfast.

From the very first page, the language struck him as pompous, filled as it was with verbal equivalents of wringing hands and brimming eyes, the hero repeatedly lamenting, in the true fashion of a humorless romantic, the "dark presentiments of a dreadful fate that hovered over him like stormy clouds." Yet little by little, Sukhanov became engrossed in the story of the young man haunted since early childhood by the image of a mysterious Sandman. The boy's mother nightly evoked the Sandman's nearing arrival as a simple metaphor for sleep, whose advent makes children's eyes heavy as if sprinkled with sand, but in Nathaniel's imagination the Sandman evolved into an eye-stealing monster from an old maid's tale—a monster the boy believed embodied in the town's sinister notary, Coppelius. When, years later, Nathaniel encountered a foreign spectacles salesman who bore a striking resemblance to the Coppelius of his childhood nightmares, his tranquil daily life gave way to a dream full of ominous forebodings, and his mind began a tortured slide toward insanity.

One aspect of the tale in particular interested Sukhanov. Were all the strange occurrences in the story merely the result of the hero's unbalanced mind—his private hallucinations—or did he lose his sanity *as a result of* strange occurrences that were indeed real but that, thanks to some dark gift of clairvoyance not unlike the artistic intuition of a genius, he alone of all his friends and family could perceive? Unfortunately, it seemed the question would be left unanswered, for Hoffmann was losing the battle with mediocrity by giving in to the cowardly impulse of supplying his readers with a happy ending. Surrounded by the tender care of his loved ones, Nathaniel was fully cured of his afflictions and, having implausibly received a substantial inheritance, began to plan a move to a country manor with his longtime sweetheart. Now the cooing couple were climbing the town hall tower to cast one last look at the place where they had lived, loved, grieved, et cetera, et cetera. Sukhanov felt bored, and heavy with sleep, as if his own eyelids had been weighed down by sand. Yawning, he flipped the page and at the same time stretched his hand to a lamp by the couch, ready to turn it off after the last sentence.

He never read the last sentence.

On top of the tower Nathaniel suffered a final outburst of madness. Spotting the notary Coppelius in the gathering crowd below, he shouted, "Lovely eyes, lovely eyes!" and flung himself over the parapet. "Nathaniel was lying on the pavement with his head shattered," Sukhanov read—and stopped, and let the book slowly drop to the floor. Lulled into drowsiness, he had not foreseen this—had not had time to erect his usual defenses—and it hit him in his most tender center with sickening precision.

For a long minute he did not move. Then, abruptly, he groped for the suddenly elusive light switch and, finding it, flooded his eyes, his mind, his soul with darkness. *Lying on the pavement with his head shattered* . . . His own dreadful fate had caught up with him after all, just as he had feared it would.

They had expected his father to return from Gorky sometime in the summer of 1938, but he did not. His presence was still needed at the factory, Nadezhda Sukhanova would say repeatedly; but as one season spilled into the next, the conviction in her voice lessened, and Anatoly began to catch that quick, cringing look in her eyes that with time would become her habitual expression. On several occasions, always on birthdays, he shouted to his father over the static of telephone lines. Pavel Sukhanov's voice, traversing a distance of four hundred thirty-nine kilometers, arrived in the boy's ear sounding muffled and somewhat distracted, as if it had collected dust along the way, but cheerful enough, and occasionally even tinged with impatient pride—an intonation that was new to him.

One conversation Anatoly remembered in particular.

"I'm close to a groundbreaking discovery that will alter the whole course of aviation," Pavel Sukhanov had told his son, but refused to divulge any details. "Best to keep it secret from everyone until the time is right," he had said mysteriously, and Anatoly could hear a smile softening the edges of his voice.

That was in the summer of 1939, and in the autumn something happened. One day the phone in the Arbat apartment rang uncomfortably early, and his mother ran into the corridor to answer it, her bare feet slapping against the floor with a newly orphaned sound. She left the door wide open behind her, and, my mind still wrapped in the thick cotton of a dream, I watched her pick up the receiver. The light that morning was like steamed milk, white and misty, and the contours of her long nightshirt seemed to dissolve in the air before my drowsy eyes. She asked a short, breathless question, then listened in silence, and I saw her put her hand up to her mouth as if to hide a yawn. Later, she slowly walked back into the room and lowered herself onto my mattress. Her eyes were standing still.

"I have some bad news," she said, her hand hovering over my forehead like a nervous bird afraid to alight. "Your father has fallen ill, and they have to keep him in the hospital for a while." The illness was going to be lengthy but not dangerous, she continued—not unlike a severe flu. He was expected to recover completely in a matter of months. "We won't be able to talk to him for some time, but that's fine, we'll just write to him, won't we?" she said with false brightness, avoiding my eyes. I was only ten years old at the time—too young to suspect the lie behind her words.

Over the next two years, the date of my father's release from the unspecified hospital kept being postponed, although, according to my mother, he was always close to getting well. He wrote to us regularly, of course, but all his letters were lost in the mail. Shortly after the beginning of the war, we left Moscow without having heard from him, joining thousands of people in a worried exodus to the east.

Then, sometime in the spring of 1942, I learned that he had been cured at last and was returning home, to work at an important defense facility in the vicinity of Moscow. A trickle of letters started between us, unpredictable and accidental like all wartime correspondence, but real, oh so real after the desperate years of silence. My mother read each precious missive aloud, clutching it tightly as if doubting its existence, and pausing often, sometimes visibly skipping a line or two with her startled, red-rimmed eyes. The letters released in me a warm burst of new hope. I knew that, after all this time, our meeting was drawing near, and, inspired by my recently discovered gift, I spent hours trying to render, on scraps of rough brown paper, margins of newspapers, discarded envelopes, and whatever else drifted into my life, everything I could remember of his laughter, his gestures, his walk, the way he squared his chin when he listened, the way my heart felt solid and warm and in place when his big hands rested on my shoulders. . . . We received his last letter in October of 1943, just as we began to prepare for our own return home. He knew we were coming. He wrote that he had a wonderful surprise planned for us—he had finally made the great discovery of his life. My mother looked queasy.

The city was slick with sleet and rain when, at two in the afternoon on the sixteenth of November, we disembarked from the overcrowded train and made our halting way across the platform. The night before, while we had waited for hours at some nameless, unlit station, I had traced my father's name in the grime of our car's window, but in the morning someone had slid the window open, and as the rain lashed inside, the letters ran down in dirty rivulets, growing slowly unrecognizable.

He himself was not there to meet us.

"That's fine, that's fine, we'll manage, that's fine," my mother kept saying in a small, fluttering voice I did not like. We had few belongings: a bag stuffed with clothes, another full of kitchen utensils, a bulky lampshade she had refused to leave behind, and a folder bulging with my drawings and watercolors, my most—my only—cherished possession, which I carried under my coat, pressed to my chest, imagining all through our journey how I would spread them out on the table before my father's eyes and wordlessly, my heart skipping with fear and joy, await his judgment. The city unwound before me like a tormentingly sluggish movie reel that seemed never to end. Then somehow it did—and there we were already, walking on our familiar Arbat street, slipping on the glistening pavement under the weight of our bags.

The deserted street is so quiet I can almost hear the liquid echo of our slushing steps. Most of the windows in the houses around us are dark, some even boarded—but I can already see that in the building ahead of us, our building, the windows on the fifth floor, our floor, are lit, lit brightly, lit bravely, overflowing with a nearing, already tangible happiness—and . . . Is it truly possible? Yes, a tall, broad-shouldered man is silhouetted against one of the windows, and as we draw closer, so close that I have to tilt my head back until my neck hurts, I see that it's him, it's really him, he is standing there waiting for us, and he is smiling, and the whole thing seems so much like a recurring dream I have had for years that I am a bit afraid to wake up. And just as I think that, the man in the window, my father, raises his hand in greeting to us, and then pushes the rain-sleeked window frame outward and, with a quick movement, steps on the windowsill; and for one brief moment, ignoring my mother's soft, horrified gasp behind me, I frenziedly try to guess the words that he is about to shout to us—the first live words I will hear from him in years.

But my father does not shout. In the next instant, still smiling joyfully, he takes a step forward, and walks off the windowsill—walks off into nothing at all.

A heartbeat wells in me, large and hollow and deafening, like the rushing sound of a monstrous waterfall, and all I know, all I believe, all I love, hangs in a confused, incredulous balance. Then, emitting a kind of strained moan, my mother grabs my head and roughly pushes my face into her coat, painfully pressing my cheek into a button, and, suddenly enveloped in her woolly darkness, I close my eyes and inhale the sharp smell of damp cloth and the faint smells of stale smoke and dried meat—the manifold odors of the rain falling on the hateful city and of our last night's train to nowhere. And as I stand without moving, it seems without breathing, my feeling of living in the present tense, my perception of reality, the very memory of my identity leave me like crumbling shells of things that have died, and the world itself falls away from my senses.

After that, the rain began to turn to snow, prickling the exposed skin of Anatoly's neck and hands like tiny cold needles, and there were people running from somewhere and shouting, and then he was suddenly running himself, faster and faster, hugging his folder of drawings with both arms, and there were darkening streets swerving before him, and an old woman who exclaimed with fright on some corner and then cursed angrily at his back, and a mangy dog that followed him for a while whimpering lightly, and after that, some quiet yard with water dripping dully, incessantly, from the branches of naked trees and all the cornices and all the windowsills—and again, the world gently slipped away like a child's clumsily folded paper boat being swept away by the current. . . .

It was in that yard, hours later, that Sashka Morozov found him, sitting motionless on the ground, watching bits and pieces of torn paper as they drowned in the downpour. Talking loudly all the while, Sashka held him firmly around the shoulders and led him somewhere, and there were more people, some of whom he probably knew, and others whom he did not, and that night they put him and his mother into a car and drove them across the river, to some place with a multitude of tiny rooms opening into one another like a series of mousetraps. He remembered oppressively low ceilings, ugly wallpaper in brown and red zigzags in the hallway, and a giant rusty bathtub resting on funny-looking clawlike feet. A skinny woman with a sharp nose kept fussing over him in visible embarrassment, pressing a cup of lukewarm soup on him and calling him "poor dear"; and a serious yellow-haired boy, no more than ten years old, surreptitiously followed him with curious, shining eyes wherever he went, whatever he did, as if expecting him to change into something strange at any moment.

Anatoly gave the boy his few remaining drawings to play with; he did not want them any longer. They must have stayed with these nameless, unnecessary people for some time, a few days at least, perhaps a whole week, because he was still there when the tenacious, numbing grief, which had paralyzed his being for so long he had ceased to understand time, began to release him slowly, breath by breath, until one evening he was finally able to sit, dry-eyed and oddly unfeeling, repeating, "There, there," while his mother cried with relieved abandon on his shoulder. That night they moved across snow-buried Moscow back to the Arbat apartment.

He never did find the surprise his father had prepared for them. There was no trace of any important discovery among the man's scanty possessions. His desk contained a neat stack of engineering manuals, a framed photograph of Nadezhda Sukhanova as a very young, touchingly awkward girl, and a volume of Pushkin's works bookmarked in a few places, with two impatient exclamation points in red pencil in the margins next to the sentence "A scientist without talent is akin to that poor mullah who cut up the Koran and ate it, thinking thus to be filled with the spirit of Mohammed." There was also a picture, torn out of some children's magazine and thumbtacked to the wall, of a brightly colored—crimson, white, and golden—hot-air balloon, one of the early models, across which Pavel Sukhanov had written in his slanting, confident handwriting: "Don't let anyone clip your wings."

In the following months Anatoly often puzzled over that phrase, wondering whether it had been a random scribble or something more meaningful, his father's personal motto perhaps, a promise of courage which in the end he had not been able to keep—for was not a self-willed departure from life, especially in the midst of so much death, the ultimate act of cowardice? Choosing to stage the exit before their very eyes seemed an additional cruelty to Anatoly, unworthy of the man he thought his father had been, and in a hidden, most childlike cranny of his mind he kept alive the possibility that none of this had been intended, that it had all been a tragic, absurdly needless accident—that his father had simply slipped on the wet windowsill in the act of some clownish, extravagant greeting. (Indeed, there would always remain this maddening touch of uncertainty, even in later years, when he well understood that Pavel Sukhanov had never been in any hospital—that, like the poor music teacher, like Gradsky and his wife, like hundreds of thousands of others, he had been arrested as an "enemy of the people" and, having survived who knew what private hell, had been subsequently freed during the war, when the country had felt an acute need for skilled officers and military special-ists, experienced aviation engineers among them, and a wave of hasty releases had swept through the labor camps—and that sometime in the preceding years of horror, his spirit must have been broken, never to mend again.)

His mother, who might have had a better understanding of what had happened, grew tearfully reproachful every time Anatoly alluded to the matter, and he soon learned to ask her no questions. Already in the first post-victory year, he watched her slightly edgy reply "My husband died during the war" change into the dignified statement "My husband died in the war," thus making their own, very private and uncertain, pain gradually seem part of a different pain, clear and bright and noble, shared by millions of people and imbued with a sense of great purpose. He let it be—it was easier that way.

Then, in May of 1947, only a few weeks before his school gradua-tion, there came a night when, in the darkness of their room, with his mother sighing in uneasy sleep behind a partition, he lay on his back watching the fireworks of the second victory anniversary light up the ceiling in uneven flares—and suddenly, just as a particularly dazzling red burst ricocheted off the chandelier stump, he understood the true meaning of the words he had come to regard as his father's farewell message to himself. "Don't let anyone clip your wings," Pavel Sukhanov had written, and it was not, as Anatoly had previously believed, a bequest of bravery, a proud expression of defiance. It was a warning instead, a cautioning reminder that the only life worth living was a life without humiliation, a free life, a *safe* life—and the only sure way to avoid having one's wings clipped was to grow no wings at all.

And that night, as the brilliant traces of celebration trailed down the sky, Anatoly saw his own choices clearly for the first time: his need to live without the fear of someone coming to pound on his door in the hushed hours before dawn; his desire to protect his mother, who could not survive another loss; his hope to watch his own child grow up one day; his anticipation of the modest achievements of some respected, quietly useful profession—a yearning, in short, for the existence of an average man who chooses not to dream, who chooses not to fly, who prefers instead the wisdom of simple, everyday living. He made a vow to himself, cemented in the grief of his previous years, to carve from the world around him a small, secure happiness, all his own. By the time morning drew near, he had compiled a mental catalogue of his abilities and, concluding that drawing was the only real skill he possessed, decided to try for the Surikov Art Institute— an education as good as any.

A ball of blazing light drew a crimson trajectory across his field of vision, interrupting the flow of his thoughts. Momentarily disoriented—were the victory fireworks still going on?—Anatoly Pavlovich blinked and peered into the obscurity around him. It took him an instant to remember that the year was 1985, that he was fifty-six, that he lay on the uncomfortable couch having yet another heart-breaking vision from the past. A damp chill pervaded the study. Realizing that his blanket had slipped off during the night, he leaned over and felt unhappily for its woolly mass on the floor—and then a fiery ball of orange-red sparks, escaping the confines of his dream, sailed past his balcony again, immediately followed by another, and another, and another after that. A soft rain of fire was falling from the Moscow skies.

He stared for a few disbelieving seconds, then, hurriedly disen-tangling himself from the sheets, ran across the room, threw open the balcony door, and rushed outside. On the balcony above, the monkey-faced madman was audibly busy tearing newspapers apart, crumpling their pages into loose balls, lighting them, and tossing them down in quick, glowing succession. Sukhanov could hear the crinkling of paper, the agitated striking of matches, and the carefree, toothless whistling. Tilting his head back, he shouted angrily toward the heavens, "Hey! Hey! Stop that right now, you hear?"

The burning balls ceased falling, and the old man's face emerged over the balcony railing, his cheeks smeared with soot, his eyes drowned in absurd happiness.

"Too late," he said blithely. "You've missed our revolution by five minutes. Didn't I tell you four o'clock sharp? Now you'll have to wait for the next one."

And before Sukhanov could think of a sensible reply, the old man ducked away with surprising agility, and a moment later an entire unfolded newspaper sheet drifted indolently past, in flames. Sukhanov could see a few words—"change," "crucial," "youth"—flare up briefly, black on melting gold, before the page disintegrated into a flock of darkly luminous shreds and landed on a balcony a few floors below. It was only a matter of time, of course, before something, somewhere, caught on fire.

Anatoly Pavlovich swore with quiet fury and went inside to call the fire station.

Eleven

"A single night of uninterrupted sleep," said Vasily. "Is that so much to ask for, really?"

For once, the entire family was present at the breakfast table, with Fyodor Dalevich, in an already established tradition, officiating at the stove. As Sukhanov stumbled into the kitchen, he could not help noticing that the man seemed especially energetic and amiable today—a striking contrast to the haunted, dark-rimmed look he himself had encountered earlier that morning in a morose, unshaved, altogether unpresentable individual in the mirror (who, to judge by his appearance, had been suffering greatly in some through-the-looking-glass world, quite possibly from tormenting memories, crazy neighbors, inefficient firemen, and a painfully prolonged acquaintance with the wires, bumps, and corners of a most uncomfortable couch). It was nice to know, Sukhanov thought bitterly, sitting down to a cup of cold coffee and trying not to look in his relative's direction, that at least *someone* was enjoying a good night's sleep—not to mention a recently acquired, wonderfully soft, imported bed.

And then Nina's question from a moment before filtered into his lagging mind.

"Do you need any help with your packing?" she had asked matter-of-factly.

He understood the meaning of her words—and felt instantly light-headed, as if his insides had filled with a swarm of exclamation points.

"Leaving us, are you?" he addressed his cousin's back in a voice of insincere regret, his tongue stumbling over the word "finally" just in time to avoid it. Strangely, Dalevich did not respond but continued to prod something sizzling in a pan with a cautious fork; and it was Vasily who dropped his cup onto its saucer with a needless clang and spoke in a tone of exasperation, "How many times do I have to tell you, Father? Honestly, do you ever listen to any of us?"

"A rhetorical question if ever I heard one," said Ksenya.

Slowly, Sukhanov turned and regarded his son with a darkening gaze.

Two hours later, he stood on a sidewalk, his briefcase in hand, and squinting against the sun, watched the chauffeur haul a gigantic suitcase into the trunk of the car. Vasily himself was already sprawled in the backseat amid more of his belongings, drawing on a cigarette and looking bored. He was going to spend the last two weeks of August with his grandfather, at an exclusive Party resort in the Crimea, doubtlessly replete with cypress-scented, starlit promenades, sonorous cicadas, and all sorts of people whom it would be most useful to meet—apparently a plan of a monthlong standing, with which everyone was well familiar and which Sukhanov alone, even after passing his memory through a sieve of intense scrutiny, could not recall ever hearing.

Vasily rolled down the window.

"Ah, you're still here," he said indifferently. "Want a lift somewhere?"

The boy acted as if he had all but forgotten their painful conversation of two nights before—and quite possibly, he truly had, the details buried in the haze of his intoxication; or else he simply had not considered the matter particularly worthy of amends. Sukhanov, on the other hand, had found neither oblivion nor forgiveness an easy proposition. After an initial, vaguely hurt reaction, the news of his son's impending absence had filled him with a feeling surprisingly like relief, and it had been in the hope of dispersing uneasy promptings of guilt that he had conceded to Vasily the use of his Volga.

"I need to go by the office to drop off a manuscript," he pointed out somewhat dryly. "The train station is nowhere near it."

"We are picking up Grandpa first," said Vasily, and having flung away his still-glowing cigarette, started to roll up the window. "But I don't care, it's up to you."

Sukhanov's father-in-law lived in a palatial apartment overlooking Gorky Street, only a few short, crooked, linden-shaded blocks from the building occupied by *Art of the World*. Sukhanov hesitated, but Vadim had already shut the trunk and was now swinging the front door open, saying briskly, "Get in here, Anatoly Pavlovich, there's no space in the back—just watch out for the dog hair." A dog, what dog? thought Sukhanov gloomily, squeezing his substantial body into the seat next to the chauffeur's.

He was accustomed to riding luxuriously spread out in the back, and the cramped quarters, permeated by the faint smell of some hirsute animal and a recent cloud of perfume, too sweet and dramatic to have been Nina's, as well as the sudden proximity of the driver, fiddling with the keys only inches away, soon began to vex him. Vasily appeared to have gone to sleep the moment the motor started. Sukhanov sighed, coughed, toyed with his wedding band, picked a few brown hairs off his trouser leg, then stared before him. From the rearview mirror, he noticed for the first time, dangled a small plastic sphere, with a tiny blue-roofed cottage inside surrounded by nail-sized fir trees. No sooner had they reached the end of their street than the car dove into its first pothole, and at the jolt a miniature storm of brightly tinted snowflakes soared inside the sphere, hung in the air for one chaotic, densely sparkling instant, then descended on the gingerbread house. Sukhanov watched with idle interest. The thing seemed embarrassingly sentimental and out of place—most drivers, after all, favored decorations of a different sort, like key-chain figurines of half-naked women—and he found himself wondering absently whether Vadim had chosen the tasteless trinket himself or it had been a gift from someone.

And all at once it occurred to him that, in truth, he knew oddly little about this man whom he saw almost daily. Vadim was a competent driver, perhaps a bit aggressive but on the whole reliable; he had the appearance of a man who liked regular exercise; he lived somewhere on the dim, desolate outskirts of Moscow with a wife named Svetlana or Galina or Tatyana, Sukhanov could not remember exactly, as well as a daughter, whose age had slipped off into the void yet again, and possibly a big hairy dog—but beyond that stretched a fog of uncertainties and conjectures. Nina's recent reproach rose unbidden in his mind. *He's worked for us for almost three years, and in all this time you haven't made an effort . . .* Wincing, he cast a quick look to his side. Vadim's profile was impassive, but as he drove he drummed his gloved fingers against the wheel as if following some nervous internal rhythm; he might have been upset about something. Resolved to be friendly, Sukhanov cleared his throat.

"I always mean to ask you, what is this?" he said casually, pointing at the sphere, in which another cheap snowstorm was subsiding. "A children's toy?"

The man shrugged. "Just a souvenir," he said.

"It's nice," Sukhanov said pleasantly. "Fun to watch."

Vadim nodded without taking his eyes off the road. A silence fell between them, as awkward as an endless elevator ride with a vaguely familiar stranger to whom one has nothing to say. They were very close now. Vasily woke up and lit a fresh cigarette.

"So," Sukhanov said in a bright tone, "did you have a good time last night?"

Vadim glanced at him sharply.

"On your evening off, that is. Do anything fun?"

"My evening off," Vadim repeated with the beginning of a frown—but just then a blue Zhiguli with a smashed door swerved wildly into their lane, and Vadim honked and swerved in turn, so abruptly that Vasily was pitched forward, bespattering his shoes with ash, and Sukhanov's glasses took a scintillating leap into the sunny, suddenly hazy space. An instant later the last traffic light turned green before them, and, grumbling about the crazy Gorky Street drivers, Vadim pulled into the cavernous courtyard of Malinin's building.

"I'll probably be a while," said Vasily, yawning, "so if you want, he can take you directly to your office and then come back here, there's plenty of—"

"No, no, that's not necessary," Sukhanov interrupted, groping for his glasses in the crevices behind his seat. "In fact, why don't I come up myself for a minute? Might as well say hello to . . . Ah, yes, here they are. . . . Well, so long, Vadim, thanks for the ride. . . . Might as well say hello to Pyotr Alekseevich, don't you think?"

And restoring his glasses to the bridge of his nose, he stepped out of the car.

Vasily opened the door to the apartment with his own set of keys, which rather surprised Sukhanov: he thought of his father-in-law as a highly territorial man not forthcoming with gestures of trust. He followed his son inside. Since his last visit here, some half a year before, the vast entrance hall seemed to have slid even deeper into the two full-sized mirrors that stood on either side of the door, and all the solid antique furnishings—an oak hat stand, a bronze umbrella stand, a carved end table, a splendidly framed portrait of a morose Polish officer with a handlebar mustache, Nina's maternal grandfather—all these genteel symbols of a well-established life, multiplying into infinity inside a diminishing progression of glass, had an unexpectedly oppressive effect on his spirit. He inhaled sharply, felt the smells of shoe polish, violet-scented hand soap, shortbread cookies, and, more delicately, old age trickle into his lungs, and was seized with an urgent desire to murmur some hasty excuse to Vasily, turn around, and leave—but the steady creaking of the hardwood floors had already announced Pyotr Alekseevich's imminent approach.

In another moment the old man emerged into the hall from one of its many doorways. Coming toward them with his straight-backed, imposing stride, he embraced Vasily in a show of warmth that struck Sukhanov as excessive and for some reason highly unpleasant. Then, with one hand outstretched, Pyotr Alekseevich turned to his son-in-law.

"Ah, Tolya. What a surprise," he said flatly. "To what do I owe the pleasure?"

Sullenly Sukhanov looked at Malinin's handsomely aged features, to which the habit of serving as a constant recipient of awards and a frequent subject of self-portraits had imparted a permanently noble, reserved expression—but then, instead of his usual irritable acquiescence, he felt a light tinge of amusement, uncertain at first, then growing more and more demanding, until a long-suppressed tide of merriment rose inside him and his mind was flooded with startling visions of his father-in-law's face. The face was already lionized but a few decades younger, and suffering endless distortions and permutations—bristling with ridiculous whiskers, sporting bushy eyebrows and elegantly curved horns, covered in poisonous, hair-spurting warts, or even balanced precariously atop a giraffe's neck, reaching for a star-shaped leaf with greedy lips. . . . Naturally, he had long since discarded all his notebooks in whose margins such secret malicious phantoms had sprouted by the dozen during so many tedious lectures, when all that had kept him from falling into a doze had been a game of rendering the lecturer as hideous as possible while keeping within the laws of portraiture. All the same, the mnemonic gift of his more successful efforts seemed revenge enough—almost enough—for all those past hours of unspeakable boredom.

He had felt bored for most of his time as a student, of course, but the class on Soviet art theory—taught in 1952, his last year at the Surikov Institute, by the recent recipient of the coveted Stalin Prize, the prominent painter, theorist, and glorified representative of state art, the forty-six-year-old star Pyotr Alekseevich Malinin—proved to be a particularly taxing exercise in patience. In truth, young Anatoly found patience to be one of the two qualities most required of him in the course of his studies; caution was the other. In his first semester, when presented, in the ranks of other eager youths, with a simple anatomical sketch or some suitably patriotic landscape, he discovered to his unease that something was wrong, that sometime previously, perhaps during the drab wartime evenings spent in the makeshift classroom with Chagall's former pupil Oleg Romanov leaning over his shoulder, he had acquired a dangerous trait it was best to do without—namely, individual style—and maybe a touch of something else besides; for as was quickly becoming apparent, his works differed from those of the others. Anatoly's paintings suffered from a fault, a twist, an uncommon streak of whimsy, and as much as he tried to follow the prescribed form, something strange, something alien, would always sneak into his renditions of Soviet reality, be it a cloud, above a perfectly ordinary industrial vista, whose shape resembled the spire of a great, sky-wide cathedral, or an incongruous herring skeleton found at the foot of a worker beaming proudly in the act of receiving a medal, or a wild riot of pearly, unearthly colors exploding in the background of an otherwise respectful harvesting scene. And all these absurdities seemed to drip from his brush so freely, so naturally, so completely apart from his conscious will, that it took him long months of diligent application to eradicate them from his canvases, from his thoughts, from the very texture of his being.

Yet gradually his efforts started to pay off, his name was increasingly mentioned among the more promising members of the new generation of artists—and only in his most private moments would he ever dream of painting enormous transparent bells raining music from the skies, or groves of springtime trees whose blossoms turned into twittering birds and flew away, or faces of women so ideal they melted as soon as you looked at them, or . . .

"I don't mean to be rude," said Pyotr Alekseevich Malinin to his son-in-law, "but I do have to finish my packing. Was there something you wanted to tell me?"

Sukhanov looked at the pompous old man standing before him, and suddenly wanted to tell him many things, not the least of them being the story of his recent meeting with Lev Belkin and the news of Belkin's exhibition. Yes, for one rebellious moment he felt a rising desire to erase the tranquil, self-assured expression on the old man's face with that name from the past that they had tacitly agreed never to mention again.

After a long pause, he spoke.

"As a matter of fact," he said, "I'd like to borrow a tie or two. Would you mind?"

Twelve

The offices of *Art of the World* occupied the two upper stories of a three-storied eighteenth-century mansion with a once magnificent turquoise façade, which had since become faded, and a cornucopia of frivolous curlicues over the windows, whose precise shape was obscured by years of relentless pigeon deposits. The first floor consisted predominantly of a maze of mysterious corridors and blank doors, which terminated, in somewhat disappointing fashion (as Sukhanov had chanced to discover upon getting lost once or twice in his first year as editor), in a glass partition with the laconic sign "Accounting" over it and a sour-looking woman knitting a sweater behind it. There was also a pet store in a corner of the building, a dark, cramped, sad little place, with somnolent guinea pigs and torpid white-eyed fish languishing in thick-walled aquariums beneath dusty plants; its proximity inevitably caused all sorts of useless, repulsive creatures to gravitate to the cubicles of the more tenderhearted of Sukhanov's secretaries and junior editors. Anatoly Pavlovich harbored a great dislike for all things scaly, crawling, and gill-breathing, and he navigated the long corridors of his private kingdom at a rather brisk pace, preferring not to look too closely at the surrounding desks for fear of meeting the stony stare of some new clammy monstrosity trapped in a mayonnaise jar or a vase too ugly for flowers.

The dinner hour was approaching, and the girls on the second floor surreptitiously powdered their noses, ready to disperse among the neighborhood cafeterias. Their conversations, swerving in shallow eddies from wall to wall, rolled back like an ebbing tide at Sukhanov's passage but left single phrases behind, to be picked up by his incurious hearing. "A pair of Italian leather boots, just around the corner!" he heard someone say excitedly. As he ascended the stairs, the chatter faded behind him.

The third floor, a yellow corridor with a stained carpet and two rows of doors whose nameplates read like the magazine's masthead, was quiet and, it struck him after a moment, oddly deserted. The doors were ajar, the offices of his senior staff empty. Quickening his steps, he walked to the far end, toward a recess presided over by Liubov Markovna, his personal secretary, a marvelously efficient woman of indeterminate years with a penchant for painfully pointy pencils. She was at her desk, whispering into the telephone. Seeing him, she abruptly let go of the receiver and, stretching out her arms as if trying to catch something hurtling toward her, began to prattle in an unbecoming manner, "Anatoly Palych, Anatoly Palych, wait a second!"— but the momentum had already carried him across the threshold.

There he stopped and looked about in puzzlement.

The managing editor, Ovseev, a tall, thin, balding man resembling a praying mantis, was sitting in his, Sukhanov's, leather chair, reading some items from a pad with a surprising air of authority, while the diminutive, wide-eyed, skittish Anastasia Lisitskaya, Ovseev's secretary and rumored mistress, tottered on nine-inch heels by his side, taking notes. Pugovichkin, the assistant editor in chief, his shape as small, rotund, and faintly comical as his name, was there too, consulting with the department heads; a few others meandered about the room. In itself, this gathering was not necessarily remarkable, since editorial meetings always took place in Sukhanov's office—but no meeting was scheduled for another three weeks, and no meeting had ever taken place without his presence.

"What is the meaning of this?" Sukhanov said in a measured voice.

Startled, the editors looked up from their pads, and a hush fell among them.

"Anatoly Pavlovich," said Ovseev, hurriedly rising from Sukhanov's chair.

"Why are you all here?"

"Anatoly Pavlovich, we had to call an urgent meeting to discuss a few last-minute changes to the current issue—and since you were supposed to be out of town—"

Lisitskaya's heels pattered across the floor as she darted to hide behind Ovseev.

Sukhanov marched to his desk, regained possession of his chair, and opened his briefcase with a harsh snap, all his gestures meant to reassert his momentarily lapsed command.

"What nonsense, I wasn't out of town," he said curtly. "How could I be, with that Dalí article on my hands? Speaking of which, someone should take it to the printers right away."

"But," said Ovseev, "surely you know . . ." He did not finish the sentence.

"I have it right here, hold on just one . . . What did you say?" Out of the corner of his eye, he noticed a few people gingerly tiptoeing out of the office, while Pugovichkin drew closer and hovered above him. Looking up, Sukhanov found an exaggerated concern wrinkling the man's kindly pancake of a face.

"Anatoly Pavlovich, I don't believe it!" moaned the assistant editor in chief. "Could it be you haven't heard?"

Sukhanov stared at him blankly.

"I'm afraid," Pugovichkin said, spreading his plump hands outward in a gesture of futility, "the Dalí piece has been postponed."

"We hope it didn't give you too much trouble," Ovseev added with an ingratiating smile. "Of course, it will be published soon, if not in the next issue, then in the one after that for sure—"

"And how, I'd like to know, could this decision be made without me?" Sukhanov thundered incredulously. "How can *any of this* be happening without me?"

Lisitskaya's heels fled into the corridor with the sound of a frantic drumroll.

"Well, you see," said Pugovichkin quickly, "we received this phone call the day before yesterday." He raised his eyes meaningfully to the ceiling, to indicate a far-off, heavenly sphere of influence—their accepted shorthand for communications from the magazine's Party liaison. "It appeared that a more . . . more timely subject had come to someone's attention, and we were to be sent a new article that very afternoon. On Chagall. We were told that, in view of his recent death . . . You know, of course, he died this past March. . . . And since you were leaving . . ."

"Chagall," Sukhanov repeated, his voice ominously steady. "They want *Art of the World* to publish an article on Chagall, and you have actually agreed to it? Be so kind as to tell me I've misheard you, Sergei Nikolaevich. Or have you lost your mind?"

The few remaining people slunk outside, and Sukhanov was left alone with his second-in-command. Pugovichkin was talking now, in a rapid, offended monotone, gathering momentum, trying to convince him of something, but for a few minutes Sukhanov heard nothing as he sat staring at the dust particles twirling before him in the stuffy, sun-lacerated air. True, he had allowed the questionable Dalí article to be forced upon the magazine, grudgingly resigning himself to this one-time challenge to his authority—but a piece on Chagall would take matters to an entirely new level. The difference between Dalí, outrageous by virtue of his foreign birth and viewed therefore as a mere curiosity akin to a two-headed goat in some little-frequented *Kunstkammer,* and Chagall, who had come from Russia's own backyard, been appointed Commissar of Fine Arts after the Revolution, taught in a Soviet art academy, and then *chosen* to leave Russia behind in order to *become* foreign and outrageous, was just as wide and impassable as the difference between some poor jungle savage who knows nothing beyond the cruel and nonsensical superstitions of his tribe and a man of civilized faith who proceeds to give it up in order to murmur incantations and slaughter chickens. Publishing an article on Chagall would be universally interpreted as an act of rebellion, an absolute break with decades of steadfast traditions of Soviet criticism, which he himself had helped to invent, and as likely as not would prove tantamount to career suicide for him and his senior staff.

Publishing such an article was impossible.

"It will be most welcome, I was assured," Pugovichkin was saying, trotting back and forth across the office. "In fact, I've been told that the Ministry is thinking of organizing a Chagall retrospective in a year or two. Wouldn't that be something?"

Sukhanov lifted his head. He was no longer angry, only tired, very tired.

"Don't be so naive, Serezha," he said quietly. "You sound just like an excitable eighteen-year-old girl I met the other day. Changes, changes, spring in the air, Soviet art is inferior, let's all say what we think! At least she has the excuse of being young—but you and I, we should know better, we went through it all once before, didn't we? Honestly, can you not see that this whole Chagall business is nothing but a provocation, a test of loyalty, if you will? The Ministry has no intention of putting on any 'retrospective.' It simply hopes to flush out the handful of enthusiastic fools who will believe in all their fine promises and start getting carried away, saying unwise things and publishing unwise articles—and before one has time to blink, they'll have lost their jobs and been sent off to the provinces, or worse, and new people in their places will say and write the same old things as before."

Pugovichkin stopped pacing and leaned over the desk.

"I understand your worries," he said earnestly, "but I think you underestimate the nature of what is happening in the country this time around. Look, Tolya, it's been less than six months since the leadership change in March, and already, the man has said some pretty radical things. His Leningrad speech, with its barbs at the old guard—"

Sukhanov waved his hand to cut him off. "You don't know what will happen any more than I do," he said, "but my prediction is, absolutely nothing. It's all smoke and no fire. Chagall, imagine that! Who's next, Trotsky? By the way, who's the author?"

"Someone with a very Russian name, like Petrov or Vasiliev . . . I'll remember in a moment. No one we've ever heard of, a curator from somewhere or other—but clearly with friends in high places. If nothing else, it may not be prudent to get them upset."

"Well, I suppose," said Sukhanov, frowning, "if written from a certain critical perspective, it might—with some heavy editing, of course—"

"It's already at the printers," muttered Pugovichkin, averting his eyes.

Sukhanov looked at his right-hand man across a sudden gap of silence, palpable and unpleasant like an acrid taste in his mouth.

When Pugovichkin spoke, his voice was almost hostile with defensiveness. "Well, what would *you* have done in my place? I was put on the spot. I was told in no uncertain terms to publish the damn piece. Think about it, the issue must be typeset by Monday, and you were going away, as far as we knew. What was I supposed to—"

"Just why does everyone think I was going away?" Sukhanov interrupted heatedly.

"Must we now belabor the obvious? I called you as soon as I heard, on Tuesday morning, and you weren't there, but—"

"Tuesday, you say? I was home most of the day."

"No, you weren't. I spoke to Vasily, and he told me you were out. I left a detailed message with him, explaining the situation. He said he was about to go to the Crimea with you."

Sukhanov sat back in his chair.

"Vasily said that?" he asked slowly.

Pugovichkin shrugged. "I think his exact words were 'with the old man.' Frankly, at the time I was rather perplexed that you hadn't mentioned your vacation. I gather you changed your mind about it? In any case, since none of us ever heard back from you, we assumed you'd received the word, agreed to the whole thing, and gone off to the sea with your son. Did he not give you my message?"

Forcing his scattering thoughts to order, Sukhanov recalled the unbearable Tuesday morning he had spent working on the article, with Vasily sulking behind his closed door and the remote telephone ringing intermittently throughout the sluggish, torturous hours. The boy had been angry with him about his failure to convey the Minister's invitation to a party, he remembered. It suddenly seemed like an event from a very long time ago.

"The issue won't go to print without my complete approval, and that's that," he said in his most formal tone. "Kindly stop the presses and get someone to bring me a copy of the article. If I don't like it, my Dalí goes instead. I'm still in charge here unless I'm told otherwise—and unless I'm told by someone *directly*. Do you understand me, Sergei Nikolaevich?"

Pugovichkin considered him bleakly.

"I understand perfectly, Anatoly Pavlovich," he said after a pause, "but if you decide to pull it, you'll be the one to do all the explaining afterward, as it's bound to make a couple of very important people very unhappy. And whatever you choose to do, you must let me know by Saturday afternoon at the latest. The typesetters are already complaining as it is."

"Of course," replied Sukhanov with a brief nod.

Pugovichkin hesitated for a moment, then walked out of the room, shutting the door behind him with pointed precision. Sukhanov remained sitting at his desk, drumming his fingers against its lacquered edge. Initially, his mind was in a whirl, his feelings undistinguished and pained, the very rhythm of his breathing punctuated by small, distressed, wordless cries of disbelief at so much betrayal— betrayal by the trusted Sergei Nikolaevich and all the rest of his colleagues, betrayal by his son, betrayal even by some nebulous influential individual whom he had probably never met but who nonetheless clearly intended to compromise him by forcing on him this impossible choice. . . .

Then, gradually, a dull premonition of dread began to steal over him like an encroaching shadow, suppressing all other thoughts and emotions; but it was not until some minutes later, when a knock so timid it was almost a scratch sounded on his door and Liubov Markovna crept inside after his second "Come in," her head pulled into her shoulders, a stack of papers in her outstretched hands, that he knew what it was he so absurdly feared—whose name he was so irrationally certain to see on the title page as a reproachful harbinger of his impending downfall. It would be a most fitting conclusion, he thought with the bitter ghost of a smile, to his disquieting slide into the past. "A very Russian name," Pugovichkin had said—and what name could be more Russian than that of a three-hundred-year-old dynasty of Russian rulers, what man better suited to write about Chagall than one of his own students? It must be, it had to be him— Oleg Romanov, the stern, courageous, maverick painter who almost half a century ago had so painstakingly fine-tuned one boy's vision in order to render it receptive to the richness of the world.

In the first few years after Anatoly's return to Moscow, Romanov had sent him frequent letters, with effortless sketches of lacelike dragonflies and demure mermaids scattered between the lines and faintly colored, oil-stained fingerprints on the margins, but Anatoly, numbed by his father's death, had tossed them indifferently, at times unopened, into a drawer, postponing his answer in expectation of a thaw in his soul, until eventually the one-sided correspondence had tapered off. Later, after he entered the Surikov Institute, his interest in life returned, but he lacked the time needed to compose a sincere, worthy reply—one that would truly explain his silence of the preceding years. Or perhaps, if he was to be completely forthcoming with himself, the time had been there all along, but the path he had chosen, his determination to use the nimbleness of his brush to secure a comfortable livelihood, his constant struggle to squeeze from his manner the last lingering consequences of Romanov's unorthodox teachings, made him feel vaguely uneasy, dishonest, unclean—a mild enough discomfort, but one that kept him from writing all through his student years, and that proceeded to intensify into a sensation of acute guilt soon after his graduation. Along with a few other promising young artists, Anatoly was appointed to teach at the Moscow Higher Artistic and Technical Institute, the very place from which Romanov had been exiled to Inza in disgrace some two decades before, accused of "undue impressionism" in his works.

With time, Anatoly's sense of guilt paled, of course, along with the memory of the man who had inspired it, and obscurely he felt the oblivion to which he had consigned his early artistic discoveries to be an essential ingredient—perhaps the basis—of his continuing peace of mind. He led a measured existence, dutifully moving between the quietened Arbat apartment (the elder Morozov, his son Sashka, and the merry construction worker had all perished in the war, and Anatoly had eventually shifted his modest belongings into one of the empty rooms), the auditoriums in which he staunchly repeated the very phrases and gestures that had once made him draw vicious caricatures of the speakers in his student notebooks, and a studio at the institute, where he produced his canvases of grimy, industrious peasants and grimly determined soldiers, with soulful vistas opening behind their broad, sturdy backs. In 1953, when Stalin died, he and his mother grieved along with everyone; he painted a small commemorative portrait for a local school. Nadezhda Sukhanova was proud of him, and appeared content. They were placed on a waiting list to receive their own flat, and at the end of 1954 moved across the city to the Liubianka neighborhood. His works were occasionally purchased by a garment factory or a Young Pioneers club. He had no close friends, but his days were busy enough without them. He was never cynical in his actions (celebrating the people's accomplishments that had come at such terrible cost was a worthy pursuit, he had no doubt), but simply uninspired and incurious; he had acquired a habit of adjusting to his surroundings with unquestioning acquiescence, and ceased to distinguish between art and craft—a difference of only two letters, after all. By the time he turned twenty-six, he believed he could follow this path into old age, obtaining in due course an amiable wife and two or three children, making a quiet, pleasant, useful way through the world.

And then came the year 1956, and everything he had once held true—all the comfortable ideas and beliefs and ways of life—was swept away. And as the past certainties melted, dizzying drops and hidden false bottoms were revealed in their stead—and in the whirlwind that followed, my soul, which had weathered the intervening years between adolescence and adulthood by retreating deep into its own rainbow-colored world and dreaming secret, fleeting, iridescent dreams of birds and flowers and stars and angels, emerged once again, and was as before, alive and demanding.

Then, awakening abruptly and discovering only emptiness where warmth and friendship should have been, I tried to find Oleg Romanov across the ravages of space and time. But neither repeated letters to the Inza school nor persistent inquiries among colleagues brought any results—the man had moved, the man had vanished, the man had probably died. . . . And now, three decades later, Anatoly Sukhanov sat in his sun-flooded office on the top floor of the eighteenth-century mansion in the heart of Moscow, trying to calculate how old his teacher would be (only a few years older than his father-in-law, so it was possible), and watching, with irregular heartbeats, Liubov Markovna's contrite approach.

"Sorry for the delay," she said in a voice so low it verged on a whisper, as she slid the manuscript across his desk. He had meant to wait until she left the room, but his eyes descended onto the page before he could prevent it. "Chagall: One Man's Universe," the title declared in capital letters. Underneath, he saw the name—D. M. Fyodorov.

Exhaling, he picked up the article and dropped it negligently into his briefcase.

The relentless advance of the past had been finally halted.

"I'm going home now," he said airily, "but tell Sergei Nikolaevich that I'll let him know as soon as I can."

"Yes, Anatoly Pavlovich," Liubov Markovna whispered behind his back. "Of course, Anatoly Pavlovich. Right away, Anatoly Pavlovich."

He had hoped to glance at the text during his metro ride home, but spent the minutes in transit with his nose pressed between the chintz shoulder blades of an elderly woman with a multitude of bags, one of which was quite perceptibly oozing a trickle of ice cream onto the floor, while a gangling, pimply fellow sank his chin meditatively into Sukhanov's neck. On the way out, mildly befuddled, he attempted to exit through a glass door that read, in mirrorlike inversion, "ꓱꓛИAЯTИꓱ," and a very large, formidable figure in a pigeon-gray uniform—whether man or woman, he could not tell—shouted at him in a booming prison guard's voice that made passersby start and turn and stare, "Where the hell do you think you're going, old man? Have you gone blind?"

He staggered into the street feeling shaky, tightly clutching his briefcase as if expecting it to be violently torn from his grasp at any moment. When he arrived at his building at last, he wanted to collapse with relief. The lobby embraced him with its familiar marble coolness, and the ancient concierge was already shuffling across the floor to summon the elevator. The two of them stood side by side without speaking, listening to the laborious creaking of the machinery floors above. Nearly a full minute later came a heavy thump, and a light shone through the crack between the folds of the door. The concierge began to swing open the gate.

"Oh, Anatoly Pavlovich, I nearly forgot," he said in a voice dry as an autumn leaf. "There have been some problems with the elevator, so they asked me to tell everyone on the upper floors to be a bit more careful."

"What do you mean?" Sukhanov asked inattentively, stepping inside.

"Oh, nothing much," the concierge replied with an ambiguous smile. "Just make sure the elevator is actually *there* before you enter it on the way down. Wouldn't want anyone falling to their deaths, would we now, heh heh heh! Had a close one, too. Two days ago, Ivan Martynovich—you know, that songwriter who lives below you—"

The elevator doors, closing with jerks and shudders, swallowed the rest of his sentence.

Sukhanov felt inordinately glad to find himself at home.

"Hello, I'm back!" he called out hopefully—but the place stayed silent, save for a few spoons that rattled dejectedly in the dining room cupboard. The air in the hallway was damp; the windows had remained open during the previous night's rain. A ghostly trace of music sent faint vibrations into the corridor from Ksenya's room. Frowning, he knocked on her door, then, not hearing a response, knocked louder. There was still no answer.

Sukhanov walked in.

The heavy green curtains were drawn, softening the room's stark, book-filled angularity, and in the semidarkness he heard the shadow of music grow to a stronger presence, more like a whisper or a persistent memory of a song. His daughter was lying flat on her bed, fully dressed, a pair of headphones on her ears, her eyes closed, a strange, tight little smile flickering on her lips. As he bent over her, the music expanded, and he could distinguish a man's voice singing, although the words remained a soft electronic blur.

"Young people nowadays," he murmured —partially to dispel with the sound of his own voice the sensation of unease that suddenly brushed him with a darting, clammy, alien touch, not for the first time in Ksenya's presence. After a moment's hesitation, he placed his hand on her shoulder. She screamed and sat up so abruptly their heads nearly collided; and for an instant her eyes, dark and veiled, were full of swinging chaos. Then, like a pair of pendulums slowly coming to a stop, her pupils became still in the gray irises.

Breathing out, she tore off the headphones.

"You scared me," she said. "I didn't hear you come in."

"Ah yes, the power of music," he said, trying to smile. "What are you listening to?"

"No one you'd know."

"Try me."

"All right then, Boris Tumanov," she replied, shrugging. "It's a homemade tape, he's part of the new underground."

"Oh. I see," he said vaguely. "By any chance, do you know where your mother is?"

"She's gone to the Tretyakovka with Fyodor Mikhailovich. He wanted to show her some of his favorite works."

"Oh, I see," he said again. "So it's just us, then. Well, well."

He turned to leave but paused with his hand on the doorknob.

"Ksenya, perhaps," he said haltingly, "perhaps we could talk?"

She regarded him without enthusiasm.

"Let me guess," she said. "You're going to deliver a lecture on how to be a good daughter. Or will this be some sort of fatherly discussion of the facts of life? 'Now that you are eighteen, my dear, you need to know there is more to boys than meets the eye'—that kind of thing? Well, don't worry, I know already. I went to school, if you recall. We had sex education."

He watched a small whirlpool of silence widen between them.

"It's nothing like that, I just . . . I just thought we'd talk, that's all," he said meekly. "We hardly ever see each other, now that you are so busy with your work. . . . I wanted to tell you, I've read that Hoffmann story you recommended the other day. Very interesting, and you were right, it doesn't have much in common with—"

Her face relaxed, and her eyes moved dreamily past him.

"Papa, I'm sorry," she said, "but if it's nothing urgent, now is really not a good time. I stayed up most of the night doing this assignment, and I was about to take a nap when you came in."

"Oh," he said brightly. "Of course. Some other time, then?"

"Some other time," she said.

She was looking away already, searching for her headphones.

He tried to read the article for the next hour, but could never get past the epigraph—an excerpt from Chagall's awkward yet oddly poignant poem, three lines of which kept alighting on the tip of his tongue like a stubborn moth, preventing him from moving any further, filling his mind with fluttering flocks of irrelevant associations.

Across the sky fly former inhabitants.

Where do they live now?

In my own torn soul.

The words circled round and round in his mind. . . . Soon he abandoned the manuscript altogether and stretched out on the couch, his gaze lost in the irregularities of the ceiling. By and by, the cumulative lack of sleep from the past few nights filled his limbs with lead and his thoughts with cotton, and the idea of a nap began to seem wonderfully appealing. In truth, he felt tired enough to sleep through several days in a row.

He had nearly drifted off when the bell rang. He went to unlock the door, pleasantly gliding just above the floor. There was no one on the landing, which was, of course, impossible, so, feeling stubborn, he strode off to check whether someone was hiding in the elevator—but the elevator itself was not there, and, losing balance, he started to fall down the shaft, and it was terrifying at first, this plummeting into the narrow, dimly glimmering abyss full of thick, creaking cables and misshapen shadows and "Do Not Enter" signs and medieval world maps hanging on the dripping walls, but gradually it became darker and darker, and easier and easier, until he found himself floating through the most delightful oblivion of blackness with a smile of full-blown happiness on his lips—and felt rather sorry when the doorbell rang again, cutting his flight short.

It appeared that he had slept for some hours, for it was suddenly late in the evening. The moon drifted brilliantly through the dining room windows as he walked past, and Nina and Dalevich, entering with the effortless laughter of two old friends, surprised him by saying they would not be joining him for supper as they had eaten already, in some nameless cafeteria upon which they had stumbled after their visit to the museum. It hardly mattered, for he did not feel in the least bit hungry, and his body still rang with an overwhelming desire for rest. Nodding agreeably, without listening (Dalevich, as usual, was trying to talk to him about some article he had written), he swam through the thickening air back to the study and, undressing this time, slipped under the blankets and fell asleep once again.

He continued to dream outlandish, not to say disturbing, dreams. Sometime in the middle of the night, he heard dogs barking incessantly in the streets. Their howling soon grew so hoarse and strained, nearly rabid with excitement, that he got up, passed through the sleeping house, and, with a presence of mind unnatural in a dream, found a coat to throw over his pajamas and some shoes in which to deposit his feet, then descended in the elevator (which was there this time), crossed the deserted, moonswept lobby, and expecting the unexpected, stepped outside. In the coolness of the August night, the mysterious woman with the exquisitely drawn features of Nefertiti was drifting aimlessly along the pavements of Belinsky Street, dressed in a diaphanous wedding gown, a pack of maddened homeless dogs following at her dainty satin heels. At his approach, she lifted her lovely, tear-stained face toward him, and said simply and sadly, "He'll never marry me, I know it. He tells me he will, but he won't. I understand now. He has a wife and a daughter. He is a very important man—a minister, no less. I understand."

As she spoke, a delicate vein pulsated in her throat, her mouth was pale and pained like a wilting petal, her eyes glistened like melting, rain-washed gems, and, bright like her eyes, two diamond cascades flowed from her ears. He stared at her with a freedom allowed only in dreams. Behind him, as if mesmerized, the dogs too ceased their barking one after another and, watching her, carefully bared their teeth, dripping saliva onto her trailing gauze train. She said nothing more, only stood there, her piano player's hands poised in an attitude of grieving supplication—and the whole world lay still and silent around them, like a starry sky's reflection in the dark waters of an abandoned pond, like a particle of time frozen for all eternity in a marvelous painting, and it was frightening and heartbreaking and beautiful, this strange encounter, woven whole as it was from the moonlit, elusive fabric of the night. . . .

It ended, as dreams must, with hasty, unbecoming absurdity. Unwinding a checkered woolen scarf left in the sleeve of his coat from some previous winter's dream, Sukhanov tossed it at the dogs in a gesture that was of course futile yet perfectly sensible at the moment, and immediately, forgetting all about them, the pack fell onto the scarf, snarling, tearing, fighting over it. Grabbing her by the elbow, he dragged her inside, and through the echoing lobby, and up a few flights of stairs, to deliver her, slightly out of breath but un-resisting, to the door of apartment number five, which he found standing wide open.

"He'll marry you, don't worry," he said generously and insin-cerely, as he gave her a gentle push across the threshold. "He'd be a fool not to."

The last thing he remembered before mounting the stairs to his own eighth floor was the sight of her face, white and streaked with two grooves of running mascara, like a tragic Venetian porcelain mask, floating above a sea of silk and lace and sparkling with dia-monds, lifted toward him from the dark cave of the gaping doorway.

After that, his duty performed, Sukhanov's dream self returned to the couch (in passing hanging the ghostly coat on its hook and removing the nonexistent shoes) and fell into an even deeper slum-ber. Sometime shortly after dawn he had another dream, not full of melancholy wonder this time, but domestic and simple, containing a promise of happiness like a seed inside its warm soil. Nina, coming into his study on tiptoes, dressed in an old pair of slacks and a faded sweater with a thick, unfeminine collar, which made her look every day of her age and so familiar, so dear, bent over him briefly to drop a light kiss onto his cheek.

"I was hoping to talk to you last night," she whispered, "but you went to sleep so early, and now I have a seven-thirty train to catch."

"But where are you going?" he asked tenderly, smiling at the kiss in his sleep.

"To the dacha," she said. "It may not have rained there. I need to check on the roses."

"Ah yes, the roses, of course, beds and carpets and fields of roses," said the dream Sukhanov. "But you'll be back, my love?"

"I'll be back," the dream Nina promised softly. "In a few days."

"The roses," he said again, and nodding joyfully, began to sail away, only opening his eyes for an instant to see Nina's hand hovering over his forehead before descending in a final, swift caress—but by then, he had already been washed onto new, unfamiliar shores.

Thirteen

But didn't she tell you?" Dalevich said, peering anxiously into Sukhanov's face.

The morning was quiet and sunny, and a bird in a nearby tree repeated its bright little song over and over in a hollow imitation of pastoral happiness.

"Anyway, it's only for a few days," Dalevich added helpfully. "She just needs to water the flowers. She should be back by Tuesday at the latest."

Sukhanov persisted in rubbing his glasses with the edge of the tablecloth, thinking of an important party to which he and Nina were invited this evening and to which he would now have to go alone. "Of course," he finally murmured, starting to stand up.

"Listen, Tolya," said Dalevich hastily, "we never finished our talk the other day, and there was something in particular I wanted to—"

"Of course," said Sukhanov again. "Except that right now I have this article I must review. Urgent work, I'm sure you understand."

"Oh, completely," said Dalevich. "And as a matter of fact, I was just about to tell you—"

"Let's talk at dinnertime, shall we, then?" Sukhanov said.

The bird continued to strain its throat with throbbing exuberance. As he trod the long corridor to his study, he felt his cousin's eyes on his back.

He spent the rest of the morning behind the closed door, in a semidarkness of tightly drawn curtains, stubbornly warding off all thoughts of Nina's desertion and poring over the Chagall article. It was, he had to admit, exceptionally well written. Instead of delivering a dutiful recital of dull biographical facts, D. M. Fyodorov (whoever the devil he was) had chosen to present the artist's development through a series of defining encounters: a stuttering meeting of the chaperoned adolescent with a kindly Judel Pan, a pedestrian but endearing Vitebsk painter who would become Chagall's first teacher and in whose studio the youth would struggle to draw plaster busts but lapse time and time again into unacceptable lilac colors; an accidental introduction to Bella, daughter of a local jewelry merchant, in whose radiant black gaze his soul would find its eternal home; then, already in the capital, a timid, excited audience with the celebrated Leon Bakst, founder of the famous St. Petersburg art school, leader in the influential World of Art movement, and proud proclaimer of art for art's sake, who to the young Chagall seemed the triumphant incarnation of all European traditions, but who, after a mere few months as his tutor, began to appear too stylized, too refined, and in the end too cold and foreign in Chagall's eyes—too small for his expanding, deepening universe of pain and joy; and finally, completing his formation as an artist, a momentous meeting in pre–World War I Paris with Anatoly Vasilievich Lunacharsky— Lenin's future mouthpiece on the subject of art in the service of the Revolution, and Bakst's ideological negative—to whom Chagall politely showed his works and, noticing the man's puzzlement, said serenely, "Just don't ask me why everything on my canvases is blue or green, or why a calf is visible in a cow's stomach. Let your Marx, if he is so smart, come back from the dead and explain everything to you."

This position of a genius whose art had grown too universal both for aestheticizing detachment and for political partiality would make it hard for Chagall to be appreciated in Russia before the Revolution and impossible for him to remain there much longer afterward, but in a sensitive omission, D. M. Fyodorov had elected not to dwell on Chagall's subsequent exile and wanderings. Instead, he had devoted the rest of the article to a poetic tribute to the master's lifelong themes—his "poignant, eternal world, radiant like a window opening from the darkness of our souls into bright blue skies, filled with flying fiddlers, green-faced lovers, and mysteriously smiling cows," as he wrote in his conclusion, "a world that seems childlike and simple and yet achieves truly biblical proportions, touching the very core of our being."

Frowning, Sukhanov tapped his pen against the stack of paper before him. Of course, he would never have allowed this piece anywhere near his magazine under ordinary circumstances, but he supposed Pugovichkin was right—it was always wiser not to cross those more important than oneself. And in any case, it could have been worse: at least it read more like a philosophical discourse on the nature of art than a subversive manifesto. All the same, it was apparent that, inspired though it might be, the text could not remain unaltered. It lacked a proper critical attitude. Even more problematic, it betrayed an openly religious sensibility, what with its constant references to the Bible, its assertion of love as the unifying principle of Chagall's universe, its comparisons between his manner and traditional iconic art, and . . . and . . .

For one uncomfortable moment, the by now familiar sensation of fleeting recognition, of his past and present endlessly reflecting off each other in a multiplying infinity of mirrors, visited Sukhanov again, disrupting the flow of his thoughts; but in a quick outburst of determination he shrugged it off and lifted his pen. The Lunacharsky scene had to go—or better yet, he would keep it (naturally, omitting Chagall's scandalous mention of Marx) in order to use it as a departure point for a stern reevaluation of Chagall's work. Perhaps something along these lines: "While the painter was able to perceive the insolvency of the bourgeois art of Bakst and his school, he lacked the maturity needed to appreciate the noble truth of Lunacharsky's position, thus failing to understand the real purpose of art as the people's weapon in their struggle against oppression." Yes, indeed, this would serve as the perfect introduction to a subsequent discussion of the artist's themes: their childish, fairy-tale nature, their total isolation from reality, their slavish reliance on religious motifs . . . As Sukhanov's pen flew across the pages, crossing out every occurrence of "biblical" and "eternal" and putting a fat question mark next to every mention of "love," he was beginning to think that it was possible, just possible, to keep the wolves full and the sheep whole. Thus occupied, he did not hear the soft knock on the door, and was presently startled by his cousin's apologetic voice close to his ear.

"Dinner's ready," said Fyodor Mikhailovich, spreading his hands in a rueful gesture. "All I do is interrupt your work."

A heap of dumplings lay steaming before them, with a dollop of sour cream sliding weightily down the bowl's rim. Ksenya helped herself to a hearty serving. Despite the early afternoon hour, the lamp was lit, and its garish orange light irritated Sukhanov's eyes. His gaze kept straying to the empty seat—Nina's seat—at the end of the table.

"Shall we resume our earlier conversation?" Dalevich suggested readily.

"Ah, yes," Sukhanov replied without much interest. "Where were we, exactly?"

"Innovation versus tradition. Or to use my example, the universe of Kandinsky versus the universe of Chagall. Which actually brings me to the very subject I was hoping to—"

Sukhanov lowered his fork.

"The universe of Chagall?" he repeated distractedly. "Why, that's a curious—"

He was about to say "coincidence," but he never did, for in the next instant his memory, with an almost perverse precision, delivered to him Dalevich's comment from two days earlier. Chagall's "child-like universe of flying fiddlers, green-faced lovers, and mysteriously smiling cows," his cousin had said. And those words—those words mirrored to an uncanny degree the phrase he had read not an hour before—the phrase written by the unknown Fyodorov. Naturally, a literal duplication was impossible, so it must have been a simple trick of the mind: under the fresh impression of the article, he must have somehow distorted Fyodor's original words. . . . Unless, that is . . . unless . . . could it be . . .

For one prolonged moment of disbelief, he stared at the man sitting across his kitchen table. He stared at the man's yellow beard, his sparkling, oddly shaped glasses, his moving thin lips—stared without hearing one word of what the man was saying. Then the possibility of truth overwhelmed him. His eyelids felt heavy and hot as if dusted with sand, and he had to close his eyes.

". . . the very subject I was hoping to address," Dalevich was saying just then. "You see, some years ago I wrote a series of essays analyzing the influence of Russian iconic art on modern artists, and naturally, one of my first studies was on . . . Tolya, are you all right?"

Slowly Sukhanov opened his eyes. It should not have come as such a shock; there had been warning signs, after all. "A curator from somewhere or other," Pugovichkin had told him, and he had indeed felt something hauntingly familiar in the unfolding of Fyodorov's arguments. Then there was the now apparent matter of inverted names, so easy to see through. . . . Yet it shocked him deeply all the same.

Sukhanov moistened his dry lips before speaking.

"So," he said, enunciating carefully, "Fyodor Mikhailovich Dalevich—or should I say D. M. Fyodorov? Seems you both had a little joke at my expense."

Ksenya's released fork clicked against her plate with an unexpected sound.

"Tolya, as I've been trying to explain—" Dalevich began with a placating smile.

"Explain?" Sukhanov interrupted. "Please, what is there to explain? You sleep in my house, you eat my food, and then you stab me in the back—really, it's very simple! Or did you not realize what the appearance of such an article in my magazine would do to my reputation? And were you even going to admit you were behind it?"

Dalevich started to talk, stammering with emotion, pressing his hands to his chest, assuring "dear Tolya" how much his good opinion meant to him and how the whole affair had simply been an accident, for, even though he had always found the notion of being published in *Art of the World* very intriguing ("Not least, Tolya, because of you, I admit"), he would never have knowingly gone behind Sukhanov's back. He had merely shown his Chagall article some time ago to a friend, who, in turn, had passed it along to another friend, who had just chanced to be quite high up in the Ministry of Culture, and then everything had happened so quickly, and almost without his consent. . . . But even setting all that aside, he had never intended to hide his authorship of the piece: "Fyodorov" had been his pen name for years, and moreover, he had tried to talk about it on numerous occasions, only each time Sukhanov had been too busy to listen. . . .

For some minutes, Sukhanov was incapable of discerning any-thing beyond the uneven hum of blood in his ears, but the absurdity of the last statement all at once intruded on his senses.

"Ah, so *that*'s the problem," he said bitingly. "I've been too busy to listen! Actually, it seems I've been too busy to do a lot of things lately—to run my own magazine, to take my wife out to museums, even to sleep in my own bed! Luckily for me, you came along, saw my sad predicament, and given all the free time on your hands, decided to help me out, yes?"

Looking dismayed, Dalevich tried to interject, but Ksenya spoke first.

"How can you talk like that to Fyodor Mikhailovich?" she said with indignation.

"Oh, so he has befriended you too, has he, Ksenya? Of course, such a nice, interesting uncle who is not afraid to voice his most unorthodox opinions on art and cooks such tasty breakfasts and—" Abruptly he stopped, then said hoarsely, "My God, it's been your plan all along, hasn't it? You've been turning my family against me!"

"Tolya, please," mumbled Dalevich, "you are angry, you don't know what you are saying, you can't possibly—"

"On the contrary, I know perfectly well what I'm saying. A long-lost provincial cousin in need of a place to stay for a day or two—heavens, I must have been blind! Not that I was ever happy about your presence, but I thought it was just a temporary, harmless impo-sition. . . . But now I see, I see it all too clearly. First, you oust me from my room, then you get my mother, my daughter, and my wife on your side—my son alone doesn't take to you, but he is soon conve-niently out of the way—and now you are trying to cost me my job!"

"Tolya, come to your senses," said Dalevich quietly. "Why would I do such a thing?"

"Yes, indeed, why would you, I'd very much like to know. Are you a disgruntled failure who envies the accomplishments of better men?

Do you have a pathological hatred of art critics? Would you like my job for yourself?" He had been throwing the words out furiously, without thinking, but now he froze, staring at Dalevich, then slapped an invisible fly against his forehead. "I don't believe it! That's it, isn't it? It's all part of your design. You mean to get my job! Your article is published under a pseudonym, I'm fired in the midst of a scandal, and once the dust settles, your influential patron appoints you to my position—and no one ever finds out that you were the author in the first place. Simple and brilliant, I have to give it to you, cousin."

"Tolya, I assure you, you couldn't be more—"

"And by the way," Sukhanov went on, his voice rising precipitously, "are you even my real cousin? I mean, isn't it rather peculiar that I don't remember meeting you or even hearing about you ever before? Why, now that I think about it, I suspect I have closer blood ties to Salvador Dalí!" He was shouting, and his face had taken on a dark brick hue. "I'm guessing that you just sat one day all alone in some roach-infested hole of a place in a godforsaken town light-years away from Moscow, saw me on a television program about an art retrospective or a university lecture series, and salivated over my existence—and that was when you cooked up your nice little plan to show up here as an imaginary relative, worm yourself into my family, and *take over my life!*"

Dalevich no longer attempted to say anything. Both he and Ksenya simply looked at Sukhanov, and their faces were all wrong somehow—wooden, tight-lipped, wide-eyed. A terrible silence descended on the brightly lit kitchen. The only audible sound was Sukhanov's labored breathing.

"Do you know, it might have worked too, had it not been for one tiny slip you made," he finally said in a voice thick with distaste. "'Mysteriously smiling cows,' was it, now? Well, that little phrase cost you dearly, didn't it, *cousin*? See, I was going to approve the article, give or take a few changes, but now I know the author's true identity and intentions, and you'll see it published only in your dreams. It appears that you've lost, dear Fedya. Imagine, all your machinations for nothing!"

Steadying himself with one hand, Sukhanov stood up and pushed away his chair; it balanced precariously on two legs, then crashed to the floor. In the doorway he stopped.

"I should turn you over to the authorities," he said, not looking directly at Dalevich, "but it's not worth the bother. You have half an hour to clear out of my place. I'm sure your important friend will happily welcome you into *his* home. Perhaps you might even try your tricks on him next, now that you've had some practice. After all, his job and apartment are probably nicer than mine."

He slammed the door on the way out. As he walked away, he heard the same ringing silence behind his back.

Some hours later, reclining in the backseat of his Volga, Sukhanov watched lit rectangles of lower-floor windows emerge from the evening shadows and then slowly glide backward and out of sight in a long, uninterrupted procession of cozy domesticity. He had left his own uncomfortably quiet apartment shortly before seven. Ksenya had followed him into the entrance hall to lock up behind him; her face, heavy in the gathering darkness, had seemed void of expression.

"The Burykins never serve their main course until well after ten," he had said, "so I don't expect to be back before midnight," and already from across the threshold, he had added with a tentative smile, "Sure you don't want to come with me? Since your mother isn't coming, it might be nice. . . . And the food's always good." She had said nothing in response, only shaken her head, and shut the door. The sound of the turning lock resonated on the landing with brisk finality.

The Burykins—Mikhail a top official at the Ministry of Culture, Liudmila his charmingly hospitable third wife—lived across the street from the massive American embassy and were famous for their dinner parties, invariably well stocked with imported liqueurs and important people. On the way, Sukhanov bade Vadim stop the car and darted out to buy a bouquet for the hostess from a portly Azerbaijani woman near a metro station. The air smelled strongly of gasoline and early autumn, and faintly of decaying stems. He could see fading red petals, slimy leaves, and shards of a rising moon floating on the surface of the dirty water in the woman's flower-filled buckets.

"Roses for the lady of your heart?" she said greedily, baring a golden tooth.

"How about that bunch of carnations over there?" he said quickly.

The lobby of the Burykins' building was even more imposing than his own, its veined marble floors slippery, its walls smooth with mirrors, the guard behind the desk bearing a disconcerting resemblance to a bulldog. He inquired after Sukhanov's name with an indifferent lift of an eyebrow and then, instead of allowing him through right away, proceeded to trace a fat finger along the list of residents, dial a number, and conduct a long conversation in a hushed voice, while Sukhanov foolishly stood before him, trying in vain to avoid looking at the hundredfold reflections of an aging man dressed in a borrowed tie and a suit that was wrinkled rather more than usual, holding a bunch of unpleasantly pink, rapidly wilting flowers in his hands.

Finally the guard issued a curt nod, and Sukhanov slid along the marble floor, soundlessly rehearsing an involved story of some ambiguous emergency that would explain Nina's embarrassing lapse of memory or manners. As alternating patches of light and darkness flitted in the crack between the elevator doors, he found himself, to his own surprise, anticipating the evening with some eagerness. In truth, his oppressive mood had started to lift shortly after his perfectly justified afternoon outburst—as soon, to be precise, as his front door had closed on one Fyodor Mikhailovich Dalevich, pseudo-cousin and first-rate scoundrel. The man had left wordlessly and without a fuss, and as

Sukhanov had leaned out the window to watch the solitary figure in the ridiculously outmoded hat lug the bulging suitcase toward the metro, he had understood Dalevich's defeated departure to be the beginning of a long-needed restoration of balance in his household. Without a doubt, now that the poisonous viper had been banished from his hearth, the vexing malfunctions in his family mechanism were bound to smooth out, and soon they would all return to their pleasant daily routines. Naturally, there remained some loose ends that still filled him with ill-defined unease. When he had subsequently attempted to reach his office with instructions to withdraw the cursed Chagall article, he had found no one there, and when he had tried Pugovichkin's home, the assistant editor's wife had announced in a phlegmatic voice that her husband had gone fishing, as if this were normal behavior on a work-day. Yet infuriating as this delay was, Sukhanov had until the next after-noon to set matters straight; and already, with each passing hour, his sense of life inching back into its customary, comforting confines grew more and more tangible. As he rang the Burykins' bell, he looked for-ward to a night of excellent food and banter in the presence of much success, sure to strengthen his quiet sense of victory.

His first ring was followed by a protracted wait. He pressed the button again, more firmly this time, and heard hurried steps inside the apartment. The door swung open, and Liudmila Burykina stood on the threshold.

"Anatoly Pavlovich! How nice, you shouldn't have," she said with a peculiar, unfocused smile as she accepted his flowers, and added unnecessarily, "The concierge just called to say you were on your way up. Please do come in."

The darkened rooms unfolded in perfect silence—no sounds of clinking glasses, no music, no voices rising toward one another in greeting. Sukhanov glanced at his watch.

"So," he said loudly, "first one to arrive, it seems. Not too early, am I?"

Ordinarily elegant, today she wore a surprisingly plain frock that made her look rather like a merchant's wife from some Ostrovsky play—the motherly kind who spends all summer making preserves and all winter sewing and who is allowed to emerge from her well-stocked pantry only two or three times for the sake of comic relief.

Her black eyes flickered uncertainly up to his face.

"Anatoly Pavlovich, I'm afraid I—"

"Lovely painting you've got there," he interrupted, pointing to an indifferent seascape. "Not Aivazovsky, is it?" And immediately, without awaiting an answer—for the silence of the place was starting to unnerve him—he asked, "Is Misha not back from the office yet?"

Her hair, he noticed, was flattened on one side, the remnant of a long nap.

"Misha's at the sauna, Anatoly Pavlovich. He won't be back until ten," she said.

"Sauna?" he repeated incredulously. "Tonight?"

She began to walk away from him, and, baffled, he followed, stepping on a trail of falling petals and feeling increasingly awkward. In the dusk of the dining room, an enormous table, bereft of a table-cloth, was stacked high with faintly gleaming, seemingly dirty china. He stole another anxious look at his watch.

"Do you mind, I must find a vase," she was saying lightly. "Please, in here, Anatoly Pavlovich. Sorry for the mess, my help has the day off, and I myself haven't yet gotten around . . . Oh, by the way, would you like something to eat? Though I'm afraid I can't offer you any-thing but leftovers from yesterday." Absolutely still now, he watched her adroit plump hands amputate the moist ends of the stems with a pair of scissors. "Too bad you and Nina couldn't . . . that is . . . Tell me, do you think they'd look better in a crystal one?"

She had slid the disheveled carnations into a ceramic vase and was glancing back at him with a questioning half-smile—and sud-denly he understood that she was chattering so rapidly because she too found the silence embarrassing. They had obviously moved the party to an earlier date and forgotten to tell him, and now here she was, the perfect hostess who for once had failed to be perfect, with nothing to give her guest but crumbs from a past feast, no doubt suffering pangs of guilt and yet not willing to acknowledge the situation out of some stubborn housewifely pride, letting them both pretend that he had simply dropped by for a little unscheduled visit.

Though displeased with the turn of events, he chose to be gracious.

"My goodness, Liudmila Ivanovna," he said in a jocular tone, slapping his forehead, "you are too polite not to set me straight—but I fear I missed your party, didn't I? I could swear it was supposed to be on Friday. How terribly absentminded of me to get the date wrong!"

He did not like the way she was searching his eyes with hers; it felt intrusive. Then, looking away, she started to pull the flowers out of the ceramic vase.

"Actually, the party *was* on Friday, Anatoly Pavlovich," she said uncomfortably. "And Nina sent your regrets. She said . . . I probably shouldn't be telling you this, since there seems to be some miscommunication here . . . but she said you were under a lot of stress and needed rest."

He barely heard anything past the first sentence.

"But it couldn't have been on Friday," he said, still smiling mechanically, yet already feeling a strange hollow sensation in the pit of his stomach. "Today *is* Friday."

"No, Anatoly Pavlovich, Friday was yesterday," said Liudmila Burykina, again studying his face. "Today is Saturday. Anyway, it doesn't matter, you are here now, so let's just forget all this, and I'll fix you a nice drink, all right? . . . Yes, the crystal vase is definitely an improvement, don't you agree? . . . Do you prefer whiskey or cognac?"

He continued to look at her without comprehension.

"But it can't be," he finally muttered. "Because I dropped off my article at the office yesterday, and it was Thursday, I remember clearly, that's when it was due, and Pugovichkin told me I had until Saturday afternoon, which was the day after tomorrow, and—"

"Or maybe a cup of tea?" she said gently, placing her hand on his sleeve.

For a moment he stared at her with unseeing eyes—and then, all at once, was seized with panic, and desperate to look at a calendar, to take full stock of his memory's transgressions, to measure his grasp on reality . . .

And the request for a calendar had nearly touched his lips when it occurred to him that the woman might merely be playing some monstrously cruel joke on him, and that, in fact, her husband, Mikhail Burykin, could easily have been the very man responsible for forcing the Chagall article onto his magazine in the first place—for hadn't someone high up at the Ministry been involved? He imagined that snake Dalevich lurking somewhere in the shadows of this still place, gleefully orchestrating his present misadventure, and the air seemed to enter his lungs in painful gasps.

"I'd love to stay, Liudmila Ivanovna," he said faintly, "but I'm afraid I can't just now. . . . Please give my regards to Misha, sorry for the confusion, you're so very kind. . . ."

And murmuring apologies, his eyes glued to the carnations so he would not have to meet her oddly compassionate gaze, he backed out of the Burykins' apartment.

In the car, under the dim light of a tiny overhead bulb, Vadim was writing something against the dashboard. Sukhanov tore the door open.

"Take me home," he said in a near-whisper, pulling at his father-in-law's tie as if it were about to strangle him. "Please."

Fourteen

On the way up, Sukhanov had to share the elevator with an unsavory character. His mind aching with increasingly futile computations of dates, he avoided looking at the man too closely, only catching out of the corner of his eye a soiled denim jacket, a shaved head, and a salmon-colored scarf wrapped around a bulging neck. The man exited without a word—Sukhanov did not bother to see on what floor—and the doors slid shut, revealing, spread diagonally on the inside, the freshly scratched word "Aquarium," the name of some semi-underground band, he seemed to recall. He shook his head at this unprecedented instance of vandalism so close to his inner sanctum, checked the time (it was almost nine o'clock), and for a moment studied the twisted corpse of a cigarette in the corner. Then it occurred to him that the thin thread of greenish light trembling in the gap above the floor had not moved and that the elevator remained where it had been. Impatiently he jabbed at the button with a fading figure eight, and was startled when the doors opened instantly: it seemed he was already on his floor. Frowning, he stepped out onto the landing, wondering mechanically what business the normally staid Petrenko family from across the hall could have with such a shady visitor—and was just in time to see the edge of the man's salmon-colored scarf disappearing inside his own apartment, admitted, he could briefly see, by an unfamiliar young girl who slouched smoking in the eerily wavering shadows of the entrance hall.

He stood frozen for a few heartbeats. The girl was about to shut the door when he shook off his stupor and, his feelings dangerously suspended, strode toward her with a demand for an explanation rising to his lips—but before he could deliver it, his hearing was assailed by a cacophony of voices and laughter and the jangling of guitar strings touched by an absent but practiced hand, all seemingly issuing from his very own living room. Taking an uncertain step inside, past the girl watching him with indifference, he saw, in the corridor's dim, hazy, diminishing depths, a crowd of people talking excitedly, some holding glasses, most with cigarettes, all casting grotesque giant shadows in the unsteady light of candles—yes, endless candles, tall and short, dripping and flickering madly, perched on counters and along shelves and even on the floor. . . .

He stared without moving, and the first thought flashing ridiculously through his disoriented mind was that the Burykins' missing party had somehow relocated itself here, with its aged wines and aging dignitaries and all the rest. . . . But already he saw that this crowd was young and strange, and the candles leapt about outlandishly, and the heavy smells of incense and some exotic spice drifted through the air in dizzying waves, and the darkly luminous space looked cavernous and foreign and not at all like an ordinary Moscow apartment—and in another breath he realized that this was all nonsense, this could never be his home, and in truth, the elevator must have taken him to the wrong floor after all, for hadn't the concierge warned him about its recent malfunctions?

Trying to inhale evenly, he stepped back across the threshold and checked the bronze number displayed above the peephole on the door.

The number was fifteen. His number.

He considered it in seething silence, gathering his thoughts. He had told his daughter he would not be back until midnight, he remembered. Her name—Ksenya, Ksenya, oh Ksenya!—throbbed in his temples like a quickly advancing migraine.

"Well, are you coming in, or what?" drawled the girl in the doorway. "They're starting in just a few seconds." She pulled at the cigarette with studied carelessness and added inexplicably, "Good thing you brought your own tie. I hear they've run out."

For a moment he debated ordering this insolent hussy out of his house—ordering all these people out, in fact, and flipping on all the light switches, and blowing out all the candles, and flinging open all the windows to air out the disgusting sweet smells, and putting a stop to the irritating singing he could now hear floating on the current of disparate guitar riffs, a man's reedy voice bleating trite lyrics, something about great poets dying tragically before their time. . . . But immediately he thought he could try to confront Ksenya first— shame her before all her friends perhaps—and maybe, having trapped her against the wall with her repentance, finally manage to have the talk with her that he had been postponing for months if not years, ever since she had begun to drift away, hiding behind her writing, her music, her books, who knew what else. . . . Suddenly decisive, with a nod to the sullen girl, he walked inside, an anonymous, harmless guest, one of many, peering into the near-darkness through his fogging glasses.

Since the singing had started, the chatting guests had begun to fall silent and gravitate toward the music, and now only one couple was left whispering in the twinkling twilight of the hallway: a slender girl with a pool of night in place of her face and a long-haired man in a leather jacket and a tie slicing across his chest like a precise slash. Taking a few more steps, Sukhanov reached the edge of a dense crowd of badly dressed youths spilling over from the living room into the corridor, some standing, others sitting cross-legged on the bare floor, rhythmically bobbing their heads like Chinese dolls, their lips soundlessly mouthing the words of the song. It was even darker here, and stuffy, and as he tried to squeeze inside, he stepped on a few feet and possibly hands, was shushed at, and in the end found himself wedged somewhere on the outskirts, with his face awkwardly pressed into the broad back of a sturdy woman whose long, slovenly hair smelled of bitter almonds, and still unable to see above the swaying heads into the room, from which an angry young voice threw the borrowed words into the smoky silence:

"And Christ was thirty-three, he was a poet, he used to say,
'Thou shall not kill! And if you do, I'll find you anywhere!'
But they put nails into his hands so he wouldn't try anything
    funny,
And into his forehead so he wouldn't write or think so much."

"Good, isn't he?" someone whispered into Sukhanov's ear, spitting with enthusiasm.

Carefully Sukhanov turned his head and encountered the yellowish grin of the man from the elevator, inches away from his face.

"Not too original," he replied dryly. "That's by Vysotsky, if I'm not mistaken?"

"Oh, he's just warming up," the man whispered back, not taking offense. "He always starts with a thing or two by Vysotsky, as a sort of tribute to the fallen. He'll sing his own stuff next. So, what's your favorite?"

His face seemed insistently familiar, but Sukhanov was learning to disregard the feeling.

"Never heard any of it," he said with distaste. "Who is he, anyway?"

The invisible singer's voice drifted toward him as if from far away:

"But present-day poets have somehow missed the deadline,
Their duel has not taken place: it is postponed.
And at thirty-three, they are crucified, but not too badly. . . ."

"Ah, stumbled in here by accident, did we now?" said the man from the elevator, his eyes glittering madly. "Well, be prepared to have your world shattered. This here is the great Boris Tumanov in person. Recognize the name, eh?"

Sukhanov remembered the drawn curtains, the echo of music, Ksenya lying on her bed with her eyes closed—yesterday, or the day before yesterday, or years ago, who knew any longer. . . .

"My daughter likes him," he said in a fallen voice.

The song ended, and everyone clapped, and the candles wavered.

"Ah yes, girls, they all like him, why wouldn't they?" the man whispered confidentially, his hot breath scalding Sukhanov's ear. "Naturally, he is taken, and twice over: has a wife and a girlfriend. His wife, well, she's kind of a youthful mistake, never even comes to his concerts, but Ksiushka—Ksiushka is a different story altogether, these are her digs, you know—a first-class girl, likes to have a good time, if you get my meaning, even if her parents are really—"

"I . . ." said Sukhanov, a scream tightly walled up in his throat, "I think I have a headache."

The man ceased whispering and, nodding, proceeded to fish for something in his pockets, but Anatoly Pavlovich did not see him any longer. All he saw was darkness.

And so perhaps—perhaps it had all been in vain. Perhaps she had already walked so far out of his and Nina's lives that they had nothing more to give her, and now she moved, unrelenting, proud, and all alone, along a path he could not distinguish through the shadows, with waves of dreamy poems splashing through her head, a married underground idol for a lover, and a burning contempt for his own world, a world of the past, a world of acquiescence and accommodation for the sake of survival—and who was to say which of them had been right, and what intervention was powerful enough to make them understand one another? I've lost her, I've lost her, I've lost her forever, little hammers of despair beat inside his heart. And so piercing was his anguish that, without resisting, without thinking, he accepted two odd-looking bluish aspirin from the grinning elevator man, swallowed them with difficulty, his mouth dry, and then stood, closing his eyes in order not to see the pulsating sea of avid faces, stood waiting for his headache to subside, for the nightmare to end. . . .

But as he waited, out of the confusion about him, out of the chaos in his mind, a voice rose, Boris Tumanov's voice—the voice his daughter loved, or thought she loved, or hoped she loved—and despite himself, he found himself listening. And now this brittle, sensitive, floating voice began to sing other songs, unusual songs, songs that flowed without a perceptible melody, one verse spilling into another, words metamorphosing in mid-syllable, sometimes drowning despondently in the troubled strumming, sometimes soaring above a quiet lull— songs that were at times incoherent, at times jarring, occasionally lyrical and occasionally terrifying, but always gripping, always exacting a toll paid in raw emotion on the roads to their meaning—songs about the true color of souls dissected on a laboratory table in a secret government project; or a one-winged angel caught and exhibited in a cage in a Moscow zoo until set free by a drunken janitor; or a despairing genius walking on shards of glass to reach the gold at the end of a rainbow, only to meet there another unhappy, lost person with bleeding feet; or a saint who had spent all his years preparing for his grand entry into heaven, only to discover on his deathbed that heaven was not some blue expanse full of angelic string quartets and opalescent clouds, but an eternity granted for reliving one's happiest moments, and that he had none to remember; or an old man who had wasted what talent he had for nothing, but now, at the very conclusion of his long, joyless, servile life, finally found the courage to fly—and was unable to stop crawling. . . .

And the more he listened, the more his head swam and the more he knew these songs to be unlike anything he had ever heard, and yet in spirit—in their high-pitched mix of hope and anger and sadness and desire to change the world, to bring beauty into it—so much like the talks that had kept him up for dizzying twenty-hour stretches at the blessed gatherings of his own youth, his slightly postponed, second youth of 1956; and the intensely expectant faces around him were the feverishly serious faces of his past companions, his teachers, his friends, his brothers in awaited martyrdom if need be; and the very air in this suddenly unrecognizable place, this oddly churchlike place with smoking incense and dancing candles, was trembling once more with the faith of old. The faith he himself had upheld for a few short, inspired, brilliant years, the best years of his life maybe—the faith he had lost when faced, at Christ's age of thirty-three, in the Year of Our Lord 1962, with his own fork in the road, his own choice between crucifixion and . . . and . . .

He caught himself tottering on the brink of the private hell to which he had long ago canceled all admission, and hastily opened his eyes, only to discover that they had always been open. The disembodied voice that had awoken such happy, such painful echoes inside him had faded away, and applause was sweeping through the world. He too clapped, trying to read his watch as he did so, but the hands seemed broken, rotating loosely and changing direction now and again. All the same, he knew hours had passed, for his soul was spent. Just as the invisible singer was announcing that in conclusion he would present the promised performance piece and nonsensically asking everyone to "please put on the ties," Sukhanov made his unsteady way out of the press of excited humanity, back into the deserted corridor.

Things were largely amiss here, he saw quickly. Candles, left without observation, were jumping mischievously from counter to counter; a few paintings had turned upside down, sending villages, forests, and lakes down the skies in rivulets of running watercolors; nearby, a flock of horses had burst out of their frame and trotted gracefully, hooves up, along the underside of a bookshelf. As he walked, he tripped over shadows that lay on the ground like unswept leaves. Worse yet, most objects had a shimmering, hazy glow about them, making him suspect that as soon as he turned his back on them, they ceased to be what they pretended and transformed into something else entirely—a shoe into an umbrella, an umbrella into an imp, an imp into a cloud—or maybe even slipped altogether into some different, fourth, dimension, melting forever in the labyrinths of existence. In a way, it seemed only appropriate that everything should be so strange and uncertain, but his head hurt more than ever, his heart tingled unpleasantly, and he felt an urgent need to immerse himself in a pool of quiet and sleep for a while—or watch the colors flitting like zigzagging dragonflies across the underside of his eyelids.

Haltingly he moved deeper and deeper, farther and farther, with each step collecting the large, humid roses that fell off the wallpaper onto his upturned palms, then offering them, in one luxurious, aromatic bouquet, to a short-haired adolescent girl in a yellow dress who at that moment chanced to walk toward him, her small boyish face as familiar as everyone else's (for, of course, he had seen them all before), her lips half open in laughter. The girl gave him a wide-eyed look and, letting the flowers drop to the floor, ran off, shouting a name he had seemingly heard before: "Ksiusha! Ksiusha!"

He followed her with tired eyes, then, crushing the delicate rose blossoms under his feet, turned into an alley, passed through a doorway almost invisible under the graffiti, rose up an evil-smelling staircase to the third floor, and after checking again the address scrawled on a tram ticket, knocked on one of the peeling doors. A fierce fellow with a spade-shaped beard let him in. Murmuring hellos, Anatoly navigated the smoky, sparsely furnished space of the crowded room and sank into a moaning couch at the back, almost out of sight, feeling a bit awkward because he knew only a couple of people here by name and no one at all closely, and the acquaintance who had invited him was running late. For almost an hour he sat quietly, nursing a glass of vodka and listening, with growing interest soon turning into excitement, to an older man with a nervously agile face, whose place this was, softly explaining his theory of art's demise.

"From its very birth at the dawn of humanity," the man was saying in a mild voice bred of generations of intellectuals, "pictorial art has served two separate functions: ritualistic and decorative. In its primitive stages, art amounted to, on the one hand, drawing pictures of slain animals on cave walls to ensure some friendly spirit's help in a hunt, and on the other, fashioning necklaces out of seashells to make savage women more bearable to look at. Gradually, as man matured, these two original functions—communicating with the spirit world and making the present world more pleasant to live in—crystallized into what I see as art's two great raisons d'être, if you will: the search for the Divine and the search for Beauty. In the Dark Ages, when man was weighed down by superstitions, the Divine predominated at the expense of Beauty, but at the very peak of artistic development—and by that, of course, I mean the age of the Renaissance—the two searches grew more and more intertwined until they became one. And for one brief moment God was Beauty, nature was God, and the Divine and the Beautiful could be found equally in Titian's voluptuous nudes and in Mantegna's emaciated saints. This miraculous balance lasted hardly more than a century, yet it brought about a flowering of genius so extraordinary that it sustains us to this day. But inevitably, as the world moved on, life gained the upper hand over art, and the seventeenth and eighteenth centuries, with their new mantras of enlightenment and reason, led to the beginning of the end. As art's two purposes drifted apart once again, creation found itself boxed into increasingly narrow compartments: portrait, epic painting, genre painting, religious painting, landscape, still life. . . . Then, with the advent of our own monstrous age of machines and secularism, Beauty was killed by industrialization, God was declared persona non grata by so-called progressive thinkers, and thus, in a blink of time, both higher artistic purposes lost all meaning. What are we left with? A sad bunch of labels and occasional pathetic attempts to recover at least something of art's previous glory, either by desperate proclaimers of art for art's sake, who try to restore Beauty but invariably end up painting poodles and shepherdesses or the aesthetic equivalent thereof, or by eager revolutionaries who seek the Divine in a red banner of humanity, hoping to use art for the common good as if it were a loaf of bread or a pair of boots—needless to say, in vain, for a purpose does not become sacred merely by virtue of being noble."

"So why continue to paint at all if art is dead?" the bearded man said, scowling.

"Christ was also dead once," replied the other sternly. "It is precisely art's resurrection that must become your mission as artists today."

Loudly they cheered, and toasted each other's health and palettes, and drank, and passed around the bottle, and drank again, and someone went off to find a jazz record a friend had just brought from Prague, and someone else was beginning to talk about a book of reproductions of some crazy Spanish artist he liked; but amid the general exuberance, no one had thought to ask the most important question—the only question really, as I saw it.

"How?" I said in an undertone, and when no one heard me, asked again, this time shouting over the noise, "How can we resurrect art? What are we supposed to *do*?"

Immediately everyone fell silent and turned toward me, perhaps trying to recall exactly who I was and who had brought me here— and just then the front door opened, and my long-awaited acquaintance walked in. Seeing them all looking at me, he said happily, with that radiant gift of a smile he possessed, "Ah, good, you've all met Tolya already." And instantly, amid the erupting shouts of "Finally!" and "Levka, come here!" and "Lev Borisovich, do us the honor of accepting this glass of disgusting home brew!" my momentous question was forgotten.

Or rather, not forgotten but postponed, for after that exulted, inebriated night, I too became a regular at Yastrebov's place. And all through the spring of 1956 we met at least weekly, and sometimes more often, and talked about history and Russia and life and death and, above all, art, the subject closest to our hearts—talked while perpetually drunk with exhilaration and daring and exhaustion, talked until tiny shards of smashed stars visible through a bleary window dissipated in the chilly white haze of another sunrise. And when we grew hoarse, we listened to jazz, the music of our private revolution, the sounds of its saxophones and trumpets filling our cramped quarters like gigantic, slowly unwinding golden coils, the sounds of its pianos soothing like cold fingers massaging away a headache; or excitedly passed around reproductions of Western painters, absently brought from abroad by well-fed and oblivious well-wishers with their diplomatic leather briefcases, or surreptitiously torn, by all of us in turn, out of those splendid art volumes we were allowed to handle briefly at the Lenin Library; or else discussed in half-whispers the precious nuggets of past truths mined collectively out of recent newspaper articles and our own, frequently misunderstood and misremembered, childhoods, comparing stories of grandfathers' and fathers' arrests—and sometime in the course of that breathtaking, galloping year, I was presented with the magnificent gift of Viktor Yastrebov's dream.

He was always the most eloquent of us all, our teacher, our leader, our host; but one night in the early summer his mind seemed to soar as never before, and he talked about art being reborn like a phoenix, rising from its own ashes in a sublime union of the earthly and the divine—a union, he said, that was possible only here, in the one truly mystical land, and only now, as the country broke out of the confines of its dark, spiritually impoverished past. He talked about our duty as artists to find Beauty without and God within, and then carry our vision to the world—"For Russia shall become the new Italy, and ours will be the next Renaissance!"—and his words spread fire through our veins and wound up our souls. Lev alone sat silent through the hours that to me felt like one brief, dazzling, inspired flight: toasting with us, and nodding, but visibly unmoved.

We parted earlier than usual that night, each of us feeling that anything said or done after Yastrebov's outburst would diminish the power of his generous message to us. By chance, Lev and I fell into step on the stairs and proceeded together along the deserted street.

"You looked bored tonight," I said to him, almost with dislike. "Don't you agree with what Yastrebov was saying?"

I had first encountered Lev Belkin a good half-decade before. Three years my junior, he too had attended the Surikov Institute, and although we had not known each other formally, our subsequent acquaintance caused me to extract a vague memory of seeing him between lectures in corridors the color of disease—I in my last year of classes, he in his second. In 1955, having graduated with distinction, Belkin was appointed as a teacher at my institute, and now introduced officially, we resumed our daily ritual of passing each

other in this or that hallway. In his first week at work, he stopped by
my studio, looked at my canvases, and left without saying anything; I
found his attitude disdainful and paid him in kind. I did not know
what prompted him one day the next spring, unexpectedly, to invite
me to a gathering of his friends—perhaps something he thought he
had glimpsed in my paintings, or more likely, the atmosphere of
reverberating revelations that was sweeping Russia, and us, off our
feet. Yet even though I owed to him my inclusion in Yastrebov's
circle, we had failed to become close and rarely, if ever, talked alone.

"It's not that I disagree," he replied thoughtfully. "It's just
that . . . Viktor is a brilliant conversationalist, of course, but . . . He
says we can't paint honestly until we find God within us—but what
does that mean, exactly? What if every time I look too deeply, I keep
seeing the devil instead of God? And even if I find God, how do I
know for sure He's the right one? Does it follow I shouldn't paint
until I figure it all out?"

"But aren't these questions ultimately important?" I asked, taken
aback.

"Important? Yes, of course," he said slowly, "but important only
to me as a human being, not to me as an artist. Man has mind and
gullet and cock to satisfy, but a true artist has only eyes with which to
see the world, soul with which to understand it, and hands with
which to render it—nothing else. Sometimes all these words we
throw at each other make me feel . . . I don't know . . . suffocated, I
guess. I keep thinking, we are not in the business of philosophy, we
are in the business of painting—and instead of devoting so much
energy to puzzling out some misty theories of God and Beauty,
shouldn't we just paint our hearts out and let the crowds, and the
future, make what they will of us and our work?"

We were alone in the whole city, it seemed. Streetlamps along the
boulevards glowed with cold lavender fire, dilapidated churches
raised their black dragon heads into the clouded skies, and in the

darkened islands of parks, drunks who were nightly tossed out of the chaos of Moscow onto vandalized benches moaned in their restless sleep. And it was precisely then that it happened—summoned to life not by all the past communal revelations of our gatherings but by Lev's simple protest. It was then that I felt a desire to paint once again—paint truly, paint freely, paint as I last had done many years ago.

And for the next half-hour, as the two of us walked through the sleeping universe in wordless companionship, passing pale ghosts of blossoming lilac bushes and dark ghosts of linden trees on our way, I sensed other ghosts following me closely in the flower-scented obscurity, their steps soundless, their smiles fleeting, their lives begging to be spilled out onto canvas—an old Arbat professor in love with Italy, a shy provincial teacher who had tasted of Chagall's blue soul, a broken man who had once been so passionate about flying, and his fourteen-year-old son who had once dreamt of discovering his own, never-before-seen colors. . . . And in that one half-hour, I understood with the utmost clarity that from now on, my existence could no longer consist of one protracted apology for my father's unknown missteps, and that I myself was no longer content to serve as a voluntary cog in a disjointed mechanism by day and dream the unearthly dreams of others by night—and that the only things that counted for me now were a blank page, a brush, and a jewel-bright assortment of oils. And already that night, as Lev, whose own apartment was too far to reach on foot, fell asleep on my bed, I tore a sheet out of an old scrapbook, found some dried-out watercolors, and tried to paint the hour before the sunrise just as I saw it through my wide-open window: a light mist swirling over blackened roofs, a soon-to-be-released warmth in the silent air, a stray cat tiptoeing along a windowsill, and a blissful drunk drawing the red edge of the sun in the lower right corner of the paling skies. . . .

During that summer, I became a less frequent presence at Yastre-bov's gatherings: I was too busy working. Lev came less often as well, not so much because of a difference of opinion, but because, as I heard it joked about repeatedly, he was preoccupied with courting some elusive flirt. After our talk that June night, he and I saw each other alone more and more, but I never asked about the girl, and he never told me—which was why in the end I was so unprepared to meet her when one day in early September he brought her to one of our evenings.

She walked into the room—and I would like to say that my friends fell silent or that the room lit up at once—but they did not, and it did not, and everyone but me continued drinking and shout-ing, and in any case, such stock phrases of a cheap novelist could never explain exactly how I felt when faced with my own perfect vision of beauty. She walked into the room, tall, thin, and graceful, and so young, a flimsy scarf the color of the sea trailing in the air after her, a pair of fluid spiral earrings dangling along her neck, the proud Lev following a step behind. Not in the least put out by the din, the crumpled newspapers, the heaps of records, the empty bottles, she moved through the room nodding to people and shaking hands and smiling as if she had always known them—and suddenly, there she was with her hand outstretched, her green mermaid eyes fully upon me.

"Nina Malinina," she said serenely. Her hand felt cool in mine, and in my stunned mind, Pushkin's immortal tribute to his beloved rang out like a clear crystal bell: *Chisteishei prelesti chisteishii obrazets.* The purest image of the purest charm.

"Malinina?" I repeated, and sensing that she was about to move on and desperate to hold on to her, hurriedly attempted to open a conversation. "Undoubtedly no connection to Pyotr Malinin," I said, ignoring Lev's wild signals behind her back, "that pompous old ass whose lectures I had the misfortune of attending at the Surikov?"

Her eyes, as she looked at me, paled to a grayer shade.

"That pompous old ass," she said quietly, "is my father. . . ."

"Damn," said a voice from the distant bottom of a well, "he seems rather badly off."

And another voice shouted, "Hey, someone, go get Borya! She says this old fogey passed out on the floor here is her father!"

A shuffle ensued, and jolted and prodded in several places at once, Sukhanov made an immense effort to raise his heavy eyelids. At first he felt he was drowning in glimmering, shifting milk, but after a while shapes began to emerge, and presently he found his fifty-six-year-old self lying on the carpet in his study, with a few curious faces leaning over him—and among them, amazingly, an eighteen-year-old Nina, her lips twisted with concern, and behind her, Lev Belkin, bright-eyed and disheveled and eternally young, for some reason clutching a guitar and wearing a wine-red tie. Sukhanov stared for a moment, then decided it was better to keep his eyes closed after all and just lie back, letting a familiar voice wash over him in anxious waves.

"Papa, Papa, are you all right?" the voice was saying. "This wasn't supposed to happen, they were all going to be gone before you got home. . . . Oh God, I'm so sorry. . . . Boris had this concert scheduled, but then the auditorium fell through at the last minute, and I thought . . . Papa, can you even hear me? Shall I call a doctor?"

He opened his eyes again. The contours of the universe had grown sharper. Ksenya, not Nina, was bending over him, and behind her knelt an unfamiliar man, still wearing the tie and, true, bearing some vague resemblance to the young Belkin—but not Belkin.

"Papa, please say something!" Ksenya kept repeating.

Sukhanov blinked and looked closer.

"Is . . . that . . . my . . . tie?" he said laboriously.

Her hand flew to her mouth. "Oh no, I forgot about those!" she said. The young man hastily started to tear the tie from his neck. "You see, Boris needed some ties . . . and by the way, this is Boris, my boyfriend. . . . He's written this piece, performance art, you know—"

" 'Song of the Bureaucrats,' " pseudo-Belkin explained contritely.

"Shut up," Ksenya said in a furious whisper, then went on rapidly. "He didn't mean any harm, he just . . . just borrowed the ties last Sunday when he stopped by, and I only found out about it tonight. It was supposed to be a joke, see? Of course, he was very upset when I told him about Valya, but don't worry, we'll fix it, and the ties are all here, they're all fine. . . ."

"I spilled some wine on mine," said someone from the back of the room. "Sorry."

And suddenly it was all too much, and he was finding it hard to breathe, and pseudo-Belkin was rushing off to throw open a window, and a short-haired adolescent girl—whose name, he somehow knew, was Lina—was pressing a glass of water to his lips, while Ksenya squeezed his hand and repeated helplessly, in a thin voice, "I'm so sorry, it's all my fault, you've fallen sick because of me—"

"Oh, I wouldn't worry too much about him, it will wear off shortly," a new voice pronounced jauntily, and the grinning face framed by the salmon-colored scarf materialized in the fog above Sukhanov. Then matters quickly disintegrated into confusion once again. In the hazy distance, he heard Ksenya asking sharp, accusing questions whose essence he could not follow, and the elevator man protesting in an offended patter, then Ksenya shouting, "Grishka, how could you, you bastard!" and a multitude of other voices rising like mist from the edges of the room. . . .

All of this, however, increasingly failed to concern him, for as he continued to look at the elevator man, he saw something wonderful happening—happening slowly but inexorably. An enormous balloon was emerging carefully, gently out of the man's shaved head. Strangely, no one else seemed to notice, but that did not bother him in the least—in truth, it made the moment all the more precious. Once free, the gorgeous yellow balloon hung in the air for one wavering minute, and then with quiet dignity swam through the open window, rose into the skies, and there turned into a most golden, most perfect full moon.

Yes, of course, thought Anatoly Pavlovich with a happy little smile—and floated out the window after it.

FIFTEEN

For a while he lay without moving. A wide patch of sunshine crept across his face, and from its brightness he deduced that it was late, at least ten o'clock, perhaps drawing closer to eleven; yet he felt reluctant to open his eyes, enjoying as he was this leisurely moment—a man half asleep, resting in his bed on a Saturday morning (here a needle of unexplained anxiety pricked his heart, but he pushed on stubbornly), yes, resting in his bed, in his freshly laundered pajamas, on a summer morning, as was his right, with nothing in particular to do, and nowhere to go, and a whole pleasant day ahead of him. He was nearly awake, but a few shadowy creatures from a recent dream still scurried about the hazy edges of his memory—and the most nonsensical dream it had been too, involving a misshapen angel in a zoo cage, a man whose head gave birth to an inflated balloon, and a crowd of hippies and rock musicians holding a disreputable concert in his very own living room. Groggily, he marveled that a mind

normally so devoid of surprises could be capable of such nightmarish notions.

A telephone began to ring, loud and insistent. After each ring
there was a pause just long enough to make him hope it would stop,
but invariably the next ring would come, torturously protracted,
filling his head with reverberations of the headache he now realized
he had. Grumbling, he groped for the nightstand on which the
telephone rested, then, not able to feel it, opened his eyes with an
effort—and found himself confronted with several truths. He was
not in his bedroom but in the living room, crammed painfully
between the armrests of a decoratively small couch. He wore a pitiful-
looking suit. The air smelled of stale incense, and his mouth tasted
as if a small animal had died somewhere inside his entrails. It was no
longer morning—the clock on the opposite wall showed half past
one; and it was possibly not Saturday either. On the coffee table, next
to the screaming telephone, lay a pile of sad remains that on closer
observation proved to be his once proud collection of ties.

And of course, he had known it, known it since the very first
moment of semiwakefulness, felt it in his nauseated, aching body,
guessed it with his sickened heart—and still had tried to move as far
away from it as possible, to hide like a frightened child in the soft
oblivion of lingering sleep—for sleep at least was peaceful, sleep at
least did not assault him with the terrifying dreams that were becoming his life, his daily life. And now his life was right here, pressing
down on him, breathing into his face, demanding that he get up and
answer the ringing telephone, and go apologize to Valya, whom he
had offended so badly, and face his daughter, whose friends were
all madmen and drug addicts and who was probably a drug addict
herself . . .

Stumbling off the couch, he yanked at the receiver.

"Well, finally!" Pugovichkin spoke cheerfully. "I was beginning to
wonder. Listen, I'm so glad you decided to keep the Chagall piece

unchanged. I promise you'll be pleased with the issue, it was all finished yesterday, a real beauty—we put his *Self-Portrait with Muse* on
the cover, and inside—"

"Ah," said Sukhanov, "then yesterday was Saturday after all."

A small silence fell. He buried his hands in the mass of his
stained, wrinkled, mistreated ties and twirled their silk corpses
about his fingers. Somehow, the Chagall controversy had lost all its
urgency in his mind, overshadowed by other, infinitely more vital
matters. He felt his whole being expanding with grief for things misplaced, and forfeited, and possibly missed forever—and where such
grief reigned, petty anger could find no place.

"Anatoly Pavlovich, is everything all right?" Pugovichkin said
uncertainly. "You sound . . . odd."

"Oh, I just woke up," Sukhanov explained. "I was drugged last
night."

His recollection of the previous night's events dissolved at some
nebulous juncture into a shimmering, emotional haze filled with
visions of himself worshipping some deceased divinity in the solemn
sonorousness of a cathedral, and his past and present ran together
confusingly; but he remembered the subsequent burn of the carpet
on his neck, the feeling of heavy, helpless humiliation, and Ksenya's
face close to his, begging him, begging him to forgive her. . . . He
wondered how he would find her today—meekly apologetic still, or
stubborn and remote, as unapproachable as ever.

"By whom? Drugged by whom?" Pugovichkin's increasingly shrill
voice repeated in the distance. "Drugged *where*?"

"Here, at my place," said Sukhanov. "There was an underground
concert, and then this fellow with a balloon inside his head—"

His eyes fell on a folded piece of paper lying on the table, with the
words "To papa" scrawled across its whiteness. As the rest of the
world faded away, he reached for it, held it in both hands for an
instant, then opened it and, swallowing, began to read.

Dear papa, what happened yesterday was ugly and unnecessary, and I'm very sorry about it. But maybe it's better to know than to stay ignorant, and now you've had a glimpse of who I really am, of the things that are important to me, of the man in my life. I should tell you that he is married, but it doesn't matter to us. . . .

Sharply he drew in his breath, and all at once became aware of a crackling void on the other end of the line.

"Listen, Sergei Nikolaevich," he said weakly, "this isn't a very good time. Unless there was something in particular you wanted to tell me—"

"As a matter of fact, there is, Anatoly Pavlovich," said Pugovichkin's hesitant voice. "Now, please don't take this the wrong way, we value your work immensely, but we've all been a little worried about you, and, well . . . we think it might be good for you to get some rest."

"Rest?" repeated Sukhanov. He kept tracing the next few lines of the note with his finger, desperately trying to uncover some other possible meaning—any other meaning apart from the one that had just slapped him in the face. *I don't expect you to like it, nor do I expect you to understand it. You have your principles, whatever they are, and I have mine. After last night, I believe you will not want to see me for a while, so I'm moving out. I think it's best for now. . . .*

"Yes, take two or three weeks off," Pugovichkin was saying uncomfortably, "even a month, if you like. Relax, go to the countryside, spend some time rereading the classics—"

"And what if I don't want to relax?" said Sukhanov flatly. *Don't worry about me, I'll be staying with good friends of mine.* "Whose idea is it? Yours? Ovseev's?"

"Yes, mine, and Ovseev's too," said Pugovichkin quickly. "Well, actually . . . Listen, I don't think I'm supposed to say anything, but what the hell, I owe it to you, Tolya. Mikhail Burykin called me confidentially this morning—you know, that big shot from the Ministry of

Culture—and . . . I can't guess who's spreading this rumor, and of course, I tried to do my best to dissuade him, but . . . he was quite convinced you were somewhat . . . er . . . unwell. A bit too . . . wound up, you know? He said *Art of the World* was better off without you for the time being, and . . . and I hate to tell you this, but it seems the Minister agrees with him. But it will be for a short time only, you understand, and your absence will of course be voluntary, just while they review your case—"

"They are letting me go," said Sukhanov slowly. "Looks like he did it after all."

"Burykin? You've had run-ins with him before?"

"Not Burykin, Burykin is just a pawn. My fake cousin is the one behind it. . . ." Sukhanov exhaled, then said after a pause, in a different, suddenly quivering voice, "Not that it matters any longer. I hate doing it anyway. Always hated it. Going through other people's texts as through dirty laundry, deleting every avoidable reference to God and lowercasing all the unavoidable ones, ferreting out the names of all the blacklisted artists, always sticking these Lenin quotes everywhere—how disgusting! Not the kind of thing that makes your children respect you, you know? Or do your children still respect you, Serezha?"

The note trembled in his hand. *I hope you feel better today. Grishka is such a—* The phrase was crossed out. *I'm sorry if I hurt you, but I think it was bound to happen, one way or another. These are my friends, and this is my life, and I'm not ashamed of it even if you are. You and I are very different people, papa. I suppose you know I love you—but as I've recently discovered, love solves nothing, nothing at all. If anything, it only causes more problems. Ksenya. P.S. Mama will know how to reach me.*

After a long, embarrassed silence, Pugovichkin was talking again, mumbling that this whole thing was temporary, he had no doubt they would let him come back to the magazine soon, of course they would, how could they not, after everything he, Sukhanov, had done for them. . . .

"Never mind all that," Sukhanov said, and folded the note. He waited for his voice to lose its sobbing edge, then asked, "How was the fishing? Catch anything good?"

For the remaining afternoon hours he wandered through his deserted kingdom like a ghost of his former self. Lost my position, lost my son, lost my daughter, he kept repeating, his voice running up and down the scale of despair, from a nearly silent whisper to a fist-smashing-into-the-wall shout. His job did not concern him any longer, but his children—his misjudged, his misguided children, his responsibility, his punishment . . . He could not bear to think how blind he had been all these years—so proud of Vasily, the smooth-talking boy with wintry eyes, so disapproving of Ksenya, with her bristling remarks and unnervingly dark adolescent poems—and all along, Vasily had been the reflection of what was worst in him, and Ksenya of what was best, and he had not stopped the one, and had not helped the other, and now it was simply too late, for they had moved forever beyond his reach. He had failed—he had failed both of them.

And then he felt tired, so very tired, of every past and present burden of guilt that all he wanted to do was collect his many failures—failure as a critic, as a father, and a few others besides—yes, collect them all and bring them to Nina, and dropping them at her feet, beg her for forgiveness, beg her for absolution. . . . He wanted, he needed her near him, as never before. His hands unsteady, his fingers repeatedly missing the digits, he dialed their dacha number, heard a hateful busy signal, waited a few minutes, and dialed again. This time he listened, with bated breath, to the faint sounds of distant ringing. There was no answer.

Sighing, he rose and slowly walked through the still rooms, everywhere seeking and finding cherished echoes of her presence: foreign fashion magazines discarded on ottomans and sofas, a lonely slipper poking its pink silky nose from underneath a chair, a face mask resting by the bathtub, her features still lightly imprinted on it. . . . But as he followed Nina's recent trail around the apartment, he felt surprisingly little comfort, and in a while found himself moving faster and breathing heavier in his chase of her shadow—for unexpectedly he had begun to perceive signs of an uncharacteristic absentmindedness, perhaps even secret restlessness, behind all her abandoned, forgotten things. He stumbled on a pair of ruby earrings tossed onto a bookshelf, a peach pit left to dry on a windowsill—inexplicable, disconcerting lapses; and as his attention sharpened, little details from the past, a whole multitude of oddly demanding trivial details, buzzed in his memory like a swarm of disturbed bees. He thought of the vague expression on her face as she had sat looking out the window, her chin running with fruit juice: when their eyes had met, he had felt he could almost see a mermaid's glistening body dive with the startled wave of a tail into the green waters of her far-off gaze. He recalled her listless movements at recent meals, and her frequent migraines, and that Sunday she had spent in bed, yet wearing a profusion of bracelets as if for an outing—the very same Sunday, he realized with a jolt, when Ksenya's boyfriend must have walked into the bedroom unseen by anyone and taken all his ties. . . . A chill crept stealthily up his spine. Had she been napping perhaps and not woken up at the sound of closet doors shutting and clothes being ripped off the hooks—she, the lightest sleeper he knew?

Ceasing to roam, he stood very still, seized with a sudden terror of losing her too. The feeling was, of course, irrational, for did not their twenty-eight years of marriage offer him reassurance enough? So she had not been home that Sunday afternoon—could she not have stepped out to buy dessert for her tea or to chat with their neighbors? Yet with so many losses wreaking devastation in his heart, he felt compelled to tread carefully now, lest he offend some envious divinity even further with undue presumptuousness and ungrateful complacency. No, never again would he dare to accept any certainty with that bovine sense of simply receiving his due. . . .

And in truth, spoke a tiny insidious voice inside him, just how certain a certainty was it, really? How confident of their closeness was he—how well did he know the inner workings of one Nina Sukhanova? She had never been easy to understand, and he had long since learned to allow her small pockets of privacy by not dwelling on her manifold silences and not pursuing to its hidden origin her every expression or gesture or even absence, habitually interpreting these mysterious lacunae as evidence of her unique brand of feminine mystique. Now, for the first time, he felt unsure. He saw that little by little, as these omissions had multiplied between them, the very essence of Nina's life had somehow become obscured, until he could guess at neither the timbre of her thoughts nor a roster of her activities. Oh, naturally, he knew all about her museum visits with his fake relatives and her theater outings with her fashionable girlfriends; yet between these major blocks of time, each day still contained numerous cracks, small enough to pass unnoticed but wide enough for . . . for . . .

And again he froze, his thoughts running aground on another disturbing half-memory he had so casually misfiled in the cabinets of his past. On the evening when Nina had gone to see the play at the Malyi, she had told him, her lips gleaming with that unfamiliar shade of lipstick, that their chauffeur had wanted the night off—yet Vadim had acted almost affronted when Sukhanov had mentioned it later. He paced along the corridor, willing himself not to panic. And he had nearly succeeded in burying the incident in a communal grave with the safely vague epitaph "Misunderstanding," when yet another unbidden recollection rose, and not for the first time, to the foreground of his mind, and he finally perceived the main reason for his feeling of unease—a feeling that had been there all along. The memory of the mangled theater bill from the Malyi's last season, which the August wind had deposited so deftly at his feet, presented him now with a clear mental snapshot of a soggy May date printed at the top—and in doing so, triggered his belated realization of a plain fact of life in Moscow. All city theaters closed their doors for the summer, reopening again only in the early days of September.

No, *most* theaters, he corrected himself in desperation—most, but not all—and it was altogether possible that the Malyi had begun its season earlier this year. What had she said she'd gone to see that Wednesday? *Three Sisters,* had it been, or *Uncle Vanya?* He did not remember. Then, before he could stop himself, it occurred to him that a Sunday newspaper would carry the list of weekly performances—and that his answer therefore lay close, only eight floors below, in the mailbox of apartment fifteen. . . .

Disgusted with his doubts, he forced himself to turn his thoughts away, to find some occupation for his restlessness. Again he walked through the rooms, picking up random novels and dropping them after reading a page or two, snacking on frozen carrots from a solitary package he discovered in the fridge, leafing through a family address book in search of he knew not whose number. Chancing upon the letter V, he was surprised to see, among a multitude of Varlamovs and Vostrikovs, most of them his work contacts (now former), a single line in Nina's delicate handwriting. "Viktor," it said next to the number. No last name, no way of knowing when the entry had been made . . . Thoughtfully he looked at it, then stood, and moving as if in a dream, picked up his keys and went out to the elevator.

Perhaps his hands shook too much, or maybe there was some unknown trick to opening the mailbox—Valya had always brought up their mail; he himself had not bothered with it in years. Whatever the cause, the key became promptly stuck in the lock, and as he tugged at it in frustration, he felt it beginning to bend. Swearing soundlessly, he looked up, and found the ancient concierge watching him with malevolent curiosity from his perch behind the desk.

"A problem, Anatoly Pavlovich?" the old man inquired, his lips rustling dryly against toothless gums.

"The key is stuck," Sukhanov replied, and shrugged with studied indifference. "No matter, I'll come back later. I just wanted to scan the newspaper."

"No point in reading newspapers nowadays," said the concierge, getting up with a great show of difficulty. "I remember the time when every day you'd wake up to read about a new hero of socialist labor or an overperforming collective farm. A man's heart was always full of joy and pride in his country." He shuffled across the hall at a funeral pace. "But the distasteful things they print today . . ." He made as if to spit, then thought better of it, and simply waved his hand. "Listen to an old man, Anatoly Pavlovich, don't read the garbage."

"I won't," Sukhanov promised. "Now, about this key . . . It appears I can't pull it out."

"Allow me," said the concierge, bending over the lock. A faint odor of smoked fish emanated from his cardigan. "Apartment fifteen, let me think. . . . Aha, just one tiny little push down, like so . . . and now a sharp turn to the right, like this . . . and here you are."

He performed the operation with astonishing agility, twisting the key in some complicated and seemingly well-practiced ritual, and Sukhanov's initial surprise turned to distaste. As the mailbox swung open, the concierge peered inside.

"That's funny—no newspaper," he said, and quickly, before Sukhanov could even move, scooped inside the box and emerged with three pieces of mail grasped firmly in his yellowing fingers. "Now, what might this be? Aha, a telephone bill, something official-looking addressed to you, and a private letter—to Nina Petrovna, by the looks of it . . . Well, here you go, Anatoly Pavlovich."

The letter, in a small white envelope, had a stamp with a golden deer on it; its address was penned in lavender ink, in handwriting Sukhanov did not recognize. As he accepted it, his hands trembled, and the presence of the old man hovering before him, watching him with those nastily glinting eyes, made him feel suddenly dirty, as if the two of them had just violated some sacred trust, irreparably damaged something fragile and beautiful. . . . Wincing, he slipped the mail into his pocket without a second glance and, with a curt "Thank you," began to walk away.

"Wait a second, Anatoly Pavlovich, I have something for you," the concierge called out from his desk. "Found it on the sidewalk this morning." From a creaking drawer he extracted a filthy rag of checkered wool and proffered it to Sukhanov. "Your scarf, I believe?"

Sukhanov looked at it for a full minute.

"No," he finally said, and turning away, pressed the elevator button. "It's not mine."

"Strange, I could swear I saw you wearing it last winter," said the concierge, smiling suggestively. "Although you probably wouldn't want it anyway. Looks like some dogs have mauled it pretty badly. Still, maybe Nina Petrovna could use it as a washrag. I mean, now that Valentina Aleksandrovna doesn't work for you anymore."

"It's not mine," Sukhanov repeated—and then, mercifully, the elevator arrived.

Back in his study, he impassively skimmed an impersonal message from the publishing staff of *The Great Soviet Encyclopedia* informing him that the planned edition with his biography was being postponed until further notice, then gave the telephone bill a cursory look, noting a call to Vologda he did not remember making, and set them aside, along with the letter to Nina. The absence of the newspaper, though irritating, was not out of the ordinary; it was at times misdelivered by the postman, and occasionally stolen, perhaps by the very concierge who appeared so skillful with locks. In any case, his brief sojourn downstairs had convinced him to abandon his distrustful pursuit, for he had sensed that it belonged in spirit to an underworld of sinister old men and disgruntled domestics who poked through people's mail and gossiped by trash chutes in search of their betters' soiled little secrets. Shuddering squeamishly, with one last glance at the letter—addressed, with a rather peculiar familiarity, to "N.S."—he left to try the dacha number again. There was still no answer.

He returned to the study later that evening. Darkness was stealing in rapidly; he switched on his Pegasus lamp. A few manuscripts were gathering dust in the corner of his desk, all of them materials to be reviewed for future magazine issues—now never to be subjected to his famously strict scrutiny, he thought, and smiling without mirth, brushed them to the floor with one sweeping gesture. A whirlwind raised by their heavy fall caused a tiny fluttering movement that caught his eye, and he found himself once again looking at the strange letter lying before him.

The deer on the stamp displayed its antlers proudly; there was no return address. The abbreviated "N.S." now struck him unpleasantly, giving the impression of someone in a feverish rush to send off the epistle—or else someone breathlessly intimate with the addressee. . . . After a moment's hesitation, he bent to pick it up, with the intention of placing it on Nina's nightstand. All at once, jolted by the precipitate movement, his glasses started to slide off his nose, and he raised his hand—the hand holding the letter—in a quick attempt to intercept them. As the envelope accidentally became positioned between his eyes and the lamp, he could not help seeing it at the precise instant when the paper grew suffused with a warm coral glow of pervading light. Two or three pages were folded inside, dense and impenetrable at their heart; but a few words, escaping to the margins, emerged to the surface like lucid watermarks. The whole thing had been completely unplanned, he told himself—it had transpired too swiftly—it could not have been prevented. He saw the loose scraps of sentences, read them involuntarily, then lowered his hand slowly, turned off the lamp, and for a long, silent while looked away into nothingness.

The words he had chanced to see were "unlike me," "marr . . . ," "know" (underlined), "just the two of us," and the last one, ". . . pture" or ". . . rture." Torture? Rapture?

As Anatoly Pavlovich sat in the darkness, sliding his finger back and forth along the edge of the envelope, he mused about choices that sometimes ambush a man so unfairly, without a moment's warning, and wresting from him an almost instinctive reaction, in the space of a mere minute change the rest of his life. He could let go of the weight in his hand and, still surrounded by blackness, feel his way out of the room, close the door on his base mistrust, and in a day or two, when Nina returned from the dacha, lightly mention that a letter awaited her on his desk—and afterward, and for all their remaining years, try not to torment himself with not knowing the truth every time he beheld her cold, unreadable, beautiful gaze—yet failing, always failing not to wonder. . . . Or, just as easily, he could flip the light switch, and right here, right now, violently rape the envelope, making it yield all its secrets in pale lavender ink—and immediately, now and for all eternity, feel ashamed, feel deeply, darkly ashamed, feel it like a bad taste in his mouth every time he looked at Nina's tired, dear face that age was already beginning to erase at the edges, forever remembering that on one late-summer evening when his heart had wavered, he had proven unworthy of her and their past—and all for some meaningless bit of women's gossip, some gushing confidence of a casual university friend.

For in the most private recess of his mind, he had no doubt that was all it was—a little note from Liusya, perhaps, dashed off self-indulgently right after the play they had gone to see and redolent with girlish affectations. *Darling Ninusya,* he would read as his hands shook and his damned soul fell, *it was so unlike me to ask you to come on such short notice—but that's what I get for marrying a reporter with a predilection for leaving on an assignment just when we have two tickets to my favorite play. But I just* know *I can always count on you! And didn't it feel so much like the old days—rushing into the theater as the curtain was rising, just the two of us, drinking in Chekhov's divine cadences, and at the intermission watching overdressed provincials and laughing and snacking on those tiny caviar sandwiches they always serve! The glass of champagne at the end was pure rapture, and I certainly hope—*

Oh, he was sure, he was sure that was all it would be—and never mind that Sunday afternoon, or Vadim's evening off, or the theater season, or the unknown Viktor in their address book . . .

Sukhanov switched on the light and ruthlessly tore at the envelope.

My beloved, the two closely written pages began, *letters are dangerous, but you don't let me call you, and in any case, I would never dare to say what I'm about to write. Seeing you so quiet and sad on our last evening together made me realize that things simply can't go on like this for much longer. You made me swear never to bring up our "fake lives," and it is unlike me to renege on a promise—but you must see that it is a much lesser crime to break a promise than to lose something as perfect as what we share. For a long time now, I've tried to do as you asked: to be satisfied with furtive meetings, whispered phone calls, poor, random snatches of your presence. But my nerves are wearing thin, my love, and the unmentionable shadow of your marriage grows darker every time I have to let go of your voice because you think you hear a noise in your entrance hall, every time you emerge from your house and pretend not to notice me waiting just down the street for fear of someone watching at the window, every time we kiss surreptitiously in some doorway.*

My heart has been broken so many times that even our dearest memories cause me nothing but pain now. Do you remember that December night when, a glamorous presence in your short fur-trimmed coat, you knocked on my car window and haughtily asked for a ride across town, and as I slowly drove through the storm, you suddenly broke down crying? The snow was falling and falling, and when I stopped the car in some alley, it soon turned into one big, white, sparkling cave . . . And every time I recall that snowfall, without you by my side, my eyes go black, and helplessness overwhelms me.

And this Wednesday, as I watched you reapply your lipstick and then walk away dejectedly—as I saw you disappear around the corner, not knowing when you would be able to get away again—I finally realized the truth. Dearest, I can no longer bear these constant farewells. I can no longer be content with having you in my present and my past only: I must have you in my future as well. Although I've never told you, you know, you must know, that I have wanted to leave Svetlana ever since that first snowbound kiss—I have just been waiting for you to ask me. I have waited for almost a year now. What are you afraid of, my beloved? Believe me, no comfortable routine of shared space and time could replace the love you and I have stumbled upon, so unexpectedly, so magically—a love that tightens one's throat, tingles in one's veins, makes every moment spent together unquestionably justified and infinitely precious. And it is in the name of that love that I must beg you now: let us be free and selfish like gods, let us leave all our habits and lies behind and start anew, just the two of us, rid of the endless torture of our double lives—and let us do so soon, before the constant humiliation of secrecy, the guilt I feel every time I look at my daughter, the pity you have for your husband slowly drain all joy from our hearts. We both know that what we have is worth any sacrifice we can offer. A long time ago, you told me your husband was kind to you. The truth is, he has never known how to love. You and I do. Please never forget what a rare gift it is.

I must hear from you soon, unless you want me showing up on your doorstep. Your V.

And so it was.

And there were no friends or lovers to whom he could pour out his heart—and no memories that he could uncork and inhale like some miraculously soothing elixir—and no forces of heaven or hell that he could invoke or curse, or to which he could pray—no benevolent divinities, no merciful guardian angels, no dark spirits of the abyss. . . . There was nothing in the whole world but the two pages crumpled in his hand, and the empty black skies of August over his head, and a trembling hole where his soul used to be. For when it finally happened, he saw he was completely alone—alone to stumble, lost, through the ruins of his past life, collecting the remaining pieces—alone to walk through the future dreariness with that gaping void in his insides—and alone to die when the time arrived.

Anatoly Pavlovich Sukhanov methodically smoothed out the pages, slipped them back into the envelope, placed it on the desk, and looked at it in silence. And after a passage of time, when his heart had stopped gasping for air, he understood the source of his deepest pain. The loss of Nina was not the most shattering loss he had suffered: it was the loss of the image of Nina that he mourned the most—that "purest image of the purest charm" he had fallen in love with and cherished for so many years in the most sacred cache of his memory. For the woman in the letter was not the reserved, quietly dignified beauty with whom he had thought he had spent his life, but rather an indecorously middle-aged femme fatale who trotted about the city, wearing her fashionably short fur coat, armed with her bright little lipstick, engrossed in an abandoned affair she had started in a parked automobile and carried on in smelly doorways, with a man so vulgar he could write of love tingling in his veins and of being free and selfish like gods. How could this unbearably trite image, which reeked of life's cheapest perfume, be the answer to the mystery of Nina's dreamy silences? How was it possible to reconcile his decades of accumulated recollections with this pitiful missive smacking of some nineteenth-century epistolary novel, from the painful grandiloquence of its contents to that theatrical "N.S." on the envelope? How could he continue to live with the knowledge that—that—

The envelope.

My God, the envelope!

Sukhanov stared, stared so intensely that the white rectangle swam before his eyes, its very fabric seemingly dissolving into a shimmering leapfrog of particles—only to reassemble a minute later (as a tear, finally released, ran down his cheek) into a creature from an altogether different dimension. The number—the number in the address line—the number he had barely glanced at before, taking it for granted, just as the postman must have done earlier—was it really, truly possible? . . . He moved his hand across the paper, brushing away the optical illusion, but it was still there: that little horizontal dash that was bending a tiny bit to the left instead of to the right and, with that one hair's breadth, granting him life yet again.

Things clicked into place like pieces of a puzzle that only moments before had appeared to suggest some surrealist atrocity—a pale Madonna rolling in a trough with swine—but now revealed a shady flowering garden on a sunny day in late summer, with dark red roses climbing a whitewashed wall. The apartment number was thirteen, not fifteen. The apartment directly below him, then—the apartment of the man who a week earlier had treated his neighbors to a sonorous church chant at four in the morning. The apartment of the songwriter Svechkin, who had had the misfortune of marrying a much younger woman.

But did the name of Svechkin's wife begin with an N?

Tossed so abruptly from such despair to such hope, he had no strength left to wrestle with the remnants of doubt in his heart. He had to know the answer now—and be rid of the darkness forever. The concierge would be able to tell him, of course, but the notion of submitting himself once again to the old man's insinuating scrutiny ("Ah, yes, a pretty lady, isn't she, Anatoly Pavlovich? So, is Nina Petrovna still out of town?") seemed too unbearably ugly a conclusion to such an unbearably ugly day.

After the briefest hesitation, Sukhanov dropped the letter into his pocket, walked out of his place, descended the stairs, and promptly rang the bell of apartment thirteen.

The door opened almost immediately, releasing onto the landing the thundering chords of Beethoven's Fifth and a faint smell of medicine. A short, plump man of Sukhanov's years, in a gabardine jacket, stood on the threshold. He looked at Sukhanov without seeing him, his eyes full of quiet anguish, and just as Sukhanov prepared to launch into a neighborly request for some kitchen utensil (designed to draw out a hollered "Natasha!" or "Nadya!"), said expressionlessly, rubbing his temples as if in pain, "I believe we did it again, didn't we? So terribly sorry, it's all these baths she takes. . . . I'll go tell her to get out, then." And leaving the door wide open, with a pathetic little wave of his hand, he wandered off down the unlit corridor.

Perplexed, Sukhanov waited. The place, or what he saw of it, looked barely lived in. The entrance, the hallway, a slice of one room visible through a cracked door mirrored his own apartment in arrangement, yet resembled a train station in appearance, so transitory everything seemed, so unloved, so full of a jumble of accidental objects—a beach towel tossed over an empty yellow suitcase, a half-peeled orange, a woman's wide-brimmed hat, a glass half full of moldy tea. An enormous brown dog emerged from the darkness and padded in his direction, its head hanging down, then veered to the side, and vanished. The music continued to pour into the corridor, its sounds pockmarked with radio static. All at once, Sukhanov felt certain that very unhappy people lived here—and when in another minute a young woman in a robe walked toward him indolently, smelling of steam and sin and some sweet, dramatic perfume, her face that of a broken porcelain doll, he knew he could leave that instant without ever hearing her name, and his heart would be at peace.

"I'm sorry we keep flooding you, Semyon Semyonovich," she started to say in an indifferent voice, "but you understand, we've been a bit preoccupied ever since Vanya had his little breakdown"— but he had already extracted the ripped envelope from his pocket and was handing it to her in silence.

She looked at it without moving, frowning nearsightedly.

"What's this?" she said, and then, swinging around sharply, shouted with startling shrillness, "Will you turn down that infernal noise? I can't hear a word Semyon Semyonovich is saying!" Her eyebrows were two thin, delicate threads painted on her face.

"I believe it's yours," said Sukhanov softly. "They delivered it to me by accident. I'm afraid I opened it. Naturally, you can count on my—"

She tore the letter out of his hand before he could finish, and carried it close to her eyes; he saw her brightly painted lips begin to tremble. Embarrassed, he nodded and, without another word, turned to leave. Rooms away, Ivan Martynovich Svechkin switched off his music, and his sorrowful voice rang out in the sudden lull behind Sukhanov's back, "Terribly sorry if it was too loud, Nellichka, but you know how I love Beethoven!"

Sukhanov slowly walked upstairs, unaccountably saddened on behalf of that meek little stranger whose life was falling apart.

Sixteen

That night he reclaimed his bedroom, but his sleep was uneasy. The seemingly boundless bed engulfed him like a dark, voluminous shroud, and for hours he wandered, crying softly, in majestic forests of giant fir trees where light barely penetrated through overgrown branches and the air smelled of loneliness, oppression, and for some unfathomable reason, violets—a smell that, surprisingly, remained in the room when, shortly after four in the morning, having just been swallowed by the yawning earth, Sukhanov awoke with a gasp and, throwing off the covers, sat peering into the shadows.

It must have been the aftershave used by Dalevich, he realized unhappily after a minute. For some time he struggled to fall asleep again, but the stillness of the world rang in his ears and the aroma of violets stole furtively into his lungs. Finally, giving up, he got out of bed, walked onto the balcony, and stood suspended between the vast, empty city and the indifferent, autumnal heavens, listening to the rarefied sounds of the night. A distant car briefly tore the fabric of communal sleep; a gust of wind rustled the trees; a crow flew cawing raggedly over the Zamoskvorechie in search of sunrise.

Then he heard a whisper trailing like smoke from somewhere above him.

"My late wife loves to waltz," an ancient voice said mournfully from the skies.

Recognizing the madman from upstairs, Sukhanov looked up warily, half expecting a burning newspaper to fly into his face; but nothing stirred on the ninth-floor balcony. Unsettled, he was about to go inside when the sad voice spoke again.

"She died forty-seven years ago. She learned to waltz in Paris. Her parents took her there when she was a young girl, before the Revolution. We met there. She still speaks French like an angel, and when she drinks champagne, she purses her lips as if for a kiss. We are celebrating her birthday today—she has just turned ninety."

The words floated down, slow and dry and broken like dead leaves from some great, invisible, heavenly trees, and Sukhanov felt strangely stirred in spite of himself.

"Hello?" he called out gently. "Are you speaking to me?"

"I am speaking to no one," said the quiet voice after a pause, "but you are welcome to listen. Perhaps you are a nobody yourself. Most people are, after all. They all think I'm crazy, but I'm the only sane one among them. Their lives are tedious and gray, but in my life, marvelous things happen all the time—ah, such adventures! My wife and I, we walked along the Seine the other night. The moon was full over Notre Dame, and she said—"

His voice fell silent abruptly, as if tripped by a sob. Sukhanov pictured the monkey-faced old man crouching in the darkness mere inches above his head, perhaps with his eyes closed, the better to see his madman's dreams, or maybe staring into the Russian night with its gloomy houses, flickering streetlights, deserted churches, frozen stars, and all the futile, thwarted lives, just like his own, that were at this moment stumbling through thousands of private nightmares under moonlit roofs—and his heart contracted with inexpressible pity.

"Forget about Paris," the hushed voice sighed. "I have better stories to tell."

And the old man talked, talked of things that were past, or more likely had never happened; and his tone held the measured, heartbroken lucidity of someone who no longer had anyone to listen to him. He talked of riding horses across the rolling hills of Andalusía, and reciting Virgil among the starlit ruins of the Colosseum, and dancing to the golden strains of Strauss on the deck of a yacht as it crossed the purple Mediterranean on its way to some forgotten tiny island of the gods—always the two of them, he and his dead wife, always basking in an illusory glow of Elysian happiness; and gradually, as the old man's whisper drifted over the sleeping city, Sukhanov found himself slipping away on the current of his own thoughts. The pain of Nina's near-loss and the joy of her miraculous recovery echoed in an oddly urgent note through his being, and the words from the intercepted letter—*Your husband has never known how to love*—constricted his heart with a feeling not unlike grief, until he knew he could not brush them aside simply because they chanced to refer to someone else.

The air was already suffused with pale light when the sad voice from the skies finally faded into an exhausted, wordless reverie. Anatoly Pavlovich walked inside, pulled a bag from a closet, and moved through the apartment, collecting shirts and socks. Shortly after noon, he left for the dacha.

The ride lasted almost two hours. Looking up, Sukhanov kept seeing Vadim's unusually bloodshot, brooding eyes flitting in the rearview mirror. Apart from an occasional clarification of directions—it had been so long since Sukhanov's last visit to the country that Vadim had forgotten the way—they did not talk. Once the congested heart of the old city with its dusty boulevards, blind bakery windows, and peeling mansions had released them, they began to pass shapeless neighborhoods with gray apartment blocks erupting dismally from empty, ill-kempt lots; then, gradually, as Moscow slid back faster and faster, the spaces between the buildings widened until precipitately, without so much as a comma, they changed into fields, bracketed by fire-tipped rowan trees and punctuated here and there by the exclamation point of a leaning bell tower or an ellipsis of dilapidated log houses—and Sukhanov envisioned the whole drive as one endless, unstructured, rambling sentence, and thinking of Nina, of the girl she had been once, of the woman she was now, was barely able to follow all of its clauses, until, veering from yet another unpaved turn in the local road, they arrived quite suddenly at the long-sought period of his country home.

Sukhanov rolled back his shoulders, exhaled, and climbing out of the car, told Vadim to return tomorrow, around three or four in the afternoon. Then, as the Volga lumbered back to the road, he pushed open the gate in a tall wooden fence and, chased by the frenzied barking of Coco, the neighbor's fat, asthmatic poodle, walked down the winding path.

Here, in the countryside, the summer still lingered as if charmed. A rich smell of cut grass rose into the air along with a midday chorus of somnolent crickets; bumblebees hovered with contented weightiness under a sky blue as the brightest faience; orchard trees rippled in the breeze, revealing flashes of the light green of Antonovka apples among the dark green of restless leaves. On both sides of the path, tumbling branches of blossoming wild roses, red and white, rained petals onto his feet, and their sweet, heavy scent unexpectedly summoned to his memory a delightful tea Valya had occasionally brewed from rose hips. In a few more strides, the white stone walls of the house gleamed through sun-dappled branches of a young oak,

reminding him of some impressionist study of color and light. Swinging his bag back and forth like an impatient child, he ran up the steps.

The front door stood ajar; he walked inside. He saw her right
away. Sitting by an open window on a glassed-in veranda, she leafed
through an art book and picked plums from a ceramic bowl before
her; a pile of pits glistened on a saucer at her elbow. The mellow
afternoon light that filtered into the room through the gently swaying reddening ivy imparted to her skin the golden glow of a Vermeer
portrait.

At the sound of his rushed steps, she looked up, and he saw a
slight wrinkle form momentarily between her eyebrows, then vanish
just as quickly.

"Tolya," she said, rising. She was dressed in a loose shirt and an
old ankle-length skirt, black with rows of bright little cherries, which
she wore only when puttering about her small vegetable garden
behind the house.

"You seem unwell," she said, coming closer. "Are you feeling all
right?"

She did not smile, but everything about her—her words, her
movements, the tone of her voice—was comforting, tender, softly
colored, and he had to fight the urge to weep with relief.

"I . . . I don't know," he said. "I guess I have a headache. It's not
important."

She put her cool hand on his forehead; her fingertips smelled of
fruits and earth.

"No, you don't feel hot," she said, taking her hand away. "Come,
I was just about to make tea. I have some wonderful apple pie, Katya
brought it over this morning. There are some leftovers from yesterday too, if you are hungry."

Realizing that he was indeed famished, he followed her inside the
sunlit house. As they drank their tea, she spoke, leisurely yet with a
touch of uncharacteristic animation, about the surprising harvest of

plums, the late blooming of roses, a tame wagtail that visited her on the terrace every morning. . . . He found himself silently watching her lips shape the words. He had planned to tell her about the rift with Dalevich, the loss of his position, the trouble with Ksenya—had, in fact, spent most of the morning rehearsing the half-indignant, half-pained expressions in which he would couch all his sufferings. Yet now, as he listened to her meandering stories, originating in a reality so different from his own and released lightly, almost lovingly, into this glowing afternoon lull, he felt his need for her pity fading away along with the last complaints of his hunger. And all at once his presence here, conceived and executed with such proprietary ease, and accepted by Nina with such unquestioning simplicity, produced in him a deliciously light-headed sensation of being freed—being rescued—from the whole of his recent existence. He felt astonished that this verdant, warm, rustic world existed not one hundred kilometers from his dark, tormented Moscow universe; and slowly, indulgently, gratefully, he allowed himself to enter the unlikely new life Nina was describing, or possibly creating, before his eyes—a life whose essence lay in the prolonged note of a bird singing in a tree, the hesitant flight of a butterfly alighting for a moment on a windowsill, its velvety brown wings closing and opening in a rhythm of deep, sleepy breathing, and the flickering advance of a dappled, aromatic shadow across a beautiful woman's face. . . .

Later she took him into the garden. Together they wandered the paths twisting among flower beds and vegetable plots and gooseberry bushes. She showed him her flaming yellow and orange marigolds, a pile of twigs in a hollow behind the toolshed where two days earlier she had glimpsed an old hedgehog, and the lacquered leaves of a rare tea rose about to bloom. He walked a step behind, nodding at the unfamiliar names of plants and weeds, feeling somehow attuned to every tentative shift in the universe—the gradual cooling of grasses, an early hint of vespertine dampness creeping through the air, the measured flow of time itself, its colors changing from the swaying green-gold of the breezy, leafy afternoon to the translucent lavender-silver of the cool, misty evening. A few houses away, someone had started a fire; a thin rivulet of smoke rose above a neighbor's roof, and the smell of burning leaves made the air tingle.

He stopped, breathed in deeply.

"Why don't we gather some branches and have a fire of our own?" he said then. "It will probably be cold enough for the fireplace."

"That sounds nice," she replied. "I think there is a bottle of red in the pantry."

The pleasingly chilly night was already pressing against the windows when he finally managed to start a good fire, fed by a three-year-old issue of *Ogonyok*. The contours of the room disappeared into wavering shadows, and darkly glowing crumbs of the disintegrating pages threw dull reflections into Nina's pale eyes as she sat staring into the flames, her wine neglected.

He watched her over the rim of his glass, then asked, "What are you thinking about, my love?"

She shrugged, not moving her eyes from the fire.

"There is an artist, I forget her name," she said. "She makes these cubes. They look like children's toy blocks, only they are upholstered in fabric, and they have texts on them—short poems, cryptic statements, that kind of thing. And sometimes a bigger cube might open up to reveal a different-colored smaller cube inside, and it might say something too, like an answer to a question posed on the outside."

"Where have you seen them?" he asked in mild surprise.

"An exhibit I went to recently. Anyway, there was this one cube. Its fabric was ugly, black with purple flowers, like an old woman's dress or a ribbon on a funerary wreath, and its label read, 'A soul.' Underneath, there was a warning: 'Don't open or it will fly away.'"

"And?" Sukhanov said after a pause.

"And nothing. The lid wouldn't open, it was glued shut. But I can't stop thinking about what might have been hidden inside. Would there be another dark cube that said, 'Too late, it's gone, told you not to open it'? Or was there instead a bright red or blue cube, or one wrapped in golden foil, perhaps, that said, 'The daring are rewarded. Take your soul, go out into the world, and do great deeds'?"

"Most likely there was nothing inside," he said, refilling his glass. "Why bother creating something if no one will see it? These kinds of trifles aren't real art, anyway."

"It's just that I can't stop thinking about it," she replied.

For a while after that, they sat in silence. The wine tasted of youth and sun; in the fireplace, hidden moisture hissed within slender aspen branches; two rooms away, in the kitchen, the cuckoo in the old clock reluctantly coughed eight times. Beyond the window, Sukhanov imagined he could see the glint of stars circling unhurriedly through the skies.

"Funny, I never liked being in the country very much," he said meditatively, emptying the last of the wine into his glass, "yet now I can almost see myself living here."

Nina stirred as if waking from her own reverie.

"I never asked you," she said. "How long are you planning to stay?"

"Vadim is picking us up tomorrow afternoon. But I think we should come back soon, don't you agree, spend a few days, maybe even a week—"

"I don't think I'll be ready to leave tomorrow," said Nina softly, almost to herself.

"More garden work?" he asked with a smile. "I thought you said you'd be done by Tuesday. Well, we could postpone our return by a day or two. I'll call Vadim."

"No, what I mean is," she said, "I want to stay here for a while."

"How long?"

"Perhaps until the first snows. Maybe longer."

His thoughts derailed abruptly. "But . . . that's at least two months! I know I just said I could live here, but frankly, I doubt I could stand it for *that* long, and even if I could, my presence in Moscow might be—"

Nina set down her half-finished wine. The glass made a small liquid chink against the floor. "Tolya, you misunderstand me," she said. "I'm not suggesting that you stay here with me. I want to be by myself. Alone."

The whistle of a train rose in the distance, piercing and solitary like the cry of a lost bird. She waited for it to die away before speaking again. Everything was moving in excruciatingly slow motion.

"I was hoping we could just have a nice day and talk about all this tomorrow, but, well . . . You haven't yet heard from Vasily, I take it?"

"No, is something the matter? Is your father ill? Is Vasily—"

The air, dense with disbelief and rasping with erratic heartbeats, was hard to inhale.

"They are both fine," she said. "As a matter of fact, they are having such a grand time together that Papa has asked Vasily to move in with him when they return. Vasily called me last night."

"And what did he . . . What did you . . ."

"He likes the idea," she said expressionlessly. "The location is much more convenient for him. More central. And it would be nice for someone to keep Papa company. He gets lonely, I think, even though he'd never admit it. So, since they both appear to want it, I don't see why—"

She bent to prod the wood in the fireplace, and he followed a flurry of tiny sparks spiraling through the darkness. Somehow he felt no surprise at the news, only bitterness and a certain vague revulsion— not unlike the unpleasant sensation he had experienced a few days before at his father-in-law's apartment when he had watched dozens of effusive old men embrace dozens of respectful youths in the gilded mirrors of the hallway. And then, as a clear snapshot of the scene emerged from the dimness of the past, he finally guessed at the source of his distaste. Pyotr Alekseevich and Vasily looked so amazingly alike that it had been rather like seeing an aged man give a young version of himself an infinite pat on the back. How odd, he wondered, that he had never noticed the similarity before—and how ironic that Vasily and Ksenya would both choose the exact same time to desert—

Sensing Nina's eyes on him, he realized with a start that he must have spoken aloud.

"Don't worry, Tolya," she said with a sigh. "I already know about Ksenya. I talked to her yesterday."

He let her words traverse his being slowly, very slowly, until he felt them coming to rest somewhere amid the chaos of his tossing thoughts. And at that precise moment, the tossing stopped, his pained bewilderment yielded, and anger began to glow hollowly in his heart—fed perhaps by a deeper current of guilt.

"Oh," he said coldly. "I see. You mean to punish me for the rift with our children, do you? Of course, I'm the only one to blame here. After all, I'm such a dismal failure as a father. Why, I should have been there for them, I should have guided, I should have prevented, I should have known—whereas you, you were always so perceptive, so loving, so—"

"Tolya, I'm not assigning blame to anyone," she said. "And anyway, Vasily is probably better off with Papa, we both know that. And Ksenya, I think she'll be all right. She'll be living at her friend Lina's, a wonderful girl. I like Boris a great deal too. Of course, I'll worry about her, but I feel it's time to let her do her own thing. She has grown up so much faster than I thought possible. That's not why I—"

"You've met that good-for-nothing boy of hers, and you think she has grown up?" he said with hasty incredulity. "Well, talk of a lapse in parenting skills! Or has our dear daughter neglected to mention that he is married, or that he writes deranged songs about angels and suicides, or that he has a following of mad hippies, or that he is the one who stole all my—"

"I said 'grown up,' not 'grown old,' " she interrupted. "Of course she makes mistakes—she is young, she and Boris both! Young and talented and in love and . . ."

Her outcry faltered, silenced by some invisible but powerful presence. When she spoke again, her voice was so low he had to strain his hearing to understand, and her words sounded oddly frail, and yet brave, as if balancing on a tightrope stretched across an abyss that only the two of them could see.

"My God, Tolya, don't you remember what it feels like?" she said in a near-whisper. "To be in a hurry to live, to dream of overthrowing conventions, to hope to make the world a gift of something beautiful and everlasting? Don't you remember, Tolya? Tolya?"

And for one hushed moment, as they sat facing each other across the night—she searching his face with a disconcerting, hopeful intensity, he struggling to find the only answer worthy of all their years together, of the past they had shared—for one brilliant, self-contained moment, everything seemed in flux, and everything was wonderfully possible, and he knew that if he could only discern the right words in the monstrous whirlwind of his mind, the universe would shift obligingly, the past and the present would merge with miraculous ease, and she would smile once more into his eyes, and their life would once again be surprising and full and precious, and . . . and . . .

"Of course, I should have known," Nina said in a tired voice, turning away. "After all, you have such a way with undesirable memories. . . . Well, I just pray that as these children sort through things in the years to come, they will be different from us and won't discard their dreams along with their messes."

And he felt time resume its progress through the world, and the present imposed itself once more on his senses—the quiet darkness dispersed here and there by the yellow squares of neighbors' lit windows, the stars dancing with chilly precision above the trees, the smells of plums and ashes in the air, the gentle scratching of aspen branches against the roof; except that now, it all began to seem strangely unreal, like a crudely painted stage decoration for some tragic and mildly ridiculous provincial play. Hopelessly he questioned the night for the expression of Nina's eyes, but saw only the lines of her profile, pale and merciless like that of a pagan goddess of justice. Then he realized that her lips were moving, that she was speaking again.

"I'm sorry, that was unfair," she was saying. "We both made our choices back then, and in all honesty, mine was probably much less admirable than yours."

Her tone was one of defeat, and her words had no meaning. He made an effort to speak.

"*Your* choice?" he said. "What choice was that? Going along with whatever I decided? Forgive me, but that's hardly a—"

She lowered her face, and the shadows closed over it greedily.

"It doesn't matter now," she said. "The time of decisions is past. And now, it seems, is our time to face the consequences. Our children leaving home may be one of them. I suppose my need to be alone is another."

"So in essence," he said after a pause filled with darkness, "you are leaving me because of something that happened almost twenty-five years ago?"

"I'm not leaving you, Tolya," she said. "I just want to be by myself for a while. I've thought about it for so long—having a leisurely stretch of time, all my own—and now, with Vasily and

Ksenya gone, I can finally do it. Don't you understand? My whole life has been devoted to other people—first Papa, then you, then our children. But none of these things has worked out quite the way I hoped, and now—now it must be my turn. I like it here. It's so silent, especially early in the morning and late at night, I can almost hear plants grow. I like making plants grow. It makes me feel alive, as if I'm part of something greater, something real. . . ."

Her speech sounded rehearsed—she must have chosen her phrases carefully in anticipation of this conversation—yet he could barely follow it. The wine was making his temples throb dully.

"My God," he said, "have you been so unhappy with me?"

She smiled a pale smile. "Happy, unhappy—these terms never really applied to us, did they? I didn't marry you in search of happiness."

And he did not dare ask the question he most wanted to ask, because now, for the first time ever, he suddenly doubted the answer—and he felt his soul dying yet another small, bleak death at the looming of the truth.

"No, I dreamt of a holy mission in life." Her words were again well practiced, and cold. "Living in close proximity to art, religiously watching over its creation, assisting at its birth with a thousand details that were in themselves mundane and yet would add up to a great, sacred trust, a short footnote next to my name for all eternity: 'Nina Sukhanova, born Malinina, the daughter of a hack, the wife of a genius.' Pathetic, isn't it—all those young Russian girls raised on nineteenth-century novels, searching for an idol at whose plaster feet they might sacrifice their own aspirations, only to wake up decades later, aged and bitter, to find their visions of vicarious greatness shattered, their husbands average, talentless nobodies . . . Only that's not exactly how it turned out with us, is it, Tolya—and to tell you the truth, I sometimes think I'd prefer such a trite, unambiguous ending to . . . to . . ."

"Please, Nina," he said thickly, "please, let's not . . ."

She stopped, looked at him in silence. The long, motionless minute that followed felt icy, crisp, multifaceted, as if time itself had hardened into crystals. Anatoly Pavlovich saw the room with astonishing clarity, from the whole of its darkened, wood-paneled expanse to the faint reflection of the dying fire on the surface of his wineglass. He saw Nina's face, the left side in dancing shadow, the right landscaped by bright light; he saw the flames gleam in her nearly transparent eyes. Irrelevantly, he thought about the colors he would use if he were to paint her portrait at this moment—the soft grays, the reserved reds, a poignant touch of liquid gold here and there—and wondered whether it would be possible to find a shade delicate enough to convey her fingernails, which glowed like so many translucent crescent moons every time she lifted her hands to the fire in that chilled gesture of hers. He also thought, disjointedly, how long it had been since she had allowed him to hold her in his arms—a dejected, months-long eternity of everyday preoccupations, distractions, headaches, which would now stretch on, stretch on indefinitely, in a glittering, echoing Moscow apartment where he was condemned to live from this day forward, exiled from his work, his family, his very existence, talking to no one for weeks at a time save his own reflection and the madman from the ninth floor . . .

In the next instant, the absurdity of the image made him laugh aloud—a bitter little laugh that startled him out of his trancelike state. Then, feeling all at once afraid to linger in this seductively warm, deceptively cozy, subtly poisonous place that belonged to him no longer, he stood up unsteadily and headed out of the room.

The air was much colder in the drafty corridor that led past the gaping cavern of an unlit kitchen to the front door. Behind him, he heard Nina ask where he was going.

"Back to Moscow," he said without stopping. The wine he had drunk—half a bottle, it must have been, or quite possibly even three-quarters—made his steps sluggish, and mechanically he chided himself for having briefly forgotten his age. As if from afar, Nina's feet pattered across the floor as she dashed after him, exclaiming, "But that's crazy! Let me make supper, we'll go to bed early, and tomorrow we can talk this over calmly. Please, Tolya, nothing's decided, we can still—"

Already on the veranda, he fished out his city shoes from a dim corner, then felt for his bag on the floor where he had dropped it just hours before. It was unnecessarily, mockingly heavy.

Catching up with him, Nina grabbed his sleeve.

"Please," she gasped, "you can't leave like this, it's already past nine, how are you going to get home, do you even know the train schedule, please . . ."

He saw her standing there, green-eyed, flushed, and out of breath like a young girl, and his heart bled with the certainty that he had been too late with her as well. And then he understood how laughable it had been to imagine, only one day ago, that the loss of some romanticized image of a thin-blooded, composed Madonna who for years had graced his idea of a perfect home with a mysterious, elegant presence would be in any way comparable to the loss of this flesh-and-blood woman before him—this woman who had once been ready to follow him to whatever amazing new horizons he might take her, this woman who could still find the strength to listen to him when he was sad and make him tea when he was tired, this woman whose fingertips smelled of fruits and earth. . . .

And for one moment, confronted with a bleak monotony of future despair, so unlike the dramatic vision of offended virtue that he had entertained over the purloined letter of a neighbor, he caught himself longing for the Nina of yesterday, furtive and unfaithful, perhaps, but still near him, instead of this new Nina, pure as always— but far away, so far away, with ninety-seven kilometers of solitude and indifference and disappointed hopes to separate them for God knew how long. . . . And simultaneously it occurred to him how surreal this parting was, how lifeless—how like a labored scene from some novel whose meaning faded amidst the flowery exchanges between unfeeling, cardboard characters—how unlike this bleeding wound that was tearing his living soul in two.

And in truth, why *was* he standing here, on the threshold of darkness, still and speechless? Shouldn't he plead with her, shouldn't he reproach her, shouldn't he remind her how much he had done for her—how comfortable her life had been with him, how successful he had become for her sake, how many lovely things she had always had at her beck and call? Shouldn't he throw her ingratitude back into her face, forcing her to remember the pitiful failure of Lev Belkin's existence, perhaps grabbing her roughly by the shoulders and shouting, "Is that the kind of life you wish we had?" Or should he confess instead how much he needed her? Should he . . . shouldn't he . . .

Still talking about train schedules, Nina was trying to wrestle away his bag. "Please understand, Tolya," she was saying rapidly, "there's no need to react like this, I only want a temporary—even brief—"

He knew with perfect conviction what an unfathomable thing it would be to walk away right now, without saying another word, without attempting to restore their life to the way it had been—yet at the same time, he felt strangely unable to break out of his stupor. And deep inside his heart, he sensed that his inaction stemmed from his ultimate acceptance of unhappiness, perhaps even a kind of perverse satisfaction at the thought that an ultimate justice was being served.

For deep inside his heart, he realized that he deserved it all.

Moving Nina's fluttering hands away, Sukhanov turned and walked through the door. The terrace steps were slippery with evening dew, and the twisting shadows of the path embroiled his shoes in dimly aromatic, faintly menacing coils of invisible rose branches. He stopped and listened briefly: she had not followed. Then, greeting his rightful fate with a quiet smile, he extricated himself from the roses, pushed open the gate—and exited into the night.

Seventeen

The station was in the nearby village of Bogoliubovka. A few summers ago, Sukhanov had gone there with Nina to meet some friends arriving by train. Beyond the gated cluster of well-appointed houses of the privileged, they had walked through a pleasant birch forest, rosy in the light of the morning sun, and on the way through the village, Nina had surreptitiously picked moist, sweet raspberries off bushes spilling over low fences—altogether an effortless little stroll through the Russian countryside in the comfortably familiar, occasionally maudlin style of Levitan.

Now, in the dark, the terrain seemed dramatically altered. The ordinarily smooth road tripped him with devious potholes; ghostly dogs strained on their chains behind his back, growling rabidly at his trespass; fat, furry moths beat a repulsively soft, flickering rhythm against streetlamps; and many-armed, troll-like silhouettes shifted feverishly in the lit windows of neighboring dachas, engaged in some dim, ugly activities of living. He passed through it all, indifferent to the strangeness of the world. But when the last of the imposing houses melted away in the wavering circle of the last streetlamp, and a watchman—a mere contour carelessly sketched by the night around the glowing pinpoint of a cigarette—pushed the gates closed behind Sukhanov's back, he was startled to see the path ahead of him swallowed by the black mass of the forest.

He hesitated before stepping under the trees.

The night was deeper here, the silence complete, the air musty with pungent smells of dampened moss and sweetly rotting leaves and poisonous mushrooms. He moved cautiously, barely able to see the ground beneath his feet. After a while, he felt the first twinge of worry. From his past walk, he had preserved an impression of this wood being transitory, nearly transparent, with dazzling splashes of clearings visible almost immediately between the birches—yet now, with every passing moment, the trees seemed to draw closer and closer together, crowding him with their motionless presence, and the infinite silence tolled in his aching head like a giant bell. He quickened his pace, and still the forest went on; and as he entered farther into its breathless darkness, he imagined it altering slowly, growing more menacing and strange with each new step. Gradually his eyes began to distinguish murky, twisted shapes, whether dead stumps and gnarled branches or some clumsy, frightening creatures of the earth, creeping after him along the ground or leaning above him from the trunks; and after some time, the profound quiet of the place filled with a multitude of insidious, secret sounds—a rustling shudder of leaves, starting unexpectedly, without wind, and falling still just as incomprehensibly; the hollow moan of an insomniac bird or else a dispossessed spirit; the sharp creak of a twig snapping under a mysterious foot . . . And all at once he knew that the sunlit birch grove of his summery recollection had long given way to the oppressive, cathedral-like woods of his recent nightmare, and he felt weak with the fear of wandering off his obscure path and becoming forever lost in a suffocating, torturous labyrinth of evil dreams.

He walked faster and faster, until he was running, hurtling head-first through the chilly blackness, heedless of roots and ghosts. His middle-aged heart pounded painfully, and his mild but persistent inebriation tangled his feet. When the trees finally started to part, revealing pale flashes of the night sky between them, his knees were about to dissolve in trembling aches, and his right shoulder was numb from the weight of his bag. Once in the open, he paused to catch his breath—and as he waited, he became aware of the unfamil-iar landscape before him. He had expected to see the lights of Bogoliu-bovka just beyond the forest, but instead, a wide meadow swayed in the blue light of a dying moon. Shouldering his bag once again, he waded across the expanse, at first simply glad to have outrun his nightmare, then increasingly uneasy. Tall grasses brushed against his legs, heavy and moist; the unseen earth yielded softly under his feet; stars rolled down the skies like drops of rain; and fog rose in uneven patches off the ground and drifted past him in an eerie procession of limbless, faceless spirits.

There was no village in sight.

His steps grew hesitant then, his thoughts wary. The meadow descended into a steep ravine, overgrown with wild hazel trees; on the way down, he stumbled and smashed his knee against a shadow of a rock. Suspecting now that he must have taken a wrong turn somewhere in the woods, he remained still for a long while, nursing his wound and watching the remote skies. But when he groped his way to the other side, he found himself presented with the gift of a solitary streetlamp on a distant hillside, spilling rarefied purple light onto an indistinct building that could only be the Bogoliubovka train station.

He limped toward it—and the anticipated station slowly under-went a shimmering, disorienting transformation, shrinking in length and growing in height, until it condensed before his eyes first into the Kremlin's Spasskaya Tower (what nonsense, he thought tiredly), then into a vanquished fairy-tale monster (Sukhanov blinked), and finally into a small church. He went closer, half awaiting another metamorphosis. The church was a pitiful ruin, with four of its domes beheaded and the fifth, central, one bereft of its cross and sagging around a shadowy gash, the whole edifice falling into the paling abyss of the peasant night. He regarded it morosely, no longer doubting that he was lost—the place was entirely new to him. Then, noticing a weed-choked path climbing past the church into the darkness, he rubbed his smarting knee and listlessly walked along it.

When he neared the ruin, the sparse, cold light of the streetlamp seeping through a yawning portal granted him a glimpse of a bare interior—the floor buried under decades of rubble, bulky shapes of sundry bales stacked high in the corners, years of indifference and misuse . . . Suddenly a puzzling flash of green alighted on the periphery of his vision. Surprised, he stopped and peered into the moldy dimness, waiting for his eyes to adjust. And then he saw the walls. Brittle under the weight of centuries, darkened by numberless summers of rains, faded by numberless winters of snows, the walls of the church were covered with frescoes.

After a moment's hesitation, he set his bag down and gingerly stepped inside. The heavens leaked starlight through the many tears in the roof, and in the wreckage of the solitary dome, wings of invisible sleeping birds rustled. The air had a heavy smell of age and oblivion, with a sour undercurrent of bird droppings, and with every halting step he made, he crushed underfoot rotting wood and damp plaster—and possibly, he thought with a start, priceless masterpieces of disintegrating medieval art.

The diffused light from outside was not enough for him to see things clearly, but gradually, as he strained his eyes, he managed to distinguish first a few colors, then a few shapes. Here an owl-eyed monk with a disapprovingly pursed mouth clutched a bricklike book, there a poorly proportioned headless beast cavorted among unconvincing fires of hell. Above a collapsed arch, a hand was raised in stiff benediction, its body long dissolved by the rains, and nearby a seraph with the features of a mean child fluttered on sharp little wings of an unlikely tangerine tint. Along a far wall, a better-preserved procession of aged saints walked with tired tread, their gowns still glowing with ghostly green and blue and crimson, their faces mostly washed away, only here and there revealing conventional traces of solemn, empty eyes. He shrugged and looked away regretfully. The frescoes he had wrested from obscurity were nothing but a recital of religious commonplaces, fading odds and ends of an unmemorable and unremembered artistic life—mediocre seventeenth-century imitations of hundreds if not thousands of other imitations currently crumbling into dust in countless former churches across the whole of Russia.

But as he turned to leave, the shadows shifted with his movement, and he glimpsed a strange figure rising in the farthest corner. He stared incredulously into the poorly lit depths of the church, doubting his sobriety, doubting his sight. Unmistakably, it was there. To one side of the obediently treading crowd of soft-hued saints, an astonishingly lifelike apparition of a tall, stooping, bearded man with wildly outstretched arms gazed from the wall. He too was a saint, yet a saint unlike the others—his face consumed by a dark, powerful passion, his eyes stark and troubled, his gaunt body draped in harsh, funereal tones; and it seemed to Sukhanov that under the heavy eyelids, the painted irises glittered with a piercing, unearthly intensity, a hundredfold more brilliant than anything ever created by the immortal hand of Goya or Rembrandt. . . .

For a long, long minute, without moving, Sukhanov blinked and squinted at the wonder before him. And then, slowly, with renewed certainty, he began to feel that his life, with all its questionable choices, all its doubts, all its pangs of guilt, was justified yet again—was it not? For here, in this stale backwater, on the outskirts of an insignificant village, in a church that now served as a warehouse for dim-witted dacha owners, on a wall ravaged by time and sun and frost, flowered a masterpiece created by an artist whom no one needed, whom no one noticed, whom no one even knew—and yet Sukhanov believed, as strongly as he had ever believed in anything, that by some miracle he had just been brought into the presence of the most original, most amazing mind ever to emerge from the dark ages of Russian art. For in the universe of stifling traditions and slavish adorations, only a genius, and one vastly ahead of his time, could have had the courage to paint such a frightening truth—to confront so boldly the beatific, pastel-colored fools of prescribed sainthood with one living, suffering, tragic human being, a man for whom faith was so visibly a struggle, a cross, perhaps even a curse. . . . An incomparable, precious gift to humanity this fresco was, yet it had been bypassed, overlooked, forgotten, exposed to the elements, diminished to a mere memory of its former, jewel-bright glory; and soon even its last few traces would be lost forever in the monstrous communal grave of all the pure talent in this damned country—this country that Sukhanov and the eternally unknown artist shared, this country that had changed so little throughout the centuries. . . .

His sharp laugh sounded like a bark in the silence of the ruined walls.

"Behold," he shouted, "the destiny of the true genius in Russia! All this beauty, all these revelations wasted! And is this the fate I too should have hoped for? My God, wasn't I right in turning away from this lot?"

All at once, the church exploded into panicked echoes as a dozen startled crows flew off into the darkness, cawing hoarsely. Still laughing, he followed their escape past the crashed domes, toward the heavens. And when the avalanche of flapping wings died away among the stars, he thought he heard a different, quieter noise behind him—a rustle of clothes, an intake of breath. . . . He turned—and was rooted to the spot, his legs filled with lead, his heart leaping through his body like a fish thrown out of water. The disheveled dark saint—the unparalleled masterpiece of the unknown creator—had walked off the wall and was standing a few paces away, looking directly at Sukhanov with that burning, penetrating gaze of his.

For a horrifying eternity of a second, all was suspended. Anatoly Pavlovich was only dimly aware of falling to his knees, of closing his eyes. . . . He thought of nothing—and at the same time, he probably thought of dying, and that he had been crazy to hurl challenges to the skies in this terrible, decomposing lair of night and art, and that, in spite of everything he had ever witnessed, God existed after all— and that, most likely, God was not pleased with the way he, Sukhanov, had lived, had wasted, his life . . .

And then the saint spoke.

"Scared me out of my wits, man," he said reproachfully. "Here I am, not bothering anyone, reflecting upon life in peace and quiet, and suddenly there's all this stomping and shouting and cawing . . . Didn't your mama teach you not to enter the house of God when you're drunk as a pig? Look at yourself, too pickled to even stand up!"

And as the world moved into sharper focus, Sukhanov dully heard a crunch of rubble as the impossibly three-dimensional saint shuffled from foot to foot, and smelled a stale odor of unwashed clothes and sweat sneaking through the air; and finally daring to open his eyes just a little, he found his vision invaded by a pair of torn shoes with the laces missing and, above them, the hem of an extremely muddy gray coat. In stricken silence, he lifted his eyes higher and higher, until he was looking fully into the saint's face— looking at the untidy beard of some months' growth bespattered with flecks of dirt and half hidden by a hideously tattered checkered scarf, the rash on the sunken cheeks, the inflamed eyelids, the unhealthy glint in the bleary, bloodshot eyes . . .

And so it was. The saint did not have the face of a saint after all. The saint had the face of a tramp, of a drunk, of a madman.

The tramp appeared troubled.

"Listen, I didn't mean to hurt your feelings," he said anxiously. "Nothing wrong with being pickled. To each his own, I say. In fact, I'm very glad you came by, I was starting to feel a bit lonely. It's been forever since anyone—"

Sukhanov heavily rose to his feet and brushed the dust off his pants. Of course, he was thinking dismally, it was really not that surprising—what with this treacherous half-light and the wavering shadows and darting birds and assorted tricks of the night—indeed, it was not at all surprising to have mistaken a peculiarly dressed, odd-looking fellow frozen in an attitude of fright in the darkest corner of a dark building for a lifeless fresco on the wall, especially for a man with imperfect eyesight and three, or perhaps even four, glasses of wine coursing through his blood. No, it was not at all surprising, and yet—and yet, there was something strange, something unsettling about the fake saint's appearance, about this whole encounter, in fact. . . . Straightening, he peered with renewed wonder into the tormented, bearded face of the stranger, feeling suddenly, unaccountably certain that if he remained with this mysterious man, in this deserted church, for just a while longer, he might in time be able to understand the precise nature of things, to decipher their eternal riddle, to finally read sense into this day, this week, this life—to see clearly, as never before—

And then he went numb with incoherent terror, and felt frantic to leave this dreadful ruin of a place, with this dreadful ruin of a person, far, far behind him.

Carefully averting his eyes, he edged toward the exit.

"Very sorry to have disturbed you," he said in a hoarse whisper, "but I really must be—"

The man regarded him sadly, without moving.

"And here I hoped you would keep me company," he said. "The nights have grown so long, and I don't have anywhere else to go. I live here, you see. Do stay for a bit, eh? We can talk, I know so many different things, I can even tell you the story of my life—you won't be bored. . . . Just don't go away, not yet, please . . ."

It occurred to Sukhanov that the man might be dangerous—after all, there was no predicting madness. He continued to back away, muttering about a train he had to catch, until he reached the moldering door. There, with the breeze brushing his neck, he felt braver, and a desperate thought stirred weak hope in his heart.

"Listen, since you live here," he said, trying to keep the pleading out of his voice, "can you tell me how to find Bogoliubovka? I was going to the station there, but I was a bit turned around on the way, and now it's late and I'm completely lost."

The stranger's fleeting smile was disconcertingly familiar.

"I wish we were all as lost as you are," he said. "You are *in* Bogoliubovka. The station is just down the hill, less than two minutes away. Only there's no sense in going there tonight, there won't be any trains until tomorrow. Plenty of space here, though . . . How about it, eh?"

But Sukhanov was already heading down the path.

"Tolya, my name is Tolya!" a disembodied voice chased after him from the echoing shadows. "Perhaps you could stop by again some day? I'm always—"

The rest was carried off by the night. Not pausing, Anatoly Pavlovich murmured under his breath, "So, my personal patron saint, no less. Just in time too—if ever I needed divine intervention!"

And he even attempted to smile at his little joke; but as he ran toward the faint village lights scattered plainly across the darkness, he strove not to wonder how he had missed noticing them before, or why he had not recognized the Bogoliubovka church, which he had seen scores of times from the window of his chauffeured car on the way to the dacha. Above all, he avoided thinking about the small pieces of plaster, suspiciously like fresco fragments, that he had glimpsed strewn here and there in the beard of his mad namesake living all alone in the abandoned house of God.

Eighteen

The hands of Sukhanov's watch had stopped at thirteen minutes past ten, but he could sense that the night had already moved into that chilly, faintly unreal stretch of transitory weightlessness that lies like mist between the deepest, most silent hour of darkness and the first timid encroachment of light. The hour, however, mattered little; the important thing was that the train had come in the end.

Shivering with exhaustion, crammed on a hard-backed bench between an ancient man asleep with his mouth open and a corpulent woman noisily extracting something vile-smelling from the folds of a newspaper, Sukhanov found himself drifting in and out of fitful dozing, his head nodding to the rhythm of the wheels. Whenever he closed his eyes, he saw the miserable train station, which hours and hours of waiting had carved indelibly into his memory—the tracks glinting under a blinking lamp; the littered length of the platform, empty save for a few shapeless figures sprawled in the shadows among bales and baskets; the drifting stench of urine; the boarded ticket window with a scribbled note glued underneath, at which he had squinted for long, dim minutes but managed to decipher nothing but "except on Tuesdays" and "without stopping at . . ."

For the first half-hour, he had paced restlessly up and down the platform. Then he stopped and intently watched the tracks, replaying in his mind the image of the train emerging from the darkness, as if trying to summon it into being. After another half-hour, growing tired, he squatted squeamishly on top of his bag and gradually allowed himself to fall asleep.

He had a strikingly vivid dream. In the dream, realizing that the train would never arrive, he abandoned his futile vigil and stumbled through the night back to the ruined church. It was empty now, and the air inside brighter; the pale frescoes floated gently above the walls. Feeling curiously lighthearted, almost happy, he swept a corner free of rubble, pulled a coat out of his bag, and wrapping himself in it, lay down and sank into merciful, tranquil sleep, until someone tapped him on the shoulder amid a rising rustle of movement. He looked up reluctantly—and saw before him the dirty platform, the lamp flickering over the empty tracks, the vague, shifting figures. His mouth was dry, his hands stiff with cold; he must have been asleep for a while, perhaps for hours. A man in a fedora, his glasses flashing bleakly, his sand-colored beard fluttering, his features indistinct in the meager light, was bending over him, talking in an urgent voice.

"Only five minutes now," the man was saying, "but they won't let you board without a ticket!"

Sukhanov sat up and blinked in confusion. The man kept pointing to a small building across the tracks, repeating excitedly that there would not be another train, that Sukhanov needed to buy his ticket while there was still time, that he would gladly watch his bag. . . . Suddenly understanding, Sukhanov scrambled to his feet and, mumbling thanks to the kind stranger, hurriedly limped off, his legs still heavy with sleep. The next few minutes moved so fast and were so perplexing that he nearly mistook them for an extension of his dream. The tracks caught at his shoes with shards of bottles and tangled wires; the village disintegrated at his gasping approach into an ugly jumble of outhouses, laundry lines, and falling fences; he tripped against an enormous sack lying in the middle of the street and almost screamed when the sack muttered a drunken oath. When he finally pushed open the door of the building indicated by the man in the fedora, he expected to see a lit room, a counter, a woman in a window saying sullenly, "One way to Moscow, four rubles, three kopecks," but was plunged instead into a darkness full of stale warmth and odors of manure and sounds of sleepy stirring. Something fluffy fled clucking from under his foot, and numerous wings broke out into frantic flapping above his head—and then, before he could gather his disoriented senses, the sharp whistle of a quickly approaching train tore through the night behind his back.

Cursing, he turned and dashed back to the station, pursued by the indignant cackling of chickens. He was still scampering over the tracks when a pair of dazzling lights blinded him in an outburst of oncoming noise. For one mad moment he stood still and stared, almost convinced that this night, this day—this whole past week, in fact—were but a disjointed nightmare, and that the shining thunder flying at him with such inevitability would bring with it a blissful promise of awakening. Then the moment passed, and he bounded in one last effort over the tracks and up the steps and, his heart flailing ominously, arrived at the platform, just in time for a powerful rush of air, a screech of brakes, a reluctant squealing of sliding doors, a dense press of people who from a few immaterial shadows had somehow grown into a shoving, pushing, striving mob. . . . He was trying to fight through the crowd in search of the man who had promised to watch his bag when a surging wave of bodies, baskets, bales, buckets lifted him forcibly and carried him off. In the next instant another whistle sounded, and as the floor skidded beneath his feet, he was hurtled forward into a thronging, reeking space.

The train had left the station.

In spite of the unreal hour, the car he found himself in was full to the point of bursting. As soon as he recovered his balance, he elbowed his way through, standing on tiptoe now and then in hopes of glimpsing the old-fashioned hat and the yellow beard. But the stranger was nowhere to be seen, and in a short while, Sukhanov started having nagging little doubts about a station office supposedly open so late at night, his stumbling through a chicken coop, the fact that no one seemed to demand a ticket from him after all. . . . And when the truth finally dawned on him, it was simple, as most truths are. He had been duped out of his bag.

He felt too worn out for anger, even when he remembered his expensive coat. Turning back in resignation, he lurched through the crammed aisle, navigating between feet and parcels, looking, with diminishing hope, for a place to sit. And it was then that he noticed, for the first time clearly, the other passengers, and his steps faltered uneasily. Pressing upon him in the unsteady light of a few bare bulbs were people in drab clothes, with stony, dark, prematurely aged faces, heads swaying loosely in time to the thudding wheels, vacant eyes staring into nothing, features distorted by grotesque deformities of sunken mouths, broken noses, monstrous warts, missing teeth . . .

These were not the people he met in the busy streets of old Moscow—they belonged rather among the medieval fiends of Bosch's tortured landscapes of hell. He glanced about, covertly at first, then almost wildly, seeking out a splash of color, a pleasant countenance, a lively expression, a natural smile; but the grim, wordless, disfigured masses enclosed him on all sides like a silent gray sea. His unease began to slide into fear. He wondered to what final destination all these perversions of human beings could possibly be heading at this hour of the night, and peering closer, thought he saw disturbing, freakish objects protruding over the rims of their draped baskets or nestled in their yawning bags—a hoof of a severed bovine leg, a drooping neck of a bird, a rusty cemetery cross with clumps of reddened earth still sticking to it. And suddenly it seemed to him that he had accidentally stumbled on some secret nocturnal world, the unseen bowels of Russia, where no outsider was ever allowed—that he was painfully, obviously out of place here—that everyone was already starting to notice his presence, to stir, to mutter, to turn around, to devour him with those heavy, empty, terrifying, alien eyes—

In the next instant he caught sight of a miraculously preserved wedge of space between a shrunken old man sleeping with his mouth agape and a fat woman fussing with a crumpled newspaper. Mumbling inaudible apologies, he squeezed through the still wall of monsters, lowered himself onto the edge of the bench, and hastened to close his eyes. Soon he was wading in and out of anxious dreams in which he again strode up and down the Bogoliubovka platform—and so real were the visions of the blinking lamp and the gleaming tracks that only the sporadic wakeful glimpses of the pink, childlike gums of the man on his left and the nauseating smell of *vobla,* the salty dried fish the woman on his right had eventually unwrapped from a *Pravda* editorial and was now eating with repulsive sucking noises, reassured Sukhanov that he was indeed on a train, moving closer and closer to Moscow with every passing moment.

Yet after some time—twenty minutes maybe, or forty, or even an hour—he wondered through the haze of his slumber why they still rumbled on, with no announcements and no stops. Forcing himself awake, he attempted to look out the window, but the old man was leaning against it, blocking his view; all he could see were wide patches of blackness superimposed with bright reflections of the man's gnarled hands. Feeling apprehensive, Sukhanov turned to his other neighbor and was met by the oily gaze of the half-eaten fish.

The woman was busy picking at her teeth. She looked astonishingly like the wife of a certain theater critic he knew, he realized now. The thought dismayed him for some reason.

"Pardon me," he said, "but do you know how soon we'll be arriving in Moscow?"

On the other side, the old man stirred.

"Moscow? We aren't going to Moscow, my friend," he said, not opening his eyes. He spoke with a funny lisp. "We are heading east—Murom, Saransk, Inza . . ."

Sukhanov swung around and stared at the man in horror.

"Don't listen to him, he's not all there," the woman's voice blustered at Sukhanov's back. "Old age will do it to you. I reckon we should be getting to Moscow in less than an hour."

"Oh," said Sukhanov faintly. "Oh."

The old man dropped off to sleep without another remark, but a calm, knowing smile played on his lips. With blank eyes, Sukhanov watched the woman unhurriedly brush the fish remains onto the floor, fake amethysts the size of walnuts sparkling in her meaty earlobes. And all at once his presence here, among these strange people, in this train hurtling who knew where, seemed so unbearable that he could no longer remain sitting still, following the passage of time in his befuddled mind, guessing at the contours of the night they traveled through, his thigh squashed against the woman's repugnantly voluminous side. . . . Nodding mechanically at the old man, he stood up and shakingly made his way back into the aisle.

Here the press of bodies had become even denser. He pushed through, intending to position himself by the nearest window, when the sight of all these heads bobbing before the expanse of the lit wall punctuated by rectangles of framed darkness struck him as an unexpectedly familiar paraphrase of some other, distant scene. He paused for a moment, attempting to place his sudden déjà vu; then, giving up, resumed his efforts to get through.

People were standing three and four deep, talking to one another in undertones, all eager to get a better look. He too felt the excitement rising from his feet, numb after so many hours of waiting in line to enter, into the tips of his fingers. Finally, there it was, unobstructed, before him: the fluid wisp of a girl acrobat balancing on a ball, with a misty desert behind her, and in the foreground, the muscular back of a man in repose, the whole scene glowing softly with pinks, blues, and grays—a poignantly lyrical metaphor of humanity as a carnival troupe of performers and freaks, a striking juxtaposition of strength and fragility, roughness and smoothness, immobility and motion. A masterpiece of Picasso's early period.

With many others, Anatoly stood and looked at the painting that had been rescued so magically from some terrible cave of a locked storage room, where it had languished for dark, musty decades. And after a while, it began to seem like a mysterious window into a new, tantalizingly foreign world where possibilities were endless, where truths were manifold, where an altogether different artistic language was spoken—a language I did not as yet know, did not as yet understand, but had been avidly trying to learn all through that year, the year of 1956. All the same, the grainy magazine reproductions and the black-and-white catalogues of across-the-ocean shows circulating at Yastrebov's gatherings had not prepared me for the shock of coming face to face with an actual paint-and-brush work of Picasso, the giant of Western art, exhibited for the first time, unbelievably, here, in Moscow, in the very Pushkin Museum of Fine Arts where as a little boy I had seen Tatlin's flying machine and where for many subsequent years one could find nothing but a dusty spread of lamps, flags, and carpets presented to Stalin on his birthdays. And even though most of Picasso's other paintings on display left me vaguely puzzled and disappointed, that first sight of *Young Girl on a Ball* sustained its precious ringing note throughout my being, and that evening, as I ran home along the quickly darkening autumnal streets, my mind strove to absorb the revolutionary freedom of modernism and my hands ached to try these new, as yet unexperienced, colors and forms. . . .

Without warning the train pulled to a screeching stop. As Sukhanov toppled forward, his glasses plunged off his nose and were instantly lost amid the shuffling of uprooted feet. Immediately everything started to float away into a fog: the cloudy faces grimacing around him, the spectral station whose black-lettered name he squinted at hopefully but was unable to read, the shimmering glow of the sky above a distant town. After a moment of agonized indecision, he crouched down and groped along the filthy floor, the muddy shoes, the flabby convexities of bags, until, against every law of probability, just as the train jolted into motion again, his fingers closed on the welcome cold of the metal frames.

Infinitely relieved, he returned his glasses to their place, only to discover, upon straightening up, that half of his world was now crisscrossed by a radiant, trembling cobweb: a star-shaped crack, the imprint of someone's vengeful step, had shattered the left lens. The crack splintered the light into dozens of cubist fragments and imparted a rainbow-tinted brightness to one side of his vision, granting unwitting haloes to a night brigade of women in orange overalls who were presently illuminated by the flickering beams of their flashlights on a parallel track, and, once the last vestiges of the unknown town had fallen into the darkness, endowing his own reflection in the window with the multifaceted eye of an insect and sending silver waves across that of a strikingly beautiful girl who had just passed behind him in the aisle.

Greedily he looked at this newly altered universe, drinking in the colors, storing up his impressions, so that at the end of the day he could unburden his fresh load of discoveries onto yet another canvas. For months after that Picasso exhibition in October of 1956, he lived as if in an experimental laboratory of art, his mind always dissecting his surroundings in search of compositions, his hands always stained by oils, his heart always on fire. There were other shows as more and more paintings crossed the loosened borders or escaped the moldering walls of Soviet prisons of forbidden creation—among them, French impressionists whose sun-spotted gardens, twirling parasols, and boating excursions he found simple but dear, and contemporary Americans whose abstract expressionism amused him with its cult of anti-art. He devoured everything he came across, and in his paintings copied, toyed with, and abandoned a multitude of techniques and styles. And all the while, my soul longed to pass through its appointed period of apprenticeship and, emerging tempered by its trials yet in essence unchanged, devise a language all its own.

For the moment, however, my search remained a private one, transpiring on a secret plane parallel to my official, seemingly unaltered, existence. Although I talked freely among my artist friends at Yastrebov's evenings, the exhilarating change in the air felt all too recent, the memories of the preceding years all too fresh, and I preferred to be careful. I still proclaimed the virtues of socialist realism in my lectures at the institute, churned out now and then the odd portrait for the leather-bound office of some factory director, and when a shrill-voiced girl stood up during a classroom discussion and denounced Picasso as a scion of capitalism, I thought it prudent not to object. For the same reason, I had chosen to paint my true works at home, while reserving the studio (visited by both my students and my superiors) exclusively for my torpid public productions. And thus it was that I had nothing to show her when she came by the institute one dazzlingly blue, gloriously fragrant, excruciatingly awkward afternoon.

The month was March, the year 1957. Since our unfortunate meeting that past September, when I had so grossly insulted her father to her face, I had glimpsed her only a few times, always in Lev Belkin's company, always from afar. I had not hoped to talk to her ever again. By now, Lev and I had grown so close that I considered him my best friend, but our almost daily contacts centered on our work, and the name of Nina Malinina never entered our conversation. I assumed he was in love with her, and attributed his silence to his private nature, or else to his innate sense of tact—for the impression she had made on me that ill-fated evening must have been apparent to everyone. For myself, I fervently continued to think of her as my unattainable ideal, and was reduced to near-stuttering when, after a cursory knock on my door, she walked into my life, the smells of melting snows in her wake.

"I came to see Lev, but he is busy with some students, so I thought I'd stop by here in the meantime," she said without a smile. "I'm curious to see the works of a man who deems himself so superior to my father."

That day, a portrait of a heavily decorated general with bushy whiskers was drying against a wall, while on my easel an uncommonly rosy-cheeked woman was proudly displaying a bucket of cucumbers. As she circled the room, she did not speak, but I saw her eyebrows rise, and my heart ached with humiliation. At the same time, I sensed it would be dangerous to tell her about my other, experimental, paintings, for she was the daughter of Pyotr Malinin, that pillar of officialdom, and I knew nothing at all about her— nothing except that she was beautiful, luminously, piercingly beautiful, moving lightly through the air alive with sunshine in that pearl-gray coat of hers, in those little black boots clicking so haughtily against the floor, her short hair the color of honey spilling in two or three curls from under a red beret, her transparent eyes distant, almost derisive, her lips—her lips—

"This isn't really what I do," I heard myself saying recklessly. "I have other kinds of things at home. I . . . I can show you if you like. I live nearby. With my mother."

I was certain she would say no at once, but she appeared to hesitate.

"I'll ask Lev to join us," I added hastily.

In silence, she pulled at the fingers of her glove, then, looking up, said, "All right." Astonished, humbled, joyful, I ran down the hall, tenderly depositing in my memory the last, expectant look of her suddenly darkened eyes. Lev's door, around the corner, was cracked. I saw him standing by an open window, gazing into the glistening yard; his students must have just left. He did not hear me approach, and I was about to call out to him—but my lips moved wordlessly and my shout died an unnatural death in my throat. For a minute I lingered in the corridor, looking at his tall, broad-shouldered silhouette pasted against the pale blue sky; then, deciding, I retraced my steps on tiptoe.

She was still there, waiting quietly, twirling the glove in her hand.

"He's too busy to come," I told her. "Of course, I understand if you don't—"

I could not read her expression. Then, abruptly, she laughed.

"No, let's go," she said brightly. "Take your scarf, it's colder than it looks."

The city was streaming, dripping, splashing around us, sailing away on a dancing wave of early spring. She walked through it heedlessly, without noticing the torrents running off roofs and the pools of water at her feet; and so unreal seemed her presence next to me that I almost expected her to melt at any instant into the lustrous air. Yet after a mortifying interval filled with our passage through a littered building entrance, her stumbling on an unlit staircase landing, my embarrassed tugging at a key that had stuck in the lock (followed by a frantic dash into the apartment ahead of her, to throw a blanket over one painting I did not want her to see), and a blundering introduction to my startled mother who had exited the bathroom in curlers—there she was at last, standing in the middle of my cluttered room, uneasily playing with her gloves.

I switched on the light.

That year, I was fascinated by trains. I painted the in-between chaos of railroad stations, stained by the palpable sorrow of partings and the sad waste of vagrant destinies, yet occasionally pierced by the dazzling ray of a joyous meeting, a pure emotion; the mechanical rhythm of robotic multitudes swallowed and regurgitated ceaselessly by metallic monsters, with a rare living, feeling person swept screamingly along within the faceless mass; foreign, at times hauntingly lovely landscapes seen only fleetingly, through a dirty windowpane, over a pathetic repast of *vobla* laid out on a newspaper editorial; random lives thrown together for one moment, squashed against each other in the dim, narrow confines of a crammed car, sharing space and time, mingling their breaths in a parody of human closeness, yet each of them remaining tragically, eternally alone. . . . Nina Malinina silently looked at the canvases propped against the walls and piled on the floor; and when she finally spoke, there was a note of surprise in her voice.

"Dark," she said slowly. "Most of these are very dark, not at all what I expected. I love this one. Strange but . . . so beautiful."

She pointed to a small painting of railroad tracks being repaired in the deep blue glimmer of moonlight by a brigade of melancholy, overweight angels with shining orange wings. And then, before I could stop her, she stepped across to my easel and in one swift movement lifted the blanket I had thrown over my latest work.

With this canvas, more challenging in composition, I had hoped to complete the railroad series and begin exploring another subject that had interested me of late, that of reflections—of houses in pools of rainwater, of shaving men in bathroom mirrors, of wives in their husbands' glasses, of constellations in cups of tea. The painting depicted a crowd of people in browns and grays standing hunched over in the aisle of a train car, all of them seen from the back. The sturdy, well-dressed man in the foreground was reflected faintly in a window. His face, hovering over a dark patch of a forest, was middle-aged and vaguely unpleasant, with a hint of a double chin, and eyes, small and furtive like insects, hidden behind metal-rimmed glasses—the face of someone who had led a comfortable, predictable, inconsequential life. At this instant, however, his bland reflected features wore an expression of shocked recognition, as if he had just glimpsed a missed dream of his youth and for one heartbeat realized the meaningless-ness of his whole existence; and his eyes stared at the silvery wisp of another, less distinct, reflection—the specter of a strikingly beautiful girl who seemed to be flitting through the air behind him but was probably simply walking along the aisle, just outside the imaginary frame, briefly positioned precisely where a viewer of the painting would be standing. The girl's face had been the most difficult thing to paint, and I had spent almost a month battling with its complexities: it had to look both real and ethereal at the same time.

"But," said Nina Malinina haltingly, "but . . . that's me."

My voice louder than necessary, I started talking about general-ized, classical features, instances of accidental similarity, the artist's subconscious use of familiar material . . . And then something strange happened: she began to cry. Unlike most weeping girls, she did not invite a comforting gesture; her face looked angry, and her tears were silent and spare.

Unsettled, I turned away, waiting for her to compose herself.

"I understand," she said quietly after a minute, "he really isn't a very good painter. I must be going now."

Our eyes met, and I had a sudden feeling that she disliked me greatly. I was surprised when she agreed to let me walk her home. She lived with her father on Gorky Street, a quarter of an hour away. When we parted, she wrote down her phone number on the back of one of my drawings.

The next day, I had a talk with Lev. I felt guilty about my encounter with Nina, and I did not want him to hear about it from her. I altered the truth ever so slightly: I told him that when I had come to invite him along, his door had been closed, and hearing the sounds of an animated discussion inside, I had decided against interrupting. He gave me an odd look, then shrugged.

"Stop sounding so damn apologetic," he said. "I don't own her or her time."

"But I thought you were . . . Aren't you and Nina . . ."

"You thought wrong," he said curtly. "We are friends. Old friends. We went to school together. The first time we talked, we were fourteen. She brought a sandwich with caviar for lunch, while I had a piece of bread spread with butter and sprinkled with sugar—the only thing my mother could afford. She was so fascinated she asked me for a trade. Good luck with her, Tolya. Now, about this last piece of yours, I've been thinking it over, and I'm not sure the composition works. Wouldn't it be better if—"

I felt relieved at having Lev's blessing, and dizzy with possibilities. After that, I saw her often. She had numerous admirers, of course, many of them in the highest ranks of society, where she moved freely because of her father, and I had no hope of impressing her with my mildly successful position in life or my unremarkable material accomplishments. Neither had I that sleek suavity acquired through experience with women, for in spite of being twenty-eight, I could brag of nothing but three or four passing flirtations in the whole of my past. But as I soon discovered, she loved art—loved it with a passion surprising in someone of Malinin's flesh and blood. Not being blessed with talent (as she herself readily admitted), she had studied art history at the Moscow State University and was now working as a curator at the Tretyakovskaya Gallery. Soon a visit to this or that museum, a walk through this or that exhibition became our habitual way of spending time together, and as I would treat her to a fiery discourse on the nature of Fra Angelico's colors or van Gogh's brushstroke, I would feel encouraged by the look of reluctant admiration I imagined at times in her wonderful mermaid eyes.

One evening in late May, I took her to the Bolshoi Moskvoretsky Bridge, to show her the garlands of liquid lights carried away by the river and tell her about a painting I had envisioned, with a mysterious city of golden churches and lacelike towers gleaming mistily under the still, dark waters of a lake, its quivering contours too incandescent to be a reality, too enchanting to be a reflection, too palpable to be a dream. And then I looked up and saw her standing there, in her narrow-waisted white dress, absently picking tiny blossoms off a branch of deep purple lilacs I had brought her and watching their twirling descent into the current below—and I could wait no longer. I told her I loved her, had loved her since the first time I saw her. She was quiet for a moment, then said expressionlessly that it was growing chilly, and could I please walk her home; but something in her face made my heart flutter like a mad butterfly—and a few weeks later, she kissed me.

It was the first real day of summer, bright and green and hot, and we went for a walk in Gorky Park. Lev came too, with Alla, a giggling nineteen-year-old with an upturned nose and eyes blue and empty as glass, whom he claimed to have met a week before in an ice cream line. The four of us rented a boat, but it proved too small to hold everyone at once, and Lev and I took turns rowing the girls around the lake; and when, distracted by the glittering waves and the sun flashing into my eyes and Nina's summery, lighthearted presence, I crashed the boat into the low branches of a willow tree, Nina began to laugh, and Lev and Alla waved and shouted from the shore, and as I tried to extricate us from the wavering, sparkling, leafy ambush, she suddenly leaned over—and kissed me.

When we parted later that day, I did not go home. Drunk with happiness, I walked the streets of Moscow, watching the darkness fall, watching windows pop up one after another and then go out, watching the sky grow thinner. When the first gray light touched the rooftops, the city unexpectedly rustled with a warm summer rain, and laughing, I ran to a nearby bus stop and waited in its glass-walled shelter. Half an hour passed, and still the rain gave no sign of abating. Realizing how close I was to the institute, I made a dash through the downpour and minutes later burst into the building.

Once in my studio, I immediately succumbed to the temptation of the virgin canvas that was stretched on my easel, for a certain image had haunted me all night—a lake, a boat, and in it, a woman—a demure, radiant nude with breasts, arms, and legs sprouting flowers, hundreds, thousands, myriad blue and white flowers whose fresh, fragrant profusion was gradually transformed into the blue, sun-dappled water on which the boat was floating gently. As I painted, I grew oblivious of the world around me—a hubbub of voices in the corridor, a patter of rain on the windowsill, a brisk knock on the door, a heavy step, a voice saying importantly, "There is a certain issue I need to discuss with you, Anatoly Pavlovich. . . ."

Then, glancing up sharply, I saw a balding man entering the room, his red face stony, his thumbs hooked in the pockets of his jacket. It took me a heartbeat to recognize Leonid Penkin, the institute director—and instantly I became aware of my unshaved chin, my rain-drenched clothes, the circles under my eyes, a possibly missed morning lecture, and worse yet, a bare breast quite visibly materializing under my brush amidst a torrent of bluebells. With scarcely a nod for a greeting, the director commenced striding back and forth across the floor, staring majestically somewhere over my head and talking—talking about certain rumors that had reached him, certain, so to speak, artistic gatherings in a certain questionable home that I surely knew about, certain actions, moreover, that he would very much regret to have to undertake in certain contingencies. . . . Praying that he would fail to notice my painting, I hardly listened to his vociferous rhetoric.

"The way I see it," he was saying, "socialist art is like a fast train into the future, and I, for one, would be rather sorry to see someone with your potential get off that train, for let me tell you, young man, it's the only train there is. But I'm afraid you must get off if . . . Are you listening to me? You must get off if you don't produce a ticket this instant!"

"A ticket?" Sukhanov repeated in confusion. "What ticket?"

"I thought as much," said the man, and pushed his red face closer to Sukhanov's. "A stowaway! Well, time to take a walk. Unless, of course, you want to pay a fine. Pay up, or get off."

The people around them murmured excitedly. Through his broken glasses, Sukhanov peered outside and saw another badly lit platform without a name, disconcertingly similar to the one he had left dreams and dreams ago, in Bogoliubovka. Shuddering, he said, "All right, all right, how much?" and hastily reached inside his pocket. He felt some loose change rolling behind the lining, but his wallet was not there. His wallet, he suddenly remembered with a sinking heart, was in a side compartment of his bag, and his bag—his bag had been stolen.

His voice trembling now, he tried to explain his predicament to the conductor, offering what coins he had, swearing he would send the rest of the money in the mail, even humiliating himself by announcing that he was a very influential man, Anatoly Pavlovich Sukhanov, the editor in chief of the magazine *Art of the World*. "And I'm the editor of *Pravda*," said a snickering voice in the crowd, "but I still buy *me* a ticket." The train exploded with ugly, malicious laughter, and the conductor grasped Sukhanov's shoulders and unceremoniously prodded him toward the door. In the quickly disintegrating mob behind him, he thought he saw the ancient man who had sat beside him earlier, now standing on the bench and frantically shouting something over the sea of heads; but his words were swallowed in the multi-throated roar, and in the next moment Sukhanov was rudely bundled off onto the empty platform. With a parting whistle, the train pulled away, all of its windows swarming with scowling, triumphant demons.

For a while after, Sukhanov stumbled up endless flights of stairs and trod along echoing passageways, emerging finally on a wide street, with a row of identical apartment buildings on one side and a park on the other. It looked like a big city. For a long time he waited aimlessly inside a glass-walled shelter by the road. (Hadn't he done this recently? He could not remember.) Eventually the darkness parted with a squeal of tires, and a rectangle of concentrated yellow light, bobbing with more demonic faces at the windows, rolled up and slid open its doors. He stuck his head inside and inquired weakly, addressing no one in particular, "What city is this, please?"—but in reply received only hooting and someone's carelessly phrased advice on public drunkenness. He was about to edge away, when a man seated by himself up front took a closer look at him and asked him where he wanted to go.

"Moscow," Sukhanov said. The demons mocked him gleefully, but the man up front did not laugh. His face was not like the others, and his middle-aged eyes were sad.

"Where in Moscow?" he asked after the demons had quieted behind his back. It appeared that the train had deposited Sukhanov on the western outskirts of the capital; and while the metro was not yet running, the man told him, all he needed to do was take night bus number 403 to Krylatskoe and there switch to the number 13 going directly to the Tretyakovskaya station. "Just wait here," said the man, glancing at his wrist. "There'll be a 403 coming any minute."

"You are very kind," Sukhanov said humbly.

"Hell, I've been there myself," the man replied, shrugging.

The doors closed, and the rectangle of light moved off into the shadows.

It must have been close to six in the morning when Sukhanov was finally spat out by the last bus into the reassuringly familiar landscape of the Zamoskvorechie. The city was still dark, the never-ending night still upon him. Almost swooning with sleep, he walked along Bolshoi Tolmachevsky Lane, and the echo of his solitary steps reverberated hollowly off aged walls. Through an open window, the faint sound of a radio reached him—many voices, remote and muffled like the buzz of an insect throng, singing the Soviet anthem, proclaiming the indestructible union of the free republics. He turned the corner, and the sprawling form of the Tretyakovskaya Gallery loomed into sight. Quickening his steps, he walked toward it, passed the main entrance, and approached a metal side door bearing the sign "Keep Out: Staff Only." When he pushed the door, it gave way soundlessly, just as she had promised. Stepping inside, he barely had time to register that singular museum smell of light dust, parquet polish, and old paper, when his elbow was seized by a swift hand, and Nina's tense face emerged from the dimness.

"Did anyone see you come in?" she whispered as she locked the door behind him.

He shook his head and tried to pull her toward him for a kiss.

"Not now," she said. "It's almost six o'clock, we must hurry. Come, this way."

We tiptoed through labyrinths of nondescript corridors, some lined with dank black pipes, others concealing bookcases in unexpected recesses. Once a red-and-white Saint George pointed a lance directly at my chest from a poster that had materialized in the air, hanging on a column that I could not see, that might not have even been there; and in another minute I almost screamed when the darkness hobbled toward us, gradually assuming the guise of a grinning custodian dragging behind a dried-out mop. "My respects, Nina Petrovna," said the museum's resident ghost, and after Nina pressed something into his proffered hand, shuffled back into the limbo whence he had come. I followed him with uneasy eyes.

"Don't worry," she said. "Anton Ivanych won't report us, he likes me."

"I still think it's too risky," I said. "What if they found out and you lost your job? It's bad enough that I'm about to—"

"What?" she asked sharply, stopping.

I had decided not to tell her about my run-in with Penkin a couple of months ago, but she was insistent, and I did not want to stand here arguing, for our presence in the bowels of the Tretyakovka was unlawful, the corridors shifted with invisible shadows, and who knew what lay lurking in wait behind all these boarded-up doors. Hurriedly I explained about the reprimand, the painting of the nude, the director's bulging eyes, the final warning. . . . She listened intently, and slowly her face assumed a determined expression.

"We'll talk about it later," she whispered. "Now let's just do this, replace the keys, and get out."

We reached the place a few wary minutes later, having passed through rooms and rooms of shoddy Soviet paintings along the way. Her hands shaking slightly, she struggled with an enormous lock. She walked in first, flipped a light switch; I heard a stifled cry. I rushed in after her, my heart pounding—and stopped, dazzled, astonished, overwhelmed, awed into silence in the presence of absolute genius.

For here, in a cramped storage space, separated by a thin partition from monstrosities and nonentities, a few dozen outlawed canvases leaned haphazardly against the walls. Canvases by Malevich, Filonov, Kandinsky, Chagall —the legendary Russian artists whose works I had never seen, whose names I had heard pronounced only rarely, and always with a self-righteous lilt of accusation. For one moment, I felt a burst of blinding, searing anger—anger at this country that had dared condemn its greatest masters to oblivion, anger at these people who had refused so ignorantly the gift of such beauty, anger at these times that appeared to change but in reality stayed the same, still forbidding us our most precious inheritance, still forcing us to steal our revelations crumb by crumb, in secret, with nervous, criminal glances. . . . And then I beheld the bright, magical world swirling about me, beckoning me softly, and discovered that my heart no longer had any place for anger—for my heart was full.

And brilliant fireworks erupted in glowing glory, and radiant skies melted with purple sunrises and green sunsets, and red and golden lovers floated on the wings of music over the roofs of their blue towns, and homeless poets flooded the nights with lyrics and stars, and the generous earth blossomed with rainbow-drenched flowers and fiery horses—and as I saw life itself dissolve into a thousand previously unseen shapes and tints, I was lost forever in the flaming flights of the purest colors, in the holy harmonies of the brush, in the deepest dreams of the soul. . . .

And when minutes or hours or years later I emerged from this glimmering, singing paradise to feel someone tugging on my sleeve, whispering that we must leave now, I felt stunned by a realization that something had happened—that I was different now—that during that color-mad stretch of eternity, I had felt in myself a mysterious, perfect affinity with the giants surrounding me—that I had glimpsed my own strength, my own voice, my own vision. At that instant, I knew at last what greatness I could demand of myself. Drunk with this knowledge, I turned around—and saw her, the woman I loved, the woman to whom I owed this gift, looking at me with a shining, wide-eyed gaze.

"You were thinking you could be one of them," she said. "I could tell."

"And what do *you* think?" I asked, laughing to hide my sudden nervousness.

"I think," she said gravely, "I think, yes, you could be. Perhaps you already are."

My heart was everywhere all at once, in my throat, in my wrists, in the backs of my knees.

"Nina," I said, "let's get married."

And smiling now, she said simply, "It was your turn to read my thoughts."

The night was finally lifting when we scrambled outside. Holding hands, we walked along Bolshoi Tolmachevsky Lane, sharing a pale, persimmon-tinted sunrise with a spluttering water truck and a solitary cat strolling home after an all-night revel. The air was brightening slowly, gloriously above our heads.

"Let's go to my place and tell Mother," I said. "She wakes up early."

She nodded wordlessly. Laughing, we chased each other down the street, across the lobby, up the stairs, all the way to the eighth floor.

On the landing, I searched for my keys.

"And tonight, if you like, I'll invite some friends over and we'll celebrate in style, with cake and champagne," I said lightly. The keys were not in my right pocket. I reached for the left. "Nina?"

But there was no answer—and when I swung around, I saw only the empty landing behind me. "Nina?" I called louder, not yet worried. "Are you hiding on the stairs?"

The keys were not in my left pocket either. Frowning, I tried to recall where I had put them last. And then I knew. The keys were in the side compartment of my bag, along with my wallet, and the bag—the bag had been stolen.

Remembering everything now, I slid onto the floor before the locked door to apartment number fifteen, building number seven, Belinsky Street, and wept.

Nineteen

Anatoly Pavlovich! Anatoly Pavlovich!"

He hesitated to open his eyes. The awakening had brought with it a flock of ugly sensations. His body felt broken, his skin seemed dusted with gritty sand, his head ached, and the right side of his mouth had developed a persistent tic. The floor beneath him was cold, and somewhere above, a worried voice was saying, "Anatoly Pavlovich, what happened? Why are you here? Are you ill?"

It could not be avoided for much longer. Sukhanov looked up unhappily and saw a landing with an elevator grille, a shaft of bleak light falling through a dusty staircase window, and looming above him, a sturdy man in his thirties, with pronounced cheekbones, a stubborn jaw, and bulging arms, dressed in a brown leather jacket.

"Oh, it's you," said Sukhanov vaguely. He knew the man—knew him rather well, in fact—but for some reason the name escaped him.

"Are you ill, Anatoly Pavlovich?" the man repeated. "Do you need an ambulance?"

Sukhanov shook his head, and immediately touched his temples to steady the pain.

"I'm fine," he said morosely. "I was just sleeping. A ridiculous situation, this. My keys were stolen, and no one's home. I've been sitting by the door for hours. I . . . I had to return to the city on an urgent matter."

The man—Volodya, perhaps, or Vyacheslav—glanced at his watch.

"How unfortunate," he said. "And where is Nina Petrovna? Here, let me help you off the floor."

Ignoring the outstretched hand, Sukhanov heaved himself up.

"My wife has decided to stay in the country for a few more days," he said stiffly. "Gardening or something."

A look of relief passed across the man's face.

"A few more days, really?" he said. "Well, that's lucky. Because as it turns out, it wouldn't be easy for me to . . . That is, I wouldn't be able to pick her up this afternoon. I was actually coming by to leave a note on your door—I was in the neighborhood anyway, and I couldn't reach you on the phone, so . . ." He crumpled a piece of paper in his hand and looked away uncomfortably. "The thing is, Anatoly Pavlovich . . . It seems I won't be driving you any longer. They've reassigned the car. A matter of departmental reorganization at the Ministry, they told me."

"Ah," said Sukhanov without surprise. It could be Vladislav, he supposed. Something with a V, in any case.

"I hope I'm not leaving you in the lurch," said the man, with another anxious glance at his watch. "Of course, you'll get a new driver in a matter of days, just in time for Nina Petrovna's return from the dacha, but if you need a lift in the meantime and I happen to be available, we could always work something out—privately, so to speak."

Sukhanov leaned against the wall and closed his eyes. The darkness under his lids was soothing, but he longed to find himself once more amid the vivid colors of a recent dream that lingered faintly in his memory—something about an empty museum in a hushed predawn hour, a violin player flying over the roofs of a turn-of-the-century town, a foretaste of greatness rising within him . . . But a stray image of rats abandoning a sinking ship in a dreary procession kept fighting its way to the foreground of his mind, and the man's increasingly impatient voice lapped at the edges of his hearing, distracting him, reminding him of a host of irrelevant, disagreeable matters that probably needed to be addressed; and he could do nothing but wordlessly wait for it all to end. Finally, as if from afar, the man said, "Well, that's settled, then," and Sukhanov heard a rustle of leather followed by steps thumping across the landing and down the stairs, raising a brief flurry of agitated barks in their wake, growing more hollow as they descended, then dissolving in the hazy midmorning silence. Alone at last, he again sank to the floor and drifted to sleep.

And he was close to catching the tail of his delightful dream when the quieted dogs renewed their barking and the steps sounded in the stairwell again, closer and closer, until the rustle of leather was all about him. Sleepily he wondered whether time had perhaps decided to play yet another little joke on him by rewinding the past few minutes—and whether he would just keep slipping deeper and deeper into the past in this terribly amusing reverse order, until he found himself once more an alert child playing with his toes on a bright green carpet, gazing down the length of his two years into the dark vortex of the unknown, so akin to death and yet so much less frightening. . . . But already he was being pulled up, and shaken awake, and the square-jawed man with the uncertain name was propping him up, saying almost belligerently, "No, Anatoly Pavlovich, I can't just leave you here like this, you seem unwell. Come, the car's downstairs, just tell me where you want to go. Does Nadezhda Sergeevna have a spare key to your place? No? How about your father-in-law? . . . All right, Gorky Street it is."

Sukhanov drowsily allowed himself to be propelled into the elevator, and across the lobby, and into the street. The familiar black Volga—once his—was parked at the opposite curb, but two people were already sitting inside, one in the passenger seat and the other in the back; he could not see them clearly for the shadowy reflections of boughs swaying ceaselessly in the windows. The man asked him to wait, then ran across the road and tapped on the glass. As the window slid down, Sukhanov glimpsed a young woman with the petulant face of a broken porcelain doll—the man's wife, most likely. For a while they appeared to argue, in fierce, inaudible voices, the man seemingly pleading. Then the woman said hysterically, "Well, if you must!" and rolled up the window.

The man turned and waved, and Sukhanov trudged toward him.

"Don't mind Prince, he's quite tame," said the man enigmatically, opening the back door. Sukhanov peered in and was startled to discover that the person in the back was not a person at all but an enormous dog with brown, matted fur and a sour expression around its unmuzzled nose; but before he could object, he was bundled inside and the car moved away, precipitating a miniature snowstorm within the plastic sphere hanging from the rearview mirror and causing a yellow suitcase on the seat next to him to bump painfully against his knee. The next few minutes were profoundly unpleasant, for the man had made no introductions, and no one said anything, and the air in the car was unbearably sweet with perfume, and the dog kept looking askance at Sukhanov, salivating mutely; and after a while, he noticed that the woman in front was making a hushed, sniffling sort of sound, and realized she was crying. He had no time to wonder about it, however, for just then they came to a skidding stop, and the man announced, "Here we are."

Hastily murmuring "Thanks" and "So long," Sukhanov clambered out of the car.

After a few steps, he glanced back. The man without the name and the woman with the face of a porcelain doll were kissing, kissing with the embarrassing, awkward hunger of adolescents—and as he quickly averted his eyes, he knew that he had seen the woman before, and that she was not the man's wife at all, and that the explanation for the whole thing was very simple and somewhat sordid and possibly a bit happy but mainly terribly, terribly sad. . . . And then the magnificent courtyard enclosed him darkly, and the necessity of facing Pyotr Alekseevich Malinin in just a few moments forced everything else from his mind.

At the mention of Sukhanov's name, the concierge waved him through: he was expected. Too impatient to wait for the elevator, he ran up the stairs to the fifth floor, stopping only once to right his tie and gather his courage. An instant later, before he had even lifted his hand to ring the bell, the imposing door opened, and Nina stood on the doorstep. She was smiling, but he could see that she too was nervous.

"Did you remember the wine?" she whispered, ushering him into the hall. "Good. We'll eat right now, it'll be easier that way, and you'll tell him later in the evening, before dessert. Don't worry, you'll like each other, he's nothing like his public persona. . . . Only please, Tolya, you promised, no art discussions."

I nodded, barely listening, suddenly disoriented by the world revealed just past the door—the brilliant expanse of polished floors, the gleaming void of enormous mirrors, a table rising importantly on leonine paws, an officer with a proud mustache gazing pensively out of a gilded frame ("Mama's father," said Nina in passing), and beyond, an infinite perspective of unfolding rooms. Even though she had charted the floor plan for me only the other day, explaining where our bedroom would be and which space I could convert into my studio, I had had no warning that the schematic drawing on the napkin would translate into a vision of all this foreign splendor, and no idea that in the year 1957 anyone in Moscow still lived in such old-fashioned luxury. Overwhelmed, I followed Nina through the vastness of the place, catching glimpses of a cupboard full of rose-tinted porcelain ("Mama used to collect china," explained Nina) and the elegant curve of a lustrously black piano ("Mama was the only one who played"); and when we finally arrived at a high-ceilinged hall with an elaborately set table, and a handsome middle-aged man in a velvet blazer rose from an armchair, his hand extended, his smile dry, I felt almost incapable of speaking—for in those few minutes I had understood, fully and for the first time, how different my life was from hers, how great a gap lay between us, and how truly uneven our union would be.

The dinner was not a success. Nina burned the main course; Malinin did not remember me from his lectures at the Surikov, visibly disliked the wine I had brought (it had cost me a week's salary), and considered it beneath him to pretend otherwise on both counts; feeling suffocatingly out of my depths, I kept discoursing lamely on the impressive growth of Moscow since the war and the accomplishments of Soviet composers. After the meal, when Nina had refilled our glasses and with conspicuous haste vanished into the kitchen to "check on that pie," I struggled to explain to this self-satisfied man who sat frowning at his wine across the table that I loved his daughter madly, that she and I were, in fact, engaged to marry, that the date had already been set for September twenty-second, less than a month away. . . . I had hoped to find words that were meaningful and sincere, but ended by simply blurting it out. He listened calmly, pressing the tips of his fingers together, avoiding my eyes. When I finished, he demonstratively pushed aside his half-full glass and cleared his throat.

"Do you know, young man, I've been hearing things about you," he said. "Leonid Penkin, your director, is an old friend of mine. He tells me he is quite disappointed in your prospects. It appears that, well, how shall I put it . . . You are not quite the stuff of which successful artists are made. Frankly, it doesn't surprise me—my daughter has never been careful in her choice of acquaintances. Though at least she's given up that awful Jewish fellow, what's his name . . ."

His voice was low—he must not have wanted Nina to overhear—and his meaning unmistakable. In stunned silence, I looked at myself through his coolly calculating eyes, and saw a pathetic little teacher breathlessly eager to enter into a lucky alliance with a race of demigods. Flushed with humiliation, I wanted to leave at once, but felt unable to move, as if trapped in a nightmare—a slow, perverse nightmare in which darkness seeped into the room through the heavy crimson curtains, seconds rustled quietly in the grandfather clock in the corner, the gold-rimmed dessert plates glittered emptily on the table, the crystal chandelier sparkled coldly, and in a precise near-whisper the man whose face resembled so much the face of my love was talking about his own position in life at my age, and some nice young man named Misha Buryshkin or Broshkin or Burykin who was also in love with Nina and promised to go far, very far, at the Ministry of Culture, and certain comforts that Nina, in the pride of her youth, might think she could do without but which were really in her blood . . .

And as he spoke, the dreary colors and communal smells of my own impoverished childhood rose unsought in my memory, and I thought of Professor Gradsky, and the twisted stump of the chandelier in the ceiling of our room, and the day I had learned that the old man and his wife had once lived alone in our vast six-room apartment—and all at once my humiliation gave way to another, more powerful feeling. The old anger, the anger of the deprived and the dispossessed, reared its righteous head inside my soul. For a minute

I tried to control it, but the conceited man in the velvet blazer went on talking in his insultingly reserved voice, and the chandelier went on sparkling, and finally, standing up so abruptly that I knocked down the chair, I told him, with the freedom of someone dreaming, exactly what I thought about his so-called comforts and his protégé at the Ministry and his unflattering opinion of his own daughter . . . As my voice climbed higher and higher, I no longer knew what I was saying. Everything was hot and swirling around me, and at first he was smiling derisively, but soon his face grew taut and white—possibly when I shouted that his success as an artist was a sham, a joke of history, that he couldn't paint worth a damn, that of the two of us—

And at that instant I saw Nina standing in the doorway, pale and wide-eyed, a soapy, dripping plate in her hands. I stopped in midsentence, looked at her, looked at her father, then picked up Malinin's glass of wine, and finished it in one gulp.

"Sorry," I said flatly, and walked across the room, past the frozen Nina, past the piano and the porcelain, along the endless corridor, and out onto the landing. Carefully I closed the door behind me and remained still for a while, waiting for the swirling to stop. But as I stood there, trying not to think, knowing full well I had lost her, I gradually became aware of a growing din, a rising tumult of incoherent voices, the sound of a broken plate; and in another minute, the door was flung open, Nina flew sobbing into my arms, and somewhere close behind, her father cried, "I swear, if you leave this house now—"

With a violence that shook the walls, Nina slammed the door shut, and his voice cut off. The two of us were left facing each other across a shocked silence.

Then someone cracked open a door on the opposite side of the landing, and a middle-aged blonde in a lacy apron edged her head around the jamb.

"What's all that noise?" she asked with disapproval, looking at Sukhanov. "No use knocking like that, Pyotr Alekseevich is out of town. He's gone to the Crimea with his grandson."

Sukhanov stared at her dully.

"Won't be returning for at least a week either," the woman added almost gleefully.

"Oh," Sukhanov muttered. "Of course. How could I have forgotten?"

And suddenly he could visualize it so clearly: a crystal bowl melting into its reflection in the still, black surface of the lion-footed table just on the other side of this wall, and in the bowl, among a jumble of many temporarily displaced but potentially useful odds and ends (a button not yet matched to a garment, a solitary cuff link, a mysterious screw), a bunch of keys, seemingly ordinary yet possessing the power of some fairy-tale genie to transport him to a marvelous, self-contained world of hot baths and fresh clothes and steaming teas and strawberry jams and maybe even strong liqueurs—a world that was now twice removed, separated from him not by one but by two locked doors. . . . He turned away and plodded toward the elevator, and the aging blonde across the landing followed his steps with such curious eyes that, glancing up with his finger already poised over the elevator button, he thought of saying something cutting—and then saw one last chance of cheating his fate.

"Pardon me," he said with all the dignity he could muster in his broken glasses and mud-stained pants, "but you wouldn't know if anyone here has a key to Pyotr Alekseevich's place? He might have left one with a neighbor."

The woman's birdlike eyes narrowed suspiciously. He hastened to explain who he was, told her in an entreating voice about his being locked out of his own house, his hunger, his need of sleep. . . . She softened perceptibly.

"You are in luck," she said after a brief hesitation. "I keep his spare key. Wait here, I'll go call the resort."

The ease of this resolution had an almost dreamlike quality to it. She returned a few minutes later. Pyotr Alekseevich, she had been told, was taking his customary promenade along the sea. She would try phoning again in a short while, for, naturally, she would not presume to release the keys without his permission, not even to his son-in-law. As she talked, she cracked her door wider, and Sukhanov smelled a rich aroma of mushroom soup and saw a stretch of cozy blue carpet in the hallway and, on the wall, a girlish fur-trimmed coat and an oversized purple jacket; and, filling in the blanks—a daughter, a son, a leisurely family dinner—he found himself envying this stranger her quiet domestic world, and longed to be a part of it, if only for an instant, if only—

"So you'll have to come back in a bit," the woman said. "Half an hour or so. I'd ask you in, but I'm in the middle of cooking."

"Oh, certainly," he said. "I understand. You're very kind as it is."

And smiling sadly, he pressed the elevator button.

Back in the street, he strolled aimlessly along the pavement. When he neared the corner by the Hotel National, where Gorky Street emptied into the square, the many-columned building of the Manège filled his view. The air had grown much colder now, and presently a snowflake melted on his cheek. He paused to file away, for some future use, the liquid reflections of headlights in the slush of the road, the powdery dust beginning to flicker in the pastel glow of streetlamps, the white columns, the black trees, the blue shadows, and above it all, the quickly darkening skies, luminously pregnant as they could be only on an evening before a snowfall. Then, at once aware of the ache in his fingers, he rapidly crossed Marx Avenue and, lowering his unwieldy parcel to the ground, prepared to wait. He was there only for a minute when Lev Belkin strode across the square, a bundle under his arm, and even at this distance I could tell he was smiling broadly.

"Glad?" Lev shouted.

"You bet!" I shouted back.

"Nervous?" Lev said, closer now.

"Not a bit," I replied, picking up my load. "I have a feeling it will all go splendidly."

Together we entered the Manège.

It was the last day of November in the year 1962, and I already imagined it emblazoned on my future memory as the date on which my prolonged apprenticeship was finally destined to end, and to the sonorous cymbals of public acclaim, my heart trembling with gladness, I, Anatoly Sukhanov, a name among names, would enter the gladiators' ring of art history, stepping into the long-awaited spotlight out of the dim shadows of anonymous toil.

I had lived in anticipation of this day for a long time. The thaw whose first astonishing inroads into the snowdrifts we had witnessed in 1956 was melting its way through history and literature, but had barely made itself felt in the arctic bleakness of Soviet art; and even though for me the preceding years had been rich with that indescribable richness of small-scale triumphs that only an artist knows in his sweaty task of creation, yet little by little my inability to share my canvases with anyone but a handful of close friends, my struggle to maintain my precarious position at the institute, the precautions I continued to take in order to conceal my real self from colleagues and chance acquaintances, the effort of teaching what I no longer believed in—in short, the pervasive duplicity of my existence— poisoned my joy in living, my joy in working, my very desire to paint; and with fading hope, I dreamt of a day when I would tear away the suffocating shroud of falsity and show them, show them all, the ripened fruits of all those years.

And then, unexpectedly, magically, the day came, at the end of a particularly trying month in a trying year, shortly after Nina's thirtieth birthday.

Nina still tried to pretend, to herself as much as to me, that she was the same girl who one day in 1957 had left her home, breaking with her father, forsaking her old life, and had stood next to me, wearing that white, narrow-waisted dress I liked so much, her back straight, her smile proud, her eyes shining, while an officious woman with thick ankles had monotonously recited solemn commonplaces from a worn compendium of Soviet marriage transactions and Lev's Alla had giggled into a bunch of wilting gladioli; but even though she continued to call herself the "high priestess" of my art and uncomplainingly slipped away to the kitchen to give me space to work, I could sense the beginning of a change, an insidious, stealthy, corrosive change, in the air between us.

On the evening of November third, the day she turned thirty, she came home from her job at the Tretyakovka wearing that slightly pinched expression I had been noticing of late, and when I unveiled her present—a portrait of her as a mermaid I had worked on in secret, to surprise her—she smiled with her lips only and said in a toneless voice, "Oh. Another painting." Then she left for a dinner party at her father's (after years of stubborn resentment, he had offered her a semblance of peace, which failed to include me). I was still up, waiting for her, when she returned, well after midnight. Her face, as she walked in, arrested me, so uncommonly animated it was, and more beautiful than I had seen it in months: her cheeks flushed, I imagined with compliments and expensive liqueurs, her gaze brightened, perhaps with golden memories of her fairy-tale youth; but my impulse to tenderly tilt her head back, look into her eyes, salvage at least something of our day together died a hurried death when I noticed a peacock-blue scintillation following her passage through the shadows of our crowded room. She was wearing a pair of sapphire earrings, and it was they, nothing else, that lent a deep blue brilliance to her gray irises and suffused her pallid skin with an excited warmth.

"What are these?" I asked sharply, knowing the answer already.

"A gift from my father."

"We can't accept such things from that man."

"He is my father," she said. "He loves me. He wanted to do something nice for my birthday. And you . . ." She stopped, looked away. "You don't know anything about him."

I had the impression she had meant to say something else but changed her mind.

"I know enough," I said. "I know what he is. I know what he does—bargains away his dignity piece by piece to the highest bidder, paints trash so he can have his cushy life—"

"You paint trash too," she interrupted. "Your studio at the institute—"

My breath caught. "I paint trash so I can do this," I said, shoving my chin at the dusty deposits of canvases in the corners, no longer bothering to keep my voice down. "What I do at the institute is irrelevant—this is who I really am."

"And how do you know who my father really is?"

"Oh, I see—after a day of prostituting himself, he plays the violin or something?"

"Have you ever considered, Tolya," said Nina slowly, "that you may actually be wrong about something or someone? You think my father is an amoral, selfish man, but maybe . . ." She paused. "Maybe he just wanted to make me and my mother happy."

Again I had the feeling that some other, harsher words had alighted on her lips, then been discarded—and it was these unspoken reproaches and accusations, combined with her unnatural calm, that sent a wave of fury crashing over me.

"Well, how noble of him," I shouted. "He sold his soul to the devil so you could have your jewelry, and your mother her piano and her gilded teacups!"

I regretted my words as soon as they had escaped me, but it was too late. Nina's face, now drawn and pale in the yellow glow of a bedside lamp, seemed suspended between expressions; then she walked to the window and, staring out into the dreary darkness punctuated by anemic streetlamps, carefully removed the earrings, balanced their tiny blue radiance on her palm, and considered them briefly before setting them down on the windowsill. When she faced me, her eyes held no love, no emotion at all.

"So my mother collected porcelain and was passionate about music," she said softly. "Is it so wrong to want to have beauty in your life? Not everyone is willing to live . . . to live like this. And is it really so contemptible to want to give beauty to someone you love?"

Then, not waiting for my answer, she turned and, usually private to a fault, started to undress as if I were not there. In silence I watched her step out of the sea-colored dress her father had brought her years earlier from a trip to Italy, which she still wore on every birthday and New Year's Eve, gently smooth its creases before hanging it in our makeshift wardrobe, then take off her stockings and, sliding her hand inside, raise them against the light and in a seemingly familiar, tired ritual check for fresh runs. As I looked at the silky shimmer spread between her fingers, I thought mechanically that stockings were very hard to come by nowadays; and on the heels of that thought, the famous words of Chekhov popped into my mind: "A human being should be entirely beautiful: the face, the clothes, the soul, and the thoughts." And suddenly I was frightened—frightened that something irreparable had happened between us. I thought of the squalor of our dingy place, which had more space for paintings than for us; and the stairs that always reeked of urine; and the anxious hovering of my mother, who kept imagining footsteps outside our door and strange clicks on our phone line, and who, in truth, did not like Nina very much and referred to her, with pursed lips and barely out of earshot—for our communal quarters were too cramped for secrets—as "your fine lady"; I thought too that none of it was ever likely to change.

And then, for one moment, I almost believed that all my creations of the past five years—all those flights of fancy, all those sleepless nights, the bouts of despair, the transports of happiness, the smuggled revelations, the full moons, the museum vaults, the lingering dreams, the stolen moments of love—all of those things were nothing but idle imaginings, youthful indulgences, rainbow dust on a butterfly's wing; and that my real life was here, now, in this unlivable room with its odors of ancient pipes, dust, and paint, with this silent woman who was lying in bed, her back toward me, pretending to be asleep. . . . And so unbearable was the thought that I did not move for a long time, and the shadows twitched and cavorted in the corners, and my mother murmured in haunted nightmares behind the wall, and my works, my gifts, my children, begged to be released into the light, and Nina's breathing gradually assumed a different, measured rhythm, and still I stood in the dark, and after perhaps an hour Nina suddenly said without turning, "You know, Tolya, there is more than one way to lose your soul."

And then, after several dismal, mostly silent weeks, the telephone rang.

For the full first minute, with Lev stuttering in his excitement and Alla shrieking in the background, I understood nothing. "Pinch me, I'm dreaming," he kept repeating. Then Nina walked into the corridor, her face remote, her eyelids swollen with insomnia.

"Please don't shout like that," she said flatly. "It's seven-thirty in the morning."

My hands were jumping so much I could not immediately fit the receiver into the cradle; then, drawing her to me, "Listen, you won't believe this," I said, already anticipating the wondrous light about to come into her eyes.

A couple of months earlier, a major retrospective—*Thirty Years of Moscow Art*—had opened at the Manège. Lev and I had gone and, having found the whole affair, with a few exceptions, staid and uninspiring, had pronounced it worthy of being displayed in the former stable. But now an event little short of miraculous had taken place. A benevolent official from the Ministry of Culture had approached a few openly experimental artists with an offer to join the show, among them Ilya Beliutin, who ran an unofficial studio, and his students; and as Beliutin happened to be an old acquaintance of our Yastrebov, the loose invitation had been extended to the members of Viktor's circle as well—the bearded Roshchin, and Lev, and myself. True, we were allowed only one work each, but all the same, it was a beginning, was it not, and one should be glad even of such—

"Oh Tolya," Nina interrupted, clasping her hands, "so what if it's only one painting—it's the Manège, millions of people will see it, and you will be noticed, I know you will be! My God, it's wonderful, just wonderful. . . . When does it start?"

It was all happening with the rapidity of a dream: we had been told to bring our paintings by tonight; Lev and I were meeting by the Manège that evening; the show was to open to the public the very next day. Mother and Nina left for work, but I quickly summoned an impressive cough for the benefit of a sympathetic secretary on the other end of the line and spent several hours in an incredulous, delightful haze, leafing through my canvases as through pages of my life, remembering each birth, at times tender and slow, at times furious and breathless, passing judgment on the sum total of my existence as an artist—my early studies of trains and reflections; the mythical and urban landscapes that had occupied me all through 1958; my subsequent fascination with surrealism, in an attempt to transplant the lessons of Dalí and Magritte to Russian soil; and in the past two years, my ultimate arrival at what I believed to be my own, truly unique style—trying to choose from among them the one painting most representative of my philosophy of art, or possibly the one most original, or the one most beautiful, or perhaps simply the one most dear to my heart. In the early afternoon, when the air had already begun to thicken into blue softness outside the window and I was still at a loss, Nina called.

"Tolya, I've been thinking," she said, and I could hear a smile in her voice. "What about that early one, with the reflection of a woman's face in a train window, you know the one? Of course, it's not as complex as your current pieces—but it may be easier for people to understand, and, well . . . It's what made me realize how brilliant you were."

"Oh," I said, smiling also. "Well, since you put it that way—"

Once inside, we unwrapped our bundles. Lev had selected an abstract piece.

"What do you think?" he said uncertainly, turning it to the light. "It's a new one."

I did not have the heart to tell him the truth. Together we watched our paintings being mounted on the walls; I found it exhilarating and almost frightening to see a deeply private vision of mine splayed across the impersonal white surface under the clinical glare of gallery lamps, with a rectangular label bearing my name underneath. Roshchin and a few others of our acquaintance were milling about, all with the same slightly disoriented look on their faces, but I did not stay to talk to them. I wanted to preserve the sonorous fullness of this day unmarred by nervous banter, insincere compliments, exaggerated camaraderie, so I could carry it, slowly, carefully, like some precious elixir, through the gleaming blue city, through the quietly falling snow, through the softly illuminated streets and the darkened courtyards, and present it, with not a single drop spilled, to her, my Nina.

She met me on the landing, kissing me quickly. She wore the white dress of our wedding day, her bare arms were goose-bumped, and her eyes were bright; she had bought a bottle of champagne, and it was lovely to hear her laugh at the dry explosion of the cork later in the evening. My mother quit the dinner table without finishing her glass, her lips tightly pressed together, and we listened to her shuffling behind the closed door of her room, muttering darkly about reprisals and retributions, until the hum of the television drowned out her voice.

"Poor woman, she never stops worrying," Nina whispered.

For a while after that, we sat silently in the cozily lit kitchen. I was watching the snow whirling outside the window, and Nina was peeling a tangerine, the first of the season. And all at once the scent of the fruit, sweet yet with the slightest hint of bitterness, and the light taste of champagne lingering on my tongue, and the soft, furry snowflakes dancing in the sky like some white winter moths, and Nina's profile bent in the gentle glow of the green lampshade, and the knowledge of this wonderful change that was drawing closer and closer, all merged into a feeling of such intensity, such completion, that I felt this to be the happiest moment of my life—happier even than that luminous, color-mad moment when, with Chagall and Kandinsky for witnesses, Nina had promised to marry me—or perhaps it was still the same moment, now in its long-awaited fulfillment. . . . Smiling, Nina looked up.

"Here," she said, holding out half of the tangerine. "It's a bit sour, but so delicious."

We did not sleep at all that night. The snow stopped soon after midnight, and immediately the sky grew dark and deep like velvet; then the grayness began to creep into the nooks and crannies of the world; and sometime later, in the pale light of a cold dawn, Nina lifted her face to mine and said, "Tolya, I'm so sorry about my birthday. I know I was unfair. It's just that as a girl I always imagined what my life would be like at thirty, and, well . . . It was harder than I had expected, that's all."

For a minute unspoken words hung between us. Then she said with a small sigh, "But I never stopped believing in your talent, not for an instant, and I would have stood by you no matter what. Still, I'm so relieved this finally happened. We've waited for this for a long time."

"Yes," I said, kissing her lightly. "A very long time. I'm sorry too. But everything will be different now, you'll see."

And then the sunrise of December first was upon us.

Twenty

When I left the house that morning, I did not go directly to the Manège. Perhaps I feared the disappointment of seeing indifferent crowds stroll with scarcely a glance past my work; or maybe I simply wanted to prolong the anticipation, sensing it to be immensely richer than the most resounding acclaim could ever be. The bleak day smelled of winter, the sky and the houses were the running gray and yellow of a spare watercolor, and rare pedestrians glided through the pale landscapes in silent, chilled preoccupation, leaving behind black garlands of footprints filled with the glistening slush of yesterday's melting snow. Wandering along the wet pavements in their wake, I did not think of the exhibition that at this very moment, perhaps, was opening its doors to eager visitors only a few streets and squares away; but a deep happiness, a kind of muted, exultant hum, underlay all my steps, all my breaths, all my heartbeats, infusing my walk with a triumphant spring and my soul with a glow of well-being.

And by the time I turned a random corner and unexpectedly saw the Manège rise into view, I had understood, with an effortless, wordless certainty, that I was finally ready to undertake my most ambitious project yet—a challenge I had cherished secretly for many years—a series of seven paintings that would merge everything I felt about Russia, and history, and art, and God.

Already impatient to return home and begin to sketch, I started toward the Manège. The sky was low before another snowfall, and the ancient towers of the Kremlin squatted morosely under the sagging clouds. Although there were more people here, it was suddenly so quiet I could hear the echoing steps of a man running along the street, heedlessly dogged by his own frantic shadow. I felt that my vision had never been sharper, as if all my artistic powers had been released at once. Happiness soared inside me like a mad angel. The first painting, I already knew, would be called *The Garden of Eden,* and its predominant color would be green—the lush, sunny green at the heart of a birch forest, the subtler, mysterious green of Nina's eyes, the simple, joyful green of the carpet I had played on as a child. . . . A snowflake pricked the skin of my hand; the running man was closer; I could see he had no hat on. At the opposite end of the spectrum, on the other side of the gates of paradise, would be the dull green of a chain-link fence, the poisonous green of a neon sign, the oppressive green of hospital walls, the . . . the . . . The running man was upon me now. His face was distorted, his eyes wild. It was Lev Belkin.

"It's over," he gasped. "Where have you been? It's all over."

"What is it? What's the matter?" I said, laughing as I arrested his flight, already anticipating some impish joke.

He shook himself free of my arms.

"Khrushchev and some bigwigs . . . showed up at the Manège this morning," he said between rasping breaths. "An official visit . . . we weren't told about. It was . . . I can't tell you what it was like. Where the hell have you been?"

It was not a joke after all. He sounded furious and, underneath it, frightened.

"I was just walking around," I said quickly. "What happened?"

"I'll tell you what happened." He kept glancing over his shoulder as if worried he was being chased. "Khrushchev hated everything he saw. Abstract paintings in particular, but the rest as well. He went all red in the face and shouted that our works were good only for covering urinals, and other things too—terrible things. . . . Real art should ennoble the individual and arouse him to action, these kinds of pictures are amoral and anti-Soviet, they have wasted money on us, we should be sent far away and put to work cutting trees so we could pay back the state for all the paper we've besmirched—"

"Did he . . . did he say anything about my painting?" I asked haltingly.

Lev grabbed my coat, so violently that I felt something rip. For a second I thought he was going to hit me. Then, slowly, his mouth softened.

"*Your* painting?" he said, releasing me. "Tolya, are you listening? Who cares what he thought about your painting? I'm sure he didn't notice it—he didn't really look at any of our things. He just saw something different and charged like a bull at a red cape. Roshchin thinks the whole affair was a provocation—that bastard from the Ministry who invited us to the show must have known about the state visit all along, and hoped that Khrushchev would have precisely this reaction. God, Tolya, don't you understand? We are *finished*, we are all finished! They are declaring war on us—prison camps and all the rest!"

For some time I studied an object lying on Lev's open palm. It was round and black and shiny, and had four small holes in it; a frayed bit of thread was sticking out of a lower hole. It looked odd, like some puzzling artifact of an ancient, forgotten civilization. Then, through the resounding silence in my mind, one thought emerged: Nina.

"Nina is coming to the Manège at two o'clock," I said dully. "I was going to show her around. I'd like her to see my painting hanging on the wall at least once. It's a painting of her, and she would really—"

Lev looked away.

"They are taking everything down as we speak," he said slowly. "Nina knows already, I called her. I've been looking for you for over an hour." After a small pause, he added, "Sorry about your coat"— and pressed the torn-off button into my hand.

The days that followed were a wretched blur. There were the rooms at the Manège, the walls bare now, with a draft off the street tossing homeless shreds of wrapping paper from corner to corner and a few square-shouldered, square-faced young men in freshly pressed suits shrugging noncommittally when a frantic, disheveled Roshchin begged them to disclose the fate of our works. There were the hours at the institute when Lev and I struggled through our meaningless lectures while the whispers of the Manège affair spread behind our backs, and that splendidly sunny morning when Leonid Penkin pushed his corpulent belly through my door and in a bored drawl relieved me of my position. There was the miserable evening I spent at Lev's place, with Lev, also fired, sitting stony-faced at the kitchen table, pouring himself glass after glass of vodka, while Alla shrilly lamented her wasted youth. Worse yet, there was the silent disapproval in my own home, with the television loudly reciting victories of socialist labor behind my mother's closed door and Nina moving about the kitchen like the ghost of a housewife doomed for all eternity to miming a multitude of imaginary chores, too busy to talk, avoiding my eyes, as if she blamed me for what had happened—but mainly, through it all, behind it all, there was an emptiness, a vast, cold, ever-present, all-pervasive emptiness inside me that kept me awake for hours every night, without thoughts, without hopes, trapped in a heavy darkness alone with the barely visible shadows of my paintings, now damned forever.

As the week neared its end, our worst fears, at least, had not been realized—though a few of us had lost our jobs, and the rest had received official reprimands, no one had been arrested, and even Roshchin, who had vanished mysteriously the day after the fateful opening, prompting his distraught mistress to make incoherent, sobbing calls to all his friends, turned up the next morning, with a black eye and reeking of drink but otherwise unharmed. Yet the sense of impending disaster continued to oppress us, and Lev kept nervously proposing extended trips to the country. "The thing to do right now," he repeated, "is to lie low until they forget about us." I would merely shrug in response. As time dragged on, irresolute and despondent, I found myself increasingly indifferent to my ultimate fate, and felt a listless calm when the telephone screamed at four in the morning on two consecutive nights and then hummed with pregnant silence into my ear, or when one evening, just as my mother and I were sitting down to supper (Nina was in bed with a migraine), there sounded a harsh knock on the door and I discovered a strange man on the landing, wearing a glossy beaver hat down to his eyebrows and carrying a bunch of artificial carnations (the kind one places on graves), who, proclaiming with a sinister smile that he must have mistaken the door, persisted in peering over my shoulder into our apartment. Nina did not share my detachment. After the man's appearance on our doorstep, she grew tense whenever she heard steps on our floor and disliked answering the telephone; and thus it was I who lifted the receiver when, exactly one week after the catastrophe, my father-in-law rang our place.

He had to name himself: in the past five years we had exchanged only a few static-filled sentences, and I did not recognize his voice.

"Nina's asleep," I said curtly—it was only nine o'clock, but I could see no light under the door to our room.

"Actually, Anatoly," he said, "I wanted to talk to you. Not on the phone, though. Would you be so kind as to come over? Take a pen, I'll give you my address."

"I remember it," I said, then added pointedly, "I have a very good memory, Pyotr Alekseevich."

"Indeed?" he said without expression. "Then I'll see you in half an hour."

The cold seeped beneath my upturned collar and damp snow slapped my face as I crossed the night between our homes. Although I tried to assure myself that I owed Nina the courtesy of this visit, my mood worsened by the minute. In the lobby I had an altercation with the concierge, who for a long time refused to let me pass; and once I reached Malinin's landing, still seething from the argument, I was stopped by a middle-aged blonde in a lacy apron who, emerging from the apartment next door, kept talking about some Crimean resort, smiling and pressing a bunch of keys into my hand. Over her shoulder hovered a pimply youth who stared at me with disconcerting curiosity, then exclaimed nonsensically, "I know you, don't I? You are that mister with the tie, from the Bolshoi Moskvoretsky Bridge, I owe you two kopecks!"—but at that moment Malinin's lock clicked, and the imposing figure of Nina's father rose on the doorstep, dressed in a floor-length robe, holding a pear-shaped goblet of cognac in his hand, reflected in the gilded mirrors.

"Please come in," he said, majestically sweeping his arm inside.

The door closed behind me.

In silence Malinin led me along the corridor. Nothing here had changed in the five years since my first, and last, visit. The Polish officer glared out of his heavy frame at the coat I tossed on the counter and the wet footprints I left on the immaculate floors; the piano, untouched in almost two decades—since Maria Malinina's premature death— glistened with its dark, useless grandeur in the depths of the drawing room; and through another half-open door I glimpsed, with a sense of oppressive recognition, the crystal chandelier, the mahogany grand-father clock, the crimson velvet curtains—the bourgeois decorations of the scene of my past outburst. No, nothing had changed—and yet, without Nina's soft domestic presence, the whole place seemed dim-mer and dustier and somehow sad; and when, still without speaking, Malinin showed me into the living room, sat me down, poured me a drink, and lowered himself into an armchair across from me, I looked at him closely and suddenly doubted why I was here. I had supposed he had invited me to gloat over my failure; now I was not sure. For a minute we sat uneasily sipping our drinks. Then he cleared his throat.

"I'll come straight to the point," he said. "I've spoken with your director Penkin, and he is willing to take you back. Naturally, upon certain guarantees."

"Such as?" Caught by surprise, I sounded sharper than I had intended.

"You understand, of course," Malinin said coldly, "he can't afford to damage his reputation by sheltering dubious elements as members of his staff. You must stop dabbling in your underground brand of art, avoid scandalous exhibitions, and stick to painting har-vests and whatnot. A few tractors in the wheat ought to make mat-ters right between you. Not unreasonable, under the circumstances, don't you think? Anatoly?"

When I swirled the cognac in my glass, it gleamed with a rich honey tint, and I thought how much I would love to find the precise color for its luxurious shade. I had planned the second painting in my series in a predominantly yellow palette—the lush saffron of Oriental carpets, the brightness of sunshine on a child's face, the translucent amber of tea rose petals, the opulent sheen of gold against the cream of a woman's throat, and perhaps, I realized now, the intoxicating smoothness of liqueurs.

"I had to pull quite a few strings on your behalf," Malinin's voice sounded in the distance, "so I would be much obliged if you would at least give me an answer."

"I've quit painting such tripe," I said indifferently, still studying my glass.

"Oh, have you, now? Must have been recent," he said.

I shrugged.

"A pity. You weren't half bad at it, from what I hear. . . . Excellent, isn't it? Our ambassador to France dropped it off the other day. A little more, perhaps? . . . Well, no matter, there are other ways of recommending yourself to your director." The clock in the next room tried to announce a quarter past the hour, but its valiant rumble was caught and promptly silenced in the folds of the velvet draperies. "How do you feel about criticism, for instance?" Malinin asked. "Simple, respected, and pays well, not to mention the possibilities for advancement. As a matter of fact, let me think—yes, I've just agreed to do an article for a good friend of mine. He happens to be the editor of our leading art magazine, *Art of the World,* I'm certain you've read it. I could arrange to add you as my coauthor; he owes me a favor. It would make Penkin happy. Of course, you'd be the one to actually write the text, I've never had much liking for this kind of—"

"What's the article about?" I interrupted.

"A subject that you are well familiar with, as I hear from Nina—surrealism. My working title is 'Surrealism and Other Western "Isms" as Manifestations of Capitalist Insolvency.' What do you think?"

"I think surrealism is the most brilliant movement of the twentieth century," I said. "In fact, I myself painted in the surrealist manner for almost two years, and even now, much of my inspiration comes from—"

"Good, good," said Malinin, standing up and walking to a bookcase. "Then it should be easy for you. Meaningless subjects, amoral disregard of communal values, decadent neglect of reality, night-mares depriving man of joy, that kind of thing. . . . Here, you can borrow this volume of reproductions, it should help you find all the indignant epithets you need. Would a month be long enough? The issue goes to print in January."

I flipped through the book he had handed me. It was in English; the pages were bright and glossy, and smelled of new print. I saw a nude with roses blossoming in her belly, a jungle metamorphosing into the ruins of a many-columned city, a bleeding classical bust . . .

"What you are suggesting," I said, pushing the volume aside, "is nothing but betrayal—of myself, of my friends, of everything I hold true."

He smiled unpleasantly.

"Such lofty words," he said. "How old are you now, Anatoly—thirty-one? Thirty-two?"

"Thirty-three," I said. "The age of Christ."

He paused in the process of pouring himself another splash, looked back at me with a raised eyebrow, and I instantly regretted my words. The drink was stronger than I had thought. Wondering hazily whether I had eaten that day—I could not remember—I watched him push the cork back into the ornate bottle.

"Is that really how you see yourself?" he said, seating himself, sweeping the folds of his robe off the floor in the grand gesture of an old Russian aristocrat. "A martyr about to make a great sacrifice? Except that Christ sacrificed himself for the people. For what would you sacrifice yourself—and not just yourself, may I remind you, but your mother and your wife as well? For some vague notion of Art with a capital A? Because let me tell you, Anatoly, the Russian people do not need you and your art. No matter how hard you beat your head against the wall—you and that woebegone friend of yours, what's his name, Rifkin, Semkin, Bulkin?—along with all the rest of those fellows, no matter how much any of you suffers, no one will

ever want to exhibit a single work of yours in this country. *My* kind
of art is what our people love. It may not be as amusing as some fantasy by Chagall, but when millions of tired, unhappy men and
women want to find a bit of light, hope, or encouragement at the end
of their hard day, they would rather look at paintings of the heroic
past and the harmonious future than puzzle over some portrait of a
man with an upside-down green face. Why, I can't tell you how many
times—"

And as I finished my cognac, he talked of all the letters he had
received from soldiers who had gone through the war carrying in
their pockets a torn-out magazine page with some landscape of his
that had reminded them of their home village, and all the teary-eyed
women who had thanked him for immortalizing their fallen fathers
and sons, and how at his age, fifty-six years, a man ought to know
whether his life had had a purpose; and somehow Andrei Rublev
came up as an artist easily accessible to the masses and mindful of
the demands of his time. . . . The grandfather clock in the next room
muttered an inaudible hour. The trapped light swung wildly in my
glass as I set it down, and the room, with its gently colored lampshades, gold-lettered spines of books lining the walls, heavy leather
chairs, and at its center, the man with Nina's face pontificating in
an arrogant voice, yet with an odd note of uncertainty creeping into
his words now and again, swayed briefly, then righted itself, when I
stood up.

"I've heard enough," I said brusquely. "I'm going home now."

Malinin stopped talking, glanced at me with something like
alarm. I was walking to the door. "I suppose all this must seem quite
sudden," he said, rising quickly, "especially since you and I haven't
exactly . . . But all I want now is to help Nina, and after this Manège
fiasco . . . Wait, just take this, will you, leaf through it, sleep on it,
discuss it with Nina, and we shall resume our conversation at a more
convenient hour, all right?"

Already in the doorway, about to stride out, I looked back at him across the congealing night, and saw, for the first time, the unmistakable traces of aging in his face, the bitter lines pulling at his mouth, the slight trembling in his hands holding out the art book, the restless, almost pleading, look in his eyes. . . . Unexpectedly I caught the faint echo of something, someone from my distant past, and hesitated, my fingers tightening around the doorknob; then, only dimly aware of my reasons, I came back, ripped the tome out of his grasp, and left without another word. On the threshold of the apartment, it occurred to me that I was forgetting something important. I paused. The entrance hall was crowded with reflections of unkempt, distraught-looking middle-aged men who did not resemble Malinin in the slightest and whom I avoided studying too closely; timid shadows were waiting in the corners, reluctant to enter their nightly dance; trapped between the mirrors, the Polish officer stared into space with stern, and somehow disappointed, eyes; the bowl on the lion-footed table overflowed with an assortment of homeless objects—a cuff link, a black button, a bunch of keys . . .

And for a second I almost had it, but the memory of the button— just like this one—that Belkin had torn off my coat interfered, dislodging some realization that in another breath would have merited a slap on the forehead and a relieved "Of course!" Shrugging, I pocketed my button's double so my mother could sew it back on, walked onto the landing, closed the door behind me, and shaking off a strange woman of forty-odd years who was tugging at my sleeve and asking with irksome insistence after some keys (and ignoring a pimpled youth who gawked at me from behind her, saying in an insolent whisper, "Looks like someone's been dipping into Pyotr Alekseevich's Courvoisier!"), descended the stairs.

Outside, the city was filled with midnight ghosts, and the December snow was still falling, damp, unrelenting, coming deviously from all directions at once. I walked with rapid steps, peering at every street corner and shuttered storefront through the white whirling. The visit had unsettled me. Without ever considering Malinin's preposterous proposal, I had been tricked into making a gesture of apparent complicity—tricked by the warm, unsteady haze of inebriation and the pity that had seized me at an inopportune moment, or else by the elusive whiff I had caught of another, long-past encounter—and now I felt soiled, as if I had shared someone's dirty secret, and anxious, increasingly anxious, to be rid of my compromising burden. The block ended; I crossed a deserted side street at a red light. There were still no trash cans in sight, and the possibility of tossing the book into a snowdrift flashed through my mind, but I hastily buried the thought and continued walking, trying to keep at bay something else that bothered me, something my father-in-law had said, something that almost had a ring of truth to it. . . . And then, mercifully, there it was, on the other side of Gorky Street, by a building even more grandiose than Malinin's—a welcome squat shape, a depository of cigarette butts, ice cream wrappers, and uneasy conscience.

As I ran toward it, I nearly collided with a woman in a full-length fur coat getting out of a magnificent black car parked by the curb. Sidestepping, I automatically raised my eyes, and saw a girl a few years younger than Nina, and rather plain; but what struck me was the expression on her face as she passed me on her way into the building, the folds of her glossy coat flying behind her—a wandering smile, directed at nothing and everything, on her lips, in her eyes. Immediately I despised her—despised her splendid clothes, the Volga at her back, her obvious and oblivious contentment—and hearing the car door slam again, turned with malice, eager to see what crimes of greed, baseness, or indifference branded her husband's face; for a life like theirs was certain to carry a price. Then, just as quickly, my contempt vanished, supplanted by another, darker feeling. A slightly stooping man of my age, with kindly eyes behind thick glasses, walked by, leading a child by the hand. I glimpsed a tiny heart-shaped face tilted upward and eyelashes instantly furry in the descending snow, and overheard the man say softly, "And so the princess and the mouse went to the tea party at the castle, and there . . ." The girl was standing in the doorway, waiting for them, smiling. The door swung open, revealing, in one moment before it slammed closed, the marble floor of a columned lobby, bronze lamps, mirrors, the fleeting reflections of silvery high heels, polished leather shoes, a three-year-old creature in a bearlike coat and red mittens, dragging a toy horse by its tail . . .

Then they were gone, and their chauffeured car slunk away into the night behind my back, leaving the street empty again; but I remained still, abruptly snatched out of my mindless drifting of the past week. My mouth tingled with the burning aftertaste of my father-in-law's cognac; the snow prickled the back of my neck, my bare hands; in the skies above me floated a few lit windows, behind which families were probably gathered around pastel-tinted lampshades, engaged in some domestic, tranquil pastimes I could not imagine, and countless dark windows, their texture indistinguishable from that of the clouds, behind which other families were no doubt sleeping the dreamless sleep of well-being. And as I stood there, looking up, I understood, for the first time since the Manège disaster, just what my life was bound to become.

There was no hope of my finding stable employment now; I would be forced into driving a night bus at best, sweeping streets more likely. My earnings would be laughable, not enough to cover even a portion of the overpriced canvases and oils I would have to obtain on the black market (for, along with my position, I had lost my access to subsidized art stores); the three of us would go on living until our dying day in this intimate, humiliating closeness, our undergarments drying communally on bathroom pipes; and in a couple of years, when my mother retired, it would be Nina, Nina alone, who would have to bear the weight of supporting us all, of paying for my secret, dangerous calling—paying with long days and longer nights, paying by parting with every small pleasure in which she still indulged on occasion—a ballet seen from the top gallery, a chocolate-covered cherry savored with an evening tea—and paying with something else besides, something she might have wanted more than my art, something we never discussed. . . .

I remembered the emptiness in Nina's eyes on her thirtieth birthday, and all the words she was always on the brink of saying yet never said, and her growing reluctance to meet her old girlfriends, and her lying in bed night after night, her face to the wall, whether counting flowers on the wallpaper blotchily illuminated by a streetlamp in an attempt to trick her insomnia or thinking bleak thoughts, I did not know. And then the words I had tried to forget, Malinin's words, sounded clearly in my mind—"For what would you sacrifice yourself—and not just yourself, may I remind you, but your mother and your wife as well?"—and I was chilled with a sudden fear that I had gotten it all wrong, hopelessly wrong, and that my heroic intent to carry on with my outlawed art was not the sacrifice I believed it to be, but merely an easy, selfish succumbing to my own desires, and that the true sacrifice lay in a seemingly craven decision to give it all up. I was still certain of the road I myself would take if offered the choice between comfort and immortality, even happiness and immortality—but did I have the right to choose it for others, for those I loved?

Then, too, exactly how confident was I of my posthumous fame, a small, cold voice inquired in my ear. Daydreaming, I used to envision a sunlit stretch of a museum corridor, precise little plaques with titles and dates, a generous chapter in art history volumes, printed on delightfully crisp, gleaming paper; but in the course of one week my vision had undergone a painful transformation and now found itself crammed into a windowless closet stacked with canvases that only janitors saw from time to time. For painting, unlike literature, was a tragic art: it could not be multiplied in a predawn hour on a rickety typewriter, or cross borders sewn into a coat lining, or live forever, weightless and unstoppable, in a dark, safe corner of someone's memory. It was eternally bound to the earthly, the material—a canvas, an easel, oils, brushes, a wall—and ultimately to time and place; and to its time and place it owed its eventual survival or destruction. Russia had not been kind to artists. I thought of all the treasures burned in wars and revolutions, of priceless frescoes washed off cathedral walls by rains and snows, of Chagall's masterpieces imprisoned in an anonymous storage room of the Tretyakovka, mildewing away brushstroke by brushstroke, inspiration by inspiration. I thought too of the persistent sadness weighing down my soul during my nightly vigils in the dusty graveyard of my own unwanted paintings, my stillborn children, and the dismal scent of failure mixing stealthily with the smell of turpentine; and then, for no apparent reason, my early memories flitted through my mind—the black shoes striding across the hushed Moscow night, the Professor holding out a trembling hand, my mother on the telephone covering her mouth as if to stifle a scream, the lonely, broken flight my father had taken from one darkness into another . . .

And already, in some deep, obscure corner of my soul, an even more terrible doubt was stirring. Was I really so sure of my talent to risk everything for it—to turn my back defiantly on this chance, this last chance, of giving Nina the happiness she deserved, all in the vague hope that one day I would create, amidst the misery and disappointment, something so unique, so beautiful, so great that it would fully justify our wasted lives?

The door of the building opened, and an adolescent came out, leading a disdainful greyhound on a leash. Beyond the dog's arched back I caught another brilliant flash of the marble, the bronze, the light dancing in the mirrors . . . And then I knew that in the few minutes I had passed standing on this sidewalk before a trash can in the whirling snow I had traveled a dizzying distance.

I looked down at the book in my hands; its cover was running with water. I wiped it on my sleeve, slipped it inside my coat, and walked home.

By the time I climbed the stairs to our apartment, I was chilled to the bone. I let myself in without a noise. Silence and wretchedness seeped from under the closed door to our room, where Nina was probably lying awake in the dark, just as I had left her, but in my mother's room the nightly news hummed faintly, and a thin streak of light leaked into the corridor. For a minute I stood hesitating; then, softly, I knocked. The noise of the television faded, and my mother's voice asked, "Yes, what is it?"

The ceiling lamp was burning, but she was in bed, dressed in a thick, salmon-colored nightgown, her head wound tightly in curlers. An aging smell of Krasnyi Oktyabr, the perfume I remembered since childhood, hung in the air.

"Tolya, what happened?" she said anxiously, leaning on her elbow. "Your hair is all wet!" The sound was off now, but black-and-white figures continued to jerk across the screen, casting sickly shadows on her face.

"Nothing happened," I said. "I was out, and it's snowing out there." Gingerly I sat down on the edge of her bed. "Mama, can I ask you something?" She was looking at me with frightened eyes. "I'm wondering," I said awkwardly, "do you like my paintings?"

Her mouth grew tight.

"It's not nice to treat your mother like this," she said in a petulant voice and, reaching over to the television, turned the volume knob. "It's late, my nerves are troubling me, you come in looking all wild, and here I'm already thinking God knows what—and you ask a silly question like that! Tolya, it's not nice."

"Mama, please," I said. "This is important. I really need to know what you think."

She looked at me uncertainly, as if trying to gauge whether I was joking.

"And now," said the bright voice of the announcer in the background, "for those who are still with us at this hour, the folk ensemble Samotsvety will perform a song from Vologda." A row of women in peasant dresses, holding the tips of their fingers under their chins, commenced wailing about some youth who refused to accept a chest of gold in place of his beloved. My mother switched the television off.

"It's because of your problems at work, isn't it?" she said with a sigh. "Well, Tolya, of course you can draw lovely things—faces, flowers, houses, just like a photograph." She gave me a pat on the hand. "Remember that one picture you did, for your graduation I think it was, of a soldier riding a horse into a village? It made me proud, such a wonderful picture! Only I wish you'd draw like that again, Tolya, because the things you do now, I must tell you, they aren't nearly as nice. It's no wonder the authorities closed down your show. . . . No, don't look away, you wanted your mother's advice, so I'm telling you, your new pictures are unpleasant. I can't imagine how your Nina even sleeps in the same room with this *art* of yours—she must have nightmares all the time."

"Nina loves my paintings," I said quietly.

"Sometimes I just don't know about you," my mother said, shaking her head. "You went to an institute, yet you don't understand simple things."

The cognac I had drunk was making the edges of my thoughts foggy. "What do you mean?" I asked. She peered at me across a small silence. I wondered if Nina was listening on the other side of the thin wall—and hoped she was not.

"I know you think I'm old, dull, and ignorant," said my mother plaintively, "no match for your fine young wife—but I can still recognize an unhappy woman when I see one, and I tell you, Tolya, Nina is unhappy. Why don't you two have children?"

"Mother, I—"

"Because of your pictures!" she interrupted. "Because you've turned our home into some sort of underground lair! Because you think a child would disrupt the important things you do! But I will say this to you, Tolya. The girl was twenty-four when you married her. She turned thirty last month. How much longer do you plan to wait? It may already be too late for her, and every day she leaves for work with her eyes red from tears, but you—you are so busy playing with your colors you don't even notice! You think she loves your pictures? Mark your mother's words, even if she pretends to now, she'll come to hate everything about them when she finds herself alone at forty."

It was not an answer to the question I had asked—but it was an answer. For a moment it was so quiet I could hear the mattress springs moaning under Nina's weight in the next room. Then, averting my eyes from my mother's reddened face, her pink and green curlers, the slightly soiled lace of her nightgown's collar, I stood up and, muttering about the late hour, slipped out into the corridor and closed her door, behind which I could already discern the renewed ululations of the folk chorus Samotsvety.

For an endless minute I waited unmoving in the dark, trying not to give in to the vast, unknown terror that crouched at my back like a beast poised to leap, fighting the desire to cry. Then the minute passed, and breathing more evenly, I picked up Malinin's book and took it into the kitchen. And in the same green circle of light in which Nina and I had shared a tangerine on that wonderfully happy night before the Manège opening—only a week ago, yet so long past—I

pored over purple deserts swarming with menacing statues, somnolent faces mutating into giant insects, musical instruments drooping
like soft organic matter, empty squares of ancient towns flooded
with harsh yellow light, contorted bodies dissected into drawers or
supported on stilts, brightly feathered canaries trilling inside rib
cages; and gradually the quiet but persistent chirping of birds filled
the shadowy crannies of my mind, and the air began to shimmer
with strange, luminous phantoms, elusive, beautiful, and terrible
like dreams; and instead of mulling over the article I was to write for
my father-in-law, I sat still for a while, vacantly gazing into the street,
where the snow was no longer falling, and seeing paintings before my
eyes—tens, hundreds, thousands of paintings that lived inside me
and that I might never paint now. . . .

Slippered footsteps dragged along the floor, and when I turned
around, I saw my mother in the doorway. I stared at her. She wore a
button-down housedress, the curlers were gone from her hair, and
her face had aged twenty-some years since the conversation we had
had only an hour earlier.

"Tolya, are you sure you are well?" she said. "You look a bit . . .
Goodness, you broke your glasses! I thought right away there was
something funny about you."

Disconcerted, I moved my eyes around the kitchen, recognizing
nothing. A kettle was about to whistle on the stove, two cups were set
out on the table amid a profusion of sugar cookies, a clock on the
wall announced five in the afternoon, and a brightly feathered
canary in a cage chirped quietly but persistently in its corner. A tranquil Arbat alley rustled with the yellowing leaves of early autumn
outside the window. I could suddenly taste cognac in my mouth.

My mother was watching me with puzzlement.

"And what's that you are reading?" she asked.

Cautiously I lowered my eyes. The book of surrealist reproductions had not been a dream within a dream, I saw then—it was still

lying open before me; I must have picked it up during my muddled visit to Malinin's place. And off the page a face looked up at me— a face almost nondescript, yet horrifying in its familiarity. . . . I blinked, pressed my hands to my temples, turned the page over and back, hoping I was mistaken, hoping to God I was mistaken—and still it was there, impossible, absolutely impossible, and yet so real.

The painting was by Salvador Dalí, dated 1936, titled *The Pharmacist of Ampurdán in Search of Absolutely Nothing.* Across the gleaming reproduction trod a small, pudgy man in a faded brown suit, with reddish-blond hair and a sharp little beard. Incredibly, there he was again, on the opposite page, carefully lifting the soft corner of a molten piano—and two pages later, peering from behind a monstrously decaying body in Dalí's *Premonition of Civil War,* wearing the same brown suit, his face bearing the same mild expression suitable for a provincial apothecary.

But the man in the Dalí paintings was not a provincial apothecary.

The man in the paintings was my pseudo-cousin, Fyodor Mikhailovich Dalevich.

Twenty-one

At first, the world was filled with an inebriated buzz. Then, slowly, out of darkness, out of chaos, islands of thought began to rise, small at first, then more and more far-reaching, forming chains, archipelagoes, merging into continents, until the fog lifted fully, and he was standing on solid ground. Of course, he had always known Dalevich for a malicious presence—but only now did he realize how much of the puzzle had been hidden from him before, and how different the completed picture was; and he felt the frightened exhilaration of a man who, after an eternity of blind groping along the narrow walls of a familiar prison, eventually stumbles upon a light switch, flips it warily, and finds himself not among the stale smells and predictable dangers of his narrow cell but in some barren landscape, caught in a blue snowdrift under a black sky, watching strange shadows weave an eerie dance in the cold, starry distance.

He had spent twenty-some years maligning, kicking, slapping, insulting, and ultimately crucifying art in general, his former god, and surrealism in particular, his former idol; now, he saw, art was simply having its revenge. With the calm, omnipotent patience of a spurned ancient divinity, some invisible force of the universe—call it God, or fate, or justice—had allowed him to rise as high as he ever would, so it might bring him down all the more harshly. And it was, of course, during that magnificently full evening of Malinin's celebration at the Manège, at the very moment when the Minister of Culture had approached him with an invitation to a private party, that the unerring and unstoppable mechanism of punishment had been triggered. Yes, he thought, as he stared with unseeing eyes at the Dalí painting before him, at that moment the cup of his success had finally run over and the walls of his long-lasting defenses had begun to shudder under the swelling pressure of unbidden synergies pushing him toward his past—another opening at the Manège, another painting of Nina, another encounter with Lev Belkin in the shadow of those neoclassical columns. . . . And then, after a theatrically sustained pause of two days, an unprepossessing phantom called Fyodor Mikhailovich Dalevich had stood on his doorstep, profusely apologetic for disturbing his supper.

Fate's modest delivery man, art's neatly efficient avenger, summoned by the hostile god from a surrealist painting, clothed in middle-aged flesh, furnished with a suitcase, a hat (painted by Magritte), a canary (courtesy of Ernst), the meek manner of a provincial relative, a wealth of provocative artistic ideas, and a transparent last name (and, indeed, it occurred to Sukhanov, the first name and patronymic of Dostoyevsky, author of *The Double*, the story of a man whose life was taken over by his own ghost), Dalí's Dalevich had clearly been dispatched into Sukhanov's well-ordered existence to wreak whatever havoc he could in the present while simultaneously orchestrating a disturbing slide into the past—a double task at which he had excelled. There was the earliest memory of Sukhanov's father, released by his mother's comment about Malvina, the surrealist bird Dalevich had presented to her; and the childhood supper culminating in the arrival of his father, which at the last instant had given way to Dalevich's arrival; and the sight of Dalevich hunched over in an armchair at night, which had brought to the surface the Morozov boys, Professor Gradsky, and his first discovery of art; and the stroll with Dalevich, which had led him to the evacuation years and his art lessons with Oleg Romanov . . .

Nadezhda Sergeevna delicately coughed into her palm.

"I think you should go home and take a nap," she said. "A nap will be good for you. I happen to be expecting someone over for tea anyway. Of course, I'm very glad you dropped by—"

"That's all right," Sukhanov said, rising. "I only wanted to say hello, I was passing—"

The bell rang in the hallway.

"Oh," she said, and glanced at him anxiously. "Oh, that must be my guest."

"Don't worry, I'm leaving already," he said. The bell rang again. She seemed about to wring her hands. "Well, aren't you going to let them in?" He attempted to smile. "Go on, I'll stay a moment."

When her shuffling steps had retreated into the dimness, he walked to the window and wrestled with the windowpane, still bound with last winter's insulating tape. Finally throwing it open, he breathed in the air of the August evening, as deeply aromatic as the evenings of his childhood, redolent of linden trees, meat pies, and tiptoeing coolness. Then, hearing hushed voices in the hallway behind his back, he lifted the birdcage in his arms—it was heavier than he had expected—and after sliding the bar on its door, held it out the window and shook it. The canary tumbled out and sank onto the windowsill, staring at him with a puzzled black eye. "Off, off you go, you evil minion!" Sukhanov whispered, slamming the window shut, then hurriedly placed the empty cage back in its corner, turned around with an absent look on his face—and was just in time to see Fyodor Mikhailovich Dalevich enter the kitchen.

"Tolya," Dalevich said softly. "Hello. Aunt Nadya told me you were here."

His expression was as mild as ever. He wore Dalí's suit and Magritte's hat, and held a boxed cake in one hand—Sukhanov could read the name "Ptich'e Moloko" on the lid—and a thin folder in the other. Nadezhda Sergeevna followed a frantic step behind.

"Well, well," Sukhanov said after a lengthy pause, filled with barely articulated, violent thoughts. "I must say, you do look marvelously convincing—just like a real person. 'Aunt Nadya' was a charming touch too."

Dalevich looked at him sadly. "I understand you are still angry with me," he said, "but I hope this meeting will give me another chance to explain. Please, Tolya, I've already told your mother everything, and she believes me. Let me just—"

"Oh, I doubt very much you've told her *everything*. I bet you've failed to enlighten her on the subject of Dalí."

"I'm sorry about your article, I really am," Dalevich protested meekly. "The whole thing was an accident, I never intended to interfere with your job. In fact, now that I've finished my research here, I'm returning to Vologda, my leave has ended anyway—"

"You know damn well I'm not talking about some article!" Sukhanov hissed, slapping his hand against the table. "And you can't even lie convincingly—it only occurred to you to say Vologda because of that idiotic folksong they were broadcasting on television just now!"

A seemingly confused look appeared on Dalevich's face. He played his role well.

"Aunt Nadya," he said haltingly, "I think I'd better be going, I don't want to upset anyone. . . . Here, I'll just put the cake on the table. And these, Tolya, I was going to leave them with Aunt Nadya, they are for you, I've meant for a long time to—"

Holding out the folder, he started to edge into the corridor.

In a high-pitched voice that did not belong to him, Sukhanov shouted, "Oh no you don't, you surrealist bastard!" and, his glasses sliding sideways, the whole room tilting, rushed wildly at the doorway.

He had imagined Dalevich ripping at the impact like a taut canvas, but the shoulders he gripped and shook had the solidity of an ordinary body. Dalevich, his eyes round with fake astonishment, weakly lifted his hands to his face, dropping the folder he had been clutching—and immediately a flock of pastel-colored pages burst out of their cardboard confinement and fluttered onto the floor.

The movement was so unexpected that Sukhanov glanced down mechanically and saw, landing on his foot, a pale watercolor of a birch tree whose leaves were transforming into translucent green butterflies and taking off on their first, quivering flight. The lines were clumsy, and the colors childish; but as he looked at it, a feeling of recognition trembled in his heart, and slowly releasing Dalevich, he bent to pick up the page, bringing it close to his face, doubting his sight, doubting it could be possible. . . .

And yet it was—one of his own first works, drawn under the tutelage of Oleg Romanov, when he had been only a thirteen-year-old boy, and subsequently lost in the whirlwind of the war. Incredulously, he turned around the kitchen, while his mother and Dalevich watched him with nervous expectation. There, under the table, rested an ink sketch he had done of their Inza street awash with melting snows, and a quick study of a weeping woman with a coarse peasant face holding a winged child in her arms; here, by the sink, lay a bleak landscape of a winter field crisscrossed by wires dotted with ruffled sparrows (which, he remembered with a start, spelled out with secret irreverence, each bird a tiny note on its wire, a musical line from a popular song about the Motherland), and next to it, a portrait of his teacher Romanov, his small figure drawn in black-and-white, the world around him blossoming into lush colors from the touch of a raised brush. He leaned to see better—and then, beneath the window, he glimpsed a drawing of a tall man in a coat, standing in a doorway with a brilliant smile on his face—that waking dream he had had so often as a boy. . . .

"How?" he said hoarsely. "How did you get these?"

"But you gave them to him yourself, don't you remember, Tolya?" said his mother hastily. "Oh, how I wish you two would stop fighting! You boys got along so well that time we stayed with Irochka Dalevich, after the . . . after we came back to Moscow in 'forty-three."

"Who on earth is Irochka Dalevich?"

"Irochka Dalevich, my second cousin—Fedya's mother! Surely you remember?"

"Mama told me not to bother you," Dalevich added readily, "but I was so fascinated by you I followed you around constantly, until you made me a present of your drawings—to get rid of me, I suspect. I was only ten at the time, but I clearly remember thinking I'd never seen anything more beautiful in my life. As a matter of fact, it's entirely to you, to these drawings of yours, that I owe my interest in art. I know you didn't pursue it as a career, but all the same, you had a real gift, Tolya, to be able to change people's lives like that—"

He continued to talk in the same soothing voice; and as Sukhanov stared at the moving lips half concealed by the blond beard, he became aware of a memory that had stirred in the recesses of his being at his mother's words and was now gathering momentum, until in a hazy sequence there began to pass before him the dismal wallpaper, the bathtub on clawed feet, the low ceilings looming over him through nightmare-ridden sleep, the skinny, sharp-nosed little woman placing a miserable succession of barely warm suppers on the table, and present through it all, a quiet yellow-haired boy, a few years younger than he, watching him, always watching him, with curious, guarded eyes. . . .

He looked again at the pages scattered on the kitchen floor—the first real evidence, delivered after a quarter of a century, that he had not dreamt it all, that he had, indeed, led a different life once—and then everything ceased to matter, everything but these drawings of a child, rescued so miraculously from the vortex of time and deposited so neatly at his feet. So perhaps Dalevich was no malevolent avenger but merely a bumbling, well-meaning relative from the misty Russian North; perhaps he himself, and no one else, was to blame for the loss of his position, his family, his sense of self; perhaps all the destruction in his life was, in fact, the inevitable, logical conclusion to the choices he had made all those years before. . . . Yet startling as these potential revelations would have seemed only an hour earlier, they were of little interest to him now. Unaware of the tense silence in the kitchen, he gathered the pages off the floor and methodically smoothed them out on the table, peering at each one closely, with eyes dimmed by decades of skimming over slick productions of socialist realism. No longer used to the sight of his own lines, his own colors, he felt suddenly anxious to test each work for timid traces of uniqueness, for an early testimony of talent—at times lifting this or that drawing against the light as if expecting to see some sign emerging through the watercolors like a transparent watermark, at times following a meandering outline with a finger—and wondering, wondering with a new, surprising sense of near-discovery, whether he could have been wrong that December night so long ago—whether paintings continued to lead their own secret, joyous, eternal lives after all, in the hidden crevices of people's memories, in the deepest drawers of people's houses, in the shadows of museum basements— and whether it was possible that once upon a time he had really had a gift. . . . And then an urgent need to confirm some truth he had just begun to suspect was upon him.

Without a word, he strode into the corridor, closed his fingers on the handle of a hallway closet, and paused, ignoring the burst of his mother's alarmed cries at his back, preparing instead for what he knew he would find just behind this door—windows into his past, windows into his soul, whole stacks of them, piled negligently this way and that, just as he had left them two decades ago, some facing away, some slightly graying, perhaps, with deposits of dust and old-woman smells, maybe even a wary touch of mildew, others certain to throw themselves at him with their wild colors and violent shapes like so many untamed beasts long in confinement. He suddenly found it uncanny that this closet had always been here—that his paintings had always been here—that there had always been only this thin partition between his present and that other world, once wholly his, now full of unfamiliar, wonderful, terrifying marvels—and that he had known it all along, yet spent years learning how to forget so he would not have to hear the muted, sorrowful call of the ghosts on those rare occasions when he sat in his mother's living room, drinking lukewarm tea, eating repulsive pastries, talking impressively about a new edition of his book, his son's excellent grades, Nina's autumn trip to Paris. . . .

Now, in a single moment, as he stood feeling in his palm the weighty coolness of the door handle, he remembered it all—all, at least, that was left to remember of a life that, with the appearance of a February 1963 issue of *Art of the World*, had started on its way to safety, constancy, tranquillity. That first article had been followed by a rapid succession of short pieces, culminating in early 1964 with a lengthy monograph, *Contemporary Applications of the Socialist Realism Method to Landscape and Still Life*, whose loudly hailed publication, as well as his timely membership in the Party, had helped him obtain later in the year, just as Nina had become pregnant, a two-room Arbat apartment for his mother. After Nadezhda Sergeevna moved out, he converted the spare room into a studio—for, of course, he had never fully intended to give up painting—but at first a steady stream of lectures and magazine assignments left him unable to work, whether from exhaustion or from some deeper, darker emotion that he did not want to define, and then Vasily was born, and Nina needed space for drying his sheets and ironing his clothes, and Pyotr Alekseevich made them a gift of a crib that was charming but unwieldy, and little by little, he found his canvases and oils relegated further and further into unobtrusive shadows, until the only painting remaining in full view was a portrait of a discreetly expectant, dreamily happy Nina, presented to them by Malinin and soon placed prominently over Sukhanov's recently acquired, gorgeously carved desk.

After that, something began to happen to the fabric of time: it grew thinner and silkier and passed through his hands so lightly that he barely noticed the patterns and colors in its smooth, flowing skin. Another year passed, Nina was pregnant again, they were awaiting a move to a significantly larger apartment, Ksenya was born, Nina left her job, those in the know whispered of his impending nomination to an important position as the head of the art criticism department at a certain well-respected institute, and a number of friendly colleagues, led by the director Penkin himself, started to drop by now and then with bottles of cognac, ostensibly to gossip and to coo over his children. He decided that it would be wiser to move his underground art out of the way for the time being, at least until the promised position materialized, and one evening crammed all his paintings into his new Zhiguli, drove over to his mother's (she had more room than she needed, anyway), and calming her fears with assurances that it was only temporary, rapidly, as if their touch burned his fingers, piled the canvases, with their manifold scents of fairy tales and nightmares, into a hallway closet. After closing the door, he stood still for a long minute, perhaps willing himself to memorize the weighty coolness of the door handle in his palm as a promise to return someday soon; then turned, and walked away. But as he walked away, he already knew in some concealed, murky layer of his soul that he would never be back to claim his dark treasure—and knowing this, tried not to listen to the chorus of disembodied voices whispering, pleading at his back, tried to ignore the strange, chilling certainty that for him the flow of time had suddenly ceased, that at this very instant his life was over, irrevocably, forever—

And of course, the feeling was ridiculous, and of course, time did not stop, and his life continued, and over the years there were plenty of changes, all for the better—the new apartment, the new position, the children growing up, the acclaimed books, the purchase of the dacha, the eventual staggering promotion to the helm of *Art of the World,* speedily rewarded by another, still more splendid apartment in the Zamoskvorechie and a personal chauffeur—yet now, as he stood so close to his past, his fingers curled around the door handle, his knuckles white, he felt that the previous two decades of his life had meant nothing, had been nothing, had vanished into the emptiness whence they had been born—and that only today, after all this waste, he finally had the power to make time flow once again.

He threw the door open.

A strong smell of mothballs escaped into the corridor. Two old coats hung on metal hangers in one corner, and in another, a monstrous vacuum cleaner, its dust bag deflated, leaned against the wall. There was a shelf he did not remember; a woolen mitten dangled off it into space. He looked at the mitten for a while, as if trying to fathom its purpose, then slowly closed the door, and returned to the kitchen. His mother had stopped talking, and was staring at him with unblinking eyes.

"How about some tea?" a funny-looking bearded man offered brightly. "I'll get another cup, don't stand up, Aunt Nadya."

Sukhanov knew the man well; he was a relative of some sort, a childhood playmate perhaps; it seemed that they had recently quarreled. It did not matter any longer.

"Mother," he said, his voice quiet and oddly strained. "Mother, where are they?"

A cup rang out against a saucer as the relative clumsily dropped them onto the table.

"Mama, please, this is important," he said, brushing away a brief sensation of repeating his own, seemingly recent words. "Where are my paintings?"

Her mouth was working convulsively.

"Well, they are not here, are they?" she said with shrillness.

"Did you move them somewhere? Why didn't you tell me? I thought—"

"I know what you thought! You thought, how convenient, turning your mother's place into a storage dump! Did it ever occur to you that I might not like it, that I have needs too, that I'm not just someone to order around?"

"Mama, what are you talking about? No one ordered you around. I just—"

"No, it never occurred to him!" She was shouting now. "And just look at him, barging in here after all this time, going through my closets without permission, expecting everything to be just the way he left it twenty years ago, as if I don't live here, as if I'm nothing to be concerned with, as if I don't have the right to do what I please in my own home—"

Perhaps she saw something strange in his face, or else she ran out of breath; all at once she fell silent. The relative, a fixed smile on his lips, finished cutting the cake into uneven slices, set the knife down, picked up his hat, and cautiously crept out into the corridor and tiptoed away; somewhere in the apartment a door opened and closed. Sukhanov stood without moving. The sun had already vanished over the rooftops, but the air was still luminous, and in its warm crimson glow the small kitchen, with its table ready for tea, its old porcelain clock on the wall, the richness of the creamy bird's-milk dessert crumbling on the plates, the leaves rustling against the windows, seemed wonderfully cozy and intimate and at the same time eternal, like some masterly painting of family togetherness, some vision of an ideal life. . . .

"So you threw my paintings away," said Anatoly Pavlovich in a flat voice, and lowering himself onto the chair, covered his face with his hands—and cried.

And for a while the world was so silent that it felt as if a deep hush, a hush of finality, of lost chances, of all the things that had gone wrong and could never be changed, enveloped it, never to lift again. Yet after some time—whether a fragment of an hour or another lonely stretch of a century—uncertainly, out of the soundless void, timid noises began to emerge: the whispering of trees, the barking of far-off dogs, the chirping of a canary on a windowsill, the trembling voice of an old woman talking, sighing, imploring someone named Tolenka to please understand, to please forgive, she had never thought he would need them again and she had been so afraid to live with all those mon- strosities, but even so, she would never have done it had she not believed that it was the best thing for him, getting rid of it all, yes, she had always feared his pictures would lead to no good, and was it not her duty as a mother to keep him safe, to help him make the best of his life, to steer him away from his father's fate—

He lifted his head, remembering his mother's presence for the first time. Her eyes were moist; her hand hovered over his, ready to descend at any instant.

"My father's fate?" he repeated blankly. "Was that why? You destroyed all my work because you were afraid I'd end up *like my father*?"

And as he spoke, he already felt the disbelief, the emptiness, the grief inside him turning into anger—anger of a heart-searing, soul-wrenching kind he had never known before, anger at this pathetic little woman with a frightened face who had once given him life.

"You don't know what I went through with your father, Tolenka," she whispered.

"What does it matter what you went through? Times have changed. You don't honestly think they throw people in jail for paintings these days?"

She pulled her hand away. "You mustn't talk to me like that," she said. "You've never heard the whole story, you can't—"

He felt as if he did not know who she was.

"What story?" he said, standing up, furiously pushing his chair away. "You and my father had the misfortune of living through a very dark period. He was arrested, they broke him, he committed suicide. Tragic things like that happened all the time in the thirties—not in the sixties or the seventies! And it certainly didn't give you the right to throw away—"

"It wasn't about that, Tolya!" she cried. "Your father wasn't arrested, I just—"

She stopped abruptly, searched the table with frantic eyes, lifted a cup of cold tea to her lips. The cup rattled loudly when she put it down, breaking the silence.

He stared at her.

"I don't believe it," he said slowly. "I always thought you produced that tale for the sake of a ten-year-old boy, but you've actually managed to convince yourself, haven't you? Hospitalized for years, is that right? With the flu! My God, and to think I never realized how the thirties warped your mind! Just what kind of a world do you live in, Mother, what kind of a sick, delusional—"

She sat averting her eyes, her hands clasped tightly together.

"Not the flu," she said, and her voice was different now, low and brittle. Taken aback by the change of her tone, he swallowed the harsh words on his tongue and leaned to look closer into her face. The early twilight had laid deep shadows along her cheeks and in the corners of her mouth, stamping her features with the unfamiliar, stark, sorrowful look of some fifteenth-century saint. Suddenly uneasy, he reached for the lamp switch.

"Please, no light," she said in the same unrecognizable voice. "It's . . . easier this way. Sit down, Tolya. I didn't mean to tell you, I always felt it was my burden alone, it just slipped out. . . . But I guess it's time you knew."

"Knew what?" he asked, his throat dry. He remained standing.

"Your father never was in prison. It's true. He was . . . ill, very ill. It happened in Gorky, they had to put him in a hospital." She swallowed audibly. "A mental hospital. His doctor telephoned me, told me the name of his condition and everything—"

"But Mama," he exclaimed in desperation, "don't you see, they did these things all the time—took people away and lied to their families! The man who called you, I'm sure he wasn't a doctor, he must have been a—"

"Tolya," she said evenly, "don't you think I considered that? But it was true. I knew it was true. I myself had noticed that he was becoming . . . well, different. Already in Moscow, he was beginning to say strange things, but I thought he was just being fanciful, joking with me, nothing more. Then, after he moved to Gorky, he became preoccupied with this crazy idea he had, only he didn't think it was crazy—it was his 'great discovery,' it was going to change the world. . . . He grew so earnest about it, working on it every night, hardly sleeping. It frightened me. He became secretive, too—always worrying that his colleagues would find out and take away his 'project,' as he called it." She was mincing the cake on her plate into chocolate dust with quick, nervous stabs of a spoon, not looking up. "The doctor told me it was common for . . . for people with his illness to become obsessed with some idea in this way, and that they would work with him, it was a good hospital, he only needed to receive some shock great enough to snap him out of it, and many other things, I forgot a lot of it, I was too upset. . . ."

A draft of silence passed between them.

"So how long was he—" he said thickly.

"Almost three years. October 1939 to May 1942. That was when they released him to work at a military factory. They thought that the war had helped him—that when he heard the country needed him he abandoned all his fantasies at last. I thought so too, until he sent me that last letter. He wrote that he had finally finished his great project but asked me to say nothing about it yet, it was all going to be such a wonderful surprise. . . . I cried all day, and it was hard, I had to hide it from you because you were so happy—we were to see him in just a few weeks. I remember I so much wanted to believe everything would be well. . . ."

The shadows lengthened along the kitchen floor, and the tangerine-colored moon, still round but already on the wane, sleepily sailed from behind a roof into the pale sky.

"His project," he said quietly. "What was it, do you know?"

"When they took him away, they found dozens of notebooks in his office, covered front to back with squiggles, drawings of birds, crazy numbers—they could make no sense of them at all. But I always knew what he was trying to do. It started in Moscow, in the early thirties. There was a museum show once, winged suits for people or something, I don't recall exactly. Your father took you to it, I think, but of course you were too young to remember. Well, something at that show must have impressed him, because that was when he first began to talk about it—whether it was possible for a man to fly without a plane or a parachute or anything—to fly as birds fly. The finest human accomplishment it would be, the perfect exercise of sheer will, he used to say, greater than anything art or science had ever invented, and other eloquent things—I'm not an educated woman, I didn't understand much, I just laughed, except that he was serious all along. . . ." She looked up, and her eyes were intent, desperate, searching for some sign in her son's face. "After . . . after he died, Tolenka, my greatest fear was that . . . that you also . . . because the doctor warned me it could happen again, these kinds of illnesses can be passed on . . . But everything was going so well for a while—and then you started to paint these dark, strange pictures of yours—and I don't know, it was as if something happened to me, as if every time I looked at them, I was staring at your father's death, and I grew so afraid, I wanted to make you stop, to make you forget, to make it all disappear, and that was why . . . They were heavy too, I had to carry them down the stairs, and I was so scared the neighbors might see me. . . . But please, Tolenka, you were right to give it up, you have a perfect life now, you make us all proud, all these books you write—"

And still she talked, but her words faded, faded, faded . . . And as he stood in the darkened kitchen, he saw once again a whirlwind of rainbow-tinted pigeons soaring into the sky over the gray monument of a mournful genius, and a three-year-old boy saying eagerly, "When I grow up, I want to fly without machines," and a decade later, his father framed by a bright, rain-sleeked window, raising his hand in a greeting, then spreading his arms, smiling a joyful smile, a smile of shared triumph—and stepping into the void. . . .

For so many years he had thought the moment of his maturity had been rooted in suicide and defeat—yet all along it had been nothing but dreams, and hopes, and one proud man who had been mad enough, or brave enough, to believe he could fly, and who had wanted to give this gift to the people he loved, his wife, his son. . . . And what had he, Anatoly Sukhanov, done with this gift? How had he understood his father's parting words, "Don't let anyone clip your wings"— he, a man who had obligingly shed his own wings and then spent decades listlessly watching ugly, atavistic stubs sprout in their stead?

Wordlessly Sukhanov bent to kiss his mother on a wet cheek, then turned, and leaving his drawings scattered about the table, walked out of the kitchen, out of the apartment, down the staircase. She did not try to stop him. The landings were unlit, the steps slippery; a sluggish headache hummed in his temples. Outside the front door, a peculiar-looking man with a canary-yellow beard grasped his sleeve and began to talk rapidly, swearing his undying devotion, inviting him to visit some museum in Vologda. . . . Just then a window swung open above, and an agitated voice shouted, "My Malvina! She escaped! My Malvina escaped!" The peculiar-looking man exclaimed, "Oh my goodness!" and threw his hands up, peering toward the commotion through his turn-of-the-century glasses.

Free of his grasp, Sukhanov quickly strode down the street.

Twenty-Two

As the city contours grew softer and hazy streetlamps began to pop out of the shadows one after another, he wandered the streets of the old Arbat, his mind churning darkly in some lonely, wordless space. His steps were aimless, directed only by a restless urge to move; but after a while, when an unexpected shortcut deposited him at the fetid mouth of an eerily familiar courtyard, he stopped, looked about, and became suddenly aware of the path his feet had followed of their own accord. Somehow, unthinkingly, he had walked along the broad, pastel-colored streets and the tree-shaded alleys where he had played as a happy five-year-old, six-year-old, seven-year-old— and the unfolding of time had led him to the spot that had marked the end of his first childhood dream.

Obeying some dimly understood impulse, he stepped through the murky, low passage into the yard. A rock-and-roll beat pulsated from one of the apartments, but at its heart the yard was still and dark, its edges lit unsteadily by the pale squares of burning windows, just as it had been almost fifty years before, when a frightened boy had slid an album of Botticelli reproductions into a snowdrift. In the corner where the snowdrift had been there was now a brand-new sandbox; but as he approached, it seemed to him that the sand gleamed with a pearly, roseate, unearthly tint in the faint light. . . . He stared for a breathless moment, then saw it was only the cast-off shadow of a garishly pink lampshade visible in the nearest window. Some child had forgotten a toy spade in the sand. His past was no longer here.

Leaving the courtyard, he walked unresisting down a deserted side street, keeping his eyes to the ground until he was almost at the end, then looking up sharply, his heart flushed with a new, trembling, imprecise feeling. He had not been here since they had moved away in 1954. The building had aged even more; the yellowish paint was peeling off the façade; the rusting balconies sagged. The fifth-floor windows were lit. On one of the windowsills an overfed cat slumbered next to a potted cactus; the curtains were splattered with merry orange flowers. The place had a quiet, almost rustic air about it. He stood still for a few minutes, wondering how different things would be now had he known the truth on that terrible day—had he believed that Pavel Sukhanov was not a coward—had he . . . had he . . .

The front door opened with a piercingly familiar squeak, and an old woman carefully hauled her overweight body toward a nearby bench.

"Are you lost, my dear?" she asked, studying him with sleepy eyes. "This is number three in Lebedinov Lane. Used to be Rozhdestvensky Passage, before the war."

Briefly he thought of telling her that he had lived in this building for years, that he was Anatoly Pavlovich, Anatoly, Tolya, Tolik. . . . The cat stretched and crept away from the fifth-floor windowsill; the old woman watched him with a heavy, indifferent gaze. He noticed the ugly, hair-sprouting mole above her upper lip.

"Thank you," he said after a silence. "I did get a bit sidetracked, but I finally know where I am."

Without another glance, he turned away from his childhood and moved off into the deepening dusk. The city felt abandoned. He crossed a dank courtyard, followed a gloomy alley into a dead end, took a wrong turn, crossed another yard, this one piled high with broken furniture, emerged onto a poorly illuminated, quiet street, and no longer noticing where he was going, quickly walked past a decrepit church, a small garden, a basement converted into an art gallery, with posters in the pavement-level windows advertising some exhibition, a neighborhood bakery, already locked for the night . . . Then, abruptly, he stopped and retraced his steps, certain that it could not be, that his fleeting glimpse had misled him—yet all the same in need of a second, reassuring look.

It could not be, and yet it was. On the posters in the gallery windows, motley letters bobbed jarringly up and down, proclaiming: "L. B. Belkin. Moscow Through a Rainbow."

The small print underneath announced that the gallery was open from eleven to six. Sukhanov's watch still showed thirteen minutes past ten of some lost, forgotten day, but he recalled hearing seven strikes of a remote clock reverberating through some alley. Relieved to find the place closed, he peered into the windows—and was startled to see a light inside and, in its bright electric circle, the indistinct blur of paintings on a wall and, shockingly, Lev Belkin himself, wearing his old velveteen blazer and bow tie, talking to someone hidden from view.

He hesitated, then, resolving to wait, moved off into obscurity on the opposite side of the street. After a passage of time he no longer had the capacity to measure, the basement door opened, and out came Belkin, supporting the elbow of a neatly dressed old man with a shrunken, hauntingly familiar face. The door slammed behind them.

"Are you sure you won't stay the night?" said Belkin, and his words rang through the empty street with the hollow emphasis of an actor on a booming stage. "My place isn't much, but I do have a moth-eaten couch."

"No, thank you, but no," replied the old man. "I should be getting home." The echoing walls amplified and carried his lisp, and all at once Sukhanov knew who he was—the chance passenger seated next to him on the nightmarish train that had delivered him from the crumbling darkness of the frescoed church to the paling dawn over the museum cell full of banished paintings. "You know how it is when work is calling, and unlike you young people, I don't have much time left. Most obliged to you for the tour of the gallery, it was highly illuminating."

Lifting a hand to the brim of a nonexistent hat, the old man turned and shuffled away. Belkin called out, "Honored to meet you! The metro will be on your left!" and for a minute watched the man's stooped back descend into the night; then, fishing out a handful of keys from his pocket, he bent to lock the door. Sukhanov remained still. In another moment, Belkin dropped his keys back into the velveteen depths of his blazer and strode down the street after the old man, whose painfully slow progress had already been obliterated by shadows.

He had nearly reached the corner when Sukhanov took a step forward and, his heart sliding sideways into a warm, indistinct fog, quietly said, "Leva." The echoes caught the name, tossed it back and forth with an increasingly empty, meaningless sound. Belkin froze, then walked back slowly, peering into the dusk.

"Tolya?" he said uncertainly. "Is that you?"

Sukhanov took another step and was trapped like a bug in amber in the watery light of the only streetlamp on the block. An incongruous thought flickered through his mind: at this instant, after the phantasmagoria of the last few days, with one lens of his glasses cracked, his shoes muddy, his clothes reeking with sour, displaced smells of stations, trains, staircases, and courtyards, he must look infinitely more pathetic than Belkin, whose worn-out blazer and maroon bow tie had seemed so amusing to him only a short while ago, on the steps of the Manège, under the aegis of the proud banner proclaiming his father-in-law's grand retrospective. . . .

He cleared his throat.

"Hello, Leva. I was in the neighborhood, visiting my mother," he said. "Thought I'd drop by. I know it's after hours, but the light was on." Belkin had halted a few paces away and was looking at him strangely. Was it possible there were still traces of tears on his face, Sukhanov wondered. He swallowed, went on loudly, "So, how is the gallery business treating you?"

"Oh, fine, thanks for asking," Belkin replied with a quick, forced laugh. "Not that I've sold anything yet, but all in good time, I say. Actually, I'm usually not here, there is a girl who runs things, but she's having a bit of a domestic crisis, her husband—one of these new underground hippie singers or something—has just left her. So I thought, why not, might as well sit here for a few days. A dose of reality is always good for the artist, and you can't imagine how humbling it is to hear what people say about your paintings when they don't know you are standing behind their back."

"No," said Sukhanov in a slightly pinched voice. "No, I can't imagine that at all."

"Yes, well, one gets used to it," said Belkin awkwardly. There was a small, awful silence. "Oh, but I did meet an extraordinary man just now. An artist of the old school, over eighty years old, and still painting as hard as ever. Lives in a small town, the devil knows where, makes all his own pigments out of spices, earth, and whatnot, can you believe it? Last month, he said, he finally began the best work of his life. 'Remember, young man,' he told me, 'it takes a lifetime to learn one's craft.' Amazing, the spirit some men have."

"What is he doing in Moscow?" Sukhanov asked, not caring about the answer, only desperate to avoid another dangerous, sob-swelling lull.

"He was a little vague about it. Said he had come to find some former pupil of his. He had a phone number, address, and everything, but I gathered no one expected him, so he spent the day going to art shows instead, 'keeping in touch with the youth,' as he put it. He claimed he had learned to paint from Chagall, but frankly, I didn't believe him—so many people nowadays . . . Tolya, are you all right? You look—"

"It's nothing, I'm just tired," said Sukhanov weakly. For an instant he struggled with a desire to sink onto the pavement and hide his face in his hands. "I . . . I've been having quite a day. Tripped and fell, broke my glasses, you see. . . . Don't let me hold you up though, you were going somewhere."

"Home, I was only going home. Nothing to rush to there," said Belkin, shrugging. "Listen, I've got an idea. If you're free right now, why not visit the gallery? We can sit and talk, I have some tea and cakes stashed in the office."

Sukhanov was silent for a moment.

"Oh, why not," he said then.

The door gave in with a pained moan. The hallway beyond was dim and small, crowded with a jumble of hats, shoes, lopsided umbrellas, greeting him with fading smells of Alla's mawkishly sweet perfume and a recently dismembered dried fish.

"Well, don't just stand there, come on in," Lev said gruffly.

"Are you alone?"

Lev nodded. He looked as if he had not shaved in a week.

"Good." Tightly clutching a sheaf of pages I had typed the night before on Malinin's typewriter, I followed the fish odors through the familiar clutter of the cramped corridor into the kitchen, Lev at my heels. In the depressingly bright light of the naked bulb dangling over the table glistened a half-empty glass of clear liquid; the bony remains of an unappetizing meal lay scattered on a greasy newspaper.

"I'm working on a still-life composition called *Repast of a Failed Artist Whose Wife Is Out with Her Girlfriends, or So She Says,*" said Lev blandly. "Sit down. Anything the matter? I'd offer you a glass, but it's really disgusting, and of course you never—"

"I'll take it," I said, and pushed the manuscript across the table. "Here, I want you to have a look at this."

Lev scanned the title.

"'Surrealism and Other Western "Isms" as Manifestations of Capitalist Insolvency'?" he said disgustedly. "Surely you don't expect me to waste my time on such—"

"Just read it, will you?"

He shrugged, took an unhurried sip, and flipped the page. I studied the patterns of melted snow forming at my feet on the yellow-and-black-checkered linoleum, watched a befuddled out-of-season fly stumble drowsily on the windowsill, drank the unpalatable vodka. Out of the corner of my eye, I saw Lev glance at me once or twice in the beginning; then he lifted his head no longer and sat silently rustling the papers and frowning. A half-hour passed, then another ten minutes. He slammed the last page against the table.

"What is this shit?" he said. "Who wrote it?"

I finished my drink at a gulp. My insides were burning.

"I did," I said. "I wrote it."

His eyes narrowed. "Tolya," he said slowly. "Is this a sick joke of some sort?"

"It's not a joke, it's going to be published. I wanted you to read it first, so I could explain . . . No, hold on, just listen for a minute, will you?" My face was burning too now. "I've been thinking more about Khrushchev closing our show. And you know what I realized? When he shut us down he wasn't acting as a representative of the state cracking down on a handful of outspoken artists. He was acting as a

representative of the people, *our* people, who do not understand—
cannot understand—the alien things we stand for. The Russian
people do not want our art, Leva. Never did, never will. They dislike
seeing Filonov's tormented faces, Chagall's flying beasts, and Malevich's black squares—they have enough tragedy, surrealism, and
emptiness in their daily lives. In the past they wanted soothing icons;
now they want the pseudo-art of someone like my father-in-law—a
pat on the head reassuring them that their future is bright, a slap on
the back letting them know that they are part of an important whole,
that their toils have a purpose—"

The fly buzzed sleepily against the windowpane; in the bluish
haze beyond, oblique snow was falling. Lev was looking at me, and
there was a new expression in his heavy gaze. I talked for a long
time—talked about the dim, oppressive centuries of Russian art
struggling against Russian history, about the walls of silence destined to surround each and every one of us forever, about casting our
pearls before swine, about our fates condemning us to this dark,
ungrateful soil, leaving us no other choice but to step away into
anonymity, into comfort, into the minute preoccupations of an uninspired, private existence . . .

And then Lev spoke.

"You've said so many clever things here," he said quietly, "but do
you know the only thing I've heard? Fear—nothing but fear. Well, I
understand fear, I'm afraid too. . . ." He was silent for a few heartbeats. "Tell you what, Tolya. Everyone has unworthy moments, and
you are my best friend. Let's go out onto the landing, throw this
abomination page by page into the trash chute, come back to finish
the bottle, and I'll promise you never to mention any of it again.
Agreed?"

The pool of water at my feet had dried out. The snow was still
whirling in the sky. The fly had ceased buzzing, falling back into its
winter stupor of sleep. I rose, gathered the pages scattered about the

table, and walked into the corridor. Lev ran after me, and when I turned at the front door, I saw that his face was transformed by that special, warm, radiant smile I loved so much. Quickly I looked away, unable to watch the light go out of his eyes. In silence, I groped on the counter for my hat, put on my coat, opened the door, and still keeping my gaze averted, stepped across the threshold and closed the door behind me. And then, though he did and said nothing to stop me, for a whole long minute, my heart beating painfully, I lingered outside on the landing, knowing that in three weeks the article would be published, knowing that Lev would never speak to me again—and still I stood there as if waiting for something, as if hoping that a miracle was somehow possible, that the door would open again at any moment, and that he would smile his wonderful, forgiving smile, and say, "Please, Tolya, come in. . . ."

"Do come in," Belkin repeated. "Watch your head, the ceiling is a bit low."

Sukhanov gingerly squeezed inside the gallery's tiny foyer. The air smelled of glue, dust, and transience; posters advertising past exhibitions were stacked on the floor in one corner.

"Not too impressive, I'm afraid," said Belkin jovially, "but it's a beginning. This way."

They passed into an adjacent room. There were canvases hanging here, most of them smallish urban landscapes done in a bright impressionist manner: a view of a slanting street with green balcony railings and a blossoming lilac bush; a single yellow leaf on a glinting bench and, in the background, passersby with purple and red umbrellas; an evening skater flying over the blue sheen of an icy pond, surrounded by merry orange windows lit in nearby buildings. Sukhanov slowly circled the walls, read a few labels: *Autumn on Gogolevsky Boulevard, Pionerskie (Patriarshie) Ponds, Winter Roofs of the Zamoskvorechie . . .*

A voice behind him spoke with a nervous chuckle: "My abstract phase didn't last, as you see, though I'm still experimenting with styles"—and Sukhanov suddenly became aware of an urgent need to say something, anything at all, about the paintings before him.

"Very lyrical," he offered hastily, "the skater especially. This night scene too—the Moscow River, isn't it? Really, congratulations, Leva, this is great. Sorry Nina and I couldn't make it to the opening, we wanted to, but you know how it is. . . ."

"Of course, of course, don't mention it," said Belkin, looking uncomfortable. "Well, this is all there is. Very modest, as you see . . . A cup of tea, then?"

"A cup of tea would be good," Sukhanov said.

The narrow, windowless space in the back—hardly more than a closet—was crowded with a desk and two chairs, their surfaces littered with crumbs of long since digested meals, tattered remnants of aged newspapers, and a nondescript overflow of paintings and sculptures from previous shows, a few price tags still dangling from pedestals and frames. While Belkin busied himself with rinsing and filling two yellowed glasses at a sink in the corner and sliding heating coils into the cloudy water, Sukhanov cleared one chair of its accumulations, sat down, and surveyed the mournful debris of bypassed art—a portrait of a man in a sailor suit with a grinning cat perched on his shoulder, a still life with a matchbox and a half-eaten herring, a number of multicolored cubes resembling children's toy blocks gathered in a flock on the desk . . . The sight of the cubes stirred some hazy recollection in his mind, and mechanically he picked one up, turned it over in his hand.

The cube was upholstered in black and purple, and the label on its side read: "A soul. Don't open or it will fly away."

And then, unexpectedly, there it was, descending on him—the whistle of a remote train, the creaking of logs in the fireplace, the motes of reflected light dancing in a glass of red wine, and Nina's quiet voice speaking into the shadows. *I can't stop thinking about what might have been hidden inside. Would there be another dark cube that said, "Too late, it's gone, told you not to open it"? Or was there instead a bright red or blue cube, or one wrapped in golden foil, perhaps, that said, "The daring are rewarded. Take your soul, go out into the world, and do great deeds"? . . .*

For a minute Sukhanov stared at the small, light object on his palm, fighting the desire to crush it. Then, setting the cube down, he slowly moved his eyes around the room until they rested heavily on Belkin.

Belkin must have felt the gaze.

"Patience, only a moment longer," he said cheerfully, glancing up. "I can't find the cakes, but the water's already—"

Noticing the expression on Sukhanov's face, he stopped uncertainly.

"Nina . . ." Sukhanov said in a halting voice. "Nina was here, wasn't she?"

Belkin hesitated briefly, then nodded.

"She was. She came to the opening last Wednesday."

"I never told her about your opening, Leva," said Sukhanov stonily.

Belkin placed the glasses of pale tea on the desk, dropped a sugar cube into each, pushed one glass toward Sukhanov, and pulled up a chair.

"I know," he said. "But you did tell her you ran into me, and she called me the next day—got my new phone number through Viktor Yastrebov. As it turns out, both of us have been visiting him from time to time, bringing him food and such, now that he is old and sick and all alone. . . . Anyway, we met that same Sunday for a stroll, and I mentioned the exhibition. She said she wanted to come, but she thought you'd be upset if you knew. Look, Tolya, I'm really sorry I didn't say anything earlier, it's just that I wasn't sure . . ."

His words trailed off. Staring into space, Sukhanov took a sip of his tea. And then, as the hot, sweet, tasteless liquid slid down his throat, he felt a new kind of calm descending on him—a calm not of detachment but rather of understanding, as if in the last few hours some invisible yet great change had been secretly wrought in the very fabric of his being and he could contemplate his life without bitterness. Perhaps it was a calm born of emptiness and despair; it hardly mattered now, he supposed. For a while he sat without moving or speaking, marveling at the swelling of the tranquil wave inside him. Then, looking up, he saw Belkin watching him tensely across the close dimness of the room.

"Leva, it's all right," he said. "Really, it is. Though I suppose I would have been angry a few days ago." He smiled without mirth. "She said she was home with a migraine all day Sunday, and on your opening night she told me she was going to a play with a girlfriend. She never mentioned Viktor either. . . . But I'm glad that she came to see you. I should have been here too."

A melting sugar cube tinkled lightly against a glass. Belkin blinked, whether relieved or embarrassed, Sukhanov could not tell.

"Well, you are here now," he said, "that's what matters. Anyway, to tell you the truth, this whole exhibition affair isn't working out quite as I imagined. And the strange thing is, having Nina at the opening made it . . . well, worse. I mean, here I am, milling about with a few of my friends who have all seen my works before, chatting about their children and vacations, nothing in particular, yet all the while basking in this pleasant glow of being somehow important— the hero of the day, you know? And suddenly the door opens, and she walks in, beautiful as always and so young-looking, in these silver earrings she used to wear in her student days, and she looks at everything so seriously, almost urgently—and after a while, I begin to see this slight hint of disappointment in her face. . . . Oh, of course she was very kind and polite, and we had tea and talked about art, and all seemed well. But after she left, after everyone left, I looked at my paintings through her eyes, and I saw just a handful of second-rate landscapes stuck in a basement."

"You shouldn't be so hard on yourself," Sukhanov said quickly. "After all, you said yourself, it's a beginning—"

"Please, what beginning, who am I fooling?" said Belkin, waving his hand. "No, I'm just not capable of anything original. Actually, I've known it for a long time, Nina's visit only made it . . . final somehow. Funny, the way life turns out. It seems only yesterday that the late fifties were here, and we were constantly on fire with our work, proud of our poverty, brave in our shared struggle against the old, drunk with our newfound gift of expression. . . . You remember, don't you, Tolya? Our days flowed into nights, our nights were endless, and every windbag who talked about Russia, God, and art was a brother, every artist a genius, every painting a miracle—and the world did not know us yet, but we were together, we were brilliant, we were destined to light up the skies. . . . And then you blink, and all at once you yourself are in your fifties, still poor but no longer so sure of all those eternal truths, and alone now, because most of your old friends have crawled into their own nooks and crannies of misery and your wife has left to have children with another man. And on occasion, when you are hungover and the only thing in your kitchen is pickled cabbage, even the colors of the rainbow all begin to seem dirty and drab—and that's when the world finally chooses to turn in your direction, and you suddenly find that after all these years, all you have to show for yourself are a few hard-earned calluses on your hands and a landscape with lilac bushes. And then all those things that seemed so earth-shattering in the past, all those experiments with religion, eroticism, surrealism, abstraction, all those exuberant departures from the commonplace, appear for what they are in the harsh light of the day—self-indulgent exercises in passing time, pathetic imitations of fashions the West tried and discarded decades ago. And you realize that all our names are fated to become only a condensed and condescending footnote to Russian history, lumped together under the heading 'Khrushchev's Thaw,' and . . . What?

Why are you looking at me like that? Wasn't always so eloquent, was I? I guess I've had a lot of practice talking to myself over the years."

"It's not that," Sukhanov said hesitantly. "It's just that I didn't expect you to sound so . . . Well, it almost seems as if you are regretting your life, the choices you made."

"Ah, that would be rather ironic, wouldn't it? After all, I despised you so much for quitting. In the beginning especially, when I kept seeing your dreadful articles in every magazine and hearing from former colleagues about your dizzying climb up the ladder of success— and I had to survive by loading and unloading vegetable trucks. Alla always complained that my clothes stank of rotting potatoes, I remember. . . . Then Yastrebov took me to a doctor acquaintance of his, and for a bottle of brandy this fellow provided me with a certificate stating that I was mentally ill. After that I lived on state allowance, pretending to be mad. Of course, it was very little money, but things were finally getting better—I had all my time to myself, I could paint all I wanted—and then Alla left me. And it's strange— I never really thought I loved her that much, but after she was gone it all somehow started to fall apart. Maybe I just grew out of my twenties, I don't know. . . . Anyway, that was when I first suspected that what I had taken for talent had been only youth and energy, nothing more. I puzzled over my last conversation with you and your decision, and, well . . . I began to have doubts. And yes, Tolya, I still do, perhaps more than ever—so much so that at times I almost wish . . . I mean, look at the two of us! At least you have your family, and I . . . I . . ."

Averting their eyes from each other, they drank their weak tea.

"It would be nicer with lemon, I think," said Belkin, lifting his glass to the light. "I used to have one somewhere, but it's gone now. . . . By the way, I went to Malinin's retrospective the other day. Saw that blue portrait of Nina. Amazing, isn't it, that even he was capable of capturing beauty on that one occasion. She made a

wonderful muse, I suppose." He smiled, but it seemed to Sukhanov
that he detected a quiver of strain in the corners of Belkin's mouth;
then Belkin leaned back, and the shadows around his lips shifted and
dissipated.

Sukhanov nodded. "My first truly original work was inspired by
her," he said. "You remember the one with her reflection in the train
window? The one lost in the Manège disaster?"

"Well, life plays funny jokes. Maybe it's now gracing some
bureaucrat's office."

"Ah, sort of like your Leda gracing mine!"

No longer smiling, Belkin carefully set down his glass. "That was
the best thing I did in my life," he said. "Perhaps the only thing. You
really have it in your office?"

"I did for a while. . . . Well, to be honest, for a day only. Nina put
it up, but . . ."

"I understand," Belkin said, and looked away.

The light moved again, and for one instant the face Sukhanov dis-
cerned through the shadows was that of a young man with dark,
mournful, beautiful eyes—the face he had known twenty-five years
ago. Feeling suddenly, unaccountably sad, he swirled the lukewarm
liquid in his glass, its brim browned with traces of countless lonely
teatimes, and thought of that painting, Lev's gift to him and Nina on
their wedding day, a mythical nocturnal landscape with water lilies
on the surface of a still lake, and a gleaming swan, and a shepherd,
and a young nude sitting on the shore, her back tense, her face
averted, her honey-colored body strangely reminiscent of someone
he knew. . . .

"You know, Leva," he said, "there is something I've always wanted
to ask you. Well, no, not always—it's really something I've wondered
about only recently—or maybe . . . It doesn't matter." Lev's gaze was
on him now, still and black and deep, and he could feel his heart fluttering in his throat. He glanced down; his hands, resting on the edge

of the desk, trembled slightly. "Were you and Nina lovers when I met her?" he asked.

Lev recoiled as if slapped.

"No, listen," said Sukhanov softly, "I won't be jealous or angry, I just need to know. You see, how can I explain this . . . For many years I thought I understood my life so well—it was all so clear, so even, so well arranged. But recently . . . recently things have been happening to me, and, well . . . Please, I just really need to know."

There was no sound, for one moment, then another, then yet another. . . . When Lev spoke, his voice was hoarse. "I loved her, Tolya. You knew that, of course. I always loved her. We met when we were in the seventh grade, and I loved her then."

"And did she . . . Was she in love with you?"

He turned away. "We were children," he said. "But yes, we thought we were in love. We started seeing each other when we were eighteen, the summer after the exams, and stayed together all through our student years. It was innocent, of course—walks in the moonlight, kisses in the shadow of blossoming jasmine branches, trembling whispers, clumsy poems—you know how first love is. Then, when I was finally appointed to my teaching position, I asked her to marry me, and that was when the quarrels began. She had all these romantic notions about my becoming the next Chagall or Kandinsky, but she said I didn't push myself hard enough, she wanted me to be more daring, she would marry me only if I showed her what I was capable of. . . . She could be very cruel at times—she knew how to make me feel so small. Of course, she only hoped to inspire me, but . . . Well, she was young then. Finally, at the end of 1956 I think it was, shortly after you'd met her, we quarreled horribly for the last time, and that was that. I saw her again only when all of us went boating the next summer, and you were with her then."

They were silent for a while. Suddenly Belkin clasped his hand to his forehead.

"Of course," he exclaimed, "that's where they are!" Throwing open a desk drawer, he rifled through its depths and extracted a plastic container with a few stale honey cakes inside. "Might as well add some more water to our tea while I'm at it."

"Please," said Sukhanov, no longer listening. He was remembering the day in March of 1957 when Nina had stopped by his studio, and for the first time he saw it all. She had not been interested in him or his works—she was there to seek a reconciliation with Lev, for she and Lev were not speaking, and she was too proud, and he was Lev's best friend; and the only reason she agreed to come to his place was that he had suggested he would invite Lev along, and the only reason she went was that she felt offended at Lev's refusal—the refusal he had invented. And later, in the crammed shabbiness of his room, as she looked at his secret paintings, at the dark fantasies he had woven for her, already for her, only for her, she said, "I understand, he really isn't a very good painter," and she cried—and the angry tears she shed and the broken words she spoke were not meant for her father, just as their first kiss, that wonderful, leafy, sunny kiss on the lake, was not meant for him. No, they were all meant for the man she loved and the artist who failed her, the ever-present, invisible shadow dogging their steps through all their museum walks, all their conversations, all their memories being created—the same man who now, thirty years later, was nervously brewing him a cup of dreadful tea over a rusty sink. And slowly, as more recollections claimed him, all the accidentally intercepted glances and bitten lips and bright, insincere intonations slid into place, all the uncertainties were made certain, all the blank spots colored—and by the time Belkin turned to him with a new glass of colorless tea, he finally knew the truth, and his whole young past with Nina, with its sleepless rambles through the city, its flights of happiness, its ecstatic dreams, shifted, changed in tint, became dimmer, sadder, more transparent, and at the same time more real.

"That painting of yours," he said quietly. "It was about us, was it not? Nina was Leda, you were the shepherd boy, her youthful, earthly love—and I was the swan, the winged divinity come to take her away with the force of my art. Except that she loved my art, but she never loved me, did she? She loved you. And to think that I quit painting for her, to make her happy . . ."

He thought now of the evening when he had told Nina of his decision, and of her spending the whole night kneeling in her thick white gown, like some medieval saint in fervent prayer, before the stacks of canvases in their room, looking at this or that one in the jaundiced light of the lamp, and crying, and begging him not to do it, promising that she would be stronger, that she would never complain, repeating over and over that he had no right to walk away from his destiny, that he had so much fire, so much power in him . . .

"Tolya, what nonsense is this?" Belkin exclaimed. "Of course she loved your art, and she was very upset about your decision to quit, but—"

"You spoke to her about it? She never mentioned it."

The spoon clanged in Belkin's glass.

"She came by my place the day your article was published. She had the magazine with her. She . . . she was crying, she needed someone to talk to. . . ."

The unnatural quiet reigned in Sukhanov's heart. They all, in the end, had their own betrayals to live with.

"Perhaps," he said, standing up, "there has been enough reminiscing for one night. I should go now. Thanks for the tea."

"Wait," Belkin said, his eyes ravaged by guilt. "What I'm trying to tell you is that Nina made a choice. She chose *you*, art or no art, don't you see?"

Briefly he thought of telling Belkin that Nina had left him, then changed his mind.

"You know," he said, stopping in the low doorway, "what I said just now, about quitting for Nina . . . Of course, I believed it at the time, and it was a big part of it, I'm sure, but . . . I've realized a few things over the last week or two, and I think you were right all along, Leva—ultimately, I was afraid. Not so much of prisons or poverty or even unhappiness, though I thought about all that—we all did. . . . But mostly, I was afraid of failure. I was so terrified that my reality would not measure up to my dreams, that I would never quite fulfill my promise, that years later I would end up—"

"Like me," said Belkin. He was looking past Sukhanov now, at the landscapes hanging on the walls of the next room. "Ironic, isn't it? I guess one discovers many ironies in one's middle age. Because if any of us had real talent, it was you, Tolya, always you—more than a talent, a gift, perhaps even genius . . ."

A small, clear voice spoke dispassionately from a darkened corner of Sukhanov's mind: "Geniuses don't sell out." Suddenly protective of his hard-won serenity, he ordered the voice silent.

"Geniuses don't quit," he said aloud.

"Geniuses are human. Humans quit," said Belkin. "Andrei Rublev stopped painting for decades."

"Andrei Rublev seems to be everyone's favorite proof of some pet theory these days. He makes a good candidate, since he probably never existed."

"Oh, I don't mean the historical Rublev. I'm talking about Tarkovsky's Rublev. Brilliance, sheer brilliance, from the very first scene. Imagine, a fifteenth-century inventor who dreams of flying leaps off a church steeple on clumsy artificial wings and smashes to his death, yet somehow one feels his triumph, if only for a second! My God, if ever there was a sure sign that times are changing, this film being allowed in our theaters is it. Haven't you seen it?"

Something caught in Sukhanov's throat. He shook his head mutely.

"But you must!" Belkin cried. "Everyone must! I saw it last week, and I can't stop thinking about it. It's one genius envisioned by another. Here is Rublev, radiant as a god, capable of turning white walls into pastures of paradise at the lightest touch of his brush, yet refusing his calling because the world around him is mean and cruel and ignorant, because people kill each other, because the rulers are unworthy, because there seems to be no place for beauty under the sun. And so for years he wanders the dark, demented Russia—the greatest artist our soil has ever formed, alone, silent, unrecognized— until one day, bent with age, he meets a boy, a mere boy, who is struggling to create the most glorious church bell in the land. And something changes in Rublev, and after all that time, he goes to Moscow to paint our Kremlin. . . . And here is the fascinating thing, Tolya. The black-and-white film ends with this incredible flowering of color—Rublev's actual frescoes and icons, the culmination of his lifelong search—the most important three minutes, really, in the whole three hours. But since the story appeared to be over, the crowds were leaving the theater in a trudging herd, never even casting a glance at the screen. And so I sat alone in the theater, and the lights began to come on while pale angels and saints were still passing before me, and I thought, yes, you were right that day, our world really is dark and ignorant, just as it was in Rublev's time—but you were also wrong, because in spite of all the injustices, and horrors, and stupidity, beauty always survives, and there will never be a higher mission than making the world richer and purer by adding more beauty to it, by making one single person cry like a child at the age of fifty-three. . . ."

He stopped, out of breath, his eyes glistening. And at that precise moment, as his former best friend fell silent, everything was finally revealed to Sukhanov, and his whole life's plan lay before him, wondrous and clear. Dazed, he stepped across the threshold and into the void. There were no landscapes with lilacs and skaters on the walls now. Other paintings hung in the dazzling space—paintings unearthly in their sublimity and terrible in their wisdom, each an amalgamation of biblical truths and the essence of Russia's soul, each a triumphant revelation in color and emotion.

Slowly Anatoly Sukhanov turned around, incredulously, gratefully soaking in the new universe unfolded before him. He saw the glorious greens of the Garden of Eden presided over by Adam, naked save for a pair of eyeglasses, absently eating a not yet ripened apple and covering himself with a thick, dusty book, while Eve, light and translucent as a breeze, danced an unconcerned, nimble-footed, solitary dance in the depths of a virginal forest, butterflies in her emerald hair. He saw the Oriental lushness of a palace, with honeyed wines flowing, and yellow roses blooming, and silk- and velvet-skinned guests lolling about on sun-drenched carpets, and Salome, still as a marble statue, her hands folded virtuously, her eyes downcast, listening with the slightest hint of a coy smile to a sermon read by John the Baptist's head residing in the place of honor on a golden platter. He saw Noah's Ark soaring into the blueness of the sky out of the blueness of the sea, its decks overflowing with strange, magnificent beasts and angels with azure wings and huge, scaly fishes gasping their last breaths with fat purple lips. He saw the blood-red fires of hell, and the sinners with blithely oblivious, ruddy faces drinking tea and playing cards and reading magazines among the flames, none of them realizing where they were. He saw an empty black cross rising into leaden skies, a pale man with pierced hands walking toward a midnight horizon, and a Madonna swathed in darkness, her face painfully white, turning away with a disappointed look in her eyes. . . .

Many, many paintings were there, and each so rich, so overwhelming, that he felt as if he were flying away into a starry whirlwind of terror and delight, and there were no words for the wild, weightless sensation in his heart. And he knew that all the women in the paintings had Nina's face, and that all these works he was seeing, all these visions of astonishing genius, were his, his own—brought into the world not by the man he had been once, but by the man he was now.

And as the ecstatic wave swelled inside him, he was sure he had uncovered the meaning of his life, its past and present and future. He had had talent once but had been too young to say anything of importance, for true wisdom could be distilled only in the retort of suffering. And it was only after twenty-three years of mute crawling through mud—only after he had felt the smooth taste of betrayal on his lips and the chilly weight of thirty pieces of silver in his sweaty palm, only after he had learned about the slow fattening of the soul, the anguish of wasted chances, the pain of love slipping away, the soft, horrifying slide into death—yes, it was only then that the elixir of life was granted him and his resurrection assured.

And that, he now knew with a lightheaded, effortless certainty, was the miraculous message of the past days, which he had misunderstood for so long—a message delivered to him again and again, with sublime simplicity, by a kind professor who, while himself vanishing in the dark whirlwind of history, had taught him that beauty was eternal; by an old teacher who had surfaced from some murky Russian depths to tell him that age was irrelevant, for it took a lifetime to learn one's craft; by a cousin whose world he had overturned with his adolescent drawings; by a father who had given him the double gift of a divine madness and the courage to fly; by a mother who, discarding all his past, clumsy attempts at greatness, had so generously wiped his slate clean, preparing it for the acceptance of new revelations; by a woman who had left her only love in the name of his brushes and oils. . . . Again and again, the truth had grazed him with a feathery touch, but he had stopped up his ears and closed his eyes, imprisoned by fear, imagining the hand of some angered deity poised above his head, ready to exact revenge. Yet there never had been a revenge—only his strengthening genius shaking off its bounds of sleep, shedding off the incidental, the irrelevant in life— only art calling him back to the fold.

And now, in one sonorous moment, he heard the call, and saw, and understood. And as his dormant talent ripened into something else, something infinitely more precious and great, he felt the itching of budding wings under his skin.

Twenty-three

An anxious voice stretched across the darkness.

"Tolya, can you hear me? Tolya? Tolya!"

He opened his eyes, though they had been open already. The perspective was all wrong: the walls with their bright little landscapes loomed over him at odd angles, and Lev Belkin crouched on the floor, sprinkling cold tea into his face.

"I'm fine," he said, restraining a sudden urge to laugh. "I must have slipped. It's nothing." Slowly he pulled himself up and walked to the door; the linoleum was overgrown with gnarled roots that kept catching at his legs—or else it was Lev trying to stop him. In the doorway, he turned, put his hands on Lev's shoulders, and looked into his face.

"Leva," he said forcefully. "Never doubt that you did the right thing. Better to know the truth, whatever it is, than to wonder forever about what might have been."

Lev's face was rapidly dissolving into the superimposed angles and planes of a cubist portrait, and his lips were opening and closing like a pair of scissors. "Tolya, you've got to listen," he was repeating, "you are ill. You need help, Tolya, do you understand me? Just wait here, I'll only be a minute, just a phone call, Tolya, you'll be fine, don't go anywhere, it will only be a minute . . ."

Stumbling, Lev turned and disappeared inside a mediocre painting of a cramped room.

Smiling to himself, Sukhanov nodded and stepped across another threshold.

Still weightless, he danced down the street. Enormous August stars were falling from the skies, violin concertos were pouring from open windows, and his soul was waltzing. In a few blocks, a taxi with a blinking green light emerged out of nowhere. Inside, there drifted a faint scent of violets, and a pair of outmoded glasses and a funny sand-colored beard leapt through the shadows in the rearview mirror.

"Voskresensky Passage, please," said Sukhanov, and obediently the car sped away through the night and the neon signs and the sounds of the city; and all he could think of were the magnificently white sheets of paper on the corner of his desk and the box of watercolors in an unfrequented drawer.

When they reached the place, he scooped the last remaining change out of his pocket, dropped it into a hand extended from the darkness, and walked inside the building, and across the lobby teeming with reflections, and toward the elevator. The elevator puzzled him briefly—the panel with its shining rows of buttons had a button for the seventh floor and another for the ninth, but none for the eighth on which he lived. Getting off at the seventh floor, he walked up a flight of stairs. It was not just the elevator, he saw then; his whole floor was missing, and the apartments jumped from number fourteen to number seventeen. He checked several times, but there was no mistake. He shrugged; it did not seem all that important in light of his new, trembling, unshakable happiness.

Taking the stairs all the way down—past the imposing leather-padded, nail-studded doors, two on each floor, every one of them hiding its own tragedy, its own madness, its own choice—he descended into the basement, traversed the unlit corridor, then stopped to knock. A sleepy girl with no eyebrows let him in and, without saying hello or asking what he wanted, wandered down a hallway that smelled of cabbage. He waited patiently, and in another minute Valya herself appeared, hurriedly wiping her hands on her apron. When she saw him, she threw her arms up, and wailed in a high, plaintive voice, "Anatoly Pavlovich, my dear, what's happened to you? Please, please, come in, are you hungry, I can make you something to eat, and while you eat, I can wash these quickly, I—"

He took her head in his hands, and she fell silent, peering at him, shyly or fearfully perhaps, out of her slightly crossed eyes.

"You are a real Russian woman, Valentina Aleksandrovna," he said earnestly. "Please forgive me."

Then he drew her toward him, kissed her on the forehead, and walked away, feeling her eyes following him closely through the basement gloom all the way to the stairs. The last expression on her face had been strangely akin to pity, and he pondered it briefly, then dismissed it. Back in the lobby, he stopped by the concierge's desk, to inform him that the eighth floor had vanished. Then he had an afterthought.

"I also need to borrow this, it belongs to my dream anyway," he said, and leaning over the strangely still concierge, opened a drawer in the desk and pulled out the tattered, formerly checkered scarf. "It might be cold where I'm going," he explained amiably, and wondering why he had never before noticed how much like a wooden marionette the old man looked, strolled outside, singing his favorite Tchaikovsky aria under his breath.

The taxi was still there, waiting at the curb. Sukhanov bent to the window.

"I don't have any money," he said, "and I need to go some distance."

"Don't worry, I'll take you for free," said the invisible driver, his yellow beard fluttering in the shadows. "I know where you want to go, I've been there before. Hop in."

The car moved off again, but this time, the journey took much longer. There were streets and lights at first, then ugly clusters of apartment buildings amid the emptiness of deserted lots with weeds swaying in the breeze, then black cutouts of trees against the sky, then endless fields, then nothing. After another hour they arrived. The air was crisp, the church silhouetted clearly against the light blue of the waning night.

"Stop here," Sukhanov said, smiling, from the backseat. "This is Bogoliubovka."

He could tell that in the darkness ahead of him the invisible man with the canary-yellow beard was smiling too. Sukhanov stepped outside; the earth smelled of daffodils and sleep.

"Be happy," said the driver, leaning forward and waving. For one instant, as the man's face passed through the ray of a solitary street-lamp, Sukhanov saw the familiar features of the apothecary from Dalí's canvases; in the next moment, the painted man and the car with its lights melted away. "It makes sense," he whispered joyously. "It's all connected."

In his excitement he ran up the hill. The church was as he remembered it, with its stale odors and pale processions of saints treading around the corners and crows cawing hoarsely in their dreams and the sky falling through the broken dome in sharp, jagged, brilliant fragments. He felt complete and at peace, as if he had never left here. The man he had seen earlier was gone, but on the threshold he stumbled against something bulky and was pleasantly surprised to discover his bag, stolen at the ghostly station who knew how long ago, he recalled, by another of Dalí's doubles. Someone had already pulled out his favorite gray coat; it lay spread on the floor a few steps away. Unconcerned, he picked it up, shook the dust off, and wrapped himself in it, for winter was drawing near, and then carefully walked through the broken glass and crunching plaster, surveying his new canvas.

It was perfect, absolutely perfect, just as he knew it would be. Here, then, on these ancient walls, he would deposit the riches of his life—here he would paint his own angels and saints and gods, and perhaps a self-portrait or two—here he would live, eternally free, triumphantly unencumbered by the muddle of tedious obligations, the shame of daily compromises, the chaos of ordinary life. . . .

Pausing in the doorway, he looked out into the night, silent, tranquil, undisturbed by human presence; only far, far below him, two or three scattered lights trembled in the invisible village. And then, as he stood watching their uncertain blinking in the darkness at his feet, somewhere in the hidden recesses of his soul a door recently closed seemed to swing open; and for a moment, for a single moment, a torrent of memories burst out of confinement. These were not the memories of his tragic, thwarted childhood or his brilliant, daring youth; these were the neglected memories of other, later times, uninspired, unremarkable, common—memories of bending with his wife over a cradle, studying, with a mixture of pride and alarm, the tiny red face of a newborn laboring over a cry; memories of strolling through a sun-sprinkled city park, laughing as his one-year-old son wobbled on unsteady legs from tree trunk to tree trunk; memories of reading a fairy tale late into the night to his six-year-old daughter, who lay in bed sick with the flu, her eyes feverishly bright, refusing to fall asleep until he turned the last page; memories of the four of them gathered in the evening around a fire on a deserted beach, listening to the breathing of the sea and the hissing of mussels in the flames. . . . And for one moment, while the door in his soul stayed open, these recollections pierced him with an unsustainable sorrow— and already in some deeper, dimmer layer of his being an ugly, unbearable suspicion was beginning to stir, and he almost wondered whether he had misunderstood everything after all—whether his newfound purpose was truly the dazzling revelation he had imagined it to be, or merely a . . . a . . .

And then the moment joined all the others on their way to oblivion. Exhaling, he slammed the door shut, this time forever, just as the last lights in the village below wavered and went out as if quickly covered by a giant hand. Everything was perfect, absolutely perfect, he told himself again. His path stretched clear before him, and he was not alone, he would never be alone—the whole world would be with him, helping him, watching over him, lending him branches for brushes, warm earth for pigments, and now and then, a falling star or two for inspiration.

He stepped outside, scooped up a handful of soil, crumbled it between his fingers, and smelled it, laughing softly. Then, once the echo of his laughter had faded, he began to mix the glorious rainbow of his new palette.

ACKNOWLEDGMENTS

I am immensely grateful to my wonderful agent, Warren Frazier, and my incomparable editor Marian Wood—without them none of this would have happened. Thanks also to my remarkable UK editor, Mary Mount; my copy editor, Anna Jardine, who is as tireless as she is skilled; and everyone at the Penguin Group who believed in this book. Finally, thanks are due to my parents, Boris Grushin and Natalia Kartseva, for their love and support and for serving as a priceless source on Sukhanov's Russia, and to my husband, Michael Klyce, who helped in more ways than I can name.

Born in 1971 in Moscow, Olga Grushin had her early schooling in Czecho-slovakia when her father, a pioneering sociologist and philosopher at odds with the Soviet regime, relocated the family to Prague. After returning to Moscow in 1981, she studied art history at the Pushkin Museum of Fine Arts and journalism at Moscow State University. In 1989, she was given a full scholarship to Emory University and became the first Russian citizen to enroll in and complete a four-year American college degree, graduating summa cum laude in 1993. Since coming to the United States, she has been a personal interpreter for President Jimmy Carter, a cocktail waitress in a jazz bar, a translator at the World Bank, a research analyst at a leading Washington law firm, and most recently, an editor at Harvard University's Dumbarton Oaks Research Library and Collection.

Her short fiction has appeared in *Partisan Review, The Massachusetts Review, Confrontation,* and *Art Times. The Dream Life of Sukhanov* is her first novel; she is now at work on her second.

Grushin became a U.S. citizen in 2002. She lives in Washington, D.C., with her husband and their son.